倍斯特出版事業有限公司
Best Publishing Ltd.

NEW TOEIC 新多益700分

閱讀特訓班

NEW TOEIC Reading is Fun!

...Gunton、連緯晏Wendy Lien ◎著

4 把鑰匙打開新多益閱讀高分之門
4 keys to a higher score in TOEIC reading

- Key -1 英語教學經驗豐富的英籍與中籍老師撰寫，符合新多益考試命題方向。
- Key -2 選題多元豐富，激發學習力讓閱讀更有趣，答題不再雙眼失焦。
- Key -3 詳細中文解說+精選單字，文法句型單字用法完整解析，考前重點整理。
- Key -4 五回500題，前兩回中英對照，後三回模擬考試，學習效果加倍。

作者序

If you want to achieve your ideal TOEIC score, you will need to take the test seriously, but that does not mean that the preparation needs to be so solemn. This book is written in the hope that the articles within it are sufficiently interesting to hold its readers' attention, so that the preparation process is not a dull experience.

Completing these review tests is not meant to simply prepare you for TOEIC, but also to teach you something. I'm sure that you will meet some new things in this book, especially vocabulary, and my intention is for you to learn from it.

Don't become disappointed from mistakes- learn from them. Many question types are repeated in later tests. If you get them right the second time, then you have accomplished the goal of this book.

I hope that this book helps you reach your desired TOEIC score.

Matthew Gunton

要達到自己理想中的多益（TOEIC）成績，就得以認真的態度準備這項測驗，但是並不代表準備過程必須是嚴肅的。本書內文題材充分展現趣味性，能成功抓住讀者的專注力，在準備測驗的過程中，不感到枯燥乏味。

做完這五回複習測驗，不只代表你已準備好應考多益（TOEIC）測驗，這些試題更是達到教授英語的目的。我確信你將在本書遇到一些沒學過的部分，尤其是字彙。本書的意涵，也是要讓讀者能從中獲得新知。

千萬別因為寫錯而感到挫敗——把它學會。會有很多類似題型在這五回測驗裡重覆出現。如果你能在第二次答對先前寫錯的類似題型，那麼你便達到了本書的目標。

我期盼本書，能助你達到心中理想的多益（TOEIC）測驗成績。

作者　Matthew Gunton

譯者　連緯晏 Wendy Lien

編者序

新多益閱讀部分共有100題，應試者需要在75分鐘答完三大類型的題組（包括單句填空、短文填空、單雙篇文章理解），而普遍考生的困擾為題目太多寫不完而失去了分數。那麼，有效得分方法是什麼呢？

有效的提高分數的策略就是閱讀技巧的提升。

最好練習英語閱讀的方法就是保持對事物的好奇心，讀自己有興趣的文章，練習時間長了後，英語閱讀的能力就會有所提升。而此書編寫的方向即為選編有趣且多元但又符合新多益考試的命題方向的題組。使練習者可以有耐心看完並答題，進而加強對英語文章寫法與語感的熟悉度。

讓你練習閱讀不苦悶，不會做題做到雙眼失焦。

多益閱讀測驗不是只有商業書信或廣告單也可以充滿趣味與活潑性，例如：

科普知識大白鯊可以活70歲，搖滾樂團宣告復出，美食部落客分享食譜，減肥營課程介紹，與社群網站Instagram的介紹……等更多有趣的文章等你來練習。

此書的每題都附有中文翻譯與解說，都將會告訴你答案在文章的什麼地方與如何推敲出答案，使你知道正確的答案外，也知道錯誤的選項不能選的原因。

要小心不要讀文章讀得太投入，這還是一個測驗，請給自己設一個鬧鐘，在安靜的地方完成一回吧！相信你的多益閱讀成績一定會有所進步，對於英語閱讀也會更有信心。

倍斯特編輯部

CONTENTS

新多益資訊

多益測驗簡介

TOEIC的全名是Test of English for International Communication（國際溝通英語測驗），這是一個專門為英語非母語的人士所設計的英語能力測驗；測驗的分數反應受測者在國際生活及職場環境中的英語溝通能力。TOEIC是目前全世界最大也是最受歡迎的職場英語能力測驗，不光是企業界用TOEIC作為同仁英語能力的標準，各大專院校、一些國際級展覽主辦單位也都以此來評定相關人員的英文能力，估計現在一年有超過600萬人接受多益測驗。

為更貼近實際職場與生活環境的需求，目前的TOEIC測驗做了以下改變：

1. **聽力方面**——面對各種英語發音是否能對答如流的能力
   (1) 題目長度增長
   (2) 連鎖題組方式呈現
   (3) 美／英／澳／加等口音
2. **閱讀方面**——受測者是否有整合句子與段落內容的能力
   (1) 題目長度增長
   (2) 以「段落填空」取代挑錯題
   (3) 閱讀測驗型態更新 → 對多篇文章的關連性理解

多益測驗方式

分「聽力」、「閱讀」兩部份進行；在測驗開始之前，受測者約花費半個小時填寫個人資料及問卷，測驗進行中不休息，真正待在考場裡的時間約為兩個半小時。以下是多益測驗的題型說明：

1. **聽力測驗**——測驗時間為45 分鐘，分4個大題，共100題。

大題	內容		題數
I	Photographs	照片描述	10題
II	Question-Response	應答問題	30題
III	Short Conversations	簡短對話	10組30題
IV	Short Talks	簡短獨白	10組30題

2. 閱讀測驗——測驗時間為75 分鐘，分3個大題，共100題。

大題	內容		題數
V	Incomplete Sentences	單句填空	40題
VI	Text Completion	短文填空	4組12題
VII	Reading Comprehension	閱讀測驗	
	* Single passage	* 單篇閱讀	7-10組28題
	* Double passage	* 雙篇閱讀	4組20題

多益測驗內容

1. 一般商務——契約、談判、行銷、銷售、商業企劃、會議……
2. 製造業——工廠管理、生產線、品管……
3. 金融／預算——銀行業務、投資、税務、會計、帳單……
4. 企業發展——研究、產品研發……
5. 辦公室——董事會、委員會、信件、備忘錄、電話、傳真、電子郵件……
6. 人事／採購——招考、雇用、薪資、應徵與廣告、比價、訂貨……
7. 技術層面——電子、科技、電腦……
8. 房屋／公司地產——建築、規格、購買租賃……
9. 旅遊——交通工具時刻表、機場廣播、租車、飯店預訂……
10. 外食——商務／非正式午餐、宴會、招待會、餐廳訂位……
11. 娛樂——電影、劇場、音樂……
12. 保健——醫藥保險、看醫生……

多益測驗分數計算

TOEIC測驗是以總分（含聽力 + 閱讀）10~990分來表現受測者的英語能力，依測驗成績有五種等級的證書：金色證書（860-990分）、藍色證書（730-855分）、綠色證書（470-725分）、棕色證書（220-465分）、橘色證書（10-215分）。

多益測驗考試時間與報名方式

1. 多益測驗時間（TOEIC官網）
   http://toeic.com.tw/tests_info.jsp
2. TOEIC測驗報名費用為1500元，報名方式有「網路報名」、「通訊報名」與「臨櫃報名」等三種，報名流程與詳細説明：http://toeic.com.tw/toeic_news_pub.jsp?type=8

考試小叮嚀

此書使用建議

此書五回的測驗，能讓你在應考時，更得心應手。請制定練習計畫，一次做完一回考試，五回的測驗裡，希望你能夠挑出兩回以不計時的方式完成；另外三回則以正式考試的時間限制（75分鐘）（要畫卡）。完成每回考試，請詳讀解析，多記不懂的字彙與文法結構（參照本書字彙與文法解說）。

第五部分——單句填空

第五部分共計40題，控制在這個部分以每30秒的速度作答一題（包括劃卡），在20分鐘內完成。答題時，不要為了幾個看不懂的字彙就停頓。先找出每個句子的主詞，才能知道動詞、助動詞、be動詞的變化，其中文法題要多留意的是詞性與時態的問題，最常出現的有介系詞、時態的動詞變化、助動詞、be動詞、動名詞、一些動詞後面只能使用動名詞的用法等。字彙題要留意語意，平常除了多補充字彙外，遇到考題不了解的字彙時，先看題意、文法，再來看選項是否有你了解的單字並使用刪去法的方式作答。

第六部分——短文填空

第六部分的短文填空共有四個題組（共12題），可以用8-10分鐘寫完，請先深呼吸，吸氣二秒、吐氣五秒（也不能太深，畢竟考試時間有限）。答題時專注在空格前後字的詞性來判斷選項，如動詞修飾名詞、形容詞修飾名詞、副詞修飾動詞、形容詞、整個句子、介系詞等文法規則。

第七部分──文章理解

第七部分文章理解共計48題，共約17篇（組）文章，分單篇、雙篇文章理解，作答時間有45分鐘。單篇文章理解有7-10篇短文，每篇建議3-5分鐘做完；25分鐘內做答完畢。雙篇文章理解有四個題組（8篇文章），每篇花5分鐘，20分鐘內做完。在做單篇文章理解時，請務必先找出主旨（大概從標題能略知一二）。接著讀題目與標題，注意題目裡的強調字（如否定的語意not、hardly、never…），然後快速閱讀文章找答案，不能因為不懂的字彙而放慢速度，同時注意文章裡出現的數字、年份、人物、時間、地點，以鉛筆淡淡圈出（多益考試規定不能在試題本做記號，所以請淡淡地畫，並在答題完記得擦掉）。如果第一題未能馬上領會找出答案，就接著下一題，有時在每題找答案的過程中，就會愈來愈清楚題意與答案。雙篇文章的題型亦相同，但要特別留意兩篇文章間主角或事件的關聯性。如果最後寫不完請記得猜題。放輕鬆運用一點邏輯去猜，或許你猜的都是對的。

重點筆記

- ✧ 答題時不要因為不認識的字就停頓太久。
- ✧ 第六部分短文填空與第七部分文章理解可以挑簡單篇幅的題目先做答。
- ✧ 第七部分文章理解先看題目與標題可先有初步文章的輪廓。
- ✧ 注意時間規劃，寫不完要猜題。
- ✧ 前晚請確保睡眠充足、當天不要餓肚子（注意力會不集中）、感冒（體力不好）。

做答把握以上建議的原則，就有可能充分表現出你的實力。

Test 1

Part 5. 單句填空

Questions 101-140

101. When given a choice, most dogs ------- eating raw meat to cooked meat.

(A) prefer
(B) continue
(C) enjoy
(D) remember

102. ------- is a major problem in many developing countries throughout the world.

(A) Connection
(B) Correction
(C) Corruption
(D) Consumption

103. She said ------- they were unable to find a parking space within walking distance of the seminar.

(A) which
(B) where
(C) what
(D) that

101. 答案 (A) 有得選擇時，大部分的狗較喜歡生肉勝於煮熟的肉。

(A) 較喜歡

(B) 繼續

(C) 享受

(D) 記得

解說 選項動詞後面都能加動名詞。本題只有用 prefer「較喜歡」才有意思。

單字 prefer（某事物）to（某事物）

102. 答案 (C) 腐敗是全世界許多開發中國家的主要問題。

(A) 連結 *(n.)*

(B) 更正 *(n.)*

(C) 腐敗 *(n.)*

(D) 消耗 *(n.)*

103. 答案 (D) 她說他們無法在研討會會場步行範圍內找到停車位。

(A) which

(B) where

(C) what

(D) that

解說 that 子句為受詞。及物動詞 say 後面需要有受詞，故選擇 (D)。She（主詞）+ said（及物動詞）+ that they were unable to find a parking space within walking distance of the seminar.（受詞）。

例句 My father always says that I am a lazy couch potato. 我父親總是說我是個懶骨頭。

104. Doctors believe that the calories you ------- affect many aspects of your health.

(A) consume
(B) assume
(C) presume
(D) contract

105. Since the earliest twentieth century, ------- from many countries have attempted to explore the underwater world around these islands.

(A) marines
(B) divers
(C) astronauts
(D) scientists

106. I wish that I ------- eaten that second dessert just before going to bed.

(A) wouldn't
(B) wasn't
(C) haven't
(D) hadn't

104. 答案 (A) 醫生們相信你吃進的熱量影響健康許多面向。.

(A) 攝取 *(v.)*

(B) 以為 *(v.)*

(C) 假定 *(v.)*

(D) 訂合約 *(v.)*

105. 答案 (B) 自二十世紀早期，各國潛水員試圖探索這些島附近的海底世界。

(A) 海軍陸戰隊隊員

(B) 潛水員

(C) 太空人

(D) 科學家

106. 答案 (D) 我希望我在剛要上床睡覺時沒有吃第二份甜點。

(A) wouldn't

(B) wasn't

(C) haven't

(D) hadn't

解說 主詞＋wish (that)＋主詞＋過去完成式——用於假設改變過去已發生的事實（實際上事實未變）。過去完成式否定用 had not＋過去分詞，答案 (D)。

例句 Harry wishes that he had bought that watch. Harry 希望他有買那隻錶。（實際上他沒買）

107. All the computers in the office - - - - - - - at the moment, but if you wait a while, one is sure to be free.

(A) are being used

(B) have been used

(C) used

(D) have used

108. Many of the country's oldest - - - - - - - have fallen into disrepair due to the lack of government funding.

(A) people

(B) services

(C) monuments

(D) rivers

109. Via webcam, thousands of interested viewers saw that the eagle - - - - - - - an egg.

(A) laid

(B) lay

(C) is laying

(D) lied

107. 答案 (A) 所有辦公室裡的電腦正在使用中，但是如果你稍待片刻，確定會有一台沒人使用。

(A) are being used
(B) have been used
(C) used
(D) have used

解說　從 at the moment（現在），可以知道這部電腦正在使用中，所以用現在進行式。現在進行式被動語態－主詞＋ be 動詞＋ being ＋過去分詞。

句子裡的時間片語為 at the moment = now 現在。不能選現在完成式被動語態選項 (B)。

例句　The windows are being washed now. 窗戶現在正在被洗。

108. 答案 (C) 許多國家最古老的遺跡年久失修倒塌，是由於政府資金匱乏。

(A) 人
(B) 公共設施
(C) 遺址
(D) 河

109. 答案 (A) 藉由網路攝影機，數千名感興趣的觀看者看見了老鷹下蛋。

(A) 下蛋（過去式）
(B) 下蛋（現在式）
(C) 正在下蛋
(D) 說謊

解說　時間片語（昨晚），表示過去式。用過去式動詞，下蛋；放置 lay 的動詞三態為：lay － laid － laid。不要搞混這兩個動詞三態：躺 lie － lay － lain／說謊 lie － lied － lied

110. Learning ------- is a big part of growing up for all children everywhere.

(A) response
(B) responsible
(C) respectable
(D) responsibility

111. The teacher warned that if he continues to show -------, he will lose many friends.

(A) up
(B) of
(C) off
(D) out

112. The guest speaker ------- many ideas that increased our understanding of the subject.

(A) introduced
(B) intruded
(C) entered
(D) conducted

110. 答案 (D) 學習責任感是各地小孩成長的一大部分。

(A) 回答

(B) 需負責任的

(C) 值得尊敬的

(D) 責任感

解說 原始句型應為 A big part of growing up for all children everywhere is learning responsibility. 所以答案必須是一個名詞。這樣的句型也可寫成以 To learn 和 Learning 做為主詞。

Learning responsibility is a big part of growing up for all children everywhere.

= To learn responsibility is a big part of growing up for all children everywhere.

111. 答案 (C) 老師警告他如果他繼續愛炫耀，他會失去很多朋友。

(A) up

(B) of

(C) off

(D) out

解說 動詞片語 show off「愛炫耀」。選項 (A) show up 出現；出席，不符合題意。

112. 答案 (A) 客座講者介紹許多增加我們了解主題的概念。

(A) 介紹

(B) 侵入

(C) 進入

(D) 引導

解說 選項 (A) 為 introduce「介紹」的過去式。

113. After the earthquake, the relief aid shipment was divided ------- the many survivors.

(A) between
(B) among
(C) with
(D) to

114. During this cold weather, those that are sick should avoid ------- out in the rain.

(A) to go
(B) on going
(C) gone
(D) going

115. Dr. Stuart was awarded the prize for ------- work in research psychology.

(A) outstand
(B) outstanding
(C) outstood
(D) outstandingly

116. Roast the turkey in the oven at 200°C for ------- one and a half hours in order to cook it thoroughly.

(A) long
(B) more
(C) above
(D) at least

113. 答案 (B) 地震之後，裝運救濟的貨物分配給許多生還者。

(A) 兩者之間

(B)（兩個以上）之中

(C) 有

(D) to

解說 among「之中」是介系詞，表示兩個以上。許多生還者表示多於兩個，故不能選 (A)。

114. 答案 (D) 在這天氣寒冷期間，那些生病的人應該避免去外面淋雨。

(A) to go

(B) on going

(C) gone

(D) going

解說 avoid「避免」後面必須用動名詞。只有選項 (D) 是動名詞。

115. 答案 (B) 史都華博士因在心理學上傑出的研究成果獲頒獎項。

(A) 突出

(B) 傑出的

(C) 突出（過去式）

(D) 傑出地

解說 outstanding「傑出的」是形容詞，形容詞修飾名詞 work「研究成果」，outstanding work 組成名詞片語。(A)、(C) 均為動詞，(D) 為副詞。

116. 答案 (D) 把火雞放入 200℃烤箱烘烤最少一個半小時，為了徹底煮熟。

(A) 長

(B) 更多

(C) 在…之上

(D) 至少

解說 不能選 (B) more「更多」，因為需要配合有 than。不能選 (C) above「在…之上」，因為只用於表示位置與立場，而非數量。

117. With immediate effect, all visitors - - - - - - - register with reception upon entering the building.

(A) are
(B) to
(C) must
(D) be

118. Our company - - - - - - - large end-of-year bonuses to our top employees on an annual basis.

(A) offered
(B) offers
(C) had offered
(D) has offered

119. Recent increases in the price of oil have been - - - - - - - reflected by prices at the pumps at gas stations.

(A) quickly
(B) quick
(C) quickness
(D) quicken

120. Antique paintings - - - - - - - by some as a good investment for the future.

(A) are seeing
(B) saw
(C) are seen
(D) see

117. 答案 (C) 此辦法即刻生效，所有訪客必須在進入大樓後向接待處登記。

(A) are
(B) to
(C) must
(D) be

解說 must「必須」在這裡當助動詞。

118. 答案 (B) 我們公司每年度提供大額年終獎金給我們的頂尖員工。

(A) offered
(B) offers
(C) had offered
(D) has offered

解說 本句時間為 annual「年度的」，是現在式，主詞是 Our company「我們的公司」，為第三人稱單數，offer「提供」是動詞。現在式，第三人稱動詞要加 "s"。(A) 是過去式動詞。(C) 是過去完成式。(D) 是現在完成式。

119. 答案 (A) 近來原油上漲，已經很快地反映在加油站加油箱上頭顯示的價格上了。

(A) 快地 *(adv.)*
(B) 快的 *(adj.)*
(C) 迅速 *(n.)*
(D) 加快 *(v.)*

解說 必須選擇副詞，因為只有副詞能修飾過去分詞 reflected。

120. 答案 (C) 古董畫作被一些人視為一項對未來好的投資。

(A) seeing
(B) saw
(C) are seen
(D) see

解說 被動語態：主詞＋be 動詞＋過去分詞。本題是現在式，主詞是複數 Antique paintings「古董畫作」所以 be 動詞用 are。see「視為；看見」的動詞三態：see － saw － seen。

例句 The dogs are fed by her. 狗被她餵。

121. Rarely has a fully intact dinosaur skeleton of this level of ------- been dug up anywhere in the world.

(A) conservation
(B) preservation
(C) maintenance
(D) upkeep

122. Despite the teachers warning, the undisciplined child ------- his classmate a cow.

(A) spoke
(B) told
(C) said
(D) called

123. Little -------about how people lived thousands of years ago.

(A) is known
(B) is knowing
(C) is knowingly
(D) is know

124. Following a short chase, the police caught a very ------- shoplifter at the local mall just now.

(A) embarrass
(B) embarrassingly
(C) embarrassed
(D) embarrassing

121. 答案 (B) 世界各地罕見這種完好無缺保存程度的恐龍骨骸。

(A) 管理

(B) 保存

(C) 維護

(D) 維修

122. 答案 (D) 儘管老師警告，沒規矩的小孩稱他的同學是母牛。

(A) spoke

(B) told

(C) said

(D) called

解說 本題四個選項中，只有 call 後面可以有受詞補語。

123. 答案 (A) 大家對關於人類如何在一千年前生活的了解不多。

(A) is known

(B) is knowing

(C) is knowingly

(D) is know

解說 被動語態：主詞＋be 動詞＋過去分詞。know「知道；了解」的動詞三態：know － knew － known。

124. 答案 (C) 隨著短程追逐，警察剛剛在當地購物中心逮捕了一位自覺丟臉的扒手。

(A) 丟臉 *(v.)*

(B) 丟臉地 *(adv.)*

(C) 感到丟臉的 *(adj.)*

(D) 令人覺得丟臉的 *(adj.)*

解說 選 (C)，過去分詞當形容詞，表示被動。embarrassed「丟臉」修飾 shoplifter「扒手」。不能選 (D) embarrassing「令人覺得丟臉的」，現在分詞當形容詞，表示主動。

125. Global Inc. announces the - - - - - - - of George Raymond as its new CEO with immediate effect.

(A) engagement

(B) appointment

(C) introduction

(D) authorization

126. In the early 20th century, travel by train - - - - - - - the fastest transport available.

(A) used

(B) be used to

(C) used to

(D) used to be

127. The new staff at the employment agency don't appear to know - - - - - - - to do.

(A) what

(B) how

(C) where

(D) when

128. Little is known about where the next outbreak will take place, but doctors in many countries are on - - - - - - - .

(A) stand down

(B) stand up

(C) standby

(D) stand off

125. 答案 (B) 全國股份有限公司宣佈任命George Raymond為新任執行長且即刻生效。

(A) 訂婚

(B) 任命；派任

(C) 介紹

(D) 授權

126. 答案 (D) 二十世紀早期，搭火車旅行曾經是速度最快的交通運輸工具。

(A) used

(B) be used to

(C) used to

(D) used to be

解說 選(D)曾經是。意指現在不是。used＋不定詞，表示以前是但現在不是。be動詞＋used to，表示習慣。

例句 I am used to cold weather. 我習慣寒冷氣候。

I used to have long hair. 我曾經是長頭髮。（表示現在是短頭髮）

127. 答案 (A) 就業服務處的人員似乎不知道該做什麼？

(A) what

(B) how

(C) where

(D) when

解說 what是代名詞，其他選項均為副詞。

128. 答案 (C) 不太知道下一次會在哪裡爆發，但是許多國家的醫生都在待命中。

(A) 退出

(B) 起立

(C) 待命

(D) 避開

129. It is impossible - - - - - - - the meeting on a new date at such short notice.

(A) rearrange
(B) rearranged
(C) rearranging
(D) to rearrange

130. Managing the national budget is - - - - - - - an important job for all government departments.

(A) such
(B) very
(C) so
(D) much

131. Dr. Livermore would like to thank everyone for their messages of support, and he hopes to return to work once he's made a full - - - - - - - .

(A) discovery
(B) recovery
(C) inquiry
(D) retrieval

132. The hotel shop, which is located in the hotel lobby, has a great variety of souvenirs and gifts all at - - - - - - - prices.

(A) extraordinary
(B) reasonable
(C) extreme
(D) rational

129. 答案 (D) 如此的臨時通知，不可能重新安排一個日期開會在臨。

(A) rearrange

(B) rearranged

(C) rearranging

(D) to rearrange

解說 (D)不定詞to rearrange「重新安排」作副詞用，修飾impossible「不可能」。(A)rearrange現在式動詞。(B)rearranged過去式動詞。(C)rearranging動名詞。

130. 答案 (A) 掌管國家預算對政府部門來説，是如此重要的工作。

(A) such

(B) very

(C) so

(D) much

解說 an important job「重要的工作」是名詞片語。such「如此地」是形容詞，必須用在名詞片語前。

例句 She is such a hardworking student. 她是個如此認真的學生。

131. 答案 (B) Livermore醫師想感謝大家支持的留言，他希望一旦他完全復元儘快回到工作崗位上。

(A) 發現

(B) 復元

(C) 詢問

(D) 取回

132. 答案 (B) 位於飯店大廳的商店，有很多各式紀念品和禮品，全都在合理的價格。

(A) 非凡的

(B) 合理的

(C) 極端的

(D) 理性的

133. Many of the young soldiers who failed the test during the recent exercise ------- expected to try again next month.

(A) is
(B) were
(C) was
(D) are

134. Due to the high volume of ------- to our website, transactions are taking longer than usual to process.

(A) vehicles
(B) trucks
(C) traffic
(D) carriers

135. If the school prom had been held last night, it ------- have been a disaster.

(A) would
(B) can
(C) will
(D) should

136. One reason that lawyers earn such large sums of money is the ever ------- size of the damages awarded in civil courts.

(A) increased
(B) increasing
(C) increasingly
(D) increase

133. 答案 (D) 許多在近期練習沒通過考試的年輕軍人，被期許下個月再試一次。

(A) is

(B) were

(C) was

(D) are

解說 many of the young soldiers who failed the test during the recent exercise 是主詞，現在式被動語態，主詞＋ be 動詞＋過去分詞，主詞是複數，be 動詞用 are。

134. 答案 (C) 由於我們網站的高流量，交易過程會比平常的處理時間長。

(A) 車輛

(B) 卡車

(C) 交通流量

(D) 置物架

135. 答案 (A) 如果學校舞會舉行在昨晚，那將會是場大災難。

(A) would

(B) can

(C) will

(D) should

解說 第三條件句。If ＋過去完成式＋，＋主詞＋ would/could/might 現在完成式。

選項 (D) should「應該」，文法是對的，但是不符合題意。

136. 答案 (B) 律師賺得如此多金額的原因之一，是因為民事法庭增加傷害賠償金額程度。

(A) 增加 *(v.)* 過去式

(B) 增加 *(adj.)* 現在分詞

(C) 增加地 *(adv.)*

(D) 增加 *(v.)* 現在式

解說 現在分詞當形容詞，修飾名詞 size「大小程度」。

137. My sister, who has been living in South Africa for the past few years, ------- return home next week.

(A) is
(B) was
(C) will
(D) would

138. A new treatment for cancer has been developed at the local university ------- center.

(A) medicine
(B) medical
(C) medicinal
(D) medieval

139. After many trials, we have found replacement equipment that seems ------- .

(A) acceptable
(B) to accept
(C) accept
(D) acceptably

140. The increased popularity of car ownership in China has placed a great strain on its road -------.

(A) surface
(B) web
(C) network
(D) lines

137. 答案 (C) 我那過去幾年一直住南非的妹妹，下週將會回家。

(A) is
(B) was
(C) will
(D) would

解說 next week「下週」表示尚未發生，是未來式，return「返回」是動詞。(C) will「將；將會」是未來式助動詞。(A) is 是現在式 be 動詞。(B) was 是過去式 be 動詞。(D) would 是 will 的過去式。

138. 答案 (B) 一種新的癌症療法已在當地大學醫學中心展開。

(A) 藥
(B) 醫學的
(C) 藥用的
(D) 中世紀的

139. 答案 (A) 在許多試用之後，我們找到了似乎可以接受的替換設備。

(A) acceptable
(B) to accept
(C) accept
(D) acceptably

解說 seem「似乎」是連綴動詞。連綴動詞後是主詞補語。主詞補語可以是形容詞故答案為 (A) acceptable「可接受的」。(B) to accept「接受」是不定詞，(C) accept「接受」是動詞。(D) acceptably「可接受地」是副詞。

140. 答案 (C) 中國擁有車子的人口增加，已造成整個道路系統上的一大負擔。

(A) 表面
(B) 網
(C) 系統
(D) 線

Part 6. 短文填空

Questions 141-143 refer to the following article.

What we all need more of.....

We all say we need more of it, and we can't get ------- of it. So, what is it? Money? Time? Expensive cell phones? Designer shoes? No. It's more sleep!

141. (A) some
(B) all
(C) any
(D) enough

In ------- around the industrialized world again and again people

142. (A) responses
(B) sayings
(C) surveys
(D) recommendations

say that they need more sleep, so why don't they spend more time sleeping?

Researchers have suggested that in our modern, hectic life, people carry their lack of sleep around with them as a badge of honor. If you get enough sleep, you can't be very busy, and so you can't be a very ------- person, so the logic goes. Do you get enough sleep?

143. (A) important
(B) good
(C) diligent
(D) respected

第 141-143 題

我們都需要更多的……

我們都說我們需要多一點，而且怎麼都不夠。究竟是什麼？是錢嗎？昂貴的手機嗎？潮鞋嗎？都不是。是更多的睡眠！

141. 答案 (D)

(A) 一些　　(B) 所有；全部

(C) 任何　　(D) 足夠

在工業化世界的問卷調查中，人們屢次說到需要更多睡眠，那麼為什麼他們不多花點時間睡覺呢？

142. 答案 (C)

(A) 回答 *(n.)*　　(B) 言論 *(n.)*

(C) 問卷調查 *(n.)*　　(D) 建議 *(n.)*

研究人員提出建議，在我們現代化、忙亂的生活中，人們四處帶著睡眠不足的樣子，像是他們榮譽的徽章。如果你睡得足夠，你就不是很忙，所以你不可能是很重要的人物，邏輯上是這樣。你的睡眠足夠嗎？

143. 答案 (A)

(A) 重要的　　(B) 好的

(C) 勤勞的　　(D) 尊敬的

字彙：

industrialize [ɪnˋdʌstrɪəˏlaɪz] *(v.)* 使工業化／ researcher [riˋsɝtʃɚ] *(n.)* 研究員；調查者／ suggest [səˋdʒɛst] *(v.)* 建議／ badge [bædʒ] *(n.)* 徽章／ honor [ˋɑnɚ] *(n.)* 榮譽／ lack [læk] *(n.)* 欠缺；不足

Questions 144-146 refer to the following staff announcement.

Staff announcement

The management of Toy World would like to thank all their staff for the great effort, ------- and teamwork shown in the busy run up to

144. (A) commitment
(B) comitted
(C) committing
(D) committedly

Christmas. Your hard work has paid off, and our December visitor numbers exceeded our most optimistic estimates. Revenue this year has set a new -------.

145. (A) recorder
(B) recording
(C) recordist
(D) record

We are aware that many of you put in double shifts on our busiest days, and we would like you all to know that the effort was noticed and appreciated. To express our gratitude all staff will be given two extra days' holiday during February in addition to their regular paid leave.

Once again thank you for your ------- to Toy World.

146. (A) help
(B) attachment
(C) truth
(D) dedication

The management: January 11th

第 144-146 題

員工公告

Toy World 的經理部，要向所有員工表達感謝，各位的努力、承擔的義務，以及團隊合作，在最忙的聖誕節期間表現得十分出色。你們的努力工作很值得，我們在十二月的來客數達到最樂觀的預期，今年的收益創下新記錄。

144. 答案 (A)

(A) 承擔的義務 *(n.)* (B) 忠誠的 *(adj.)*

(C) 託付 *(v.)* 現在進行式 (D) 忠誠地 *(adv.)*

解說 句中敘述員工們的工作表現，effort「努力」teamwork「團隊合作」均為名詞，所以要選一個名詞。

145. 答案 (D)

(A) 錄音機 *(n.)* (B) 錄影 *(n.)*

(C) 錄音員 *(n.)* (D) 記錄 *(n.)*

解說 四個選項皆為名詞，但是放入題目，意思皆不相同。(D) 是最符合題意的答案。

我們留意到你們之中很多人，在最忙的那幾天都輪了兩班工作，我們要你們知道，你們的努力我們都注意到也很感激。為了表達我們的謝意，所有員工享有在正常薪水之外，還可以在二月期間多休假幾天。

再次地，感謝你們對 Toy World 的奉獻。

146. 答案 (D)

(A) 幫忙 *(v.)* (B) 附件 *(n.)*

(C) 事實 *(n.)* (D) 奉獻 *(v.)*

解說 dedication + to「專心致力於」(某事物)。

經理部　元月十一日

字彙：

announcement [ə`naʊnsmənt] *(n.)* 公告／ effort [`ɛfət] *(n.)* 努力／ commitment [kə`mɪtmənt] *(n.)* 託付；委任／ appreciate [ə`priʃɪˏet] *(v.)* 感謝／ gratitude [`grætəˏtjud] *(n.)* 感激

Questions 147-149 refer to the following article.

Volunteers needed to help with reindeer in Finland

We are a small family owned farm in northern Finland. My wife and I run the farm, but - - - - - - - our children have grown up and moved away,

147. (A) since
(B) for
(C) if
(D) although

we offer free accommodation for anyone willing to put in a little hard work on the farm.

Our farm has reindeer and horses, and also some dogs. We particularly need help in wintertime taking care - - - - - - - the horses,

148. (A) with
(B) by
(C) for
(D) of

especially with feeding and cleaning of the stables. Any work with the reindeer will be done together with us.

We have two empty bedrooms, and horseback riding is possible when things are not too - - - - - - -.

149. (A) busily
(B) busy
(C) busyness
(D) busier

第 147-149 題

需要志工幫助芬蘭的馴鹿

我們是芬蘭已部一處小型家庭自營農場。我的妻子和我一起經營農場，但是自我們的孩子長大並搬離家之後，我們提供任何願意替農場盡點勞力的人，提供免費膳宿。

147. 答案 (A)

(A) 因為 (conj.) (B) 在 *(prep.)*

(C) 如果 *(conj.)* (D) 雖然 *(conj.)*

解說 since「因為」，是連接詞，故選 (A)。

我們的農場有馴鹿和馬，也有一些狗。我們在冬季尤其需要幫手照顧馬，特別是餵食和清潔馬廄。任何與馴鹿有關的工作，會和我們夫妻倆一起完成。

148. 答案 (D)

(A) with (B) by

(C) for (D) of

解說 take care of「照顧」。

我們有兩間空房，而且當事情不是太忙時，在馬背上騎馬是可能的。

149. 答案 (B)

(A) 忙碌地 *(adv.)* (B) 忙碌的 *(adj.)*

(C) 忙碌 *(n.)* (D) 忙碌的（形容詞比較級）

解說 too「太」，是副詞，副詞可以修飾形容詞，故選 (B)，busy「忙碌的」。

字彙：

willing [ˋwɪlɪŋ] *(adj.)* 願意的／ particularly [pɚˋtɪkjələlɪ] *(adv.)* 尤其；特別／ stable [ˋstebḷ] *(n.)* 馬廄／ empty [ˋɛmptɪ] *(adj.)* 空的／ horseback [ˋhɔrsˏbæk] *(adv.)* 在馬背上

Questions 150-152 refer to the following newspaper article.

Councils to sell off land

Environmental campaigners are up in arms over proposals by local councils to ------- green belt land around our towns and cities to

150. (A) hand over
(B) give over
(C) bring over
(D) talk over

property developers.

Previously protected by law, these areas of trees and parks are, in many places, the only open spaces where local children can play away from traffic and pollution. They are also home to many plants and small wild animals. Recent changes to the law have ------- local councils to

151. (A) allowing
(B) allowed
(C) been allowed
(D) allows

decide for themselves which areas to protect and which to turn over to construction companies. Many hard up councils have voted to allow development on the previously protected land. This is thought to be mostly due to the revenue that will be generated by the sale of the land.

Campaigners have ------- that many councils are more interested

152. (A) debated
(B) compromised
(C) complained
(D) discussed

in balancing their books in the short term than long term sustainability.

Protests are expected.

第 150-152 題

議會出售土地

環境保護人士反對當地議會提案交出在我們鄉鎮及城市的綠地，給房地產開發商。

150. 答案 (A)

(A) 交出　　(B) 停止

(C) 把…帶過來　　(D) 商議

以前受法律保護，在很多地方，這些樹林和公園區域，是當地小孩唯一可以玩耍在遠離交通與污染的空曠場地。也是許多植物和小型野生動物的家園。最近法律的修改，已允許當地議會可自己決定哪些區域要保護，以及哪些要轉賣給建設公司。許多缺錢的議會已投票贊成票允許開發先前保護的土地。這被認為最可能是因為銷售土地的產生的錢，會成為議會的收益。

151. 答案 (B)

(A) 允許（現在分詞）　　(B) 允許（過去分詞）

(C) 允許（被動語態）　　(D) 允許（現在式動詞）

解說　現在完成式：主詞＋ have/has ＋過去分詞。只有選項 (B) 是過去分詞。不能選 (C)，因為是現在完成式的被動語態，不符合題意。現在完成式被動語態：主詞＋ have/has been ＋過去分詞。

例句　He has shown the photos to me.　他已經給我看過照片了。

環境保護人士抱怨道，很多議會對短期平衡帳冊上的不足金額較感興趣，而不是長期的永續平衡。

152. 答案 (C)

(A) 辯論　　(B) 妥協

(C) 抱怨　　(D) 討論

預期一定會有抗議。

字彙：

council [ˋkaʊnsḷ] *(n.)* 議會／ up in arms *(ph.)* 反對／ proposal [prəˋpozḷ] *(n.)* 提案／ hard up〔俚語〕缺錢；經濟拮据／ sustainability [səˏstenəˋbɪlɪtɪ] *(n.)* 永續性／ protest [ˋprotɛst] *(n.)* 抗議

Part 7. 單篇／雙篇文章理解

Questions 153-154 refer to the following memo.

December 5th

To all employees,

I'm happy to inform you that this year's Christmas party will take place on the evening of December 22nd at Basil's Steak Grill. For those of you not familiar with it; it's on Holland Road just up from the hospital. There will be plenty of food and drink, all accompanied by a small band playing traditional Christmas carols….. Feel free to sing along!

Don't be surprised if our CEO turns up dressed as Santa Claus bearing gifts for a few lucky partygoers. This would also be a great time to exchange any gifts of your own, although none should be over $20.

Merry Christmas to you and all your family.

Sherry Alcott

Director Human Resources- Rebound Engineering

153. Who would you NOT expect to be at the Christmas party?

(A) Sherry Alcott
(B) Santa Claus
(C) The company CEO
(D) Employees of Rebound Engineering

154. Whose Christmas party is this notice about?

(A) Basil's Steak Grill
(B) The hospital's
(C) Sherry Alcott's
(D) Rebound Engineering's

第 153-154 題

12月5日
致全體員工，

我開心的通知你們，今年的聖誕派對將會在12月22日傍晚，在 Basil's Steak Grill 牛排館舉行。不熟悉該地點的人，該牛排館是在 Holland 路上，就從醫院再往上面走。將會有充足的食物和飲品，派對全程伴著小型樂團演奏傳統的聖誕歌…請隨意地跟著高歌。

請不要驚訝，若是執行長裝扮的像聖誕老人出席，帶著禮物給幾個來參加派對的幸運兒。這也會是你們想交換自己禮物的好時機，然而這些禮物不應該超過20美金。

祝你與家人聖誕快樂
人力資源部主管 Sherry Alcott
Rebound Engineering 公司

153. 答案 (B) 你不會預期誰在聖誕派對裡？

(A) Sherry Alcott　(B) 聖誕老人
(C) 公司的執行長　(D) Rebound Engineering 公司的員工

解說 (A) 從倒數第二行，知道 "Sherry Alcott" 是發佈邀請消息的人，所以預期她也會出席。(C) 從原文第二段第一句 "Don't be surprised if our CEO turns up"，可以知道有預期公司的執行長可能會出席。(D) 從原文第二句 "To all employees"，以及原文最後一句，發佈的消息是來自 "Rebound Engineering"，就可以知道這間公司員工受邀參加派對。

154. 答案 (D) 這個通知是說關於誰的聖誕派對？

(A) Basil's Steak Grill 牛排館　(B) 醫院的
(C) Sherry Alcott 的　(D) Rebound Engineering 公司的

字彙：
take place *(ph.)* 舉行／ plenty [ˋplɛntɪ] *(adj.)* 充足的（＋of）／ accompany [əˋkʌmpənɪ] *(v.)* 伴隨／ traditional [trəˋdɪʃən!] *(adj.)* 傳統的／ carol [ˋkærəl] *(n.)*（聖誕）頌歌／ turn up *(ph.)* 出席／ bear [bɛr] *(v.)* 攜帶／ exchange [ɪksˋtʃendʒ] *(v.)* 交換

Questions 155-156 refer to the following warning.

WARNING!!!
DANGER OF DROWNING
NO SWIMMING
NO DIVING

This lake is deceptively deep water - over 20m deep.
All swimming, diving, paddling or playing in or near this lake is strictly prohibited.
There is a steep underwater cliff near the water's edge with a sudden drop of over 18m. Do NOT enter this water.
Quick response from emergency services is not available in this isolated location.
In an emergency call the ranger station on 0453 73835433.
Camping within 200m of the lake is also not allowed.
Stay safe and stay away from this water!
National Park and Ranger service

155. What is an underwater cliff?

(A) A place where the water suddenly gets very deep
(B) A place that looks good to dive from
(C) An isolated place
(D) The edge of the lake

156. Why is this lake so dangerous?

(A) Because it is in an isolated place.
(B) Because quick response from emergency services is not available.
(C) Because the water is deeper than it looks.
(D) Because many people have drowned there.

第 155-156 題

警告！！！
有溺水危險
禁止游泳
禁止跳水

這座湖是外表讓人看不出來的深水——水深超過 20 公尺。
所有游泳、跳水、划船、在湖裡玩水，或靠近這個湖，都是在法令上嚴格禁止的。
水的邊界處有個突然驟降 18 公尺的水底陡峭峭壁。不要進入這個水域。
緊急服務的快速回覆，在這個孤立的地點無效。
遇到緊急情況，請撥打國家公園森林護林處電話 0453 73835433。
在湖的 200 公尺內範圍也不允許露營。
保持安全，並遠離這個水域！
國家公園與森林護林服務處

155. 答案 (A) 什麼是水底峭壁？

(A) **水深突然變得很深的地方**　(B) 看起來是很好跳水地點的地方
(C) 孤立的地方　(D) 湖的邊界處

解說　從原文第七句"with a sudden drop of over 18m"可以得知是水深會突然驟降。

156. 答案 (C) 為什麼這座湖如此危險？

(A) 因為它在孤立的地方　(B) 因為緊急服務的快速回覆在這裡不管用。
(C) **因為水深比看起來的還深**　(D) 因為很多人在這裡溺斃

解說　這個警告標示從原文第五句"This lake is deceptively deep water-over 20m deep"，可以知道危險的原因，是因為湖水本身的水深極深。選項 (A)、(B) 兩個原因，皆不是湖本身危險的因素。(D) 未提。

字彙：

paddling [ˋpædl̩ɪŋ] *(v.)* 划船／ strictly [ˋstrɪktlɪ] *(adv.)* 嚴格地／ prohibit [prəˋhɪbɪt] *(v.)*（法令上的）禁止／ steep [stip] *(adj.)* 陡峭的／ cliff [klɪf] *(n.)* 峭壁／ ranger [ˋrendʒɚ] *(n.)* 國家公園森林護林員

Questions 157–158 refer to the following advertisement.

Introducing the new extraordinary PowerVac vacuum cleaner

More powerful than any other vacuum cleaner on the market today!

Four times the suction of its nearest rival.

Including our CleanBag dust collection system. Never get your hands dirty changing a vacuum cleaner's dust bag again.

Cordless use for up to 15 minutes.

ONLY $199

Not available in any shops- order online at www.powervac/cleaners.com or telephone 017 92831414.

Limited stocks available, so call soon to avoid disappointment.

Satisfaction guaranteed or 100% of your money back!

157. What does this advertisement claim?

(A) That PowerVac is cheaper than other vacuum cleaners.
(B) That PowerVac's suction is stronger than its competitors.
(C) That you can buy PowerVac at your local electrical store.
(D) That you will be satisfied.

158. What does this advertisement say about PowerVac?

(A) That you will never have to change the dust bag.
(B) That it's 100% free.
(C) That you won't get dirty changing the dust bag.
(D) That the vacuum cleaner only works for 15 minutes.

第 157–158 題

介紹令人驚奇的新上市 PowerVac 吸塵器

比任何其他現今市面上的吸塵器更強大！
吸力比接近可相比的他牌吸塵器大四倍。
包括我們的 CleanBag 集塵系統。再也不把您換吸塵器集塵袋的雙手弄髒。
可在不用電線插電的狀態下，使用 15 分鐘。
價格只要 199 美金。
任何實品商店均無展售——只採網路訂購 www.powervac/cleaners.com 或電話訂購 017 92831414。
供應的存貨有限，所以儘快打電話，才不會買不到失望。
滿意保證，否則全額退費！

157. 答案 (B) 這則廣告宣稱什麼？

(A) PowerVac 比其他品牌吸塵器更便宜
(B) PowerVac 吸塵器的吸力比它的競爭者大
(C) 你可以在當地電器行買 PowerVac 吸塵器
(D) 你會感到滿意

解說 第三句 "Four times the suction of its nearest rival"，說明廣告向消費者宣稱此產品的特點。不選 (A)，並未跟他牌價格做比較。不選 (C)，在實體商店均無展售。不選 (D)，最後一句，如果不滿意可以全額退費，不是你一定會對產品感到滿意。

158. 答案 (C) 這則廣告說什麼關於 PowerVac 吸塵器？

(A) 你永遠不用換集塵袋
(B) 完全免費
(C) 你在更換集塵袋時不會把雙手弄髒
(D) 吸塵器只能用 15 分鐘。

解說 "Never get your hands dirty changing a vacuum cleaner's dust bag again"，是特點。選項 (A)、(B) 未提到。選項 (D) 錯誤，在未插電使用的狀態下能夠用 15 分鐘。

字彙：

extraordinary [ɪkˋstrɔrdnˏɛrɪ] *(adj.)* 令人驚奇的／ suction [ˋsʌkʃən] *(n.)* 吸力／ cordless [ˋkɔrdlɪs] *(n.)* 不用電線／ disappointment [ˏdɪsəˋpɔɪntmənt] *(n.)* 失望／ stock [stɑk] *(n.)* 存貨／ guaranteed [ˋgærənˋtid] *(adj.)* 必定的；保證的

Questions 159–161 refer to the following article.

Instagram- The new Facebook?

Instagram- the online photo and video social network has increased in popularity many fold in recent months. It now boasts over 100 million regular users. This is still only a fraction of the 1.2 billion that Facebook has, but it's still giving it a run for its money in some markets.

Instagram was launched in October 2010. It allows users to upload their photos and video to the website and then to digitally alter them through various filters to give them a different look. Its user base rapidly grew and it soon started grabbing attention as it became one of the world's most successful social media start-ups.

Much of Instagram's popularity is due to its attraction to a younger age group. Facebook may seem rather outdated to the next generation, and so Instagram is particularly fashionable with teenagers who maybe don't feel comfortable being on the same social media site as their parents.

Should Facebook be worried? Probably not. In April 2012, Instagram was acquired by Facebook for US$1 billion. Maybe some teenagers will need to be looking out for a new place to hang out, if they don't want to be 'friends' with their parents.

159. According to this article which is NOT true?

(A) Most teenagers like to share their Facebook profile with their parents.

(B) Facebook has more users than Instagram.

(C) Instagram helps you modify photos.

(D) Instagram is popular with teenagers.

160. Why does this article suggest that Facebook doesn't need to be worried about Instagram?

(A) Because Facebook has more users

(B) Because Instagram is growing very fast

(C) Because Facebook owns Instagram

(D) Because young people prefer Instagram

161. What does Instagram help its users to do?

(A) It helps them take better photos and videos.

(B) It teaches them about digital photography.

(C) It helps them make their photos look better.

(D) It helps teenagers hide from their parents.

第 159–161 題

Instagram——新的臉書？

Instagram 是線上照片與影片社交網站，已經在最近幾個月增加好幾倍的用戶。它現在擁有超過一億常用用戶。這仍只是 Facebook 擁有的十二億用戶的一小部分，但是它仍在一些市場能與 Facebook 相比。

Instagram 在 2010 年 10 月發行。它允許使用者上傳他們的照片與影片至網站上，並且後續透過多種濾光器數位修改，讓他們看起來不一樣。它的使用者基於快速地成長，所以它很快開始抓住大家的注意，因為它成為了全世界其中一個成功的新堀起的社群媒介。

很多 Instagram 受喜愛的原因，是由於它對年輕族群的吸引力。Facebook 在下一世代看來，也許顯得有些過時，所以，Instagram 對於跟自己父母在同一個社群媒介，感到不自在的青少年來説，是特別流行的。

Facebook 應該要擔心嗎？大概不用。在 2012 年 4 月，Instagram 被 Facebook 以十億美金取得。也許一些青少年會需要再找新地方閒聊，如果他們不想跟父母成為「好友」的話。

159. 答案 (A) 依據這篇文章，以下哪一個不是事實？

(A) 大部分青少年喜歡跟他們的父母分享在 Facebook 上的概況

(B) Facebook 有比 Instagram 更多使用者

(C) Instagram 幫你修飾照片

(D) Instagram 受青少年喜愛

解說 選項 (A) 不是事實，從原文第三段第二句，"Instagram is particularly fashionable with teenagers who maybe don't feel comfortable being on the same social media site as their parents"，可以知道青少年並不喜歡跟父母同在 Facebook 社群。選項 (B) 在本文中是事實，原文第一段第三句，"This is still only a fraction of the 1.2 billion that Facebook has"。選項 (C) 在本文中是事實，原文第二段第二句，"the website and then to digitally alter them"。選項 (D) 在本文中是事實，原文第三段第一句 "Much of Instagram's popularity is due to its attraction to a younger age group"。

160. 答案 (C) 為什麼這篇文章暗指 Facebook 不需要擔心 Instagram？

(A) 因為 Facebook 擁有較多使用者

(B) 因為 Instagram 成長快速

(C) 因為 Facebook 持有 Instagram

(D) 因為青少年比較喜歡 Instagram.

解說 原文最後一段第二句，"In April 2012, Instagram was acquired by Facebook for US$1 billion"，說明 Facebook 已買下 Instagram，所以不用擔心它帶來的競爭。

161. 答案 (C) Instagram 幫助它的使用者做什麼？

(A) 它幫助他們拍好看一點的照片和影片

(B) 它教他們關於數位拍照

(C) 它幫助他們把照片弄得比較好看 .

(D) 它幫助青少年躲父母

解說 原文第二段第二句，"digitally alter them through various filters to give them a different look"，正常來說，修改就是想讓東西變得更好，所以是把相片與影片修改得更好。

字彙：

boast [bost] *(v.)* 擁有／ fraction [ˋfrækʃən] *(n.)* 小部份；些微／ upload [ʌpˋlod] *(v.)* 上傳／ filter [ˋfɪltɚ] *(n.)* 濾器；濾光器／ digitally [ˋdɪdʒɪtḷɪ] *(adv.)* 數位／ start-up [ˋstɑrt͵ʌp] *(n.)* 起始；新運作的公司／ popularity [͵pɑpjəˋlærətɪ] *(n.)* 討人喜歡的特點／ acquire [əˋkwaɪr] *(v.)* 取得

Questions 162-165 refer to the following letter.

159 Lodge Road
Columbus Ohio
Sept 17th
Dear Angela

My family and I would like to thank you so much for the wonderful time we had staying with you during our vacation last month.

The whole family agrees that this was the best vacation ever. It was made all the more memorable by staying in your home instead of a hotel.

Auckland is such a beautiful city. We met so many people and visited so many places with you as our guide. Now that we are back home, it makes Columbus seem quite dull.

We have hundreds of photos and many souvenirs. I'm enclosing some of the best shots with this letter for you. But most important are all the amazing memories of our time with you that we have brought home with us.

We particularly enjoyed visiting Sky Tower, the views were unforgettable; however, we all agree that the best day was the BBQ we had in your backyard with your extended family. What an astonishing family you have. We can't believe that you mother-in-law is 75. She looks so young.

We were planning to visit Australia next summer, but the children are now demanding that we return to New Zealand again next year. They say that they want to see a glacier and climb Mt cook.

Once again we would all like to say a very big thank you to you and all your children, but most of all to your husband, John, for making us feel so welcome. Remember that you are all welcome at our home here in Columbus any time.

Sincerely yours
Rachel Hughes

162. Apart from those already staying at the house, who came to the BBQ?

(A) John's mother
(B) Rachel's mother
(C) Angela's mother
(D) John's father

163. Where do Angela and her family live?

(A) Columbus
(B) Australia
(C) Mt Cook
(D) Auckland

164. What does Rachel offer Angela's family?

(A) To take them to see a glacier
(B) To host a BBQ for them
(C) A place for them to stay in Columbus
(D) To visit them in Australia next year

165. What should Angela find with this letter?

(A) tickets to Columbus
(B) some souvenirs
(C) some memories
(D) some photographs

第 162-165 題

Lodge 路，159 號
俄亥俄州，哥倫布市
九月十七日
親愛的 Angela，

我和家人想謝謝你，上個月我們在假期間暫住在你家，度過了美好的時光。

全家人都一致贊同這是我們有始以來最棒的一次假期。住在你們家而不是飯店，讓一切記憶更深刻。

奧克蘭是如此美麗的城市。有你當我們的嚮導，我們遇見如此多的人，並造訪了如此多的地方。現在我們回到家了，它讓哥倫布市顯得蠻單調。

我們拍了好幾百張相片，也有許多紀念品。我在這封信裡封入一些最棒的相片給你。但是最重要的是，我們帶回家的所有與你在一起美妙的回憶。

我們尤其喜愛造訪天空塔，那個景色是永生難忘的；然而我們一致同意很棒的一天，是與你其他的家庭成員在你家後院烤肉。你的家人是多麼令人驚豔。我們不相信你的婆婆 75 歲了。她看起來是如此年輕。

我們計畫明年夏季造訪澳洲，但是現在孩子們現在要求，明年要再次回到紐西蘭。他們說他們想要看冰河，也想爬庫克山。

再次地，我們想向你和你的孩子們說聲最大的感謝，但最感謝你丈夫 John，讓我們感到如此被歡迎。記得，你們全都歡迎隨時來我們位於哥倫布市的家。

誠摯的
Rachel Hughes

162. 答案 (A) 除了已經暫住在房子裡的人，還有誰來烤肉？

(A) John 的母親　　(B) Rachel 的母親
(C) Angela 的母親　　(D) John 的父親

解說　原文第五段，"the BBQ we had in your backyard with your extended family.... We can't believe that you mother-in-law is 75"，說明是 Angela 的婆婆，原文最後一段第二句，"to your husband, John"，得知 Angela 的先生是 John，表示婆婆就是 John 的母親。

163. 答案 (D) Angela 與她的家人住在哪裡？

(A) 哥倫布市 (B) 澳洲

(C) 庫克山 **(D) 奧克蘭**

解說 從原文第二段 "staying in your home instead of a hotel" 與原文第三段，"Auckland is such a beautiful city. We met so many people and visited so many places with you as our guide"，可以知道 Angela 的家是在奧克蘭。選項 (A) 是寄信者 Rachel Hughes 居住的地方。選項 (B) 是寄信者計畫明年要去的地方。選項 (D) 是寄信者的孩子想爬的山。

164. 答案 (C) Rachel 提供 Angela 的家庭什麼？

(A) 帶他們去看冰河

(B) 為他們辦一場烤肉

(C) 一個他們來哥倫布市可以暫住的地方

(D) 明年去澳洲拜訪他們

解說 原文最後一段，"Remember that you are all welcome at our home here in Columbus any time"。選項 (A)、(B)，在本文均未提供這樣的建議。選項 (D)，原文第六段，"but the children are now demanding that we return to New Zealand again next year" 應是明年他們會應孩子要求會回到紐西蘭拜訪他們，而不是澳洲。

165. 答案 (D) Angela 應該會在這封信發現什麼？

(A) 到哥倫布市的票

(B) 一些紀念品

(C) 一些回憶

(D) 一些相片

解說 從原文第四段，"I'm enclosing some of the best shots with this letter for you"，可以知道信裡附上一些相片。

字彙：

souvenir [ˋsuvə͵nɪr] *(n.)* 紀念品／enclose [ɪnˋkloz] *(v.)* 封入／amazing [əˋmezɪŋ] *(adj.)* 驚人的／guide [gaɪd] *(n.)* 嚮導／unforgettable [͵ʌnfɚˋgɛtəbl̩] *(adj.)* 難忘的；永遠記得的／extended [ɪkˋstɛndɪd] *(adj.)* 延伸的／astonishing [əˋstɑnɪʃɪŋ] *(adj.)* 令人驚豔的／demand [dɪˋmænd] *(v.)* 要求

Questions 166–169 refer to the following article.

Creek Lake Science University Summer Lectures

Creek Lake Science University is proud to announce its summer line up of guest lectures. These popular and creative talks aim to inspire the imagination of the audiences and create greater interest in the sciences. All lectures are free and open to the public; however only limited seating is available and will be strictly allocated on a first come first served basis.

Monday, August 4th
Dr. John Lepont, Professor of Astronomy
Dr. Lepont will lecture on black holes. What have we learnt about them from space telescopes in the past decade? Is there really a giant black hole at the center of our galaxy? Do they hold the key to our galaxy's future?

Wednesday, August 6th
Mrs. Judith Syths, Director of Research at Rockwell Labs
And Dr. Paul Owens, Professor of Physics
As modern physics probes ever deeper into the mystery of the atom, more and more questions are starting to be asked. Join the debate as two of the rising stars of modern physics debate, "Was Einstein right?"

Friday, August 8th
Dr. Richard Hawkins, Botanist and Explorer
The origins of life. Where did we all come from? And where are we going? From Darwin to DNA, what does the future hold for mankind?

All lectures are introduced by the Dean of Studies, Professor Vincent Lee, and conclude with time for audience questions.

166. If you wish to attend one of these lecture, what does the article suggest you do?

(A) Buy your ticket in advance
(B) Arrive early
(C) Enroll in the university
(D) Bring a seat

167. Ashed Hazeed likes to hear both sides of things, whose lecture is he most likely to enjoy?

(A) Dr. John Lepont's
(B) Dr. Richard Hawkins'
(C) Mrs. Judith Syths and Dr. Paul Owens'
(D) Professor Vincent Lee's

168. Who can attend these lectures?

(A) Students of Creek Lake Science university
(B) Anyone
(C) Professors of physics and astronomy
(D) Darwin and Einstein

169. What are you unlikely to learn about from these lectures?

(A) The future of the human race
(B) Space
(C) Einstein's theories
(D) Life on other planets

第 166–169 題

Creek Lake 科學大學夏季講座

Creek Lake 科學大學很驕傲宣佈本校夏季系列講座。這些受歡迎跟有創造力的談話，目標要鼓舞聽眾的想像力，並創造在科學的更多興趣。所有講座皆免費，而且是開放給公眾參加的；然而，只有座位數是有限制的，將會嚴格地以先來的人先有位置的方式分配。

八月四日，星期一

John Lepont 博士，天文學教授

Lepon 博士將會演講關於黑洞。我們在過去十年來，從太空望遠鏡學到了什麼關於他們的事？真的有巨大的黑洞在我們的銀河中心嗎？他們有我們銀河的未來重要關鍵嗎？

八月六日，星期三

Judith Syths 女士，Rockwell 實驗室研究執行長

以及 Paul Owens 博士，物理學教授

因現代物理學前所未有地深入探測原子的謎，愈來愈多問題開始被提出質疑。參加這兩位現代物理學新起之星的辯論，「愛因斯坦是對的嗎？」

八月八日，星期五

Richard Hawkins 博士，植物學家與探險家

生命的起源。我們所有的人是從哪裡來的？我們要去哪裡？從達爾文到 DNA，未來有什麼人類需要面臨的結果？

所有講座均由研究協會 Vincent Lee 教授介紹，並且結束會有時間讓觀眾發問。

166. 答案 (B) 如果你想出席這些其中一場講座，文章中建議你該怎麼做？

(A) 事先買好票　　(B) 早一點到

(C) 註冊該大學　　(D) 帶一個座位

解說　原文第一段第三句，"only limited seating is available and will be strictly allocated on a first come first served basis"，說明座位有限，沒了就沒辦法參加，而且是先到的人有座位，所以建議要早一點到。(A)

不正確，原文第一段第三句，"All lectures are free"。說明講座不用錢，所以也不需要去買票。選項 (C)、(D) 文章內容未提及。

167. 答案 (C) Ashed Hazeed 喜歡聽雙方對事情的看法，他最有可能參加誰的講座？

(A) John Lepont 博士的

(B) Richard Hawkins 博士的

(C) 女士 Judith Syths 與 Paul Owens 博士的

(D) Vincent Lee 教授的

解說 原文第三段第四句，"Join the debate as two of the rising stars of modern physics debate"，表示該場演說有兩位演講者，並且會在看法上做出辯論，故選 (C)。

168. 答案 (B) 誰可以出席這些講座？

(A) Creek Lake 科學大學的學生

(B) 任何人

(C) 物理學與天文學教授

(D) 達爾文和愛因斯坦

解說 從原文第一段第三句，"open to the public" 可以知道，這些講座是開放給大眾，沒有身份限制，任何人都可以參加的。

169. 答案 (D) 你從這些講座不太可能學到什麼？

(A) 人類的未來 (B) 太空

(C) 愛因斯坦的理論 **(D) 其他星球上的生命**

解說 選項 (A)，原文第四段第三句，"what does the future hold for mankind"，知道講座內容會提及人類未來。選項 (B)，原文第二段第二句，"Dr. Lepont will lecture on black holes" .，知道該場講座會談論外太空。選項 (C)，原文第三段最後一句，"Was Einstein right?"，知道會討論愛因斯坦的理論。選項 (D)，在本文並未提及。

字彙：

allocate [ˋæləˏket] *(v.)* 分配／ astronomy [əsˋtrɑnəmɪ] *(n.)* 天文學／ lecture [ˋlɛktʃɚ] *(n./v.)* 授課；講座；演講／ physics [ˋfɪzɪks] *(n.)* 物理學／ conclude [kənˋklud] *(v.)* 結束（＋ with）／ debate [dɪˋbet] *(n.)* 辯論

Test 1 Test 2 Test 3 Test 4 Test 5

Questions 170–172 refer to the following advertisement.

Boot Camp's Workout:
A Week by Week, 3-Month Exercise Program

Start your new year off with this 12-week fitness program by Boot Camp. Designed to build body strength, lose weight, enhance endurance, and improve health and energy levels. It's a great beginner-level program for those new to exercise, or it can be used as a warm-up for the more advanced. The first phase, lasting 30 days, can be done in the comfort of your own home, and by the end of phase three the target is to be able to jog for thirty minutes.
Weeks 1-4 (Phase 1)

Complete the following exercise routine once a day in the first week, increasing to four times a day by the fourth week.

1. Slowly stretch all limbs for one minute.
2. Perform 100 step-ups onto a stepping stool.
3. Perform 10 sit-ups whilst lying down.
4. Five minutes of brisk walking around the house or garden.
5. Repeat 100 step-ups onto a stepping stool.

Rest for one minute between each step.

To receive phases two and three please register for our newsletter at www.bootcamp/fitnesss.com

170. What is Boot Camp's main purpose in this article?

(A) To help people get fit

(B) To sell stepping stools

(C) To get people to sign up for their newsletter

(D) To sell their exercise program

171. By week four how many step-ups should a participant in the exercise program be doing each day?

(A) 800

(B) 100

(C) 400

(D) 200

172. What is the target for a participant in the exercise program after three months?

(A) To be able to run

(B) To be able to run slowly for thirty minutes

(C) To be healthy

(D) To be thin

第 170–172 題

魔鬼訓練營體能訓練：為期三個月的每週課程

用這個魔鬼訓練營為期 12 週的健身課程，來開始你嶄新的一年。課程設計為了增進體力、減重、增加耐力，並且改善健康與精力程度。對那些運動新手來說，是個很棒的初級者程度課程，或是也可以當成進階健身的暖身練習。第一個階段，為期 30 天，你可以在家裡舒適的完成，然後在第三階段結束之前，目標是能夠慢跑三十分鐘。

第一至四週（第一階段）

在第一週，每天一次完成以下運動程序；到第四週，增加至每天四次。

1. 慢慢地伸展四肢一分鐘。
2. 在踏步凳上做 100 次走台階。
3. 躺著做 10 次仰臥起坐。
4. 在房子四周或花園快走五分鐘。
5. 在踏步凳上重覆做 100 次走台階。

在每個程序之間休息一分鐘。

要收到第二與第三階段，請至 www.bootcamp/fitnesss.com，註冊我們的時事通訊。

170. 答案 (C) 魔鬼訓練營在本文中的主要目的為何？

(A) 幫助人變瘦

(B) 賣踏步凳

(C) **要人註冊他們的時事通訊**

(D) 賣他們的運動課程

解說 選項 (A)、(B)、(D) 並未在文章中提及，亦無收費資訊。選項 (C) 在原文最後一句，"To receive steps two and three please register for our newsletter"，他們的目的是要有興趣得到進一步資訊的人，至他們的網站註冊。

171. 答案 (A) 到了第四週，這項運動課程的參與者每天應該要做幾次走台階？

(A) 800

(B) 100

(C) 400

(D) 200

解說 在原文第九行，"increasing to four times a day by the fourth week"，知道到了第四週要增加至四倍。原文第十一行，"Perform 100 step-ups onto a stepping stool"，是運動程序第 2 項，要做 100 次；原文第十四行，"Repeat 100 step-ups onto a stepping stool"，是運動程序第 5 項，要再重覆做 100 次，所以是 200 乘以四倍，等於 800 次。

172. 答案 (B) 給運動課程的參與者，在三個月後達到什麼目標？

(A) 能夠跑步

(B) **能夠慢慢地跑三十分鐘**

(C) 變健康

(D) 變瘦

解說 選項 (A) 在原文第六行 "by the end of phase three the target is to be able to jog for thirty minutes" 提到跑步，是 jog「慢跑」，故不能選 (A)。選項 (C)、(D) 並未在文章裡宣稱有這樣的效果。

字彙：

endurance [ɪn`djʊrəns] *(n.)* 耐力／ warm-up [`wɔrm,ʌp] *(n.)* 準備練習／ phase [fez] *(n.)* 階段／ routine [ru`tin] *(n.)* 程序／ complete [kəm`plit] *(v.)* 完成／ limb [lɪm] *(n.)* 肢；臂／ perform [pɚ`fɔrm] *(v.)* 做；履行／ register [`rɛdʒɪstɚ] *(v.)* 註冊；登記

Questions 173-176 refer to the following report.

LOCAL VILLAGE CHERISHES PAIR OF ENDANGERED FALCONS

Residents have launched daily patrols to monitor and protect a pair of endangered falcons found nesting in a tree outside their village. Locals hope that the birds will increase tourism to their village and already a trade in bamboo model falcons has taken hold providing a boost to the local economy.

First noticed in early September, and initially kept a closely guarded secret; however, after villagers noticed four young falcons also in the nest, word got out in the nearby town. Patrols were then started for fear that someone might try to capture the falcons and their young. Every night, for over three months now, a pair of volunteers spends the night guarding the tree which houses the nest.

As more and more visitors came to the village, locals constructed a hide near the tree, so that the birds could be viewed more easily without disturbing them.

Local community leader, Amy Lin, commented that under the care of the village the falcons have thrived and the young are now learning to fly. Lin continued, "At first we feared for their survival, but the response from the local community couldn't have been better. We have no trouble finding volunteer for our patrols, and it has even become something of a social event. I couldn't be prouder of my village."

Falcons have long been known to nest in the local forests, but with increased deforestation in the area, bird numbers have been steadily decreasing over the past decade. It is hoped that this nesting pair will be the first of many that will visit the area and that the four young falcons will return next year to nest and raise their own young.

Ornithologists who have visited the site have praised the response of the village and say that this should be used as an example of how humans and birds can not only coexist but also benefit from each other.

173. What does an ornithologist do?

(A) Study forests

(B) Guard the tree

(C) Study birds

(D) Find volunteers

174. What does "it has even become something of a social event" mean?

(A) People enjoy doing it.

(B) Volunteers must spend all night there.

(C) The whole village takes care of the birds.

(D) The villagers feed the birds.

175. Which of the following does Amy Lin NOT say?

(A) The young falcons are doing well.

(B) She is proud of her village.

(C) Volunteers are easy to find.

(D) She is worried about the birds now.

176. Why were patrols started?

(A) Someone tried to steal the falcons.

(B) A hide had been built.

(C) To sell more model falcons.

(D) People outside the village heard about the birds.

第 173-176 題

本地村莊保育一對瀕臨絕種的獵鷹

村民已展開每日巡邏，保護一對被發現在村莊外築巢，瀕臨絕種的獵鷹。當地民眾希望獵鷹能增加造訪的遊客，竹編的手工獵鷹模型，振興了當地經濟。

一開始是在九月初注意到這件事，起初他們小心地保守這個祕密，然而在村民察覺也有四隻年幼獵鷹在鳥巢裡時，風聲就傳到了鄰近村莊。起初巡邏是因擔心也許有人會試圖補捉這些獵鷹。至今已超過三個月，每晚兩人一組志工會花整晚時間，守護這棵築了巢的樹。

因為造訪村莊的遊客愈來愈多，當地村民建造一間觀鳥亭在樹附近，以利觀察鳥而不打擾牠們。

當地社區領導人 Amy 林評論道，在村民的照料下，獵鷹已茁壯成長，而年幼獵鷹現在正在學飛。林小姐繼續說，「一開始我們擔心他們能否生存，但是當地社區民眾的反應再好不過了。我們沒有找不到志工來巡邏的問題，它甚至變成一種社區裡的大事。我對我的村莊倍感驕傲。」

長久以來，大家都知道獵鷹在當地森林築巢，但是隨著該區域砍伐森林增加，鳥類數量過去十年來持續下降。盼望這對築巢的獵鷹能是眾多鳥類中首先造訪該森林區的鳥類，也希望這四隻年幼獵鷹明年能回來築巢，養育牠們的下一代。

造訪過該地點的鳥類學家，對該村莊的反應讚譽有加，還說這應該被用來做為人類與鳥類不只能共存，也能互利的範例。

173. 答案 (C) 鳥類學家做什麼？

(A) 研究森林
(B) 守護樹木
(C) 研究鳥類
(D) 尋找志工

174. 答案 (A) 這句「它甚至變成一種社區裡的大事」意思為何？

(A) **大家喜愛這麼做**

(B) 志工必須花了整晚在那裡

(C) 全村莊的人照顧鳥

(D) 村民餵鳥

解說 原文四段第三句 "We have no trouble finding volunteers for our patrols,"，足以得知大家喜愛這麼做。

175. 答案 (D) Amy 林沒有做出下列哪項敘述？

(A) 年幼的獵鷹成長得很好

(B) 她為她的村莊感到驕傲

(C) 志工很容易找到

(D) **她現在擔心這些鳥**

解說 (A) 在原文第四段第一句 "the young are now learning to fly"。(B) 在原文第四段最後一句 "I couldn't be prouder of my village."。(C) 在原文第四段第三句 "We have no trouble finding volunteers for our patrols"。

176. 答案 (D) 為什麼開始巡邏？

(A) 有人試著偷獵鷹

(B) 建造了觀鳥亭

(C) 為了多賣一些獵鷹模型

(D) **村莊外的人聽到關於這些鳥的消息**

解說 只能選擇 (D)，因為他們是擔心有人會偷獵鷹，並非在已經發生這件事之後才開始巡邏。

字彙：

falcon [ˋfælkən] *(n.)* 獵鷹／ initially [ɪˋnɪʃəlɪ] *(adv.)* 最初／ patrol [pəˋtrol] (v./n.) 巡邏／ comment [ˋkɑmɛnt] *(v.)* 發表評論／ deforestation [ˌdifɔrəsˋteʃən] *(n.)* 砍伐森林／ ornithologist [ˌɔrnəˋθɑlədʒɪst] *(n.)* 鳥類學家／ coexist [ˋkoɪgˋzɪst] *(v.)* 共存

Questions 177-180 refer to the following introduction.

THE BRISTOL INTERNATIONAL BALLOON FIESTA

The Bristol International Balloon fiesta is held annually just outside the city of Bristol in the south west of England. It has become one of the region's most popular and spectacular tourist attractions. Held in August on a large country estate on the edge of Bristol, it is now Europe's biggest balloon festival. Regular crowds of over 100,000 attend daily for the four days of displays.

Mass launches are held every morning and evening where hundreds of balloons can be seem taking off almost at the same time. You will have to be up early to see the morning launch as it's held at 6am. The evening launches are at 6pm.

One of the most popular events is the night glow. Usually on two evenings during the fiesta dozens of tethered balloons are lit and inflated in the early evening. They then glow in the dark timed to music. This is followed by a spectacular fireworks display. Many people say that the night glow is the highlight of the whole fiesta.

The fiesta, which was first held in 1979, used to be held in September, but due to poor weather leading to muddy grounds and canceled flights the fiesta was moved to its present August dates.

Over the years the fiesta has become well known for its strangely shaped balloons. At first locally manufactured balloons in the shapes of bottles, cartoon characters and even supermarket trolleys were regularly seen. Now international teams, from all over the world, visit bringing their own local designs. Recently there have been UFOs from the US and Kiwis from New Zealand.

The entertainment is not only limited to the balloons. With fairground rides, air displays and plenty of stalls to keep children happy during the day.

And finally possibly the best part of the fiesta is that it is totally free. There is no charge to enter the event. With around half a million visitors expected through the gates this year, if you do make the trip, you certainly won't be alone.

177. Why was the fiesta moved from September to August?

(A) More international teams can visit in September.

(B) It rains less is August.

(C) The nights are darker

(D) Children are happier.

178. What is the most popular event at the fiesta?

(A) The night glow

(B) The mass launches

(C) The air shows

(D) The fairground rides

179. What has the balloon fiesta become famous for?

(A) Spectacular air shows

(B) Food stalls for children

(C) Fireworks displays

(D) Balloons that look like other things

180. What reason might discourage someone from visiting?

(A) The cost

(B) The night glow

(C) The crowds

(D) The UFOs

第 177-180 題

布里斯托國際熱氣球節

布里斯托國際熱氣球節，每年於剛好位於該市外的英國西南部舉行。它已成為該地區其中一個最受歡迎的活動，也是一股最吸引遊客的吸引力，每年八月舉辦在布里斯托邊界的廣大腹地，是現在歐洲最盛大的熱氣球節。一般前來參加的民眾，在為期四天的展期中，每日累計超過十萬人次。

每日早晨與傍晚開始做彌撒時，也幾乎能同時看見數以百計的熱氣球升空。你必須夠早起床才能看見早場的熱氣球升空，因為是在早上6點舉行。傍晚場的熱氣球升空在晚上6點。

最受歡迎的一個項目是晚間點燈秀。通常在該節慶期間會有兩個晚上，在較早的傍晚時分將許多拴好固定住的熱氣球充氣並點上火源。然後就在黑暗中閃耀光芒，替音樂會揭開序幕。這也伴隨著壯觀的煙火。很多人說晚間點燈秀是整個節慶最精彩的部分。

第一次舉辦這個節慶是在1979年，以前在九月舉行，但是由於天候不佳導致滿地泥濘取消飛行，所以現在節慶才移到八月舉行。

多年以來，熱氣球節以奇形怪狀的熱氣球聞名。一開始，當地製造瓶子形狀、卡通角色造型的熱氣球，還有甚至超級市場購物車造形的也很常見。現在來自世界各地的國際團隊，帶著他們自己的設計與會。最近還有自美國帶來的飛碟造形，以及紐西蘭產鷸鴕鳥造型。

娛樂節目不只限熱氣球。有露天遊樂團的乘座設施、飛機飛行表演，以及超多攤位讓小孩們開心地度過一整天。

最後，可能是這節慶最棒的部分，那就是完全免費。進入會場不需收費。今年預估湧入五十萬名遊客進入會場，如果你有要到那裡的旅程，你必定不會孤單。

177. 答案 (B) 為什麼節慶從九月移到八月？

(A) 較多國際團隊能在九月造訪

(B) 八月較少下雨

(B) 夜晚比較暗

(C) 小孩比較開心

解說 原文第四段第一句 "due to poor weather"。

178. 答案 (A) 節慶中最受歡迎的項目是什麼？

(A) 晚間點燈秀

(B) 開始做彌撒

(C) 飛機飛行表演

(D) 露天遊樂團的乘座設施

解說 原文第三段第一句 "most popular events is the night glow"。

179. 答案 (D) 熱氣球節有名的原因為何？

(A) 壯觀的飛機飛行表演

(B) 為小孩設置的食物攤位

(C) 煙火秀

(D) 熱氣球看起來像別的東西

解說 從原文第五段第一句，"has become well known for its strangely shaped balloons"，足以得知。

180. 答案 (C) 什麼原因也許讓想造訪的人怯步？

(A) 價錢

(B) 晚間點燈秀

(C) 擠滿了人

(D) 飛碟

解說 依原文最後一段第三句 "With around half a million visitors expected through the gates this year" 的陳述，足以推測遊客想法，如此多遊客湧入會場，也許會造成塞車與飯店不好預訂的問題。

字彙：

fiesta [fɪ`ɛstə] *(n.)* 節慶；喜慶日（與 festival 同義）／ region [`ridʒən] *(n.)* 地區／ spectacular [spɛk`tækjələ˞] *(adj.)* 壯觀的／ attraction [ə`trækʃən] *(n.)* 吸引；吸引力／ tether [`tɛðə˞] *(v.)* 栓／ display [dɪ`sple] *(n./v.)* 陳列；表演／ manufacture [ˌmænjə`fæktʃə˞] *(v.)* 製造（大量）

Questions 181-185 refer to the following advertisement and email.

MISSING

LOST DOG

Reward $100

Four-year-old brown male mongrel

Answers to the name Rodney

Last seen on Friday, March 13th in the park behind Redgate Elementary School.

He has a black collar with his name on it.

Rodney is a very friendly dog. He loves to play with anyone and chase anything. He rarely barks and will never bite, so don't be afraid to try to catch him if you find him. His favorite treat is a carrot.

There is a reward of $100 for anyone who finds Rodney.

Call 0634 7849381 ask for Celeste.

Email lostrodney@gmail.com

To:	Celeste
From:	Bonnie

I think that I know where Rodney is. I've seen a brown mongrel near my house quite a few times these past few days. I'm not sure of its gender, but it's spending the nights in the small woods behind my house on Park Avenue, just by the horse stables.

Last time I saw it, it looked very hungry and I left it some dog food.

I was afraid to look at its collar because I'm not very good with animals and I never approach stray dogs.

It is limping. It appears to have a problem just above one of its paws.

I wouldn't accept anything for helping you. I just hope you can find Rodney.

I'll look out for you tonight in the woods behind my house.

181. Other than where Rodney is, what information does Bonnie have that Celeste doesn't?

(A) That Rodney has injured a leg
(B) That Rodney is in the park behind Redgate Elementary School
(C) That Rodney likes to eat carrots
(D) That Rodney is wearing a collar

182. What isn't Bonnie sure of?

(A) Where the dog she has found is sleeping
(B) Whether the dog she has found is a boy or a girl
(C) If the dog she has found has a collar
(D) If the dog she has found is hungry

183. What pet does Bonnie probably have?

(A) a dog
(B) a cat
(C) a horse
(D) no pet

184. After reading this email, what would you expect Celeste to do?

(A) Go to the park to look for Rodney
(B) Visit the woods on Park Avenue tonight
(C) Telephone Bonnie
(D) Buy Rodney a new collar

185. After Celeste finds Rodney, what will she probably do?

(A) Give Bonnie $100
(B) Sleep in the woods
(C) Take Rodney to the vet
(D) Give Bonnie some dog food

第 181-185 題

失蹤

走失的狗

懸賞 100 美金

四歲棕色公的混種狗
會對 Rodney 這個名字有回應
最後一次看見是在三月十三日星期五，Redgate 小學後面的公園。
牠戴有印著牠的名字的黑色項圈。
Rodney 是隻非常友善的狗。牠愛跟任何人玩，也追逐任何東西。牠很少吠，而且從不咬人，所以，如果你發現牠，請不要害怕去抓牠，牠最愛的小款待是紅蘿蔔。
這裡有懸賞 100 美金給任何找到 Rodney 的人。
請打電話至 0634 7849381 找 Celeste。
電子信箱 lostrodney@gmail.com

收件者:	Celeste
寄件者:	Bonnie

我想我知道 Rodney 在哪裡。過去這幾天，我在我家附近看見一隻棕色混種狗相當多次。我不確定牠的性別，但是牠晚上都在我位於公園大道住家後面的小林地，就在馬廄旁。
上次我看見牠時，牠看起來非常餓，而我餵牠一些食物。
我很害怕去看牠的項圈，因為我不擅長跟動物在一起，我從未接近流浪狗。
牠一跛一跛的走路。看起來似乎就在其中一個腳爪上面有問題。
幫助你，我不會接受任何東西。我只希望你能找到 Rodney。
今晚我會幫你留意找我家後方的林地。

181. 答案 (A) 除了的所在位置之外，Bonnie 擁有什麼 Celeste 沒有的資訊？

(A) Rodney 一腿受傷了　　(B) Rodney 在 Redgate 國小後面的公園
(C) Rodney 喜歡吃紅蘿蔔　　(D) Rodney 有戴項圈

解說　在第一篇並未提到 Rodney 有受傷。在第二篇第四段，"It is limping. It

appears to have a problem just above one of its paws" 走失後可能如此。

182. 答案 (B) Bonnie 不確定什麼？

(A) 她找到的狗是否在睡覺　(B) 不知道她找到的狗是公的還是母的

(C) 她找到的狗有沒有戴項圈　(D) 她找到的狗是不是餓的

解說 從第二篇第一段第三句，"I'm not sure of its gender" 故選 (B)。選項 (A)，文章中並未提到。選項 (C)，從第二篇第三段，"I was afraid to look at its collar"，可知狗有戴項圈。選項 (D)，從第二篇第二段，"It looked very hungry"，可知狗是餓的。

183. 答案 (D) Bonnie 可能會有什麼寵物？

(A) 狗　(B) 貓

(C) 馬　(D) 沒有寵物

解說 在第二篇原文第三段，"I'm not very good with animals"，可以猜想到 Bonnie 因不擅長跟動物在一起，所以不會養寵物，故選 (D)。

184. 答案 (B) 在讀完這封電子郵件之後，你預期 Celeste 會做什麼？

(A) 去公園找 Rodney　(B) 今晚去公園大道的林地

(C) 打電話給 Bonnie　(D) 幫 Rodney 買一個新項圈

解說 第二篇原文最後一句 "I'll look out for you tonight in the woods behind my house"，還有第二篇原文第一段第三句，"my house on Park Avenue"，表示今晚 Bonnie 會去幫她留心的找狗，而她是住在公園大道，身為主人一定也會想去公園大道的林地找自己的愛狗，故選 (B)。

185. 答案 (C) 在 Celeste 找到 Rodney 之後，她大概會做什麼？

(A) 給 Bonnie 100 美金　(B) 睡在林地裡

(C) 帶 Rodney 去看獸醫　(D) 給 Bonnie 一些狗食

解說 從第二篇原文第四段 "It is limping"，知道狗可能受傷了，所以需就醫治療，故選 (C)。第二篇原文倒數第三句，"I wouldn't accept anything for helping you"，可以知道不會給 Bonnie 任何東西，故不能選 (A)。

字彙：

reward [rɪˋwɔrd] *(n.)* 獎賞；懸賞／ collar [ˋkɑlɚ] *(n.)* 項圈／ treat [trit] *(n.)* 小款待／ gender [ˋdʒɛndɚ] *(n.)* 性別／ approach [əˋprotʃ] *(v.)* 接近／ stray [stre] *(adj.)* 流浪的／ limp [lɪmp] *(v.)* 跛行

Questions 186-190 refer to the following Health Announcements.

Rosworth County Health Department Family Flu Clinic

The Rosworth County Health Department will have a Family Flu Clinic on Friday, January 15th from 2pm to 7pm.

Children in pre-school through twelfth grade and pregnant women will be vaccinated FREE of charge.

Vaccine supply is limited and will be given on a first come, first served basis.

All other family members can get vaccinated at this clinic for a $10 fee.

If you can't come to the flu clinic on this day, you can still get the vaccination, but an appointment will be necessary.

Remember, flu vaccinations are the best protection against the flu!

Advisement from the Health Officer

We will soon enter the influenza season. Influenza cases usually begin in November, but the highest number of cases occur in January and February. In an average year influenza is the eighth leading cause of death in the country and leads to approximately 750,000 hospitalizations.

People 65 and older are most likely to die from complications of influenza (the flu). Although it is extremely important for seniors to get vaccinated, we know that the vaccine is not as effective as people get older. This makes it even more important for children to get vaccinated, so that they are less likely to spread the virus to their parents and grandparents.

Pregnant women are also at greater risk of complications from influenza than non-pregnant women. All health officials agree on the safety and importance of vaccination during pregnancy. Vaccination protects not only the mother, but also the unborn child.

186. Mary is expecting her fourth child. She, her husband and all of their children, who are in elementary school, want to get vaccinated at the clinic. How much will it cost them?

(A) $60
(B) $50
(C) $10
(D) It will be free

187. According to these articles, who are most at risk from the flu?

(A) Old people
(B) Pre-school children
(C) Pregnant women
(D) Grandparents

188. What should someone who wants to get vaccinated, but is unable to attend the flu clinic do?

(A) Telephone the clinic and arrange a time
(B) Go to the clinic anytime
(C) Take a child with them to the clinic
(D) Pay $10

189. According to these articles, what is the best way to avoid the flu?

(A) Keep away from children
(B) Get vaccinated
(C) Don't go near pregnant women.
(D) Telephone the clinic to arrange an appointment

190. According to these articles, what is one of the reasons for children to get vaccinated?

(A) Because the flu is most likely to kill children
(B) Because they may infect their mother who may be pregnant
(C) Because they may infect their older relatives
(D) Because it's free

第 186-190 題

Rosworth 縣立健康部門暨家庭流感會診

Rosworth 縣健康部門將會在一月十五日，從下午兩點至七點，有家庭流感會診。

兒童從幼兒園至高中生，以及懷孕婦女，施打該疫苗免費。

疫苗供應有限，將採取先到先施打的分配方式。

所有其他家庭成員可以在這次會診，以 10 美金費用施打疫苗。

如果你在這一天不克前往流感會診，你仍可以施疫苗，但是會需要預約。

切記，流感疫苗是對抗流感最好的保護！

來自健康部長的宣導

我們不久將進入流行性感冒季節。流感病例通常從十一月開始，但是病例件數最高是在一月和二月。普通的一年來說，流行性感間是國內前八大死因，並導致大約七十五萬人住院治療。

65 以上的人，最可能死於流行性感冒（流感）併發症。雖然對年長的人來說，施打疫苗極為重要，不過我們知道疫苗對愈年長的人，不是一樣有效。這讓兒童施打疫苗更為重要，所以他們比較不可能傳播病毒給他們的父母與祖父母。

懷孕婦女也比未懷孕婦女，有更大因流行性感冒產生併發症的風險。所有健康官方機構皆同意以安全與重要性考量，在懷孕期間應施打該疫苗。該疫苗保護的不只是母親，也保護了未出生的嬰兒。

186. 答案 (C) Mary 現在懷了第四胎。她、她的先生，以及她全部都在就讀小學的孩子們，想要在會診時施打疫苗，他們要花多少錢？

(A) 60 美金

(B) 50 美金

(C) 10 美金

(D) 將會是免費

解說 第一篇原文第二段，"Children in pre-school through twelfth grade and pregnant women will be vaccinated FREE of charge"，知道以 Mary 的家庭狀況，只有先生需要自費施打疫苗。從第一篇原文第四段，"get vaccinated at this clinic for a $10 fee"，得知自費為 10 美金，故選 (C)。

187. 答案 (A) 依據這些文章，誰得到流感會有最大風險？

(A) 老人

(B) 幼兒園學童

(C) 懷孕婦女

(D) 祖父母

解說 第二篇原文第二段，"People 65 and older are most likely to die from complications of influenza"，可以知道是老人，故選 (A)。不能選 (D)，因為不一定祖父母的年齡為 65 歲以上。

188. 答案 (A) 如果有人想施打疫苗，但是無法出席該流感會診，應該怎麼做？

(A) 致電會診所預約時間

(B) 別的時間再去會診所

(C) 帶一個小孩一起去會診所

(D) 付 10 美金

解說 第一篇原文第五段，"If you can't come to the flu clinic on this day, you can still get the vaccination, but an appointment will be necessary"，故選 (A)。選項 (D)，是也許後續會需付費的金額，但是錯過這期間仍要施打疫苗的人，必須預約時間。所以不是最好的答案。

189. 答案 (B) 依據這兩篇文章，避免流感的最好方式為何？

(A) 遠離兒童

(B) 施打疫苗

(C) 不要靠近懷孕婦女

(D) 打電話給會診所預約時間

解說 從第一篇原文最後一句，"Remember, flu vaccinations are the best protection against the flu"，第二篇原文第二段第二句，"it is extremely important for seniors to get vaccinated"、第三句，"even more important for children to get vaccinated"，以及第三段第二句，"All health officials agree on the safety and importance of vaccination during pregnancy"，可以知道這兩篇文章強調施打疫苗預防流感的重要性。

190. 答案 (C) 依據這兩篇文章，兒童應該施打疫苗的其中一項原因為何？

(A) 因為流感最可能讓兒童致命

(B) 因為他們可能傳染給懷孕的母親

(C) 因為可能會傳染給他們年老的親人

(D) 因為是免費的

解說 從第二篇原文第二段第三句，"This makes it even more important for children to get vaccinated"，這個this是指第二篇原文第二段，"People 65 and older are most likely to die from complications of influenza (the flu). Although it is extremely important for seniors to get vaccinated, we know that the vaccine is not as effective as people get older"，因此 (C) 為最好答案。

字彙：

clinic [ˋklɪnɪk] *(n.)* 會診／ vaccinate [ˋvæksn͵et] *(v.)* 給…注射疫苗／ appointment [əˋpɔɪntmənt] *(n.)* 預約／ occur [əˋkɝ] *(v.)* 發生／ hospitalization [͵hɑspɪtl̩ɪˋzeʃən] *(n.)* 住院治療／ complication [͵kɑmpləˋkeʃən] *(n.)* 併發症／ spread [sprɛd] *(v.)* 傳播／ unborn [ʌnˋbɔrn] *(adj.)* 未出生的

Questions191-195 refer to the following newspaper articles.

Dear Debra

First I would like to say thank you for your newspaper advice column. It's the first thing that I read every day and I always try and follow your advice when I experience the same situations. I never thought that I would need to write to you to tell you my problem though, but I do.

It's our daughter. My husband and I love her very much, but as she is growing up through her teenage years, she is getting harder and harder to live with. She barely even speaks to us anymore.

When not at school, she is either out with friends, or in her room listening to music. We never know if she is going to be home for meals or not, and we often don't even know where she is.

Her friends are another matter. We don't even know who many of them are. Some of them seem much older than her, too. We think one of them is her boyfriend, but we don't even know that for sure.

We've tried talking to her many times, but she just doesn't listen.

What do you suggest that we do?

A worried mother

Dear Worried Mother

I'm sure that many of my readers out there are experiencing the same problems as you and your husband, so the first thing to say is that this is probably just an ordinary part of growing up and the way that many parent-child relationships develop during the teenage years.

Other than just waiting it out, there may be a few strategies that you could try. Your letter says that she doesn't listen. This just may be a hint as to what is needed. Everybody does things for a reason, so you need to find out what hers is. Maybe she would like to be heard. Try asking her what's on her mind, and then listen and meet her half way. Give her a little more respect and then ask her to respect some house rules like letting you know if she will be home for meals.

As to her friends, there is probably very little that you can do. You can't choose someone else's friends no matter how much you may want to, so I think you will have to just live with that one and have some trust in your daughter that she will do the right thing.

Please let me know how things turn out.

Debra

191 What does Debra do?

(A) She helps parents with their children.
(B) She talks to troublesome teenagers.
(C) She writes a newspaper advice column.
(D) She listens to teenager's problems.

192. What does the worried mother complain that her daughter DOESN'T do?

(A) Speak to them very often
(B) Listen to music
(C) Go to school
(D) Follow Debra's advice

193. After reading this response, what might the worried mother do?

(A) Ask her daughter to talk about her worries and problems
(B) Tell her daughter to respect some house rules
(C) Ask her daughter to explain who her friends are
(D) Tell her daughter to grow up faster

194. What comfort does Debra offer to the worried mother?

(A) She tells her that her daughter will make the right decisions.
(B) She tells her not to worry.
(C) She tells her that this is an ordinary part of raising children.
(D) She tells her to write to her again if things get worse.

195. Who will read the worried mother's letter?

(A) Only Debra
(B) Any reader of the newspaper
(C) The troubled daughter
(D) The worried mother's husband

第 191-195 題

親愛的 Debra

首先我想謝謝你在報紙上建言專欄。它是我每天第一個讀的東西，而且每當我經歷相同處境時，我總是試著跟隨你的建言。我從沒想過我會需要寫信給你，告訴你我的難題，但是我的確需要。

是我們的女兒。我先生與我非常愛她，但是當她長大，她整個青少年時期，變得愈來愈難與她共同生活。她甚至幾乎再也不開口跟我們說話。

不是上學期間時，她不是跟朋友出去，就是在她房裡聽音樂。我們從來不知道她會不會回家用餐，我們也常常不知道她人在哪裡。

她的朋友們也是另一個問題。我們甚至不知道他們是誰。他們其中一些人也看起來比她年長很多。我們認為其中一位是她的男朋友，但我們不確定。

我們試著跟他聊很多次，但是她就是聽不進去。

你建議我們該怎麼做？

憂心的母親 留

親愛的憂心母親

我確信很多我的讀者們，也正經歷著你與你先生面臨的相同問題，所以，首先我要說的是，這也許只是正常的成長部分過程，也是許多親子關係，在孩子青少年期間發展的方式。

與其只是等這段時期過去，這裡也許有幾件你能試試看的策略。你在信中說道她聽不進去。這個也許暗示著需要些什麼。每個人行為都有其理由，所以你需要找出她這麼做的理由是什麼。也許她想要自己的想法被聽見。試著問她在想什麼，然後聆聽並從中了解她。多給她一些尊重，然後要求她尊重一些家規，像是讓你知道她是否會回家用餐。

至於她的朋友，你能做的大概很少。你無法幫人選擇朋友，無論你有多想這麼做，所以我認為，你將必須接受，並且對你的女兒有點信心，相信她會做正確的事。

請讓我知道事情結果變成如何。

Debra 留

191. 答案 (C) Debra 的職業為何？

(A) 她幫助父母教養孩子

(B) 她與令人煩惱的青少年談話

(C) 她寫報紙上的建言專欄

(D) 她聆聽青少年的問題。

解說　從第一篇第一段 "I would like to say thank you for your newspaper advice column"，而且該信件收件人是 Debra，可以知道她的職業是報紙建言專欄作家。

192. 答案 (A) 這名憂心的母親抱怨女兒不做什麼？

(A) 常跟他們說話　　(B) 聽音樂

(C) 去上學　　(D) 跟隨 Debra 的建言

解說　從第一篇原文第二段第三句，"She barely even speaks to us anymore"，知道女兒幾乎不跟他們說話，故選 (A)。選項 (B)，在第一篇原文第三段第一句，"in her room listening to music"，知道聽音樂是女兒會做的事，故不能選 (B)。選項 (C)、(D) 在文章裡皆未提及。

193. 答案 (A) 在讀完這個回覆後，這名母親大概會做什麼？

(A) 要求她的女兒告訴她，她在擔心的事和問題

(B) 告訴女兒尊重一些家規

(C) 要求她的女兒解釋她的朋友是哪些人

(D) 告訴她女兒要她快點長大

解說　從第一篇原文第一段第二句，"I always try and follow your advice when I experience the same situations"，可以知道這名母親會聽從 Debra 的建議。在第二篇原文第二段倒數第二句，"Try asking her what's on her mind, and then listen and meet her half way."，Debra 建議她試著這麼做，故選 (A)。選項 (B)，在第二篇原文第二段最後一句，"Give her a little more respect and then ask her to respect some house rules"，是建議母親給予女兒尊重後，才來要求女兒尊重一些家規。選項 (C)，第二篇原文第三段第二句，"I think you will have to just live with that"，是要她就此接受她對女兒交友狀況的疑問。選項 (D) 在文章中並未提及。

194. 答案 (C) Debra 提供這名憂心母親什麼安慰？

(A) 她告訴她，她的女兒將會做出正確的決定

(B) 她告訴她不用擔心

(C) 她告訴她這是養育小孩的正常部分

(D) 她告訴她如果情況變更糟再寫信給她

解說　第二篇原文第一段，"this is probably just an ordinary part of growing up and the way that many parent-child relationships develop during the teenage years"，讓這名母親知道這是正常的過程，安撫了她憂心的情緒，故選 (C)。選項 (A) 錯誤，第二篇原文第三段第二句，"trust in your daughter that she will do the right thing"，是建議相信自己的女兒，而不是向她保證女兒會做對的事。選項 (B)，文章中未提及。選項 (D) 錯誤，第二篇原文最後一句，"Please let me know how things turn out"，意思是不管情況如何都要再寫信給他。

195. 答案 (B) 誰將會讀這封憂心母親的信？

(A) 只有 Debra

(B) 任何報紙的讀者

(C) 麻煩的女兒

(D) 憂心母親的先生

解說　信是寫至報紙專欄，所以回覆與信件大概會刊登在報紙上。

字彙：

column [ˋkɑləm] *(n.)* 專欄／ situation [ˏsɪtʃuˋeʃən] *(n.)* 處境／ barely [ˋbɛrlɪ] *(adv.)* 幾乎沒有／ relationship [rɪˋleʃənˋʃɪp] *(n.)* 關係／ respect [rɪˋspɛkt] *(n./v.)* 尊重／ live with *(ph.)* 接受；容忍某件事 (＋ sth) ／ either…or [ˋiðɚ][ɔr] (conj.) 不是…就是（兩者其一）／ suggest [səˋdʒɛst] *(v.)* 建議

Questions 196-200 refer to the following two articles.

Mrs. Cook's Recipe for Sausage Rolls

Here's my recipe for the week. It's my favorite recipe for sausage rolls. It's simple and traditional, no fancy ingredients. As I always say the old ways are always the best. I love to receive your comments, or even send me a picture of how yours turn out. Enjoy!

Ingredients:

200g sausage meat
25g onion, finely chopped
1g dried sage
Salt and pepper
1g flour
1g sesame seeds
1 egg, beaten
500g puff pastry

Makes: 12

Preparation time: 20 minutes

Cooking time 20-25 minutes

Steps:

1. Preheat the oven to 180°C.
2. Add a little salt and pepper to the sausage meat.
3. Mix the sausage meat, onion and sage.
4. Roll the pastry into a rectangle that is about 3mm thick. Cut in half along the length, and sprinkle the flour over the pastry.
5. Divide the sausage meat into two equal portions. Roll each portion into a long sausage about the same length as the pastry, and place down the center of a pastry strip. Spread the sesame seeds over the sausage meat.
6. Dampen one long edge of each pastry strip and fold the pastry over the sausage mixture. Press the pastry edges together and gently roll until the join is underneath.
7. Brush the beaten egg over the pastry and cut into 3cm lengths.
8. Place on a baking tray and stab each sausage roll a few times with the point of a sharp knife.
9. Bake for 20-25 minutes until golden brown.
10. Allow to cool before eating

📖To:	Mrs. Cook
From:	Anne Rogers
Subject:	An email to Mrs. Cook

Thank you for your recipes. I love cooking them. I always try them out on my husband. He gets one for dinner every Friday evening, and he thinks they are great, too.

I've been meaning to email you for a long time to tell you how much I enjoy them, but I didn't want to bother you. Then I thought that my attempt at your latest recipe might amuse you.

The recipe for sausage rolls was excellent. I did make one mistake however. While mixing the onion with the sausage meat, I accidentally added a little mustard powder instead of the herb. Surprisingly it tasted great! Maybe you would like to try it.

Thanks again for your recipes. They are always the first thing that I look for when I turn the computer on in the morning. Keep the recipes coming!

196. Who is Anne Rogers?

(A) A chef

(B) A newspaper food critic

(C) A regular reader of Mrs. Cook's recipes.

(D) A writer of food recipes

197. How often does Anne Rogers cook Mrs. Cook's recipes?

(A) Every day

(B) Once a week

(C) Once a month

(D) This was the first time.

198. What didn't Anne Rogers do that Mrs. Cook suggested?

(A) Send her a photograph

(B) Try her recipe

(C) Send her comments

(D) Bake sausage rolls

199. What did Anne Rogers fail to put in her sausage rolls?

(A) The onion

(B) The salt and pepper

(C) The flour

(D) The sage

200. What may Mrs. Cook do after she reads Anne Roger's email?

(A) Cook for her husband

(B) Preheat the oven to 180°C

(C) Bake some sausage rolls Anne Roger's way

(D) Write her next recipe for publication

第 196-200 題

庫克太太的香腸肉捲食譜

這是我本週食譜。這是我最喜歡的香腸肉捲食譜。它簡單又傳統，沒什麼花俏的材料。就像我常説老方法總是最好。我樂意收到你的評語，或是甚至寄給我你試做的照片。享受它吧！

材料：

200 克 香腸肉
25 克 洋蔥，切細碎
1 克 乾燥鼠尾草
適量的鹽和黑胡椒
1 克 麵粉
1 克 芝麻
1 顆蛋、打散
500 克 酥皮
份數：12 個
準備時間：20 分鐘
放烤箱時間：20-25 分鐘

步驟：

1. 將烤箱預熱至 180℃。
2. 在香腸肉中加適量鹽和黑胡椒。
3. 將香腸肉、洋蔥、鼠尾草混合。
4. 把酥皮捲成長方形，大約 3 公厘厚。對切一半，並灑上些許麵粉。
5. 把香腸肉分成兩等分。將每等分香腸肉捲成長形，大約跟酥皮一樣長，然後放入酥皮中央。在香腸肉上灑一些芝麻。
6. 將每條酥皮的兩個較長的邊稍微弄濕，把酥皮包在香腸肉混料上。把酥皮的邊輕輕地壓在一起，直到接合處在下面。
7. 將打好的蛋刷在酥皮上，並切成每條 3 公分的長度。
8. 將它們放在烤盤上，並在每個香腸捲上用刀尖戳幾下。
9. 烤 20-25 分鐘直到呈金黃色。
10. 食用前靜置冷卻。

收件者:	庫克太太
寄件者:	Anne Rogers
主旨:	給庫克太太的一封信

謝謝你的食譜。我喜愛煮你食譜內的菜色。我總是讓我先生試吃。他每週五晚上都能吃一道菜色當晚餐。他也覺得這些菜很棒。

我很久之前就想寄郵件給你，向你表達我有多享受你的菜色，但是我不想打擾你。然後我想在試做過你最新食譜後寫給你，也許會讓你開心。

香腸肉捲食譜很棒。然而我有做錯一步驟。當我把洋蔥和香腸肉混在一起時，不小心加了一些芥茉粉而不是藥草。令人驚訝的是，它嚐起來很棒！也許你也會想試試看。

再次謝謝你的食譜。他們總是我早上打開電腦第一個尋找的東西。請繼續把食譜放上來！

196. 答案 (C) 誰是 Anne Rogers ？

(A) 廚師

(B) 報紙美食評論家

(C) 庫克太太食譜的定期讀者

(D) 食譜作家

解說 從第二篇原文最後一段 "They are always the first thing that I look for when I turn the computer on in the morning." 足以得知。

197. 答案 (B) Anne Rogers 多常煮庫克太太的食譜？

(A) 每天

(B) 每週一次

(C) 每月一次

(D) 這是第一次

解說 第二篇原文第一段 "I love cooking them. I always try them out on my husband. He gets one for dinner every Friday evening," 的敘述，可以得知 Anne Rogers 每週煮一次食譜菜色。

198. 答案 (A) Anne Rogers 沒有做庫克太太建議的哪一件事？

(A) 寄照片給她

(B) 試做她的食譜

(C) 寄給她評語

(D) 烤香腸肉捲

解說 第一篇原文第一段第五句 "I love to receive your comments, or even send me a picture of how yours turn out." 庫克太太提到評語跟試做的照片。(B) 第二篇原文第一段第一句 "Thank you for your recipes. I love cooking them." ，表示試做了一些食譜；(C) 第三段第一句 "The recipe for sausage rolls was excellent."，為評語；(D) 第二篇原文第二段第二句 "I thought that my attempt at your latest recipe might amuse you"，表示已試做了香腸肉捲。

199. 答案 (D) Anne Rogers 沒有放什麼在香腸肉捲裡？

(A) 洋蔥

(B) 鹽和黑胡椒

(C) 麵粉

(D) 鼠尾草

解說 第二篇原文第三段第二句 "I accidentally added a little mustard powder instead of the herb." 第一篇原文第八行的材料中有 "1g dried sage"，為一種藥草。

200. 答案 (C) 庫克太太讀完 Anne Roger 的郵件後也許會做什麼？

(A) 煮飯給她先生吃

(B) 預熱烤箱至 180℃

(C) 用 Anne Roger 的方法烤一些香腸肉捲

(D) 寫她下一個要公佈的食譜

解說 從第二篇原文第三段最後一句 Anne Roger's 的建議，"Maybe you would like to try it." 可以猜想。

字彙：

stab [stæb] *(v.)* 戳；刺／ dampen [ˋdæmpən] *(v.)* 弄濕／ edge [ɛdʒ] *(n.)* 邊；邊緣／ equal [ˋikwəl] *(adj.)* 相等的／ divide [dəˋvaɪd] *(v.)* 分；劃分／ ingredient [ɪnˋgridɪənt] *(n.)*（烹飪的）原料；材料／ instead of *(ph.)* 代替／ amuse [əˋmjuz] *(v.)* 使開心

Test 2

Part 5. 單句填空

Questions 101-140

101. There was a fire at the hotel when a candle was knocked over -------.

(A) accidental
(B) accidentally
(C) accidentalness
(D) accident

102. The coast guard has been ------- to reach the stricken ship, but they will continue trying as long as there is hope of saving survivors.

(A) stopped
(B) able
(C) relieved
(D) unable

103. The addition of the new data greatly ------- our financial calculations.

(A) complicated
(B) complication
(C) complicating
(D) complicatedly

101. 答案 (B) 蠟燭意外不慎被撞倒時飯店發生火警。

(A) 意外的 *(adj.)*
(B) 意外地 *(adv.)*
(C) 意外的 *(n.)*
(D) 意外事情 *(n.)*

解說　要選擇副詞，修飾動詞片語 knock over「撞倒」。

102. 答案 (D) 海巡員已無法到達沉船地點，但是只要有營救生還者的一絲希望，他們會繼續試。

(A) 停止 *(adj.)* 過去分詞
(B) 能；可 *(adj.)*
(C) 放心 *(adj.)*
(D) 無法 *(adj.)*

解說　連接詞 but 表示連接兩個相異意思的子句，", but they will continue trying" 是肯定句，所以前一子句必須是否定，故選 (D) unable「無法」。選項 (A) 文意不對，stop + to-V 的意思是，停下來然後去做別的事，這句選 (A) 會把意思變成，「海巡員已停下來，然後再到達沉船」。

103. 答案 (A) 新資料的附加物件，讓我們的財務計算變得極其複雜。

(A) 複雜 *(v.)* 過去式
(B) 複雜 *(n.)*
(C) 使複雜 *(v.)* 現在分詞
(D) 複雜地 *(adv.)*

解說　必須選一動詞，因為 greatly「極其」是副詞，修飾動詞。簡單過去式，主詞＋過去式動詞。

例句　A friend of his opened the window for no reason. 他的一位朋友沒來由地打開窗戶。

104. The link between new house building and land prices has long been understood by - - - - - - - .

(A) economists
(B) communists
(C) ecologists
(D) receptionists

105. After the hurricane, there wasn't one house - - - - - - - a roof left.

(A) that
(B) which
(C) with
(D) without

106. Neither Mr. Thomas nor Mr. Brooks - - - - - - - present at the new client meeting last week.

(A) is
(B) are
(C) was
(D) were

107. Regardless of the weather, we are determined - - - - - - - the repairs to the roof today.

(A) completely
(B) to complete
(C) complete
(D) completed

104. 答案 (A) 新房子跟土地價格之間的關聯性，很久之前就被經濟學家了解了。

(A) 經濟學家
(B) 共產主義者
(C) 生態學者
(D) 接待員

105. 答案 (C) 颶風過後，沒有一間房子有屋頂。

(A) that (B) which
(C) with (D) without

解說 選 (C)，名詞＋with（介系詞）＋名詞，with 表示「有」。(A)、(B) 是關係代名詞，需要有子句。(D) without「沒有」是介系詞。there wasn't one house 是否定句，without 是否定，所以若是選 (D)，就會把題意改成「颶風過後，沒有一間房子是沒有屋頂的」＝每間房子都有屋頂。不符題意。

106. 答案 (C) 上週的新客戶會議，Thomas 先生和 Brooks 先生都不在場 。

(A) is (B) are
(C) was (D) were

解說 neither ～ nor ～「兩者都不；既不～也不～」＋動詞 /be 動詞。動詞 /be 動詞必須隨 nor 後的主詞變化。last week「上週」，就表示要用過去式，nor 後面的主詞是 Brooks 先生，為單數，故選過去式 be 動詞 was。

例句 Neither Ashley nor Blake is a naughty boy. Ashley 和 Blake 都不是頑皮的男孩。

107. 答案 (B) 無論天氣如何，我們下定決心今天完成屋頂修繕。

(A) 完全地 *(adv.)*
(B) 完成 *(inf.)*
(C) 完成 *(v.)*
(D) 完整的 *(adj.)*

解說 不定詞當副詞，修飾 determined「下定決心」形容詞。

108. Following the power outage, it ------- five hours to complete the equipment inspection.

(A) took
(B) cost
(C) spent
(D) suffered

109. Life on other planets has long been -------, but never proven.

(A) doubtful
(B) suspicious
(C) certain
(D) suspected

110. Although great effort was made to stop people lighting fires in the protected area, ------- success was very disappointing.

(A) their
(B) theirs
(C) its
(D) they

111. Stock market prices were volatile in the third ------- of last year.

(A) quarter
(B) half
(C) cycle
(D) circle

108. 答案 (A) 隨著停電，花了五個小時才完成設備檢查。

(A) took　　(B) cost

(C) spent　　(D) suffered

解說　(A)、(B)、(C) 的中文意思相當，但是在英文用法上不同。(A) take＋時間。(B) cost＋錢。(C) 人（主詞）＋ spend ＋時間。本題主詞是 It，指「設備檢查」這件事，所以選 (A)。(D) suffer「受苦」過去式動詞。過去式動詞：take － took；cost － cost；spend － spent

例句　This article took me 5 hours to type. 這個文章花了我五小時打字。

The bag cost me 500 dollars. 包包花了我五百元。

Robert spent 2 hours jogging. Robert 花了兩小時慢跑。

109. 答案 (D) 其他星球上的生命已經很久被懷疑可能存在，但是從來沒有被證明。

(A) 懷疑的 *(adj.)*

(B) 猜疑的 *(adj.)*

(C) 確信的 *(adj.)*

(D) 懷疑可能存在的 *(adj.)*

110. 答案 (C) 雖然已做出極大努力來停止人在保護區點火，它的成效十分令人失望。

(A) their

(B) theirs

(C) its

(D) they

解說　its 是所有格形容詞，代表句子裡的主詞 great effort。

111. 答案 (A) 股票市場價格在去年第三季是反覆無常的。

(A) 四分之一；季度

(B) 二分之一

(C) 週期

(D) 圓圈

112. If I - - - - - - - you, I wouldn't accept that job offer at such a low salary.

(A) was

(B) were

(C) am

(D) be

113. The chef had all the ingredients ready, but was unable to find a big enough - - - - - - - bowl.

(A) mix

(B) mixed

(C) to mix

(D) mixing

114. We are - - - - - - - that you like the gift which we sent you to thank you for hosting the event.

(A) good

(B) delighted

(C) happily

(D) successful

115. There is no point waiting, as the tour bus - - - - - - - away just now.

(A) has driven

(B) is driving

(C) was driven

(D) is driven

112. 答案 (B) 假如我是你，我不會接受那個如此低薪的職缺。

(A) was (B) were

(C) am (D) be

解說 第二條件句，用來假設或預測現在或未來發生的事。第二條件句，be 動詞文法，If ＋主詞＋ were ＋，＋主詞＋ would/could/might/should。

例句 If you were a bird, you could fly in the sky. 假如你是隻鳥，你能在天空飛。（實際上，你不是鳥）

113. 答案 (D) 廚師已經準備好所有食材，但是找不到夠大的攪拌碗。

(A) 攪拌 *(v.)*

(B) 攪拌 *(v.)* 過去式

(C) 攪拌 *(inf.)*

(D) 攪拌 *(v.)*

解說 (D) mixing bowl「攪拌碗」是一個字。mixing 是現在分詞作形容詞用，修飾名詞 bowl「碗」。

114. 答案 (B) 我們感到很高興你喜歡我們為了感謝你舉辦大活動而寄的禮物。

(A) 好的 *(n.)* (B) 感到高興的 *(adj.)*

(C) 快樂地 *(adv.)* (D) 成功的 *(adj.)*

解說 關係代名詞 that 領導的子句，在這裡是形容詞補語，修飾形容詞，因為主詞是人 we「我們」，所以這個形容詞必須是一種情緒，故選 (B)。

例句 Maggie is pleased that you love the book which she wrote.
Maggie 感到很快樂你喜歡她寫的書。

115. 答案 (C) 等待沒有意義，因為遊覽車就在剛才開走了。

(A) has driven

(B) is driving

(C) was driven

(D) is driven

解說 過去式的被動語態：主詞＋過去式 be 動詞＋過去分詞。本句主詞 the tour bus 為單數，所以用過去式 be 動詞 was。

例句 The banana was eaten last night. 香蕉昨晚被吃了。

116. The recent increase in visitor numbers to National Parks has caused ------- damage to many pathways.

(A) unexpected
(B) undiscovered
(C) unexplained
(D) unauthorized

117. The environment in which ------- are raised has a great effect on their future prospects.

(A) animals
(B) children
(C) livestock
(D) adults

118. Despite his age, the local mailman ------- his bike to work for many years.

(A) was ridden
(B) has ridden
(C) was riding
(D) is ridden

119. The launch of the new satellite into space will bring communications in many isolated regions ------- .

(A) up-to-date
(B) out-of-date
(C) up-market
(D) upside down

116. 答案 (A) 近期增加的國家公園遊客，已經對許多小徑造成意想不到的損傷。

(A) 意想不到的

(B) 未發掘的

(C) 未經說明的

(D) 未授權的

117. 答案 (B) 兒童的成長環境，對他們未來的前途有極大影響。

(A) 動物

(B) 兒童

(C) 家畜

(D) 成人

解說 (A)、(C) 皆為動物，不會有未來的前途。(D) 成人已經長大了。故選 (B)。

118. 答案 (B) 儘管他的年紀很大，這名當地的郵差已經騎腳踏車上班多年。

(A) was ridden 過去式被動語態

(B) has ridden 現在完成式

(C) was riding 過去現在進行式

(D) is ridden 現在進行式

解說 介系詞 for ＋時間，用在過去式或是現在完成式，這題時間為「三年了」，ride「騎」的動詞三態為 ride － rode － ridden 。不能選 (A)，因為主詞＋過去式 be 動詞＋過去分詞，是過去式的被動語態。

例句 I cooked the chicken for 1 hour. 我煮了一小時的雞肉。

Celeste has loved Rob for 20 years. Celeste 已經愛 Rob 二十年了。

119. 答案 (A) 新的衛星發射至太空，將能帶來許多偏遠地區傳達的最新訊息。

(A) 最新的訊息

(B) 過期的

(C) 高價的

(D) 上下顛倒的

120. The newspaper reported that the billionaire gave all his money ------- before he passed away.

(A) up

(B) in

(C) away

(D) from

121. ------- the documents arrived before the end of the working day.

(A) Fortunate

(B) Fortune

(C) Fortuitous

(D) Fortunately

122. The new road layout has caused much confusion among motorists, especially during the ------- hour.

(A) fast

(B) rush

(C) busy

(D) hurry

123. The announcement said that all assembly workers can stop ------- lunch at 12pm.

(A) to eat

(B) eating

(C) eat

(D) eaten

120. 答案 (C) 報紙報導億萬富翁捐出他所有的錢，在他過世之前。

(A) up　　(B) in

(C) away　　(D) from

解說　give ＋名詞＋ away ＝ give ＋ away ＋名詞。away 是副詞；give away「贈送；捐贈」。(A) give up「放棄」。(B) give in「讓步」。(D) give from 沒有任何意思。

例句　Wendy gave her old clothes away before Lunar New Year.

＝ Wendy gave her old clothes away before Lunar New Year.

Wendy 在農曆新年之前把她的舊衣服捐贈出去。

121. 答案 (D) 有幸地，文件在工作天結束之前到達了。

(A) 幸運的 *(adj.)*

(B) 財富 *(n.)*

(C) 偶然的 *(adj.)*

(D) 有幸地 *(adv.)*

解說　副詞 fortunately 用在主詞 the documents 前面，表示你的觀點。

122. 答案 (B) 新的道路設計造成許多駕駛人間的混亂，尤其是在交通尖峰時間。

(A) fast

(B) rush

(C) busy

(D) hurry

解說　rush hour「尖峰時間」，是名詞。

123. 答案 (A) 公告上說所有組裝工人，不能在中午 12 點停止工作去吃午餐。

(A) to eat

(B) eating

(C) eat

(D) eaten

解說　stop「停止」可以加不定詞或動名詞，但是意思不同。stop to eat「停止某事然後去做另一件事」。stop eating「馬上停止做你現在正在做的事」。

124. Owen Brookes is the founder of the company; however, he no longer refers to - - - - - - - as its leader.

(A) him

(B) himself

(C) it

(D) he

125. The police are searching for the man - - - - - - - car was found near the scene of the attack.

(A) where

(B) who

(C) which

(D) whose

126. The New York Symphony Orchestra - - - - - - - a concert in Central Park attended by over 50,000 people.

(A) showed

(B) achieved

(C) performed

(D) accomplished

127. If they had followed the - - - - - - - which was given, the accident would not have happened.

(A) advice

(B) advise

(C) inform

(D) warn

124. 答案 (B) Owen Brookes 是公司的創始人；然而他再也不提及他自己是公司的領導者。

(A) him

(B) himself

(C) it

(D) he

125. 答案 (D) 警察正在尋找車子被發現在攻擊現場的男人。

(A) where

(B) who

(C) which

(D) whose

解說 本題的關係代名詞必須是所有格，whose「指某 (人 / 物) 的東西」，修飾 the man「男人」，故只有選項 (D)。

例句 The dog whose legs are hurt is my dog. 腿受傷的狗是我的狗。

126. 答案 (C) 紐約交響樂團在中央公園的音樂會演奏，有五萬人出席。

(A) 展示 *(v.)*

(B) 達成 *(v.)*

(C) 演奏 *(v.)*

(D) 完成 *(v.)*

解說 音樂要用 perform「演奏」。

127. 答案 (A) 如果他們跟隨著給予的勸告，意外就不會發生。

(A) 勸告 *(n.)*

(B) 勸告 *(v.)*

(C) 告知 *(v.)*

(D) 警告 *(v.)*

解說 答案必須是名詞。其他三個選項皆為動詞。

128. It is with - - - - - - - that we agreed to the new contract.

(A) reluctant

(B) reluctance

(C) reluctantly

(D) reluct

129. Doctors have noticed a big increase in patients suffering - - - - - - - the flu this month.

(A) about

(B) for

(C) over

(D) from

130. Despite her parents warnings, Lily still wrote homework while - - - - - - - to music on her cell phone.

(A) listening

(B) listen

(C) listened

(D) to listen

128. 答案 (B) 我們不情願的同意新合約。

(A) 不情願的 *(adj.)*

(B) 不情願 *(n.)*

(C) 不情願地 *(adv.)*

(D) 反抗 *(v.)*

解說 with「有」是介系詞，後面一定要加名詞，只有選項 (B) 是名詞。

129. 答案 (D) 醫生已經留意到，本月受到流行性感冒之苦的病患，有大幅增加。

(A) about

(B) for

(C) over

(D) from

解說 全部都是介系詞，但是 suffer「受…之苦」後面要加 from，及物動詞＋介系詞＋名詞。

例句 William suffered from malaria. William 受瘧疾（帶來的病痛）之苦。

130. 答案 (A) 不管她父母的警告，Lily 仍舊邊功課邊聽音樂。

(A) listening（現在分詞）

(B) listen*(v.)*

(C) listened（過去式動詞）

(D) to listen*(inf.)*

解說 副詞子句的主詞與主要子句主詞相同時，可將副詞子句中的連接詞與主詞改成現在分詞，即為分詞構句。while listening = while she was listening「當她在聽音樂時」。

例句 He was angry, while doing his homework. = He was angry while he was doing his homework. 他在做他的功課時是生氣的。

131. I am - - - - - - - that Miss Thompkins is not in the office today, but she will be tomorrow.

(A) afraid
(B) scared
(C) feared
(D) nervous

132. The rescheduled flight from Atlanta will not arrive on time, - - - - - - - .

(A) too
(B) neither
(C) either
(D) so

133. It is rumored that the discount that is - - - - - - - offered to new customers will be discontinued.

(A) rarely
(B) recently
(C) usually
(D) equally

134. Failure to follow these - - - - - - - during assembly will render the guarantee invalid.

(A) destructions
(B) orders
(C) commands
(D) instructions

131. 答案 (A) 恐怕 Thompkins 小姐今天不在辦公室，但是她明天會。

(A) 恐怕 *(adj.)*

(B) 感到害怕 *(adj.)*

(C) 感到恐懼 *(adj.)*

(D) 緊張的 *(adj.)*

解說 只有用選項 (A)afraid「恐怕」在文中表示「抱歉」，而非「恐懼」之意。

例句 I'm afraid that I have to leave earlier. 我恐怕要提早走。（表示歉意）

132. 答案 (C) 從亞特蘭大重新安排時間的航班，將也不會準時抵達。

(A) 也 *(adv.)*

(B) 兩者都不 *(adj.)*

(C) 也（用在否定句中）*(adj.)*

(D) 如此地 *(adv.)*

解說 是否定句，所以必須用 either「也」，故選 (C)。不能選 (B) 是因為 neither 本身為否定。

例句 He doesn't like noodles, and I don't either. = He doesn't like noodles, and neither do I. 我們兩個都不喜歡麵。

133. 答案 (C) 傳言說通常提供給新顧客的折扣將不會繼續。

(A) 很少地 *(adv.)*

(B) 最近地 *(adv.)*

(C) 通常地 *(adv.)*

(D) 相當地 *(adv.)*

134. 答案 (D) 組裝期間不跟隨這些操作指南，將會給予保證無效。

(A) 破壞 *(n.)*

(B) 訂購 *(n.)*

(C) 命令 *(n.)*

(D) 操作指南 *(n.)*

135. The article stated that it is best for children to learn - - - - - - - to swim at a young age.

(A) what
(B) how
(C) which
(D) who

136. A revolutionary airplane - - - - - - - the future of aviation took to the skies last week.

(A) is demonstrating
(B) demonstrated
(C) has demonstrated
(D) that demonstrated

137. With hindsight the company wishes that it had recalled the product much - - - - - - - than it did.

(A) earlier
(B) early
(C) the earlier
(D) more early

135. 答案 (B) 文章闡述在年幼時學習如何游泳，對小孩最好。

(A) 什麼

(B) 如何

(C) 哪一個

(D) 誰

解說 how「如何做；怎麼做」是副詞，指做這件事的方式、方法，to swim「游泳」在這裡是不定詞。選項 (A)、(C)、(D) 皆為代名詞，如果本句選擇這三者其一，文法結構會讓 swim「游泳」看起來像是做及物動詞用，what, who, which 就會變成受詞，意思就不符題意。

例句 Can you tell me how to cook? 你可以告訴我怎麼煮飯嗎？

Can you tell me what to cook? 你可以告訴我煮什麼嗎？（what 是受詞）

136. 答案 (D) 展示航空界未來的革命性飛機，上週開始飛行。

(A) is demonstrating

(B) demonstrated

(C) has demonstrated

(D) that demonstrated

解說 需要關係代名詞 that，帶領形容詞子句 demonstrated the future of aviation「展示航空界未來」，修飾主詞 A revolutionary airplane「革命性飛機」。選項 (A)、(B)、(C) 會讓句子到 aviation 就完成句子，無法再從 took 接下去，不符合文法與完整題意。

137. 答案 (A) 有了事後的了解，公司希望當初更早一點召回產品。

(A) earlier *(adj.)*

(B) early *(adv./adj.)*

(C) the earlier

(D) more early

解說 形容詞比較級，形容詞是兩個音節且字尾是 y，要刪掉 y 加 ier。

138. Managers whose ------- exceed $50,000 are expected to work over the weekend.

(A) pay
(B) riches
(C) salaries
(D) income

139. ------- in 1995, the album remains one of the greatest of all time.

(A) Releasing
(B) Released
(C) Having released
(D) Release

140. Typhoons are a/an ------- occurrence in the western Pacific from June to November each year.

(A) common
(B) often
(C) extraordinary
(D) unnatural

138. 答案 (C) 薪資超過五萬美金的經理，被期盼週末也要工作。

(A) 薪俸 *(n.)*

(B) riches（沒有意思的字）

(C) 薪資 *(n.)*

(D) 收入 *(n.)*

解說 選項(B)沒有意思。選項(A)、(D)符合題意，但是因為本句的動詞exceed「超過」並未以主詞為第三人稱的形態加s，所以知道主詞為複數，故選(C)。

139. 答案 (B) 於1995年發行，這唱片仍是一直以來最棒唱片之一。

(A) Releasing

(B) Released

(C) Having released

(D) Release

解說 應該選擇能構成分詞構句的選項。句中主詞是the album「唱片」，而唱片又是「被發行的」，因此被動語態為being released，而分詞構句可省略being只寫released，故選(B)。

140. 答案 (A) 颱風是普遍發生在西太平洋，每年從六月至十一月間。

(A) 普遍的 *(adj.)*

(B) 常常 *(adv.)*

(C) 異常的 *(adj.)*

(D) 不自然的 *(adj.)*

解說 必須選擇形容詞，修飾名詞occurrence「發生」。句中提到時間為「每年從六月至十一月間」，足以得知是為常態，故選(A)。

Part 6. 短文填空

Questions 141-143 refer to the following article.

The V-type electric cars

The latest edition of the V-type electric car from Kryon Motors hits the roads this week. Powered by its onboard -------, its driver will never need to fill this car up with gas again.

141. (A) engine
(B) generator
(C) battery
(D) power plant

The revolutionary car sets new benchmarks in endurance. From just a two-hour charge it can run for over 300km or about five hours' -------. This sets it apart from its competitors which reach nowhere near this capacity.

142. (A) driven
(B) drove
(C) to drive
(D) driving

It's not just its performance that is so high though, it's also the price. The entry level V-type starts at $70,000. At that price, it ------- not be as revolutionary as we thought.

143. (A) maybe
(B) might
(C) perhaps
(D) likely

第 141-143 題

V 型電動車

Kryon 車業最新版的 V 型電動車，在本週成為路上最風行的一個話題。以內裝機載的電池提供動力，駕駛人將永遠不需要再替這輛車加汽油。

141. 答案 (C)

(A) 引擎　　(B) 發電機
(C) 電池　　(D) 發電廠

革命性的汽車替車的耐久力設立新的水準點。只要充電兩小時，它就能跑超過 300 公里，或是能行駛五個小時。這點讓他把其他不能到這種能力的競爭對手比下去。

142. 答案 (D)

(A) 行駛（過去分詞）　　(B) 行駛（過去式動詞）
(C) 行駛 *(inf.)*　　(D) 行駛 *(n.)*

解說　選 (D)，因為 hours'「小時的」，後面要加名詞。driving「行駛」是動名詞，動名詞屬名詞。

不只是它的表現如此高水準，價格也是如此。V 型入門款從七萬美金起跳。那個價位，也許不如我們想的那麼有革命性。

143. 答案 (B)

(A) 可能；也許 *(adv.)*　　(B) 也許 *(aux.)*
(C) 大概；也許 *(adv.)*　　(D) 很可能 *(adv.)*

解說　選 (B)，因為本句 It 為主詞，後面需要一個助動詞，might「也許」是助動詞。

字彙：

edition [ɪ`dɪʃən] *(n.)*（發行物的）版／ benchmark [`bɛntʃ͵mark] *(n.)* 水準點；基點／ charge [tʃardʒ] *(v.)* 充電／ competitor [kəm`pɛtətɚ] *(n.)* 競爭者；對手／ revolutionary [͵rɛvə`luʃən͵ɛrɪ] *(adj.)* 革命的

Questions 144-146 refer to the following notice.

Bar staff wanted

Crystal Cocktail Bars is looking for experienced cocktail barmen for their seafront and their newly refurbished city center bars.

Working hours are three nights a week 9pm to 2am with one night each week always being either Friday or Saturday. Salaries are to be ------- according to experience.

144. (A) debated
(B) organized
(C) negotiated
(D) argued

At Crystal Cocktail Bars, we believe in taking care of our employees. We offer a ------- and relaxed working environment suitable for

145. (A) friendly
(B) friendless
(C) friendship
(D) friendlessness

energetic and outgoing individuals.

To apply please send your ------- along with a letter explaining why you are right for the job to:

146. (A) data
(B) information
(C) report
(D) resume

Jackie Peterson
Crystal Cocktail Bars
247 Greek Road
Santa Monica

第 144-146 題

酒吧徵人

Crystal Cocktail 酒吧，正為了他們位於海邊且重新整理刷新好的市中心酒吧，尋求有經驗的雞尾酒吧台人員。

工作時間是每週三個晚上，從晚上九點至凌晨二點，其中一個工作天總是在星期五或星期六。依照經驗，薪資可議。

144. 答案 (C)

(A) 辯論 *(v.)* (B) 組織 *(v.)*
(C) 協商 *(v.)* (D) 爭吵 *(v.)*

在 Crystal Cocktail 酒吧，我們相信照顧好我們員工能帶來的效用。我們提供一個友善與輕鬆的工作環境，適合活力充沛與外向的人。

145. 答案 (A)

(A) 友善的 *(adj.)* (B) 沒有朋友的 *(adj.)*
(C) 友誼 *(n.)* (D) 沒有朋友 *(n.)*

解說 friendly and relaxed「友善與輕鬆的」，皆為形容詞，修飾後面的名詞 working environment「工作環境」。不能選 (B)，因為 and「和；與」連接的應是同性質的形容詞。

要應徵，請寄履歷並附上為何你是適當人選的函件。

146. 答案 (D)

(A) 數據 *(n.)* (B) 資訊 *(n.)*
(C) 報告 *(n.)* (D) 履歷 *(n.)*

Jackie Peterson
Crystal Cocktail 酒吧
Greek 路 247 號
聖莫尼卡市

字彙：

refurbish [riˋfɝbɪʃ] *(v.)* 重整理刷新／ salary [ˋsælərɪ] *(n.)* 薪資／ according to [əˋkɔrdɪŋ tu] *(ph.)* 根據；按照／ energetic [ˌɛnəˋdʒɛtɪk] *(adj.)* 精力充沛的／ individual [ˌɪndəˋvɪdʒʊəl] *(n.)* 個人；人

Questions 147-149 refer to the following advertisement.

Concert by the Water

Tickets are now on sale for the much anticipated annual classical Concert by the Water on July 7th.

This year The National Orchestra - - - - - - - by the acclaimed Sir

147. (A) led
(B) escorted
(C) guided
(D) conducted

Richard Charles will perform a varied collection of both contemporary pieces and old favorites. Also featuring a - - - - - - - violin performance by

148. (A) lonely
(B) alone
(C) solo
(D) single

Janet Lou. Don't miss this annual spectacular set along the beautiful river Lye.

Tickets from $25 including pre-concert refreshments. Alternatively bring your own picnic and - - - - - - - in the magnificent surrounding park

149. (A) relax
(B) relaxed
(C) relaxing
(D) relaxedly

and watch the concert for free.

Tickets available at your local ticket office.

第 147-149 題

水岸音樂會

現在開始售票這場十分令人期待，將在七月七日於水岸邊舉辦的年度經典音樂會。

今年，國家管弦樂由受到讚譽的 Richard Charles 爵士擔任指揮，將會演出一系列不同曲風的音樂，有當代的作品與經典老歌。也以 Janet Lou 的小提琴獨奏表演為特色。不要錯過這場在美麗的 Lye 河畔的年度鉅獻。

147. 答案 (D)

(A) 引導　(B) 護送
(C) 指引　(D) 指揮

148. 答案 (C)

(A) 孤獨地 *(adv.)*　(B) 單獨的 *(adj.)*
(C) 獨奏的 *(adj.)*　(D) 單一的 *(adj.)*

解說　名詞片語 a solo violin performance，形容詞修飾名詞 violin performance「小提琴表演」，故選 (C)。

票價 25 美金起，包含音樂會前的小茶點。另一個選擇，你也可以帶自己的野餐，並在四周的偌大公園裡放鬆，免費聽音樂會。

149. 答案 (A)

(A) 放鬆 *(v.)*　(B) 放鬆的 *(adj.)*
(C) 令人輕鬆的 *(adj.)*　(D) 輕鬆地 *(adv.)*

解說　選項 (B)，過去分詞做形容詞，表示被動。選項 (C)，現在分詞做形容詞，表示主動。

購票可洽當地售票處。

字彙：

anticipate [æn`tɪsə͵pet] *(v.)* 期待／ conduct [kən`dʌkt] *(v.)* 指揮／ acclaim[ə`klem] *(v.)* 稱讚／ contemporary [kən`tɛmpə͵rɛrɪ] *(adj.)* 當代的／ spectacular[spɛk`tækjələ˞] *(adj.)* 壯麗的／ refreshment [rɪ`frɛʃmənt] *(n.)* 小茶點

Questions 150-152 refer to the following advertisement.

Dylan Express couriers the number one name in - - - - - - - express couriers in the state.

150. (A) in time
(B) over time
(C) on time
(D) out of time

With our Super Express Service* send any size, any weight anywhere in the state of Florida for next day delivery for only $25.

Open a business account and the first ten deliveries are on us.

Out of state deliveries within 48 hours to anywhere in the US. Call for a/an - - - - - - -.

151. (A) quote
(B) cost
(C) bid
(D) offer

Special delivery where we guarantee the time of - - - - - - - to within 30 minutes available for an extra $10.

152. (A) delivery
(B) delivered
(C) delivering
(D) deliver

All deliveries insured up to $500 and delivered as promoted or your next delivery is free.

*25kg weight limit on Super Express delivery offer

第 150-152 題

Dylan 快遞信差，州內第一名的準時送達快遞。

150. 答案 (C)

(A) 及時 (B) 超時
(C) 準時 (D) 沒時間

用我們的超級快遞服務 * 寄送任何尺寸、重量，至佛羅里達州內任何地方，今天寄隔天送達，只要 25 美金。

開一個商用帳號，前十個寄件算我們招待。

州外寄送至美國境內，會在 48 小時內送達。打電話給我們為你報價。

151. 答案 (A)

(A) 報價 *(n.)* (B) 成本 *(n.)*
(C) 投標 *(n.)* (D) 提供 *(n.)*

有特別的遞送，額外多付 10 美金，我們保證 30 分鐘內送達。

152. 答案 (A)

(A) 遞送 *(n.)* (B) 遞送（過去式動詞）
(C) 遞送（現在完成式動詞） (D) 遞送 *(v.)*

解說 of 是介系詞，後面一定要用名詞，故選 (A)。

所有遞送已投保最高至 500 美金的保險，並依廣告宣傳的內容與方式進行遞送，否則下一次的遞送服務就免費。

* 超級快遞服務限重 25 公斤

字彙：

courier[ˋkʊrɪɚ] *(n.)* 送急件的信差／ state [stet] *(n.)* 州／ quote [kwot] *(n.)* 報價／ bid [bɪd] *(n.)* 投標／ insured [ɪnˋʃʊrd] *(adj.)* 已投保的／ promote[prəˋmot] *(v.)* 宣傳

Part 7. 單篇／雙篇文章理解

Questions 153-154 refer to the following memo.

📖To:	All accounts department personnel
From:	Mr. Burns, Accounts Manager

This week's accounts staff meeting will be held on Thursday morning at 10am instead of the usual Friday morning.

The change is due to the visit of the company chairman, Burt Saunders, to our offices on that day.

I know that this will cause some inconvenience to those of you who have computer training that morning, but I have arranged for that to be postponed for a week.

As I'm sure you are aware, a visit from such a high company figure to our offices is a very rare event, so I expect the office and all employees to look their best on that day. The normally relaxed Friday dress code will not apply.

153. What should accounts department personnel wear to work on Friday?

(A) Casual clothes
(B) Suits and ties
(C) Jeans
(D) T-shirts

154. What would you expect accounts department personnel to do on Thursday before going home?

(A) Tidy their desks
(B) Greet Mr. Sunders
(C) Review the day's computer training
(D) Prepare for tomorrow's accounts department meeting

第 153-154 題

📖收件者:	會計部全體人員
寄件者:	會計部經理 Burns 先生

本週會計員工會議將會在星期四早上 10 點舉行，而不是往常的星期五早上。

這個改變是由於公司總裁 Burt Saunders 先生，那天要造訪我們部門。

我知道這將會造成你們那些當天早上有電腦訓練的人的不便，但是我已經安排讓那延遲一星期。

我確信你們意識到，有如此公司高層的人物到我們部門，是個十分罕見的大事，所以我期待部門與所有員工，在當天看起來皆為最佳狀態。按慣例的週五輕鬆裝扮規則，當天將不適用。

153. 答案 (B) 會計部人員星期五應該穿什麼去上班？

(A) 非正式的服裝　　(B) 西裝及領帶

(C) 牛仔褲　　(D) T 恤

解說　最後一段，"I expect the office and all employees to look their best on that day. The normally relaxed Friday dress code will not apply"，說明當天要穿正式服裝。

154. 答案 (A) 你預期會計部人員會在星期四下班回家前做什麼？

(A) 整理好他們的辦公桌桌面　　(B) 向 Sunders 先生打招呼

(C) 複習那天的電腦訓練　　(D) 準備明天會計部的會議

解說　原文最後一段第一句，"I expect the office and all employees to look their best on that day"，知道整理環境是預期他們會做的事，故選 (A)。原文第一段，"meeting will be held on Thursday morning at 10am"，表示改成星期四舉行會議，故 (D) 錯誤。原文第二段，"The change is due to the visit of the company chairman, Burt Saunders, to our offices on that day"，表示總裁星期五才造訪會計部，故 (B) 錯誤。(C) 錯誤，在原文第三段，"I have arranged for that to be postponed for a week"，表示電腦訓練已延期。

字彙：

personnel [ˌpɝsn`ɛl] *(n.)* 員工／ postpone [post`pon] *(v.)* 延遲／ casual [`kæʒuəl] *(adj.)* 非正式的

Questions 155–156 refer to the following advertisement.

STAMP OUT THE STRESS

OF SECOND HOME OWNERSHIP

Unlike any other form of home ownership, 88 Park Street offers you a second home in London-Mayfair, for the amount of time you personally require each year – at a fraction of the cost of whole ownership.

Without many of the drawbacks usually associated with property ownership and with the additional benefits of 24-hour room service, dedicated concierge, valet and twice-daily maid service, let your time be yours. Limited number remaining. Price starting from ￡115,000.

Contact us or visit our virtual show apartment

+44 (0) 20 7663 8888 Mon-Fri 8:30am~4:30pm

www.88parkstreet.co.uk/house

88 PARK STREET

London-Mayfair

155. Who will be the main target of this advertisement?

(A) Housewives

(B) Valets

(C) Businessmen

(D) Scholars

156. What does "Stamp Out" mean in this advertisement?

(A) Reduce

(B) Refuse

(C) Eliminate

(D) Encompass

第 155–156 題

排除擁有第二個寓所的壓力

有別於其他寓所的持有方式，88 PARK STREET 提供您在倫敦上流住宅區擁有第二個寓所，依照您每年所需入住的次數而定，只需負擔部分金額，就能享有完全的使用權。

沒有一般置產的相關繁雜程序，但卻享有許多附加有利條件，二十四小時客房服務、專職櫃台服務人員、衣物洗熨侍者、以及每日兩次房務整理服務，讓你全然擁有自己的時間。席次有限。價格從 115,000 英磅起。

聯絡我們或想造訪我們的實境展示寓所

電話＋44 (0) 20 7663 8888　　週一至週五 早上 8:30 至下午 4:30

www.88parkstreet.co.uk/house

88 PARK STREET

倫敦上流住宅區

155. 答案 (C) 誰會是這則廣告的主要目標？

(A) 家庭主婦　　(B) 衣物洗熨侍者

(C) 商務人士　　(D) 學者

解說　依原文，“for the amount of time you personally require each year”，以及“let your time be yours”，可推測是較適合商務人士的生活型態，因為也許常需出差，或是忙碌至極，所以時間寶貴，無法分擔家務。

156. 答案 (C) 本則廣告中的“STAMP OUT”意思為何？

(A) 減輕　　(B) 拒絕

(C) 排除；消除　　(D) 包含

字彙：

ownership [ˋonɚ͵ʃɪp] *(n.)* 所有權／ drawback [ˋdrɔ͵bæk] *(n.)* 不利條件／ associate [əˋsoʃɪɪt] *(v.)* 與…聯結在一起 (+with) ／ virtual [ˋvɝtʃʊəl] *(adj.)* 實際上的／ valet [ˋvælɪt] *(n.)*（旅館中的）衣物洗熨侍者／ eliminate [ɪˋlɪmə͵net] *(v.)* 排除；消除／ encompass [ɪnˋkʌmpəs] *(v.)* 包含

Questions 157-158 refer to the following builder's quote.

Quote for work

With regard to my visit to Grove Lodge Apartments on March 28th, here is my quote for the maintenance work you requested.

Repair to roof tiles- $490, including new tiles and labor- It is imperative that this is repaired before it rains as further water damage will increase the cost of repair.

Replacement of 3rd floor window- $150 for a wooden framed window or $250 for a PVC double glazed window.

Painting of entrance doorway- $100

Repair of broken floorboard in hallway- $100

Repair of backyard fence- $120

TOTAL $960+tax or $1,060+tax depending on which window you choose.

Please advise me if you accept this quote, and we can arrange a day for the work to be done.

Jack Gough

Builder

157. Grove Lodge Apartments choose the wooden window, how much will the work cost?

(A) $900

(B) $960

(C) $1,060

(D) more than $960

158. What does Jack Gough advise Grove Lodge Apartments to do?

(A) to accept his quote

(B) not to delay in the repair of the roof

(C) to choose the PVC window

(D) to paint the entrance doorway

第 157-158 題

工程報價

關於我在三月二十八日至 Grove Lodge 公寓看現場，這裡是我對你要求的維護工程報價。

修繕屋瓦要 490 美金，包含新屋瓦與工錢——在下雨前修好是當務之急，因為更進一步的水所造成的損壞，將會增加修繕費用。

更換三樓窗戶，換成木框邊窗戶要 150 美金，換成聚氯乙烯的雙層玻璃窗戶要 250 美金。

油漆入口處要 100 美金。

修繕玄關壞掉地板要 100 美金。

修繕後院圍籬要 120 美金。

總計 960 美金再加稅金，或是 1,060 美金再加稅金，視你選擇哪一種窗戶而定。

如果你接受這個報價，請告知我，我們會安排一天完成工程。

Jack Gough

裝修工程行

157. 答案 (D) Grove Lodge 公寓選擇木框邊窗戶，工程將會花費多少錢？

(A) 900 美金　(B) 960 美金

(C) 1,060 美金　(D) 比 960 美金多

解說　原文倒數第五行，TOTAL $960+tax，這是木框邊窗戶的報價，其中表明稅金是外加的，但並未提到稅金的比例，所以知道金額會比 960 美金多。

158. 答案 (B) Jack Gough 建議 Grove Lodge 公寓做什麼？

(A) 接受報價　(B) 不要延遲屋頂的修繕

(C) 選擇聚氯乙烯的窗戶　(D) 油漆入口處

解說　第二段，"It is imperative that this is repaired before it rains as further water damage will increase the cost of repair"，是裝修工程行提供的建議，其餘為業主要求的工程範圍。

字彙：

quote [kwot] *(n.)* 報價／ maintenance [ˋmentənəns] *(n.)* 維護／ request [rɪˋkwɛst] *(v.)* 要求／ imperative [ɪmˋpɛrətɪv] *(adj.)* 必要的；緊要的／ replacement [rɪˋplesmənt] *(n.)* 更換／ frame [frem] *(v.)* 給…裝框子

Questions 159–161 refer to the following letter.

57 Broak Lane
Ashfield
Seattle
March 11th

Mobil Inc.
215 High St
Seattle

Dear Sir

I am writing to you with reference to my repeated calls to your call center between March 7th and March 10th regarding my cell phone bill.

I have been charged over $300 for 19 calls between January 3rd and February 1st. These calls were made from France to Japan, but I have not visited France. Neither my cell phone nor I have left the country. I don't even have a passport.

Every time I call your call center, your operator doesn't seem to understand the problem, and even went so far as to say that I must be mistaken and have made the calls myself. This is impossible. One operator even went on to say that if I didn't pay the bill in the next couple of days, my phone would be blocked. I have no intention of paying this bill, and will be very angry if my phone is blocked.

I am giving you until the end of the month to correct my bill and apologize or I will take legal action.

Sincerely yours
Brian Dean

159. How does Brian Dean say that he can prove that he wasn't in France?

(A) He doesn't have a passport.

(B) He knows nobody in France.

(C) He didn't use his cell phone at all.

(D) He called the call center many times.

160. What does Brian Dean suggest that he will do if his telephone bill is not corrected?

(A) He will pay the bill.

(B) He will call the call center again.

(C) He will get a passport.

(D) He will contact a lawyer.

161. Apart from having his cell phone bill corrected, what else does Brian Dean ask for?

(A) He wants his money back.

(B) He wants Mobile Inc. to apologize.

(C) He wants to visit France and Japan.

(D) He wants to call center operator to understand the problem.

第159–161 題

Broak 巷 57 號
Ashfield
西雅圖市
三月十一日

Mobil 股份有限公司
High 街 215 號
西雅圖市
親愛的先生／長官，

我寫信給你，是因為我已在三月七日至三月十日屢次打到你們電話中心，就是關於我的手機帳單問題。

我已經在一月三日至二月一日間的十九通通話被收取 300 美金。這些電話是從法國打到日本，但是我從未造訪過法國。我本人與手機都未離國。我甚至連護照都沒有。

每次我致電你們中心，你們的客服似乎不了解問題，甚至很過份地像是說一定是我弄錯了，還說我是自己打這些電話。這是不可能的。其中一名客服甚至繼續說，假使我在接下來兩天不付帳單的錢，我的電話就會被封鎖住。我不打算付這個帳單，而如果我的電話被封鎖住我會十分生氣。

我只給你們到月底的時間來更正我的帳單並道歉，否則我將會採取法律行動。

誠摯的
Brian Dean

159. 答案 (A) Brian Dean 說他能如何證明他不在法國？

(A) 他沒有護照

(B) 他在法國沒有認識的人

(C) 他完全沒用他的手機

(D) 他致電中心很多次

解說 原文第二段第三句，"I don't even have a passport"，可以證明不在法國，因為根本沒出過國。選項 (D)，在原文第一段第一句，"my repeated calls to your call center"，是事實，但是不符合本題要問的問題。

160. 答案 (D) Brian Dean 暗示他將會做什麼，如果他的帳單沒被更正？

(A) 他會付帳單

(B) 他會再致電電話中心

(C) 他會辦護照

(D) 他會與律師聯絡

解說 原文最後一段，"I will take legal action"，表示尋求法律途徑，大概就會先與律師聯絡。選項 (A) 是錯誤的，因為原文第三段第四句，"I have no intention of paying this bill"，表明不會付帳單。

161. 答案 (B) 除了要他的手機帳單更正之外，Brian Dean 還要求什麼？

(A) 他要把錢要回來

(B) 他想要 Mobile 有限公司道歉

(C) 他想造訪法國和日本

(D) 他想要電話中心客服了解問題

解說 原文最後一段，"correct my bill and apologize"，提到除了帳單更正之外還需要向他道歉。

字彙：

regarding [rɪˋgɑrdɪŋ] (prep.) 關於／ passport [ˋpæsˏport] *(n.)* 護照／ operator [ˋɑpəˏretɚ] *(n.)* 接線生；客服／ impossible [ɪmˋpɑsəbm̩] *(adj.)* 不可能的／ block [blɑk] *(v.)* 封鎖／ intention [ɪnˋtɛnʃən] *(n.)* 意圖；打算／ legal [ˋligm̩] *(adj.)* 法律的／ action [ˋækʃən] *(n.)* 行動

Questions 162–165 refer to the following itinerary.

Here is your itinerary for your Grand Canyon tour.

Overview:

On this 3-day, 2-night tour of the Grand Canyon, you'll travel through the desert before exploring the scenic Oak Creek Canyon; finally arriving at the Grand Canyon to admire the ever-changing colors of this national landmark.

Day 1:

Travel through the Sonoran Desert to the red rock county of Sedona, before enjoying a two-hour scenic tour of the historic area. The afternoon ends with a wilderness jeep excursion, before witnessing the beautiful colors of a desert sunset. Overnight at the Sonoran Desert Inn.

Day 2:

After breakfast, your guide will take you for a tour of the Oak Creek Canyon. Often called the smaller cousin of the Grand Canyon, it's known for its scenic beauty. Your guide will take you on a morning hike inside the canyon. Travel to the Grand Canyon stopping at various lookout points along the way after which the more adventurous are free to take a helicopter ride over the canyon. Overnight at the Canyon Park Lodge.

Day 3:

Witness the sun rising over the Grand Canyon. Walk along the canyon's rim and visit the Canyon Museum and Visitor Center, before traveling to an authentic trading post on the Navajo Indian Reservation to learn about the Navajo people and their arts and crafts.

162. Which activity on the tour is optional?

(A) overnight at the Canyon Park Lodge
(B) visiting the Navajo Indian Reservation
(C) a wilderness jeep excursion
(D) a helicopter ride

163. What does this itinerary describe as a national landmark?

(A) the Oak Creek Canyon
(B) the Grand Canyon
(C) the Sonoran Desert
(D) the Navajo Indian Reservation

164. When will those on the tour view dawn over the Grand Canyon?

(A) in the morning of day 3
(B) in the evening of day 2
(C) in the morning of day 2
(D) in the evening of day 1

165. Which is true about the tour?

(A) Your guide will be an Navajo Indian.
(B) The helicopter tour is too dangerous for some.
(C) The tour includes two nights' hotel accommodation.
(D) You will hike to the Grand Canyon.

第 162–165 題

這是你的大峽谷旅行計畫

概要：

在這個三天兩夜的大峽谷旅程，你們將會在探索景色秀麗的橡樹溪峽谷之前穿越沙漠區；最後抵達大峽谷，來欣賞這顏色瞬息萬變的國家的地標。

第一天：

在享受兩小時歷史上著名的區域美景之前，先行經索諾蘭沙漠至紅岩聞名的喜多娜鎮。下午會在目睹沙漠美麗日落之後，在荒蕪地帶的吉普車短途旅行作為結束。在索諾蘭沙漠小旅館過夜。

第二天：

早餐過後，你們的導遊將會帶你們至橡樹溪峽谷遊覽。這個地方常被稱為大峽谷的堂弟，以美景聞名。你們的導遊將會帶領你們在峽谷內進行晨間健行。遊歷大峽谷，停止在沿途多樣化的景色，後續還有更冒險的，你可自由參加搭乘直昇機鳥瞰峽谷。在峽谷公園小屋過夜。

第三天：

目睹旭陽昇起在大峽谷上。沿著峽谷邊走，在旅行至印第安納瓦伙族保護區裡可靠的小店，學習納瓦伙族人的藝術與手工藝之前，先至峽谷博物館與遊客中心。

162. 答案 (D) 這個旅遊有什麼可供選擇的活動？

(A) 在峽谷公園小屋過夜

(B) 造訪保護區內的印第安納瓦伙族

(C) 荒蕪地帶的吉普車短途旅行

(D) 搭直昇機

解說　第三段 "after which the more adventurous are free to take a helicopter ride over the canyon"，說明搭直昇機，是可自由參加的選項。

163. 答案 (B) 這個旅行計畫形，把什麼形容得像是國家的地標？

(A) 橡樹溪谷

(B) 大峽谷

(C) 索諾蘭沙漠

(D) 印第安納瓦伙族保護區

解說　原文第一段最後一行，"arriving at the Grand Canyon to admire the ever-changing colors of this national landmark"，指出大峽谷為國家的地標。

164. 答案 (A) 那些在旅程上的地點何時會有曙光照耀在大峽谷？

(A) 第三天的早晨　(B) 第二天傍晚

(C) 第二天早晨　(D) 第一天傍晚

解說　原文第四段，"Day 3"，"Witness the sun rising over the Grand Canyon"，說明是在第三天的早晨，目睹旭陽昇起，所以必須是在早上的時間。

165. 答案 (C) 關於遊覽行程，下例何者是事實？

(A) 你的導遊將會是第安納瓦伙族人

(B) 對一些人來說直昇機導覽太危險

(C) 遊覽行程包含兩晚旅館住宿

(D) 你將會健行至大峽谷

解說　原文第二段最後一句，"Overnight at the Sonoran Desert Inn"，以及第三段最後一句，"Overnight at the Canyon Park Lodge"，知道行程中兩位住宿含在內。選項 (D)，原文第三段第三句，"hike inside the canyon"，是指在峽谷內健行，不是健行至大峽谷。

字彙：

itinerary [aɪˋtɪnəˏrɛrɪ] *(n.)* 旅行計畫／ overview [ˋovəˏvju] *(n.)* 概要／ explore [ɪkˋsplor] *(v.)* 探索／ scenic [ˋsinɪk] *(adj.)* 景色秀麗的／ admire [ədˋmaɪr] *(v.)* 欣賞／ historic [hɪsˋtɔrɪk] *(adj.)* 歷史上著名的／ excursion [ɪkˋskɝʒən] *(n.)* 短途旅行／ Lodge [lɑdʒ] *(n.)* 小屋／ authentic [ɔˋθɛntɪk] *(adj.)* 真正的；可靠的

Questions 166-169 refer to the following article.

LEGO- The building blocks of childhood

Lego, the ubiquitous toy of choice for millions of children around the world. Look in most children's toy box and you are sure to find some of the brightly colored plastic construction bricks.

First appearing in Denmark in 1949, they soon became an international hit. More recently Lego has faced competition from cheap imitations, but real Lego still retains its appeal.

Originally Lego was sold simply as bricks of various sizes for children to create their own designs; now it is more likely to be marketed as a set to make a specific airplane, rocket or truck with many intricate pieces and even motors, gears and other moving parts. These sets will undoubtedly include full step-by-step instructions so every child constructs exactly the same model.

Lego competitions are held in many countries, where those who venture beyond the instruction booklet can pit their imaginations and skill against other like-minded modelers. Often huge life-sized models are created or even replica cars, planes or ships. You can even visit one of five Legolands.

Don't throw yours away. They're sure to still be around when your children are old enough to start building.

166. What does the article say has changed about Lego over the years?

(A) The colors of Lego
(B) The size of models that can be built
(C) The age at which children like to play with Lego
(D) That Lego sets have become more complicated

167. What does the article suggest that modern children prefer?

(A) To design their own models
(B) To follow instructions during model construction
(C) To buy poor quality imitations
(D) To use bricks of the same color

168. What does the article advise you to do?

(A) Keep your Lego for the next generation
(B) Build a model rocket
(C) Paint Lego bright colors
(D) Build huge life-sized models

169. If you purchased Lego in 1949, what wouldn't you have got?

(A) Brightly colored bricks
(B) Different sized bricks
(C) Motors and gears
(D) Plastic bricks

第 166-169 題

樂高——童年時期的建築積木

樂高，對全世界好幾百萬小孩來說，是普遍存在可供選擇的玩具。去看大部分小孩的玩具箱，確定你會找到一些色彩鮮明的塑膠建造積木。

首先在 1949 年的丹麥出現，他們很快成為國際上紅極一時東西。較近期的樂高，面臨來自便宜仿製品競爭，但是貨真價實的樂高仍舊保有它的吸引力。

原始的樂高單純賣許多不同尺寸的積木，讓小孩創造他們自己的設計；現在行銷的方式比較是整組的特定組合，像是有許錯綜複雜組件的飛機、火箭或是卡車，甚至有像是馬達與排擋，以及其他可行進移動的組件。這些組合將無疑地含有每個步驟的指示，所以每個小孩建造出一模一樣的相同模型。

樂高比賽在許多國家舉行，那些在說明書以外的冒險，能夠使他們的想像力和技術，與其他志趣相投的製造模型者相競爭。常常實體尺寸的大型模型被創造，甚至是複製的汽車、飛機，或是船艦。你也可以造訪五個樂高樂園中的其中一個。

不要把你的丟掉。他們確定在你的孩子夠大能開始建造時，仍舊存在。

166. 答案 (D) 這個文章說關於樂高在這幾年改變了什麼？

(A) 樂高的顏色

(B) 能被建造的模型尺寸

(C) 小孩開始喜歡玩樂高的年紀

(D) 樂高組合開始變得複雜

解說　原文第三段"with many intricate pieces and even motors, gears and other moving parts"，說明樂高組合變得較複雜。

167. 答案 (B) 文章暗示了現在小孩較偏好什麼？

(A) 設計他們自己的模型

(B) 在建立模型時跟隨指示

(C) 購買品質不好的仿製品

(D) 用相同顏色的積木

解說　原文第三段第一句，“now it is more likely to be marketed as a set”，與第三段最後一句，“include full step-by-step instructions” 表示改變成現在的行銷方式，就是因為小孩較喜歡跟著指示建造模型。

168. 答案 (A) 文章建議你做什麼？

(A) 把你的樂高留給下一代

(B) 建造一個火箭模型

(C) 把樂高漆上亮麗的色彩

(D) 建造真實尺寸的模型

解說　原文最後一段，“Don't throw yours away. They're sure to still be around when your children are old enough to start building”，建議你把你的樂高留給自己的小孩夠大能玩時。

169. 答案 (C) 如果你在 1949 年買樂高，你不會得到什麼？

(A) 顏色鮮明的積木

(B) 不同尺寸大小的積木

(C) 馬達

(D) 塑膠積木

解說　原文第三段第二句，“now”，指現在，與第三段第一句，“even motors, gears and other moving parts”，表示不會在 1949 年時買到這些。故選 (C)。原文第一段，“brightly colored plastic construction bricks”，表示選項 (A)、(D)。原文第三段第一句，“Originally Lego was sold simply as bricks of various sizes”，表示選項 (B)。

字彙：

ubiquitous [ju`bɪkwətəs] *(adj.)* 普遍存在的／ construction [kən`strʌkʃən] *(n.)* 建造／ international [ˌɪntɚ`næʃənl̩] *(adj.)* 國際性的／ imitation [ˌɪmə`teʃən] *(n.)* 仿製品／ retain [rɪ`ten] *(v.)* 保有／ appeal [ə`pil] *(n.)* 吸引力／ intricate [`ɪntrəkɪt] *(adj.)* 錯綜複雜的／ venture [`vɛntʃɚ] *(v.)* 冒險

Questions 170-172 refer to the following letter.

Highfield High School

Dear parents

Following a successful and very educational trip to Paris during summer vacation this year, we are pleased to announce that Highfield High School will be taking a group of students to the Swiss Alps on a skiing trip during winter vacation. The trip will be from January 6th to January 14th.

Limited places are available for thirty students and two parent helpers. Two teachers will also accompany the party.

Everyone who wishes to participate needs to have some skiing experience, and to be able to ski at a competent level without close supervision. In Switzerland the party will be accompanied by a qualified local ski instructor, but there will be no formal lessons.

Those wishing to take advantage of this exciting opportunity must be in possession of an up-to-date passport and return the enclosed application form together with a deposit of $100 to school reception by Thursday, October 3rd. A further payment of $825 must be paid before the end of November.

Unfortunately those students who are in their final year and are still waiting for confirmation of the dates for their university interviews will be unable to participate, as they must be available for interview at the time of the trip.

Mr. Ralph Taylor
The principal, Highfield High School

170. Who can't participate on this skiing vacation?

(A) Parents

(B) Beginners at skiing

(C) Teachers

(D) Students who don't plan to go to university

171. John plans to go on the trip. What should he check?

(A) How much money the trip costs

(B) When his passport expires

(C) If his mother wants to go with him

(D) If he has thirty friends who want to go with him

172. How many adults will accompany the students on the ski slopes?

(A) Three

(B) Four

(C) Five

(D) Six

第 170-172 題

Highfield 高中

親愛的貴家長們，

隨著今年暑假，成功及十分具教育意義的巴黎之行，我們很開心宣佈 Highfield 高中，將會在寒假期間帶一團學生至瑞士阿爾卑斯山脈滑雪，旅行期間自一月六日至一月十四日。

名額限定為 30 名學生，以及兩名隨行幫忙的大人。兩名教師也會隨同出遊。

每個想參加的人需要有一些滑雪經驗，並且能夠勝任不需隨時監督的程度。在瑞士當地，本團將會由一名合格的當地滑雪指導教練陪同，但是將不會有正式的課程。

那些想把握機會參加這個難得機會的人，必須持有效期內的護照，並且與申請表附件連同 100 美金訂金，一併在十月三日星期四之前，送回學校管理室。更進一步的 825 美金款項，必須在十一月底前支付。

不幸地，那些在校最後一年，仍在等待他們大學面試日期確定的學生，將無法參加，因為他們必須在這個旅行期間能夠參加面試。

Ralph Taylor 先生
Highfield 高中校長

170. 答案 (B) 誰無法參加這個滑雪假期？

(A) 父母

(B) 滑雪初學者

(C) 老師

(D) 不打算讀大學的學生

解說 原文第三段第一句，"to be able to ski at a competent level without close supervision"，初學者會需要時時的注意監督，故選(B)。原文第二段第一句，"thirty students and two parent helpers. Two teachers"，表示(A)、(C)、(D)皆可參加。

171. 答案 (B) John打算要參加旅行。他應該檢查什麼？

(A) 旅行要價多少錢

(B) 護照何時過期

(C) 他的母親是否與他同行

(D) 他是不是有三十個朋友跟他一起去

解說 原文第四段第一句，"must be in possession of an up-to-date passport"，參加者需要持有效期限內的護照，故選(B)。

172. 答案 (C) 有幾名成人將會陪同學生在滑雪坡上？

(A) 三名

(B) 四名

(C) 五名

(D) 六名

解說 原文第二段第一句，"two parent helpers. Two teachers"，表示四名大人，以及第三段第二句，"accompanied by a qualified local ski instructor"，表示一名合格滑雪指導教練，共計五位成人。

字彙：

educational [ˏɛdʒʊˋkeʃənḷ] *(adj.)* 教育的／ competent [ˋkɑmpətənt] *(adj.)* 能勝任的／ supervision [ˏsupɚˋvɪʒən] *(n.)* 監督／ instructor [ɪnˋstrʌktɚ] *(n.)* 指導教練／ application [ˏæpləˋkeʃən] *(n.)* 申請／ confirmation [ˏkɑnfɚˋmeʃən] *(n.)* 確定／ accompany [əˋkʌmpənɪ] *(v.)* 伴隨；陪同／ slope [slop] *(n.)* 坡

Questions 173-176 refer to the following report.

ICE STORM FREEZES US AND CANADA

Freezing weather across large parts of the northeastern US and eastern Canada have sent repair crews into overdrive trying to restore power to over half a million customers who face a cold and dark weekend without either light or heat.

Respite does not seem to be on the way however, as the National Weather Service is warning of further freezing temperatures and more snow in the coming week.

With temperatures around -15°C around Toronto authorities reported a massive increase in calls to emergency services. "We've experienced around a six fold increase in calls for assistance over the last 24 hours," reported the local mayor, "and we don't expect things to get any easier very soon." He also asked for those affected to stay indoors and to keep warm.

In the US travel chaos was reported in northeastern states with numerous traffic collisions reported on a number of different highways. All train services have been canceled in the affected states, although airports and airlines were reporting only minor delays at the region's airports.

Meanwhile fire officials have warned residents trying to heat their homes to avoid using anything that burns inside the house especially candles. A fire official spokesman said, "In these freezing conditions there is always a tendency to keep warm by any means possible, but it's not just the risk of fire that has to be taken into account, but also carbon monoxide poisoning."

At their home outside Witchurch, John Lyne and his family of five said that they lost electricity in the middle of Sunday night and he has been trying to keep the family happy and warm in one room while they wait for power to return. "We're all staying in sleeping bags all day. The children thought it was fun at first, but now they are getting more and more irritable," he said.

For those in the Midwest who were spared the initial storm the need to be vigilant remains as temperatures there are also expected to plunge over the coming few days.

173. If you need to travel out of this area which method of transport would be the best?

(A) By car
(B) By airplane
(C) By train
(D) By bus

174. What shouldn't residents burn inside their house to keep warm?

(A) Coal
(B) Wood
(C) Candles
(D) All of the above

175. Which are John Lyne's children most likely to be doing now?

(A) Arguing with each other
(B) Sleeping in their beds
(C) Building a snowman in the yard
(D) Watching TV

176. What does the fire official spokesman suggest is more important than keeping warm?

(A) Restoring power
(B) Using candles for lighting
(C) Staying safe
(D) Keeping the family together

第 173-176 題

冰暴風急凍美國與加拿大

急凍的氣候橫掃美國東北部與加拿大東部，已經派維修組員長時間奮戰，試圖替五十多萬名在週末面臨沒燈或暖氣，又黑又冷顧客們修復電力。

儘管看起來電力似乎不會那麼快恢復，然而國家氣象服務站正警告會有更冷的氣溫，而且本週還會有更多降雪。

氣溫大約零下 15℃ ，多倫多市當局報導，撥打緊急服務的電話量大幅增加。「在過去的 24 小時，我們經歷大約六倍打來尋求協助的電話。」當地市長說道，「我們也不期望情況很快就會獲得改善。」他也要求那些受疾病侵襲的人留在室內，保持溫暖。

美國東北部報導旅程一片混亂，有許多交通部撞事故在很多不同高速道路上發生。所有火車在受影響的各州均停駛，然而機場與航班報導，只有在該區域機場有輕微誤點。

同時，官方火災中心警告居民，試著讓家裡溫暖時，避免在屋內使用任何燃燒的物品，尤其是蠟燭。一位官方火災中心的發言人說，「在這些寒凍的天氣情況裡，用任何可行方法保持溫暖一直是我們的天性，但這不只是有導致發生火災的風險，也會有一氧化碳中毒的風險。」

John Lyne 一家五口在他們位於 Witchurch 城市外的家中，他們在星期日晚上中途停電，當他們在等待電力恢復時，他試著讓家人保持開心，並擠在同一間房間保暖，「我們整天留在睡袋裡。孩子們一開始認為很好玩，但是後來他們愈來愈煩躁，」他說道。

那些在美國中西部，逃過這最初暴風的人需要警戒，因為那邊的氣溫也預期會在接下來的幾天急降。

173. 答案 (B) 如果你需要在這個區域外旅行，哪一種方式的交通運輸會是最好的？

(A) 開車　　(B) 搭飛機

(C) 搭火車　　(D) 搭公車

解說　原文第四段第二句，"airports and airlines were reporting only minor delays at the region's airports"

174. 答案 (D) 居民不應該在屋內燃燒什麼來保持溫暖？

(A) 木炭　　(B) 木頭

(C) 蠟燭　　(D) 以上皆是

解說　原文第五段第一句，"avoid using anything that burns inside the house especially candles"。意指任何可燃的東西都不要在屋裡燒。

175. 答案 (A) John Lyne 的孩子們現在最有可能在做什麼？

(A) 彼此爭吵　　(B) 睡在他們自己的床上

(C) 在院子裡堆雪人　　(D) 看電視

解說　從原文第六段最後一句 "now they are getting more and more irritable" 推斷，孩子們現在最有可能因為煩躁而爭吵。不選 (B)、(C)，在原文第六段 "trying to keep the family happy and warm in one room" 與 "We're all staying in sleeping bags all day" 得知他們留在睡袋裡並且在同一間房間。試圖保暖，不可能出去房子外堆雪人。不選 (D)，原文第六段第一句，"they lost electricity in the middle of Sunday night"，說明他們有停電，停電不能看電視。

176. 答案 (C) 官方火災中心發言人暗示什麼是比保持溫暖更重要？

(A) 修復電力　　(B) 用蠟燭當照明

(C) 確保安全　　(D) 全家人聚在一起

解說　從原文第五段 "to keep warm by any means possible, but it's not just the risk of fire that has to be taken into account, but also carbon monoxide poisoning" 可得知，發言人強調安全的重要性，不是只有引發火災，更要小心一氧化碳中毒。(A)、(B)、(D) 在文章中均未提到。

字彙：

restore [rɪˋstor] *(v.)* 修復／ authority [əˋθɔrətɪ] *(n.)* 當局／ mayor [ˋmeɚ] *(n.)* 市長／ chaos [ˋkeɑs] *(n.)* 混亂／ condition [kənˋdɪʃən] *(n.)* 情況／ carbon monoxide [ˋkɑrbən] [mɑnˋɑksaɪd] *(ph.)* 一氧化碳／ irritable [ˋɪrətəbl̩] *(adj.)* 煩躁的／ vigilant [ˋvɪdʒələnt] *(adj.)* 警戒的

Questions 177-180 refer to the following statement.

YOUNG ASIAN BUSINESSMAN OF THE YEAR

Kai Rai Loi has always been interested in computers and has just won the title of Young Businessman of the Year at this year's Asian Business Awards. Ever since he was a child growing up in a suburb of Seoul, South Korea, he has been programing computers, and always dreamed of turning his hobby into a career.

Kai's hardworking parents wanted him to follow them into the hotel business, so out of respect for his parents, he went to university to do a hotel management degree. He never felt quite at home on the course, but despite his misgivings, he graduated with honors.

After university however, while working for a major hotel chain in Busan, his passion for computers was reignited. He started writing apps in his free time for the newly developed smart phones. He soon realized that he could make more money after work than he could during his day job, so he quit it.

Soon back in Seoul, one of his first apps- that turned your contacts into a musical game, hit one million downloads. Since then Kai hasn't looked back. "Back then apps were quite simple and easy to write," he said, "but now there is so much more that goes into them. It's more of a team effort."

Kai has managed where so many others have failed by turning programming skills into sustained business success. Kai's company, AllApps, has gone from strength to strength and now employs over fifty people and has an annual turnover of over US$5,000,000.

Kai says that his parents have now forgiven him for not continuing with his career in hotels, in fact they are now very proud of him. When asked what his next app would be he just smiled and said that we'd have to wait and see just the same as everybody else.

Still just in his twenties, it's no wonder he has been chosen as this year's Young Asian Businessman of the Year.

177. What did Kai win the Young Asian Businessman of the Year for?

(A) His app which turned contacts into a musical game

(B) His hotel business

(C) The success of his company AllApps

(D) Because he is still in his twenties

178. Why did Kai study hotel management?

(A) His parents wanted him to do it.

(B) He thought this would be a successful career.

(C) He dreamed of opening his own hotel.

(D) He wanted to write a hotel app.

179. What did Kai do that many other good programmers couldn't?

(A) His app hit one million downloads.

(B) He created a long term successful business.

(C) He quit his day job.

(D) He wrote a musical app.

180. When did Kai learn to program computers?

(A) At university

(B) During childhood

(C) While working at a hotel in Busan

(D) After university

第 177-180 題

本年度年輕亞洲商人

Kai Rai Loi 一直以來都對電腦有興趣，而且才剛贏得今年亞洲商業獎的年輕商人頭銜。從他小時候在南韓首爾郊區長大時，就一直在寫電腦程式，也一直夢想把嗜好變成事業。

Kai 辛勤工作的雙親，希望他跟隨他們一同進入飯店業，所以為了達到雙親期盼，他進大學修飯店管理學位。他在課程中一直不覺得這是他在行的，但是僅管他的不安，他仍以優等成績畢業。

大學畢業後儘管進入釜山的主要連鎖飯店工作，他對電腦的熱情再次點燃。他開始在空閒時間，寫最新發展智慧型手機的應用程式。他很快地了解到，他可以在下班後賺的錢是比正常工作還多，所以他辭去工作。

他很快回到首爾，他的其中一個首批應用程式——把你的通訊錄變成音樂遊戲，下載率達一百萬次。從此以後，Kai 不再回首過去。他說，「以前的應用程式還蠻容易寫的，可是現在有太多要寫在裡面的東西。比較像是要團隊努力的事。」

Kai 把寫電腦程式技術變成一個成功的永續事業，很多人這麼做卻是失敗。Kai 的公司 AllApps 不斷進步，現在員工人數超過 50 人，而且每年度營業額超過 500 萬美金。

Kai 說他的雙親現在已原諒他沒有繼續他在飯店的事業，事實上，他們現在十分以他為榮。當問到他個應用程式要做什麼時，他只微笑說，我們必須跟每個人一樣觀望。

他只有二十幾歲，也難怪他被選為本年度的年輕亞洲商人。

177. 答案 (C) Kai 因為什麼贏得當年度年輕亞洲商人獎？

(A) 他寫的應用程式把通訊錄變成音樂遊戲

(B) 他的飯店事業

(C) 他的公司 AllApps 的成功

(D) 他只有二十幾歲

解說 原文第五段，第一句 "Kai has managed where so many others have failed by turning programming skills into sustained business success"，可知道他的 AllApps 公司很成功，所以贏得當年度年輕亞洲商人獎。

178. 答案 (A) 為什麼 Kai 讀飯店管理？

(A) 他的雙親想要他從事這方面的工作

(B) 他認為這是個成功的事業

(C) 他夢想開一間自己的飯店

(D) 他想寫一個飯站的應用程式

解說 原文第二段第一句，“so out of respect for his parents, he went to university to do a hotel management degree”。

179. 答案 (B) Kai 做到了什麼其他優秀寫程式者做不到的事？

(A) 他的應用程式有一百萬次下載率

(B) 他創造了長期經營的成功事業

(C) 他辭去工作

(D) 他寫了音樂的應用程式

解說 原文第五段第一句，“Kai has managed where so many others have failed by turning programming skills into sustained business success”。

180. 答案 (B) 何時學會寫電腦程式？

(A) 讀大學時

(B) 童年時期

(C) 在釜山飯店工作期間

(D) 大學畢業後

解說 第一段第二句，“Ever since he was a child growing up in a suburb of Seoul, South Korea, he has been programming computers”，得知是從年幼時期就會寫。

字彙：

suburb [ˋsʌbɝb] *(n.)* 郊區／ graduated [ˋgrædʒʊˏetɪd] *(adj.)* 畢業了的／ reignite [ˏriɪgˋnaɪt] *(v.)* 再點燃／ application[ˏæpləˋkeʃən] *(n.)* 應用程式，app 是縮寫／ sustained [səˋstend] *(adj.)* 持久的；永續的／ from strength to strength *(ph.)* 不斷進步／ turnover [ˋtɝnˏovɚ] *(n.)* 營業額／ wonder [ˋwʌndɚ] *(v.)* 懷疑；納悶 (no wonder 難怪)

Questions 181-185 refer to the following advertisement and email.

Computer programmer wanted: Tech Solutions Ltd. is looking for a full time computer programmer. Experience in programming graphics and familiarity with the latest games consoles a must. Preferable a degree in computer science, but all applicants who possess the skills to program will be considered. Send resume and any supporting documents by August 28th to Anna Wong, Tech Solutions, 29 Ark Street, Edinburgh, Scotland or email techsolutions@game.co.uk

To:	Anna Wong
From:	Tony Logan

I am writing to you with reference to the advertisement at the local job center for a computer programmer. I am currently working as a computer trainer for a major bank, but my passion is programming.

Please find enclosed my full resume and work experience. I am also sending you some examples of my programming because, as you will see from my resume, I didn't study computer science while at university. I am sure that these programs will give you a good idea of the high level of my skill as a programmer.

Please do not hesitate to contact me if you require any further information or examples of my work.

Sincerely

Tony Logan

181. What is Tech Solutions Ltd.?

(A) A software developer
(B) A maker of games consoles
(C) A bank
(D) A graphics design company

182. What does Tony Page say demonstrates his qualifications for the job?

(A) His computer science degree
(B) His job as a computer trainer
(C) The example programs that he includes
(D) His resume

183. What does the advertisement say is NOT necessary required for the job?

(A) Knowledge of games consoles
(B) A resume
(C) Skills as a programmer
(D) A computer science degree

184. What kind of software does Tech Solutions Ltd. want to develop?

(A) Games for personal computers
(B) Games for games consoles
(C) Software for bank training
(D) Software for art students

185. What DOESN'T Tony Logan say in his email?

(A) What he studied at university
(B) Whether he went to university or not
(C) What his current job is
(D) Why he wants the job at Tech Solutions Ltd.

第 181-185 題

徵電腦程式設計師：Tech Solutions 有限公司正在尋找全職電腦程式設計師 。有製圖程式設計經驗，並且熟悉近期的遊戲操縱台是必備條件。有電腦科學學位尤佳，但是所有擁有技術的申請人，將皆會列入考慮。

請在八月二十八日之前，將履歷與任何所需次要文件寄至，Tech Solutions 公司 Ark 街 29 號 愛丁堡 蘇格蘭，Anna Wong 收，或是寄電子郵件至 email techsolutions@game.co.uk。

🕮收件者:	Anna Wong
寄件者:	Tony Logan

我寫信給你，是看見本地工作中心的徵求電腦程式設計者廣告。我目前的工作是一間大銀行的電腦訓練師，但是我熱愛的是程式設計。

請參閱我附件的完整履歷與工作經歷。我也寄給你一些我設計的程式範例，因為，就如你會在我履歷中看見的，我在大學時並非主修電腦科學。我確定這些程式將會讓你對我的程式有高程度的概念，甚至認為我是位電腦程式設計師。

如果你需要任何更進一步的資訊，或是我的工作例子。請不要猶豫聯絡我。

誠摯的

Tony Logan

181. 答案 (A) Tech Solutions Ltd 是什麼？

(A) 軟體開發商　(B) 遊戲操縱台製造商

(C) 銀行　(D) 圖像設計公司

解說　第一篇第一段 “looking for a full time computer programmer”，可以得知公司是軟體開發商。

182. 答案 (C) Tony Page 說了什麼來展示他有資格故這份工作？

(A) 他的電腦科學學位　(B) 他的電腦訓練師職務

(C) 他附在郵件裡的程式範例　(D) 他的履歷

解說　第二篇第二段第一句，“I am also sending you some examples of my programming” 與第三句，“I am sure that these programs will give you a good idea of the high level of my skill as a programmer”，

表示他對此有信心具這項職缺的資格，故選 (C)。選項 (A) 在第二篇第二段，"I didn't study computer science"，故不正確。選項 (B)，不符合職缺需求。選項 (D)，未從事同性質工作過，所以履歷不符合職缺需求。

183. 答案 (D) 廣告上說什麼不是這項工作的必備條件？

(A) 擁有遊戲操縱台的知識　(B) 履歷

(C) 有程式設計師的技術　(D) 電腦科學學位

解說 第一篇第三句，"Preferable a degree in computer science"，擁有電腦科學學位「尤佳」，並非必備條件，故選 (D)。選項 (A)，第一篇第二句，"familiarity with the latest games consoles a must"，是必須條件。選項 (B)，第一篇第四句 "Send resume"，是必須條件。選項 (C)，第一篇第三句，"all applicants who possess the skills to program will be considered"，是必須條件。

184. 答案 (B) Tech Solutions 有限公司想要開發什麼種類的軟體？

(A) 個人電腦用的遊戲軟體　(B) 操縱台遊戲用的遊戲軟體

(C) 給銀行訓練用的軟體　(D) 給美術學生用的軟體

解說 從第一篇第二句，"familiarity with the latest games consoles a must"，可以知道需要程式設計師來設計的是操縱台遊戲軟體，因為它為需求資格的必要條件。

185. 答案 (A) Tony Logan 沒有在他的電子郵件中說什麼？

(A) 他在大學主修什麼

(B) 他是否讀過大學

(C) 他目前的工作

(D) 為什麼他想要在 Tech Solutions 有限公司工作

解說 第二篇原文第二段第二句，"I didn't study computer science while at university"，說明大學不是主修電腦科學，並未進一步說明主修的科目，故選 (A) 選項 (D)，在第二篇原文第一段尾，"my passion is programming"，可以知道這是他熱愛的事，所以想從事這方面的工作。

字彙：

graphics [ˋgræfɪks] *(n.)* 製圖法／ console [ˋkɑnsol] *(n.)* 操縱台／ familiarity [fə͵mɪlɪˋærətɪ] *(n.)* 熟悉／ possess [pəˋzɛs] *(v.)* 持有／ degree [dɪˋgri] *(n.)* 學位／ hesitate [ˋhɛzə͵tet] *(v.)* 猶豫／ passion [ˋpæʃən] *(n.)* 熱愛的；熱情／ further [ˋfɝðɚ] *(adv.)* 更進一步地

Questions 186-190 refer to the following emails.

📖To:	Jim
From:	Dan

Hi Jim

How's it going? Hope the new job is going well. How are Rose and the twins? We haven't seen you in months.

The holiday season is coming soon. I bet the twins are getting excited. This is what I want to ask you about. Every year we go to Mom and Dad's for Thanksgiving, but how about giving them a rest this year, and everyone comes here instead? You can drive down from Atlanta and I'll get tickets to fly Mom and Dad in from Dallas. We've got the whole big house and yard here, and only the two of us, so plenty of room for everyone.

Thought I'd see what you think before mentioning it to anyone else. Everyone is welcome to stay as long as they like.

Let me know what you think, as I'll need to reserve the plane seats soon.

📖To:	Dan
From:	Jim

What a great idea. It will be good to go somewhere else for a change. I do miss Dallas sometimes, but then we did spend so many years there while we were growing up, and Rose and I really don't know Mobile that well, so it will be nice to get to know the city a little better.

It will be better for Jessica and Jasmine, too. They can play out in the yard at your house. Ever since Mom and Dad moved into that apartment, it's never been the best place to have children running around.

The only problem I see is convincing Mom and Dad. It is a bit of a family tradition to spend Thanksgiving in Dallas after all. But I'm sure if you ask them just after they come back from their vacation in Hawaii, they'll be ok with it.

Rose is doing great. She did have a busy Halloween, especially helping at the school party. Jessica and Jasmine love their new school, and think that they are very grown up now that they go to elementary school.

186. What is the relationship between Jim and Dan?

(A) They are father and son.
(B) They are twins.
(C) They are Rose's sons.
(D) They are brothers.

187. Where do Jessica and Jasmine live?

(A) Dallas
(B) Atlanta
(C) Mobile
(D) Hawaii

188. What do we know about Jim?

(A) He recently changed his employment.
(B) He lives in Dallas.
(C) He has no children.
(D) His daughter is called Rose.

189. How many children does Jim have?

(A) Four
(B) Three
(C) Two
(D) He doesn't have any.

190. Which of the following statements is true?

(A) Dan and Jim spent their childhood in Dallas.
(B) Rose knows Mobile well.
(C) Dan and Jim's parents live in a big house.
(D) Jim lives in an apartment.

第 186-190 題

收件者: Jim
寄件者: Dan

嗨 Jim，

近來如何？希望你新的工作順利。Rose 和雙胞胎們好嗎？我們已好幾個月沒和你們見面了。

假期的季節快到了。我打賭雙胞胎們開始感到興奮。這就是我想問你的事。我們每年感恩節都去媽媽和爸爸的家，但是要不要今年讓他們休息一下，換成讓每個人來我們這裡？你可以從亞特蘭大開車下來，我會幫媽媽和爸爸買機票從達拉斯搭飛機過來。我們在這裡有大房子和院子，而且只有我們兩個，所以有充份的房間給每個人。

在我向任何人提起之前，我想先知道你的想法。歡迎每個人來要停留多久都可以。

讓我知道你的想法，因為很快會需要預訂機位。

收件者: Dan
寄件者: Jim

多麼棒的主意。有時換去不同的地方是好的。我有時候想念達拉斯，我們的確有幾年是在那裡長大的，但是 Rose 和我真的不是很熟悉摩比港市，所以多了解一下該城市將會是很不錯。

這也將對 Jessica 和 Jasmine 比較好。他們可以在你們家的院子玩耍。自從媽媽和爸爸搬到那間公寓後，就不再是小孩們可以跑來跑去的最好地方了。

在我看來的唯一的問題，是說服媽媽和爸爸。感恩節要在達拉斯渡過，畢竟是有點像家裡的傳統。但是我確定，如果你在他們從夏威夷的假期回來後問他們，他們會對這個安排沒問題。

Rose 很好。她的確有個很忙碌的萬聖節，尤其是幫忙學校的派對。Jessica 和 Jasmine 愛他們的新學校，而且他們覺得他們上了小學就是長很大了。

186. 答案 (D) Jim 和 Dan 之間是什麼關係？

(A) 他們是父子　　(B) 他們是雙胞胎
(C) 他們是 Rose 的兒子　　(D) 他們是兄弟

解說　從第一篇第二段第四句，"Every year we go to Mom and Dad's for Thanksgiving" 可以知道他們是兄弟，故選 (D)。

187. 答案 (B) Jessica 和 Jasmine 住在哪裡？

(A) 達拉斯　　(B) 亞特蘭大

(C) 摩比港市　　(D) 夏威夷

解說　在第一篇第一段第一句，"How are Rose and the twins"，知道 Jim 有雙胞胎小孩；在第二篇第二段第一句，"It will be better for Jessica and Jasmine"，知道小孩的名字。再從第一篇第二段，"drive down from Atlanta"，知他們居住的地方。

188. 答案 (A) 我們知道關於 Jim 的什麼事？

(A) 他最近換了工作　　(B) 他住在達拉斯

(C) 他沒有小孩　　(D) 他女兒的名子叫 Rose

解說　第一篇第一段，"Hope the new job is going well"，可以得知，故選 (A)。

189. 答案 (C) Jim 有幾個小孩？

(A) 四個　　(B) 三個

(C) 兩個　　(D) 他沒有任何小孩

解說　在第一篇第一段，"How are Rose and the twins"，知是雙胞胎。

190. 答案 (A) 以下哪一個陳述是事實？

(A) Dan 和 Jim 童年在達拉斯市長大　　(B) Rose 非常熟悉摩比港市

(C) Dan 和 Jim 的父母住在大房子　　(D) Jim 住在公寓裡

解說　選項 (A)，第二篇第一段，"we did spend so many years there while we were growing up"，是事實。選項 (B)，在第二篇第一段，"Rose and I really don't know Mobile that well"，表示 Rose 不熟悉摩比港市。選項 (C) 第二篇第二段，"Ever since Mom and Dad moved into that apartment"，知他們的父母住在公寓，且下一句，"it's never been the best place to have children running around"，推測是空間不大的公寓。選項 (D) 未提。

字彙：

instead [ɪn`stɛd] *(adv.)* 作為替代；反而／ mention [`mɛnʃən] *(v.)* 提起／ reserve [rɪ`zɝv] *(v.)* 預訂／ apartment [ə`pɑrtmənt] *(n.)* 公寓／ convince [kən`vɪns] *(v.)* 說服／ after all *(ph.)* 畢竟

Questions 191-195 refer to the following bank statement and email.

ALL UNION BANK

Mr. R Reynolds	**Statement**	74
57 Birchfield Road	**Date**	November 28th
Highfield	**Branch**	Washington
Washington	**Account**	867937365
	Call us	0473 67653256
	Write to us	675 Lincoln St Rose Hill Gardens Washington
	Online	www.allubank.com

REGULAR CHECKING ACCOUNT **September 28th to November 28th**

Opening Balance	$1,245
Total in	$1,768
Total out	$2,173
Balance on November 28th	$840

Date	Payment type	Details	Money out	Money in	Balance
		Opening balance			1,245
29 Sept		Branch deposit		250	1,495
2 Nov	Debit card	Hill Gas station	70		1,425
5 Nov	Check	Tax department	325		1,100
7 Nov		Salary		1,505	2,605
11 Nov	Debit card	Shark's Mall	45		2,560
11 Nov	Debit card	Shark's Mall	45		2,515
11 Nov	Debit card	Rider Bikes	130		2,385
15 Nov	Transfer	Mortgage	890		1,495
18 Nov		Interest		13	1,508
21 Nov	Debit card	Rose Supermarket	163		1,345
25 Nov		Check	250		1,195
27 Nov	Transfer	Regular Saver	200		895
27 Nov	Debit card	Online shopping	55		840
		Closing Balance			**840**

Your Interest Rate 2.5%
Open a new savings account online today at www.allubank.com
Call us 24hr on 0473 67653256 for all your personal banking, business banking and financial services.
All Union Bank. A proud member of the Better Bank Association

📖To:	All Union Bank
From:	Mr. Reynolds
Date:	November 30th

I have just received my monthly statement for my checking account 867937365, and I think there has been a mistake with one of my debit card payments. I appear to have been charged twice when I used my debit card to make a purchase on November 11th.

I am not sure how to deal with a situation like this. Is it up to me to contact the store myself and to ask for a refund of the second payment or is this a banking problem and I should leave it to you to sort out?

I would also like to change my regular savings transfers. At the moment I am saving $200 a month, but due to my current financial situation I would like to reduce this to $100. Can you tell me if I can do this online, or if I have to fill in a form and sign it?

Thank you for your help in these matters.
Mr. R Reynolds

191. Who is Mr. Reynolds?

(A) An employee of All Union Bank
(B) An employee at Shark's Mall
(C) An account holder at All Union Bank
(D) A tax department worker

192. Which payment is Mr. Reynolds querying?

(A) The payment at Shark's Mall
(B) The payment at Hill Gas Station
(C) The payment at Rose Supermarket
(D) The payment at Rider Bikes

193. What would be an appropriate reply from All Union Bank to Mr. Reynolds' email?

(A) We have no record of your payment at Shark's Mall.

(B) We no longer offer savings accounts.

(C) Sorry about the double payment. It will be corrected on your next statement.

(D) Please contact the tax department yourself to sort out the problem.

194. What might be a reason for Mr. Reynolds reducing his monthly savings to $100?

(A) He was charged twice at Shark's Mall.

(B) He is opening a new business.

(C) He doesn't have a job.

(D) He spent more than he earned during the month.

195. What might Mr. Reynolds expect to receive in the mail from All Union Bank?

(A) A check for closing his regular savings account

(B) A form to sign to change his regular saving

(C) A new debit card

(D) A request for payment from Shark's Mall

第 191-195 題

ALL UNION 銀行

R Reynolds先生
Birchfield路57號
Highfield市
華盛頓州

對帳單	74
日期	九月二十八日
分行	華盛頓
帳號	867937365
分行聯絡電話	0473 67653256
寫信至分行	Lincoln街675號 Rose Hill Gardens 華盛頓州
網站	www.allubank.com

支票活存帳戶

自九月二十八日至 十一月二十八

本期開始餘額	$1,245
總存入	$1,768
總支出	$2,173
十一月二十八日餘額	$840

日期	付款型態	細目	支出	存入	餘額
		本期開始餘額			1,245
9/29		至分行存入		250	1,495
11/2	簽帳卡	Hill加油站	70		1,425
11/5	支票	稅務部	325		1,100
11/7		薪資		1,505	2,605
11/11	簽帳卡	Shark's 商場	45		2,560
11/11	簽帳卡	Shark's 商場	45		2,515
11 /11	簽帳卡	Rider 腳踏車店	130		2,385
11/15	轉帳	房貸	890		1,495
11/18		利息		13	1,508
11/21	簽帳卡	Rose 超級市場	163		1,345
11/25		支票	250		1,195
11/27	轉帳	定期轉存	200		895
11/27	簽帳卡	線上購物	55		840
		本期結束餘額			840

您的存款年利率為 2.5%。
開立新的存款帳戶，請至網站www.allubank.com。
個人電話銀行理財服務、商業電話理財服務，以及財務規畫服務，請撥打24小時服務電話0473 67653256
All Union銀行——是Better Bank 機構引以為傲的會員。

📖收件者:	All Union 銀行
寄件者:	Reynolds 先生
日期:	十一月三十日

我剛才收到我支票活存帳戶的每月對帳單，帳戶號碼為 867937365,，但是我想在我的簽帳卡付款項目，出了一個錯。我似乎在十一月十一日當天，使用簽帳卡購買商品時被收費了兩次。

我不確定怎麼處理像這樣的情況。是看我要不要自己聯絡該商店，然後要求退回被二次付款的款項，還是這是銀行的問題，我是否應該留給你們去處理？

我也想要更改我的定期轉存轉帳。目前我每個月存 200 美金，但是由於我目前的財務情況，我想要把金額減少至 100 美金。你能告訴我我是否可以在網路上做這個，或是我必須填寫表格並簽名？

感謝你幫忙這些問題

R Reynolds 先生

191. 答案 (C) 誰是 Reynolds 先生？

(A) All Union 銀行的員工

(B) Shark's 商場的員工

(C) All Union 銀行的帳戶持有人

(D) 稅務部的工人

解說 從第一篇原文的銀行對帳單收件人是 Mr. R Reynolds，可以知道是該銀行客戶。

192. 答案 (A) 哪一個款項是 Reynolds 先生提出疑問的？

(A) 在 Shark's 商場的款項

(B) 在 Hill 加油站的款項

(C) 在 Rose 超級市場的款項

(D) Rider 腳踏車店的款項

解說 第二篇第一段，"I appear to have been charged twice when I used my debit card to make a purchase on November 11th"，知他提出疑問，第一篇 "11 Nov" 的部份，在 "Shark's Mall" 共有兩筆款項。

193. 答案 (C) All Union 銀行回覆給 Reynolds 先生的電子郵件，應該怎麼樣才是合宜的回覆呢？

(A) 我們沒有你在 Shark's 商場的付款記錄

(B) 我們不再提供存款帳戶

(C) 關於兩次扣款的款項我們十分抱歉。將會在您下一期帳單上做更正。

(D) 請自己聯絡稅務部來解決問題

194. 答案 (D) 什麼可能是 Reynolds 先生把他每月存入款項減至 100 美金的原因？

(A) 他在 Shark's 商場被兩次扣款

(B) 他正要創業

(C) 他沒有工作

(D) 他本月花的錢比他賺的還多。

解說　第一篇原文的 "7 Nov"，"Salary" 是 1,505，但是自 11/7 後的支出是 1,778 元。表示本月入不敷出，第二篇原文第三段第二句，"due to my current financial situation"，表示是目前的財務問題而已。

195. 答案 (B) 從電子郵件裡知道 Reynolds 先生，可能預期從 All Union 銀行那裡收到什麼？

(A) 結束他活期存款帳戶的支票

(B) 變動他固定存款需簽名的表格

(C) 新的簽帳卡

(D) 來自 Shark's 商場的要求付費款項

解說　第二篇原文第三段第三句，"or if I have to fill in a form and sign it"，表示他想過也許可能會需要填表並簽名。

字彙：

debit card [ˋdɛbɪt] [kɑrd] *(n.)* 簽帳卡／ purchase [ˋpɝtʃəs] *(n.)* 購買／ deal [dil] *(v.)* 處理 (+with) ／ check [tʃɛk] *(n.)* 支票／ sort [sɔrt] *(v.)* 整治；處理 (+out) ／ due to [dju] [tu] (prep.) 因為；由於／ financial [faɪˋnænʃəl] *(adj.)* 財務的／ reduce [rɪˋdjus] *(v.)* 減少；降低

Questions 196-200 refer to the following articles.

Obesity nearly quadrupled in developing countries.

The following table displays a regional guide to the percentage of overweight and obese adults in both 1980 and 2008.

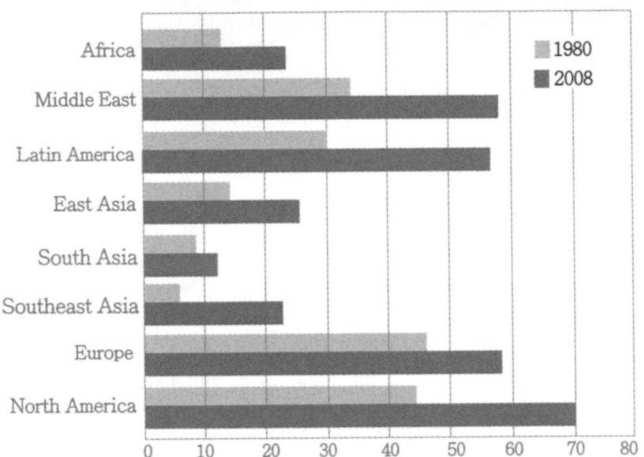

The number of overweight and obese adults in the developing world has nearly quadrupled to nearly one billion since 1980 according to a recent report. Nearly one in three people worldwide is now overweight. The report predicts a huge increase in strokes, heart attacks and diabetes, which will put a huge strain on health systems in coming years.

The report also points out that as developing countries continue to get fatter, malnutrition is still a major problem for hundreds of millions of people in less developed countries.

While North America still has the largest percentage of overweight adults at 70%, other regions like Latin America and the Middle East are rapidly catching up.

The biggest increase has been in Southeast Asia. Despite starting the study at only 7%, by 2008 the overweight had reached 22%.

One of the report's authors, John Logan, suggests that the data can be largely explained by the rises in urban populations in these developing countries. Urbanization leads to changes in lifestyles and eating habits. The newly created middle classes are turning away from traditional foods, and eating more high fat, sugary foods.

The report concludes that governments need to recognize the problem and start taking action.

Diet- The South Korean Way

As many parts of the world grapple with issues of the increasing size of their waists, one country seems to be bucking the trend. South Korea has avoided the worst of the obesity epidemic even as it has swept the region surrounding it.

The traditional Korean diet seems to be the key to keeping South Korean's weight under control. Their low fat cuisine means that they are now one of the least obese countries in the world.

Many are crediting government policy for playing a major part in this success. Government action to preserve the country's traditional diet has included public campaigns and, at a more local level, teaching women how to cook traditional dishes. These are skills that are being slowly lost in modern generations in many other countries.

Another country which is often cited as an example of a success story in fighting the fat is Denmark. Lawmakers there started legislating against some of the more harmful ingredients in processed foods long before the problems were accepted elsewhere.

196. What do both articles agree on?

(A) That public campaigns have little effect on people

(B) That the Middle East has a big problem with obesity

(C) That government policies are needed to fight obesity

(D) That Denmark has been successful in fighting obesity

197. According to the report, which region still had the lowest level of obesity in 2008?

(A) South Asia

(B) Europe

(C) Southeast Asia

(D) Africa

198. What has Denmark been a good example of?

(A) Making laws that reduce problem foods

(B) Preserving the traditional diet

(C) Helping reduce malnutrition in developing countries

(D) A country with a large increase in obesity

199. What do the articles link?

(A) Obesity with malnutrition

(B) Obesity with health problems

(C) Government policy and urbanization

(D) The middle classes and the Korean diet

200. According to the articles, which statement is true?

(A) Latin America has the world's highest obesity problem.

(B) People in Denmark still eat mainly traditional foods.

(C) Obesity is not a worldwide problem.

(D) One third of humanity is overweight.

第 196-200 題

肥胖人口在開發國家將近四倍。（圖表是以人口換算成比例）

以下圖表，顯示 1980 和 2008 年這兩年，成人過重和肥胖比例的地區性指標。

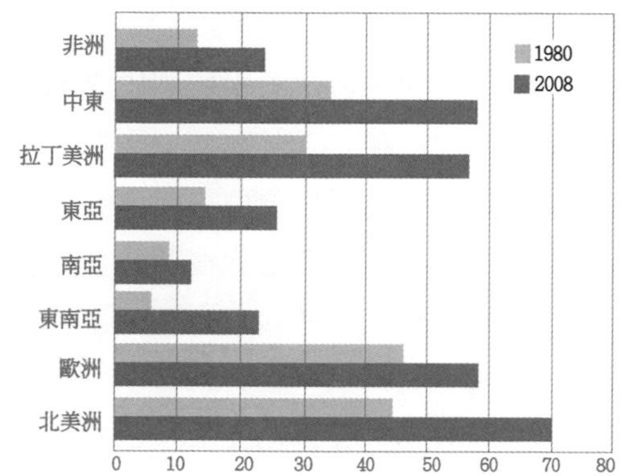

根據一項近期報告，在開發中的世界裡，自 1980 年起，成人過重與肥胖人口數幾乎成長四倍，達到將近 10 億人。現在全世界將近三分之一的人是過重的。報告中預測中風、心臟病病發，以及糖尿病將大幅增加，這將會讓接下來幾年的健保系統不堪負荷。

報告也指出，因為開發中國家的人持續愈來愈胖，營養失調仍是在低度開發國家中，好幾百萬人民的主要問題。

然而美國北部仍是擁有最高比例，百分之 70% 的成人肥胖人口，其他像是拉丁美洲裔美國人地區，以及中東國家，也正迎頭趕上。

在東南亞國家的增加幅度最大。儘管研究一開始的數據是 7%，到了 2008 的過重人口達到 22%。

其中一份報告的作者 John Logan，他提出這個資料可從這些開發中國家，城市的居住人口上升來說明。都市化導致生活型態和飲食習慣改變。新創造出的中產階級，不再吃傳統食物，而是去吃更高脂、高糖的食物。

報告的結論是，政府需要認清問題，並開始有所行動。

飲食——南韓的方法

全世界許多地方努力解決腰圍尺寸增大的問題，但是有一個國家似乎躲過這個趨勢。南韓已經避免掉最糟糕的肥胖流行，甚至還把鄰近地區的肥胖問題一掃而空。

傳統的韓國飲食似乎是保持南韓的體重受控制的關鍵。他們的低脂餐點，代表他們現在是全世界，擁有最少肥胖人口的其中一個國家。

許多政府，有部分在主要扮演這成功角色的政策優點，政府保存國家傳統飲食的行動，包括公共活動，還有，以較本土的程度來看，教導女人如何烹調傳統的菜。這些是許多其他國家現代化的世代中，逐漸被遺忘的技能。

另一個常被引用為成功戰勝肥胖故事範例的國家，是丹麥。那裡的重大事件是，早在其他地方接收這些問題時，就開始立法禁止加工食品裡，一些比較對人體造成損害的原料 。

196. 答案 (C) 兩個文章均同意什麼論點？

(A) 公眾活動對人的影響很少

(B) 中東有很大的肥胖問題

(C) 需要政府政策來對抗肥胖

(D) 丹麥在對抗肥胖是成功的。

解說 只有選項(C)在第一篇原文最後一句，“governments need to recognize the problem and start taking action”，以及第二篇原文最後一段第一句，“Another country which is often cited as an example of a success story in fighting the fat”，和第二句，“started legislating”，這兩篇文章中均表示需要政府的作為對抗肥胖。

197. 答案 (A) 根據報告，哪一個地區仍在2008年有最低程度的肥胖程度？

(A) 南亞 (B) 歐洲

(C) 東南亞 (D) 非洲

198. 答案 (A) 丹麥是什麼的好範例？

(A) 制定降低問題食物的法律

(B) 保留傳統的飲食

(C) 幫助降低開發中國家營養失調問題

(D) 肥胖大幅增加的國家

解說 第二篇原文最後一段，"cited as an example of a success story in fighting the fat is Denmark. Lawmakers there started legislating against some of the more harmful ingredients in processed foods"。

199. 答案 (B) 文章有什麼相聯結之處？

(A) 有營養失調的過胖

(B) 有健康問題的過胖

(C) 政府政策與都市化

(D) 中產階級與韓式飲食

解說 第一篇原文第二段第三句，"increase in strokes, heart attacks and diabetes, which will put a huge strain on health systems"， 以及第二篇原文最後一句，"more harmful ingredients in processed foods"，均表示是有關影響健康的肥胖問題。

200. 答案 (D) 依據這兩篇文章，下例哪一項陳述是事實？

(A) 拉丁美洲有全球最高的肥胖問題

(B) 丹麥的人仍舊主要吃傳統食物

(C) 肥胖不是全球性的問題

(D) 三分之一的人類是過重的

解說 第一篇原文第二段第二句，"one in three people worldwide is now overweight"，故選 (D)。選項 (A)、(B) 並未明確在提及。選項 (C)，在第二篇原文第一句，"As many parts of the world grapple with issues of the increasing size of their waists"，足以知道是全球性的問題，故不正確。

字彙：

quadruple [ˋkwɑdrʊpl̩] *(v.)* 成為四倍／ billion [ˋbɪljən] *(n.)* 十億／ overweight [ˋovɚ͵wet] (n./adj.) 過重的／ malnutrition [͵mælnjuˋtrɪʃən] *(n.)* 營養失調／ urban [ˋɝbən] *(adj.)* 城市的／ conclude [kənˋklud] *(v.)* 做出結論／ grapple [ˋgræpl̩] *(v.)* 努力解決問題 (+ with) ／ epidemic [͵ɛpɪˋdɛmɪk] *(n.)* 流行

Test 3

Part 5. 單句填空

Questions 101-140

101. We - - - - - - - to inform you that we are unable to find a buyer for your property at this time.

(A) regretted
(B) regretting
(C) regret
(D) regretful

102. Due to - - - - - - - snow in southern England, many flights from Heathrow Airport have been delayed for up to seven hours.

(A) large
(B) heavy
(C) abundant
(D) oversized

103. Without a good attitude, it is very unlikely that you will achieve anything at this company - - - - - - -.

(A) at all
(B) at least
(C) at most
(D) at last

104. We have been informed that service will be - - - - - - - as soon as the fault has been repaired.

(A) resume
(B) resuming
(C) resumed
(D) resumes

105. As a general rule, employee breaks cannot - - - - - - - twenty minutes during each four hour shift.

(A) exceed
(B) last
(C) be
(D) extend

106. - - - - - - - to pay this bill on time may lead to a penalty or to the disconnection of your telephone.

(A) Failure
(B) To fail
(C) Fail
(D) Failed

107. Following the disorganized product launch, either Mr. Peters or Mr. Abraham - - - - - - - expected to be fired at the board meeting next week.

(A) are
(B) was
(C) is
(D) were

108. The recent relaxation of visa restrictions has resulted in a lack of airline capacity on many European - - - - - - -.

(A) lines
(B) routes
(C) roads
(D) tracks

109. Star Fashion is an institution that is famous in many countries for - - - - - - - use of bright colors and patterns.

(A) their
(B) them
(C) they
(D) its

110. Fire fighters have been battling the blaze all night, but hope to finish ------- out the fire very soon.

(A) washing
(B) blowing
(C) putting
(D) fighting

111. Passersby ------- save the old man who had an accident on Main Street.

(A) tried
(B) attempted
(C) helped
(D) hoped

112. I ------- of the winner of this year's Nobel Peace Prize before I saw him on TV last night.

(A) didn't hear
(B) don't hear
(C) hadn't been heard
(D) hadn't heard

113. If you don't know how to spell the word, you should look ------- in a dictionary.

(A) up it
(B) it up
(C) for it
(D) it for

114. Farmers around the world are growing more and more ------- fruits and vegetables in order to meet growing consumer demand.

(A) fresh
(B) whole
(C) healthy
(D) organic

115. Television is often used by parents to keep their children - - - - - - - when they are busy.

(A) entertained
(B) entertaining
(C) entertain
(D) entertainingly

116. Whether the economy recovers or not interest rates are expected to remain low - - - - - - - the foreseeable future.

(A) with
(B) since
(C) for
(D) before

117. Despite repeated requests for the documents, I am still unable to obtain - - - - - - - I asked for.

(A) what
(B) that
(C) which
(D) who

118. - - - - - - - are happy to announce the birth of their second child, Maria, on October 14th.

(A) Lloyds
(B) The Lloyd
(C) Lloyd
(D) The Lloyds

119. According to the report the - - - - - - - of CO_2 in the atmosphere is a leading cause of climate change.

(A) concentrate
(B) concentration
(C) concentrated
(D) concentrating

120. The note said that if the ------- is not paid promptly, the hostage will not be released.

(A) research
(B) ransom
(C) bill
(D) rescue

121. The company ------- the number one computer manufacturer for ten consecutive years when the current chairman retires in the fall.

(A) will be
(B) will have been
(C) will have
(D) will be being

122. The department has spent a large part of its budget ------- its new computer system.

(A) on buying
(B) to buy
(C) buy
(D) buying

123. Mr. James has extensive ------- of the inner workings of the motor industry.

(A) learning
(B) knowledge
(C) wisdom
(D) literacy

124. Had the sailors not discovered the leak in the hull, the ship might ------- sunk.

(A) have
(B) has
(C) been
(D) be

125. The accident at the construction site was very serious; however, all the injured are expected to make a full -------.

(A) recover
(B) recovered
(C) recovery
(D) recovering

126. ------- like to start their day with a cup of coffee with their breakfast.

(A) Some people
(B) Somebody
(C) Some person
(D) Any people

127. In order for the seminar to start on time, all participants must be ready ------- 2pm.

(A) until
(B) after
(C) during
(D) by

128. Any ------- behavior towards our employees will not be tolerated and will be immediately reported to the police.

(A) threat
(B) threatening
(C) threaten
(D) threatened

129. All delegates in the forum have to register with the organizing committee at least three weeks in -------.

(A) forward
(B) advance
(C) approach
(D) arrival

130. Our antivirus software was being updated when the hackers broke ------- our database.

(A) out of
(B) off
(C) into
(D) at

131. We have been advised to invest cautiously, and we will act -------.

(A) accordingly
(B) according
(C) accord
(D) accorded

132. New research has shown that habitat destruction has affected the ------- in the area, but less than expected.

(A) nature
(B) culture
(C) wilderness
(D) wildlife

133. The company CEO ------- a briefcase with a lot of important company documents in it while riding on the subway.

(A) lost
(B) lose
(C) has lost
(D) was losing

134. The parents' committee ------- that the annual school dance will not be subsidized by any school funds this year.

(A) decides
(B) decided
(C) has been decided
(D) is deciding

135. By the time we got to the front of the queue, all the tickets for the concert had been sold -------.

(A) up
(B) of
(C) out
(D) off

136. The assistant ------- we employed last month is to be offered a new permanent position in another department.

(A) which
(B) that
(C) where
(D) what

137. The introduction of the new sales technique had a ------- effect on the company's market share.

(A) notice
(B) noticing
(C) noticed
(D) noticeable

138. Without proper training security guards are forbidden from ------- firearms in public places.

(A) bringing
(B) carrying
(C) taking
(D) getting

139. ------- is unfortunate that you missed your train and were unable to attend the meeting.

(A) It
(B) This
(C) That
(D) Its

140. Eyewitnesses to the accident report ------- a deep rumbling sound prior to the collapse of the building.

(A) hear
(B) to hear
(C) hearing
(D) heard

Part 5. 單句填空

第 101-140 題

101. 答案 (C) 我們遺憾告訴你，我們這次沒找到你房地產的買主。

(A) 遺憾（過去分詞）　　(B) 遺憾（現在分詞）

(C) 遺憾（現在式動詞）　　(D) 遺憾的 *(adj.)*

解說　本題時間是 this time，文法為現在式，故選用現在式動詞。

102. 答案 (B) 由於英國南部劇烈的降雪，許多從希斯洛機場的航班延誤七小時以上。

(A) 大的　　(B) 劇烈的

(C) 豐富的　　(D) 過大的

103. 答案 (A) 沒有好的態度，你根本不會在這間公司達到任何成就。

(A) 根本　　(B) 至少

(C) 至多　　(D) 最後

104. 答案 (C) 我們被告知，一旦問題修復好就會馬上恢復服務。

(A) resume　　(B) resuming

(C) resumed　　(D) resumes

解說　未來式被動語態，主詞＋ will be ＋過去分詞，故選 (C)。

例句　Wendy will be a superstar in ten years. Wendy 十年後將會是超級明星。

105. 答案 (A) 如一般的規定，每四小時一班的輪班裡，員工休息時間不得超過二十分鐘。

(A) 超過 *(v.)*　　(B) 持續 *(v.)*

(C) 是 *(v.)*　　(D) 延長 *(v.)*

106. 答案 (A) 不履行準時付這個帳單，會導致罰款或切斷電話線。

(A) 失敗 *(n.)*　　(B) 失敗 *(inf.)*

(C) 失敗 *(v.)*　　(D) 失敗了的 *(adj.)*

解說　“to pay”「付」，是不定詞作形容詞，形容詞修飾名詞，所以需要一個名詞，故選 (A)。

107. 答案 (C) 隨著無組織的產品發表，預計不是 Peters 先生就是 Abraham 先生，會在下週的董事會議被開除。

(A) are　(B) was
(C) is　(D) were

解說　"either ~ or"「不是…就是」，所以知道主詞為單數，所以須用 be 動詞 "is" 或 "was"，是現在式，故選 (C)。

例句　Either Maya or Nancy was hit by a car last night. 不是 Maya 就是 Nancy 昨晚被車撞。

108. 答案 (B) 最近放寬的簽證限制，導致許多歐洲路線航班供不應求。

(A) 線　(B) 路線
(C) 路　(D) 軌道

109. 答案 (D) 星流行是一個機構，在許多國家有名，因為它的亮色系和圖樣。

(A) 他們的（所有格）　(B) 他們（受格）
(C) 他們（主格）　(D) 它的（所有格）

解說　"its"「它的」，代表 "Star Fashion"「星流行」。

110. 答案 (C) 消防員整晚撲擊火焰，希望很快撲滅火勢。

(A) 洗　(B) 吹
(C) 滅　(D) 滅

解說　put out a fire「滅火」，finish「完成」，後面的動詞必須是動名詞 。也可以用 fight a fire「滅火」，但是不能寫成 fight out，故不能選 (D)。

例句　The candle fell down and caused a fire. Luckily the fire was put out immediately. 蠟燭倒下造成火災，幸運地火勢馬上被撲滅。

111. 答案 (C) 過路人幫忙救了在 Main Street 發生事故的老人。

(A) 試　(B) 企圖
(C) 幫助　(D) 希望

解說　"helped save = helped to save"，只有 "help" 可以省略掉 "to"，直接加動詞。

112. 答案 (D) 在昨晚看見今年諾貝爾和平獎得主之前，我從未聽過這個人。

(A) didn't hear（過去式）

(B) don't hear（現在式）

(C) hadn't been heard（過去完成式被動語態）

(D) hadn't heard（過去完成式）

解說 過去完成式，主詞＋ had ＋過去分詞。

例句 I had heard the news before it was on TV. 在電視播報之前，我就聽過這則消息。

113. 答案 (B) 如果你不知道怎麼拼單字，你應該查字典。

(A) up it (B) it up

(C) for it (D) it for

解說 "look it up"「查」(表示已知道要找東西的所在位置)，look 是及物動詞，it是代名詞，up是副詞。代名詞必須在副詞前面。如果是名詞，放在副詞前或後均可，如look the word up = look up the word.「查單字」。選項(C)，look for是尋找某個東西的意思，不適用在本句。

114. 答案 (D) 世界各地的農夫正種植愈來愈多的有機的水果與蔬菜，以迎接日益成長的消費者需求。

(A) 新鮮的 (B) 完整的

(C) 健康的 (D) 有機的

115. 答案 (A) 電視常被父母用來保持他們的小孩娛樂，在他們忙碌的時候。

(A) 娛樂（過去分詞） (B) 娛樂（現在分詞）

(C) 娛樂 *(v.)* (D) 娛樂地 *(adv.)*

解說 過去分詞作形容詞，當受詞補語，修飾 their children「他們的小孩」。

116. 答案 (C) 無論經濟復甦與否，在可預見的未來，預期仍保持低利率。

(A) 有 *(prep.)* (B) 自從 *(prep.)*

(C) 在 *(prep.)* (D) 在…之前 *(prep.)*

解說 介系詞 "for"「在」，指一段時間。

117. 答案 (A) 儘管再三的要求文件，我仍無法獲得我要求的東西。

(A) what　(B) that
(C) which　(D) who

解說 “obtain”「獲得」是及物動詞，“what I asked for”是名詞子句。及物動詞後面需要一個受詞，名詞子句可作受詞。

例句 I love what you made. 我喜愛你做的。

118. 答案 (D) Lloyd 一家人很開心宣佈他們第二個小孩，Maria，十月十四日誕生的喜訊。

(A) Lloyds　(B) The Lloyd
(C) Lloyd　(D) The Lloyds

解說 “The Lloyds”「 Lloyds 一家人」。表示一家人時，需加定冠詞 the，並將姓氏寫成複數。

119. 答案 (B) 根據報告，大氣層的二氧化碳濃度，是造成氣候變遷的主要原因。

(A) 濃縮 *(v.)*　(B) 濃度 *(n.)*
(C) 濃縮的 *(adj.)*　(D) 濃縮（現在分詞）

解說 定冠詞 the，後面要是名詞。

120. 答案 (B) 紙條説如果不立即支付贖金，人質將不會被釋放。

(A) 研究 *(n.)*　(B) 贖金 *(n.)*
(C) 帳單 *(n.)*　(D) 援救 *(n.)*

121. 答案 (B) 當目前的主席在秋天退休時，公司將會已是連續十年第一名的電腦製造商。

(A) will be　(B) will have been
(C) will have　(D) will be being

解說 未來完成式，主詞＋ will ＋ have been。

例句 Next month, I will have been the best car salesman in the company for 2 years. 下個月，我就會是公司連續兩年的最佳售車員。

122. 答案 (D) 部門花了該部門很大一部分的預算，購買新的電腦系統。

(A) on buying (B) to buy

(C) buy (D) buying

解說 "spend"「花」＋錢＋on(*prep.*)＋名詞＝"spend"「花」＋ 錢 ＋ on (*prep.*)＋ 動名詞。

例句 My daughter has spent all her money on her bedroom. My daughter has spent all her money decorating her bedroom. 我的女兒花了全部她的錢在（佈置）她的房間上。

123. 答案 (B) James 先生有汽車業內部運作的廣大知識。

(A) 學習 (*n.*) (B) 知識 (*n.*)

(C) 智慧 (*n.*) (D) 識字 (*n.*)

124. 答案 (A) 如果水手沒有發現船身的裂縫，船可能就沉了。

(A) have (B) has

(C) been (D) be

解說 "had the sailors not" = If the sailors hadn't「如果水手沒有」，第三條件句，表示假設改變過去發生的事實。If ＋過去完成式子句＋，＋主詞＋might/would/could ＋現在完成式。

例句 If Sara hadn't lost all her money, she would have lived in a bigger house. 如果 Sara 沒有輸了她所有的錢，她就能住更大的房子。

125. 答案 (C) 建築工地的事故十分嚴重，然而期待所有受傷的人完全復元。

(A) 復元 (*v.*) (B) 復元（過去分詞）

(C) 復元 (*n.*) (D) 復元（現在分詞）

解說 "full"「完全的」，是形容詞，後面必須是名詞。

126. 答案 (A) 一些人喜歡在早餐喝一杯咖啡作為一天的開始。

(A) 一些人 (B) 某人

(C) Some person (D) Any people

解說 現在式，主詞為第三人稱時，動詞要加 s，本句的動詞 "like"「喜歡」並沒有加 s，故主詞必須是複數。選項 (B) 為單數。選項 (C)、(D) 均為錯誤的英文。

127. 答案 (D) 為了讓討論會準時開始，全部的參與者必須在下午兩前之前準備好。

(A) 直到…時 *(prep.)* (B) 在…以後 *(prep.)*
(C) 在…期間 *(prep.)* (D) 在…之前 *(prep.)*

128. 答案 (B) 任何對我們員工脅迫的行為，將不會被容忍並馬上報警。

(A) 威脅 *(v.)* (B) 脅迫的 *(adj.)*
(C) 威脅 *(v.)* (D) 受到威脅的 *(adj.)*

129. 答案 (B) 討論會裡的所有代表人，必須在至少三週前，事先跟組織委員會登記。

(A) 轉交 *(v.)* (B) 事先 *(v.)*
(C) 接近 *(v.)* (D) 到達 *(n.)*

130. 答案 (C) 我們的防毒軟體被升級，當駭客闖入我們的資料庫。

(A) out of (B) off
(C) into (D) at

解說 選項 (C)，break into *(ph.)* 闖入。選項 (A) break out of *(ph.)* 逃出。選項 (B) break off *(ph.)* 中斷。選項 (D)，沒有意思。

131. 答案 (A) 我們被建議謹慎的投資，而我們也將照做。

(A) 照著 *(adv.)* (B) 相符的 *(adj.)*
(C) 符合 *(v.)* (D) 符合（過去分詞）

解說 “act”「做事」，是動詞，副詞修飾動詞，故選 (A)。

132. 答案 (D) 新研究顯示動物棲息地破壞，影響了該區的野生生物，但影響程度不如預期大。

(A) 自然 *(n.)* (B) 文化 *(n.)*
(C) 荒野 *(n.)* (D) 野生生物 *(n.)*

133. 答案 (A) 公司執行長在搭地鐵時，遺失了有許多重要公司文件的公事包。

(A) lost (B) lose
(C) has lost (D) was losing

解說 過去式，主詞＋過去式動詞。

例句 Linda missed her favorite TV program while tidying her desk.
Linda 在整理書桌時錯過了她最喜愛的電視節目。

Test 1 Test 2 Test 3 Test 4 Test 5

134. 答案 (B) 家長會決定學校的年度舞會，今年將不會被任何學校基金資助。

(A) decides　　(B) decided

(C) has been decided　　(D) is deciding

解說　過去式，主詞＋過去式動詞。

135. 答案 (C) 到了我們排到隊伍的前面時，所有演唱會的票都已被賣完了。

(A) up　　(B) of

(C) out　　(D) off

解說　選項 (C)，sell out *(ph.)* 賣完。選項 (A)，sold up *(ph.)* 為還債變賣一切。選項 (B)，沒有意思。選項 (D)，sell off *(ph.)* 廉價出售。

136. 答案 (B) 我們去年雇用的助理，上個月另一個部門提供她新的永久職位。

(A) which　　(B) that

(C) where　　(D) what

解說　關係代名詞 who 或 that 都可用來引導形容詞子句，代表在它前面的人。選項 (A)、(C) 皆為關係代名詞，但各代表它前面的東西和地方。選項 (D)，不是關係代名詞。

例句　The boy that my son is talking to is Jim. 我兒子正跟在他說話的那個男孩是 Jim。

137. 答案 (D) 新的銷售技巧介紹方法，在公司的市佔率上有顯著的影響。

(A) 注意 *(v.)*　　(B) 注意（現在分詞）

(C) 注意（過去分詞）　　(D) 顯著的 *(adj.)*

解說　"effect"「影響」，是名詞，形容詞修飾名詞，故選 (D)。

138. 答案 (B) 沒受過專業訓練的保全人員，禁止在公共場合攜帶槍枝。

(A) 帶來　　(B) 攜帶

(C) 拿走　　(D) 獲得

解說　槍枝要用動詞 carry「攜帶」。

139. 答案 (A) 不幸的你錯過了火車，而且無法參加會議。

(A) It　　(B) This

(C) That　　(D) Its

解說　"It"，代名詞，可以當假的主詞。

例句　It is important that you listen to my advice. 你聽我的勸告是很重要的。

140. 答案 (C) 事故的目擊證人記述，在建築物倒塌先前，聽到一個深厚的隆隆聲。

(A) 聽到 *(v.)* (B) 聽到 *(inf.)*

(C) 聽到（動名詞） (D) 聽到（過去式動詞）

解說 "report"「記述」，是動詞，report 後面只能用動名詞。

例句 The teacher reported smelling smoke before the fire started. 老師記述在火災開始之前聞到煙味。

Part 6. 短文填空

Questions 141-143 refer to the following article.

Global Stocks see new highs

2013 was a stellar year for many of the world's stock markets. Contrary to most professional's predictions, it wasn't the emerging markets that benefited the most, but the more mature markets of the US and Europe where despite continued economic problems, especially in Europe, markets - - - - - - - around 20%.

141. (A) rise
(B) rose
(C) risen
(D) rising

Meanwhile 2013 couldn't have come to an end sooner for many of the emerging markets with - - - - - - - of around 10% for the year. Markets

142. (A) lose
(B) lost
(C) losing
(D) losses

in Latin America being the worst affected.

So what does 2014 have - - - - - - - store for investors? We'll

143. (A) by
(B) on
(C) in
(D) for

probably know in January for as traders say, "As goes January, so goes the year."

Questions 144-146 refer to the following school announcement

Poetry competition for schools

Elementary school students in the Omaha school district are invited to submit ------- poems for the city's seventh annual poetry

144. (A) originate
(B) original
(C) originally
(D) origin

competition. All children aged 10-13 who attend any of the city's 56 elementary schools are eligible to enter. The topic for this year is "Winter."

This year's total prize money has been increased to $10,000. The winner will receive $5,000 and five runners-up will each receive $1,000. All prizes will be presented to the winners' schools for funding their school libraries. The top 100 poems will also be published and copies will be given to all the top writers ------- every school within the state.

145. (A) over and above
(B) also
(C) besides
(D) as well as

Last year's winning poem was "A Rose Petal" by Jermain Dexter, who went on to represent the state at the National Poem Writing Competition where he placed third. His poem can be read on our website- www.poemcomp.omaha.com. Or if you need some -------, why not borrow a copy of last year's top 100 from your school library. All entries must be received before the end of the semester. Your teacher has full details of how to submit a poem.

146. (A) inspire
(B) inspired
(C) inspiration
(D) inspiring

Get writing, and good luck!

Questions 147-149 refer to the following announcement.

It is with a mixture of ------- and pleasure that we announce the

147. (A) sad
(B) sadden
(C) sadly
(D) sadness

retirement of Alex Chapman, our longest serving employee, coworker and friend. Alex's last day is March 20th.

Alex joined the company in 1978 and brought about a revolution in the way that our products were ------- including our first use of

148. (A) marketed
(B) marketing
(C) markets
(D) marketable

television advertising. His career has mirrored the development of the company from a local manufacturer to an international brand. We are indebted to him for his talent and commitment for propelling the company ------- the position that it is in today. His leaving marks an end of an era.

149. (A) on
(B) to
(C) at
(D) from

We will be honoring Alex with a retirement party in the ballroom of the Royal Lake Hotel on March 19th. We invite everyone who has worked with Alex over the years to attend as we extend our best wishes to Alex and his wife, Jane. We all wish them a long and happy retirement together.

Questions 150-152 refer to the following article.

What you need to know about getting married in Bali

Many people are ------- the tropical Indonesian island of Bali as

150. (A) chosen
(B) choose
(C) choosing
(D) chose

the location for their wedding. It is possible and in most cases easy to get legally married in Bali. You will need to hire the services of a local wedding planning company and to plan ahead to have all the necessary documents prepared. Then all you need to do is to choose the -------, almost anywhere from a hotel villa to the beach is suitable.

151. (A) scene
(B) location
(C) region
(D) position

Another alternative which is becoming popular is to do all the paperwork for a ------- marriage back home and to have a wedding

152. (A) legal
(B) legally
(C) good
(D) authorized

without actually getting legally married in Bali. If you choose this option it is not only cheaper, but there is no involvement with the authorities in Bali, and you can choose for anyone from a friend to a relative to officiate at the service.

Part 6. 短文填空

第 141-143 題

全球股市創新高

2013 年是對許多世界上的股市來說，是主要的一年。跟大部分專家的預測相反，受益最多的不是新興的市場，而是儘管持續有問題的美國和歐洲較成熟的市場，尤其在歐洲，市場價格漲了 20%。

141. 答案 (B)

(A) rise (B) rose
(C) risen (D) rising

解說 簡單過去式，用過去式動詞，rise「上升」的動詞三態為 rise-rose-risen，故選 (B)。

同時，2013 年對許多同年損失大約 10% 的新興市場來說，過得太慢了。在拉丁美洲的市場受到最不好的影響。

142. 答案 (D)

(A) lose (B) lost
(C) losing (D) losses

解說 with「有」，是介系詞，後面一定要是名詞，故選 (D)。選項 (A)，lose「遺失」是動詞。選項 (B)，lost「遺失」是過去式動詞。選項 (C)，losing「失敗的」是形容詞。

所以對投資者來說，2014 年即將會發生什麼事？我們大概會在一月知道，就如商人說的，「只要一月順利，整年都順利。」

143. 答案 (C)

(A) by (B) on
(C) in (D) for

解說 in store for「即將要發生」，是片語，故選 (C)。第 141-143 題

字彙：

stellar [ˋstɛlɚ] *(adj.)* 主要的／ contrary [ˋkɑntrɛrɪ] *(adj.)* 相反的／ emerging [ɪˋmɝdʒɪŋ] *(adj.)* 新興的／ meanwhile [ˋminˏhwaɪl] *(adv.)* 同時／ loss [lɔs] *(n.)* 損失／ trader [ˋtredɚ] *(n.)* 商人

第144-146 題

校際詩文競賽

阿馬哈市行政區的國小學童受邀提交原創詩文，此為第七屆年度詩文競賽。年齡介於 10 至 13 歲的該市 56 所國小學童，符合參加資格。今年的詩文主題為「冬季」。

144. 答案 (B)

(A) 發源 *(v.)* (B) 原創的 *(adj.)*
(C) 原創地 *(adv.)* (D) 起源 *(n.)*

解說 必須選形容詞，修飾名詞 poem「詩文」。

今年的總獎金增加至 1 萬美金。第一名將會獲得 5 千美金，五位第二名將會獲得 1 千美金。所有獎金將會被送至優勝者就讀學校，做為學校的圖書館基金。前 100 名入選的詩文也將會集結出版，該書會贈予這前 100 名作者，也會贈予該州每間學校。

145. 答案 (D)

(A) 在…之外 *(prep.)* (B) 也 *(adv.)*
(C) 除此之外 *(prep.)* (D) 也 *(prep.)*

解說 介系詞後面可以是名詞片語，every school「每間學校」為一個名詞片語。文章內容以選項 (D) 為最通順答案。

去年第一名的詩文是 Jermain Dexter 創作的《玫瑰花瓣》，他繼續代表該州參加全國性詩文寫作競賽，獲得全國第三名。他的詩文可以在我們的網站 www.poemcomp.omaha.com 看到。或者如果你需要一些靈感，何不去學校圖書館。

146. 答案 (C)

(A) 激勵 *(v.)* (B) 有靈感 *(adj.)*
(C) 靈感 *(n.)* (D) 激勵人心 *(adj.)*

解說 some「一些」，在本句為形容詞，必須加名詞。選項 (D)inspiring「有靈感」通常是形容詞，很少做動名詞用。

借一本去年的前 100 名入選詩文集。所有參賽作品必須在本學期未前收件。你們的老師有如何提交詩文的完整細節。

開始寫作，並祝你好運！

字彙：

annual [ˋænjʊəl] *(adj.)* 一年一次的／ eligible [ˋɛlɪdʒəbḷ] *(adj.)* 有資格的 (＋ to-v) ／ runner-up [ˋrʌnəˋrʌp] *(n.)* 第二名；亞軍／ publish [ˋpʌblɪʃ] *(v.)* 出版／ represent [ˏrɛprɪˋzɛnt] *(v.)* 代表／ semester [səˋmɛstɚ] *(n.)* 一學期

第 147-149 題

我們宣佈 Alex Chapman 的退休，是悲喜交雜的，他是我們服務最久的員工、同事，以及朋友。Alex 的最後一天上班日是三月二十日。

147. 答案 (D)

(A) 悲傷的 *(adj.)*　　(B) 使悲傷 *(v.)*
(C) 悲哀地 *(adv.)*　　(D) 悲傷 *(n.)*

解說　of 是介系詞，後面一定是名詞，故選 (D)。

Alex 在 1978 年進公司上班，並引進我們革命性的產品行銷方式，包括我們第一次採用電視廣告。他的職業生涯映照出公司的發展，從一間當地的製造業者變成國際的品牌。我們受惠於他，因為他的才能和奉獻，把公司推進到今天的地位。他的離開，代表一個時代的結束。

148. 答案 (A)

(A) 銷售（過去式動詞）　　(B) 行銷 *(n.)*
(C) 銷售 *(v.)*　　(D) 可銷售的 *(adj.)*

解說　過去式被動語態，過去式 be 動詞 + 過去分詞，故選 (A)。

149. 答案 (B)

(A) on　　(B) to
(C) at　　(D) from

我們會在三月十九號，在 Royal Lake 飯店宴會廳舉辦一場向 Alex 致敬的退休派對。我們邀請每位曾跟 Alex 共事過的人參加，當作致上我們的祝福給 Alex 以及他的妻子，Jane。我們都希望他們在一起享有長久快樂的退休生活。

字彙：

mixture [ˋmɪkstʃɚ] *(n.)* 混合／ announce [əˋnaʊns] *(v.)* 宣佈／ retirement [rɪˋtaɪrmənt] *(n.)* 退休／ revolution [ˏrɛvəˋluʃən] *(n.)* 革命／ manufacturer [ˏmænjəˋfæktʃərɚ] *(n.)* 製造業者／ indebted [ɪnˋdɛtɪd] *(adj.)* 受惠的

第150-152題

在峇里島結婚需要知道的事

很多人選擇熱帶的印尼峇里島作為舉行婚禮的地點。在峇里合法結婚是可以辦到的，在大多數的例子中也容易辦到的。你將會需要雇用當地婚禮籌辦公司的服務，並事先計畫，才能準備好所有必需的文件。然後你只需要選擇地點，幾乎從飯店別墅到海灘的任何地方都很適合。

150. 答案 (C)

(A) 選擇（過去分詞） (B) 選擇 *(v.)*
(C) 選擇（動名詞） (D) 選擇（過去式動詞）

解說 are 是現在式 be 動詞，後面可以是名詞，choosing 是動名詞，動名詞是名詞，故選 (C)。選項 (A)，be 動詞＋過去分詞，是被動語態，不合題意。

151. 答案 (B)

(A) 場景 *(n.)* (B) 地點 *(n.)*
(C) 地帶 *(n.)* (D) 職位 *(n.)*

另一個可供選擇的方式變得很受歡迎，那就是在自己的國家做好所有合法婚姻的書面作業，然後在峇里島舉行婚禮，並不是真的在峇里島合法結婚。如果你選擇這個方式，不只是花費較少，也不會牽涉在峇里島授權的問題，然後可以從朋友到親戚中，選擇任何人來主持婚禮儀式。

152. 答案 (A)

(A) 合法的 *(adj.)* (B) 合法地 *(adv.)*
(C) 好的 *(adj.)* (D) 授權的 *(adj.)*

解說 a legal marriage「合法婚姻」，marriage 是名詞，形容詞修飾名詞，必須選擇一個形容詞，故選 (A)。選項 (C)，也是形容詞，但不符合題意。

字彙：

tropical [ˋtrɑpɪkḷ] *(adj.)* 熱帶的／ location [loˋkeʃən] *(n.)* 地點；場所／ hire [haɪr] *(v.)* 雇用／ alternative [ɔlˋtɝnətɪv] *(adj.)* 可供選擇的／ paperwork [ˋpepɚˏwɝk] *(n.)* 書面作業／ legal [ˋligḷ] *(adj.)* 合法的

Part 7. 單篇／雙篇文章理解

Questions 153-154 refer to the following email.

To: Christine Taylor
From: High Pacific Bank

Your request to reset your password has been received. To complete the process, please click on the link below and enter your temporary password. The link and temporary password will work only one time.

Your temporary password: Mj459AtvQ

Click Here to Reset Your Password

This email is only to confirm your email address. Please delete it after resetting your password.

If you have any further problems please email: customerassist@hpbank.com or call the 24hr Customer Assistance Desk on 677 4446749

Thank you

High Pacific Bank Administration Center

153. What has most probably happened?

(A) Christine Taylor has forgotten her bank password.

(B) Christine Taylor is opening a new email account.

(C) Christine Taylor has forgotten that her password is Mj459AtvQ.

(D) Christine Taylor is unable to contact the Customer Assistance Desk.

154. What should Christine Taylor do next?

(A) Enter the password Mj459AtvQ

(B) Check her email

(C) Call the Customer Assistance desk

(D) Click on the link

Questions 155-156 refer to the following advertisement.

Watson's Computer Stores

The specialists in business and home computing

personal computers	printers	cables
business computers	tablets	software
laptops	networks	supplies

Extended guarantee on all computers we sell

Full repair service

Free advice for anyone anytime

Lessons available- we will teach you to use what you buy

Two locations within the city

Broadoak Mall	219 Claire Street	(271) 483-1294
Oldgate Park	57 Badminton Hill	(271) 483-2479

Open: Monday – Saturday 9am – 5pm

Email: watson@computers.com

Tel: (271) 483-7184 (24h helpline)

Visit our website for special offers at
www.watcomputers.com

155. If you buy a computer at Watson's computers, what do they give you for free?

(A) Free advice
(B) Free lessons
(C) A longer guarantee
(D) Free repairs

156. It's late on a Monday evening, and your computer isn't working properly, what could you do?

(A) Visit Watson's Computer Store's website
(B) Take your computer to a Watson's Computer Store
(C) Buy a new computer
(D) Telephone Watson's Computer Stores

Questions 157-158 refer to the following email.

📖To:	Jackie Lang
From:	Samui Resort

Thank you for your booking at Samui Resorts on the beautiful Thai island of Koh Samui.

February 3rd to February 8th one Standard Double room including breakfast.

Payment has been received from Visa card 7856********

Your booking reference is SR5078976

Please accept a complimentary upgrade to our Club Double room.

Full details of our hotel facilities along with a guide of thing to do on Koh Samui are available on our website: www.samuiresort.com.th

We look forward to welcoming you on February 3rd. If we can be of any assistance before then, please contact us and we will be happy to help.

157. What has Samui Resort given Jackie Lang?

(A) Free breakfast

(B) A better room

(C) A guided tour of Koh Samui

(D) Assess to their website

158. What should Jackie Lang do upon receipt of this email?

(A) Go to the airport

(B) Check that her credit card has received payment

(C) Contact Samui Resorts about the confusion about her room type

(D) She doesn't have to do anything.

Questions 159-161 refer to the following article.

Davos- The World Economic Forum

Up in the freezing mountains of Davos must feel like a great climate to reflect on the problems of mankind far below. The ski resort in the Swiss Alps is where the global business and political elite are heading to this week for the annual World Economic Forum (WEF) for four days of pondering on the planet's future. This year's forum will debate the challenges of wealth, poverty and economic growth all with the usual aim of trying to make the world just right.

Much of this year's debate will be focused on how globalization is reshaping the developing economies with many in the investment community skeptical about prospects in many emerging markets such as China where the pursuit of growth often comes at the expense of shareholder profit.

Also to be discussed is the widening gap between rich and poor with a WEF survey suggesting that this is the biggest risk to the world in the coming year. The survey warns both those in business and politicians that the income disparity and its related social unrest will increasingly shape the world economy in the next decade. It warns of a "lost generation" who enter working age lacking skills, jobs and opportunities.

159. What is Davos?

(A) The World Economic Forum
(B) An emerging market
(C) A ski resort in Switzerland
(D) A problem for mankind

160. Which is NOT mentioned as a concern for debate at this year's World Economic Forum?

(A) The planet's future climate
(B) Emerging markets
(C) Young jobless people
(D) Poor people

161. What has been highlighted at this year's World Economic Forum as possibly the most important issue?

(A) Globalization
(B) Social unrest
(C) Differences in income between people
(D) A lack of young people

Questions 162- 165 refer to the following email.

🕮To:	Orchid Flowers
From:	Mrs. Green

Thank you for the twenty-four red roses delivered to us on Saturday. They are very beautiful. The only problem is that I have no idea why I have received them.

My husband and I were not at home when they were delivered on Saturday morning, and your deliveryman left them with our neighbor. When we arrived home in the afternoon, we received the flowers and were curious to read the card. The card was addressed to a Mrs. Green of New Road, Summerfield, Ireland. I am Mrs. Green of New Road, Summerfield, England.

Upon reading the card, I immediately tried to telephone the number on the delivery receipt, but only got your answering machine which said that you only open on Saturday morning during the weekend. I have no other way of contacting you until Monday, and so I'm sending you this email. The flowers look very nice in my living room, but I'm afraid that Mrs. Green in Ireland is still waiting for hers.

162. Why is Mrs. Green emailing Orchid Flowers?

(A) To complain about the delivery of flowers
(B) To inform Orchid Flowers of their mistake
(C) To find out why the flowers she sent to Ireland were not delivered
(D) To try to contact Mrs. Green in Ireland

163. Why was Mrs. Green unable to contact Orchid Flowers by telephone?

(A) Because she cannot find the telephone number for Orchid Flowers
(B) Because Orchid Flowers' telephone is only answered by an answering machine
(C) Because Orchid Flowers' deliveryman is not in the office
(D) Because by the time Mrs. Green received the flowers, Orchid Flowers had already closed

164. What is the connection between the two Mrs. Greens?

(A) They share the same name.
(B) They are friends.
(C) They send each other flowers.
(D) They live on the same street.

165. Who ordered the twenty-four red roses?

(A) Mrs. Green in England ordered them.
(B) Mrs. Green in Ireland ordered them.
(C) Orchid Flowers ordered them.
(D) The article does not say who ordered them.

Questions 166-168 refer to the following article.

Yellowstone National Park

Yellowstone National Park is a national park in the northwestern United States. It is primarily located in the state of Wyoming but also has areas that straddle the border into the neighboring states of Idaho and Montana. Yellowstone is credited with being the world's first national park. It is now one of the world's most popular with over three million visitors each year.

The Yellowstone area has been inhabited by Native Americans for thousands of years, but it wasn't until the mid 19th century that European settlers first explored the area.

The park encompasses mountain ranges, canyons, rivers and lakes; however, Yellowstone is best known for its volcanic activity. The whole park is centered around a volcano, and it is this that gives rise to one of its most famous features - the geyser Old Faithful. Sometimes called the most predicable geological feature on Earth, it sprays boiling water into the air approximately once every ninety-one minutes.

It is not only its geology that Yellowstone is famous for, but also its ecosystem which is home to countless species of plants and animals some of which are endangered.

166. What does the geyser's name "Old Faithful" refer to?

(A) That it can be relied upon to perform
(B) That it sprays boiling water into the air
(C) That it performs many times every day
(D) That it is part of a volcano

167. What does Yellowstone hold a world record for?

(A) It is the world's biggest national park.
(B) It is the world's oldest national park.
(C) It has more visitors than any other national park.
(D) It has been inhabited for longer than any other national park.

168. According to the article, which statement is true?

(A) Old Faithful is the name of a volcano.
(B) European settlers arrived before the Native Americans.
(C) Most of Yellowstone's ecosystem has died out.
(D) The park is not all in one state.

Questions 169-172 refer to the following article.

Online Passport Application

You can complete an online passport application to renew your existing passport or to update details on an existing passport. Please do not use this form to apply for your first passport.

If you are traveling within the next fourteen days, do not use this form. Contact your nearest passport office for details of our express over-the-counter service for which an appointment will be necessary.

After completing the application form online, print and sign the document. Then attach all the necessary supporting documents including two photographs and send it to the address at the top of the form.

Please read the supporting notes carefully when filling in your passport application. Failure to attach all the necessary supporting documents or sending photographs that do not meet our strict standards will delay your application. More applications are rejected because the photographs do not meet requirements than for any other reason.

Passport applications can take up to six weeks to process especially during busy holiday periods, so apply early.

CLICK HERE TO APPLY

169. If someone without a passport wishes to travel abroad next week, what should they do?

(A) Send the passport application and ask for the express service
(B) Take the passport application straight to the nearest passport office
(C) Telephone the nearest passport office to arrange when to go to the passport office
(D) Apply online

170. What is the most common reason that passport applications are rejected?

(A) There is a problem with the photographs.
(B) People only send one photograph, not two.
(C) People don't read the supporting notes carefully.
(D) People send the incorrect supporting documents.

171. According to the article, which statement is true?

(A) You can complete the entire passport application process online.
(B) Most passport applications are rejected because of problems with the supporting documents and photographs.
(C) If you are renewing your passport, there is no need to sign the application form.
(D) It may take longer to receive your passport during holiday periods.

172. After downloading the online application form, what is the next step?

(A) Print the application form
(B) Sign the application form
(C) Attach the necessary supporting documents
(D) Send the application form to the nearest passport office

Questions 173-176 refer to the following article.

BANK ROBBERIES- A THING OF THE PAST

Traditional bank robberies are rapidly becoming a thing of the past according to statistics from both the United States and Europe. Bank robberies are down 90% in the UK over the last decade with only 66 holdups reported in 2011. A similar trend can also be seen in the US with 3,870 reported nationwide in 2012, the lowest in a decade.

One reason for the dramatic fall seems to be the security in the banks themselves making it hard for traditional tactics to work. Besides the usually CCTV coverage, banks now have better protective screens and barriers that rise in under a second.

More high tech equipment is also available in the form of a DNA fog. At first the fog disperses the robbers, but it also leaves the thieves coated with a unique traceable material that is very hard to wash off the skin. It can later be used to prove that a suspect was at the crime scene.

A second and probably more important factor in the drop in robberies is that it is now often easier to target a bank through cyber-crime than with a gun. With millions of online bank and credit card transactions every day, this is rapidly becoming the crime of choice.

Every day we are hearing in the news of the mass theft of credit card details and of banks that have been hacked. Recently a US lawyer remarked, "Instead of guns and masks, they're using laptops and malware. It's also becoming much more of a cross-border crime by international criminal gangs, and it's worth millions of dollars."

Whatever the reasons for the change in criminal behavior, it all comes as good news for bank employees and customers who no longer have to go through the trauma of armed bank robberies so often.

While the armed bank robbery may still make great TV dramas and movies, the reality is that they may soon be confined to history.

173. In paragraph five, what does "cross-border crime" mean?

(A) The robbers cross a border into another country.
(B) The robbers are not in the country that they steal from.
(C) The robbers are careful not to cross a border.
(D) The robbers can't be found.

174. What does the writer suggest is the biggest cause for the drop in bank robberies?

(A) More robbers are getting caught.
(B) Some banks have DNA fog.
(C) The increase in online crime.
(D) More international gangs are doing the robbing.

175. Where are armed bank robberies still popular?

(A) In the United States
(B) In movies
(C) In border towns
(D) In the UK

176. Why do bank robbers fear the DNA fog the most?

(A) It can link them to the crime.
(B) They can't see clearly in it.
(C) Only the police can see through it.
(D) It makes them dirty.

Questions 177-180 refer to the following article.

Who is Banksy?

Banksy is the secret street name or pseudonym of a British graffiti street artist. His works can be found on street walls and bridges in cities all over the world from London to New York. The art which is often political and humorous never fails to generate debate, but despite regular speculation in newspapers and magazines, nobody actually knows for sure who he is.

What is known is that he grew up in Bristol in the southwest of England and it is in that city that his artwork began to appear in the early 1990s. His early work seemingly greatly influenced by the underground graffiti and music scene there.

Banksy started his graffiti career painting the established way using spray cans, but soon moved to stenciling where the outline is cut out of paper beforehand and simply sprayed over to create the work. This stenciling technique meant that much less time was needed to complete a piece. Banksy has claimed that the stenciling idea came to him while hiding from the police under a garbage truck and seeing the truck's serial number stenciled underneath it.

Banksy has always been controversial. Is his graffiti art or vandalism? Many local councils call it vandalism and try to remove it, but whenever the public have been consulted the response has almost invariably been supportive of the paintings.

Banksy's work can now be found in many unexpected places around the world even in disputed territories, but always the scenes depicted have local meaning and cause debate as well as bringing international attention to the issue.

Banksy's art has been reaching higher and higher prices at auction, especially since the purchase of a number of pieces by international celebrities including singers and Hollywood actresses. However as most of Banksy's work is simply left on a brick wall, sale is impossible, although this has not stopped some building owners who have even gone as far as to remove whole sections of walls from buildings in order to try to sell the paintings on them.

Recently while in New York Banksy set up a stall on a street corner and disguised as an old man put his work for sale at just $60. Only four sales were made during the day with the lucky purchasers getting work valued at over $30,000 for just $60!

The true identity of Banksy may not be known, but the value of his work most definitely is.

177. Who/what do not appreciate Banksy's art?

(A) Local councils
(B) Building owners
(C) Hollywood actresses
(D) The public

178. What inspired Banksy to use stencils?

(A) The police
(B) A garbage truck
(C) Music
(D) Local councils

179. What is a "pseudonym"?

(A) A type of graffiti
(B) The name of a newspaper
(C) The name of a street
(D) A made-up name to protect someone's identity

180. What happens to most of Banksy's art?

(A) It is sold for a lot of money.
(B) It is left outside.
(C) It is sold on street corners.
(D) It is left on garbage trucks.

Questions 181-185 refer to the following advertisement and email.

Real World Publishers are looking for talented writers of short stories for publication. We are interested in original short children's stories of around one thousand words in the following categories: musical worlds, talking animals, monsters or fairy tales.

Email a sample story by August 15th to sherry@rwp.com

Please include your name, address and phone number, and let us know about any previous writing experience you have.

All successful applicants will be notified by telephone in September.

📖To:	Sherry
From:	Tony James
Date:	August 16th

I am replying to your advertisement looking for talented writers.

I have written many short stories, and have even had some published in magazines. I was the winner of The Young School Writer of the Year competition when I was in high school, and I have always had a passion for writing as my hobby.

I am including one unpublished story as an attachment with this email. It is called "A Word with a Mouse." I hope you like it. I have many more like it already written.

My telephone number is 756 35433438

181. What did Tony forget to include in his email?

(A) His example story

(B) His writing experience

(C) His address

(D) His age when he won The Young School Writer of the Year competition

182. Why will Tony be lucky to be considered for the writing job?

(A) He doesn't have enough writing experience.

(B) Children do not like stories about mice.

(C) He missed the deadline to submit his story.

(D) Because he has had stories published before

183. Which category would Tony's story be suitable for?

(A) Talking animals

(B) Musical worlds

(C) Fairy tales

(D) Monsters

184. Tony receives a telephone call from Sherry in September, what is it possibly about?

(A) She likes his story.

(B) To ask why he thinks a mouse can speak

(C) To ask him his telephone number

(D) To ask him about his writing experience

185. What do the articles tell us about Sherry?

(A) That she likes children's stories about musical worlds, talking animals, monsters and fairy tales

(B) That she writes children's stories

(C) That she works for Real World Publishers

(D) That she wants to publish stories in magazines

Questions 186-190 refer to the following two articles.

New England Park Lake Golf and Spa Hotel

Rates for May-June. All prices per room per night, excluding breakfast.

Deluxe Suite - **$450**

Standard Suite - **$375**

Club Double - **$310**

Standard Double - **$290**

Grand Twin (two single beds) - **$295**

Standard Twin (two single beds) - **$199**

Single (one single bed) - **$125**

Breakfast **$25** per person

Special Evening Spa **$99**- Must be reserved at time of booking.

Special Weekend Golf Package for two **$800**- includes Club Double or Grand Twin for two nights and two rounds of golf, breakfast included.

All prices include tax

To: Mike
From: Carlos

Great news about your promotion. You really deserve it after all the hard work and overtime you've been putting in recently. Does the new job mean that you are going to be too busy to hang out with me anymore, or can you start taking it a little easier?

Have a look at the flyer I'm attaching to this email. You owe me a trip after all. Are you free for a golfing weekend in June? You'll need to practice your swing, as I've been playing a lot recently.

We used to play almost every weekend, but since you started working for Global Technology a couple of years ago, you never seem to have enough free time. You should try working for yourself; then you might have as much free time as me!

If you feel too guilty about spending your free weekend away with me instead of with Susan, I can bring Lynette along too, and we can send the wives to the spa while we play golf.

Have a look in your diary and give me a call.

186. Which statement is true?

(A) A golf package weekend for two costs over $800.

(B) Room rates do not include breakfast.

(C) Women cannot participate in a golfing weekend.

(D) A single room costs $125 in July.

187. If Mike and Carlos decide to take their wives with them on their golfing weekend, what do they need to do?

(A) Arrange the spa when they reserve the Golf Package

(B) Book a single room for Susan and Lynette

(C) Reserve breakfast for everyone

(D) Practice how to play golf

188. Where does Carlos work?

(A) He works for Global Technology.

(B) He works for New England Park Lake Golf and Spa Hotel.

(C) He works for Mike.

(D) He works for himself.

189. Who will pay for this trip?

(A) Mike and Carlos

(B) Global Technology

(C) Mike

(D) Carlos

190. What do these articles tell us about the relationship between Mike and Carlos?

(A) They used to work together.

(B) That Mike is now Carlos' boss

(C) That they have known each other for many years

(D) That Carlos used to work for Mike.

Questions 191-195 refer to the following articles.

The BRICS countries

BRICS is an acronym (a word formed from the first letters of each word in a phrase) that refers to the countries Brazil, Russia, India, China and South Africa. The term was first used by the British economist Jim O'Neil in 2001. These five countries are all at a similar stage of rapid economic development. They are distinguished not only by their large, fast growing economies, but also by their growing influence in world affairs. Together they have become a symbol of the shift in economic power away from the traditional western countries to the newly developing ones.

South Africa was a late inclusion in the grouping and resulted in an "S" being added to the original BRIC. Many have argued that South Africa doesn't deserve to be included due to its mixed economic record and comparatively small population, and that it was only added as it would conveniently fit into the acronym.

The BRICS countries seem to appreciate the acronym and have even formed an association to further their mutual aims. But despite all the attention that the world's media gives to the BRICS, their combined economies are not expected to surpass those of western countries until around 2050.

The MINT countries

MINT is the latest acronym given to us by Jim O'Neil the economist famous for grouping the BRIC countries together. The MINT countries are Mexico, Indonesia, Nigeria and Turkey. O'Neil has identified them as potential economic powerhouses of the twenty-first century.

What set the MINT countries apart are their people. They have a younger population, and so, at least for the next twenty years, they will have more people entering the workforce than leaving it. This is seen as key to economic success and is the envy of not only developed countries, but also many of the rapidly developing ones.

We will have to wait to see whether or not the MINT countries will attempt to form some kind of political association as the BRICS countries have. Meanwhile as the arguments continue over which country should or should not be included in which grouping, the number of acronyms increases. Two new ones are MIKT and TIMBI. Can you guess who they represent?

191. What do these articles suggest that the rise of the BRICS and MINT countries will result in?

(A) The creation of more acronyms
(B) The movement of power away from the BRICS and MINT countries
(C) The movement of power away from western countries
(D) The movement of power to younger people

192. Which reason is given that South Africa should NOT be a member of BRICS?

(A) That its economy is not strong enough
(B) That it doesn't fit into the acronym
(C) That its population is too large
(D) That it is not a member of the association

193. According to these two articles, what is the main difference between BRICS countries and MINT countries?

(A) Their growing economies
(B) The sizes of their populations
(C) The ages of their populations
(D) Who created the acronyms

194. What did Jim O'Neil do?

(A) He invented the term "acronym".
(B) He grouped the BRICS countries together.
(C) He formed an association of BRICS countries.
(D) He argued over which counties to include in BRICS.

195. Which country might also be included in MIKT and TIMBI?

(A) Nigeria
(B) South Africa
(C) Russia
(D) Mexico

Questions 196-200 refer to the following book reviews.

The Cliff's Edge, by Larry Cameron

Reviewed by Simon Adams

"We met on one of those coastal paths that twist along the cliff's edge one blue October dawn." And so we begin the epic tale of Theo and Eleanor in Larry Cameron's masterpiece The Cliff's Edge. Three hundred and fifty pages of love, deceit, loss and betrayal, and all with a twist at the end.

Theo and Eleanor are growing up in a coastal village in late 18th century America. Eleanor is a milkmaid from a humble family, while Theo is the poacher son of a local landowner. Their story over the following twenty years both chronicling their lives in their isolated community mirrored against the newly industrializing and rapidly changing world around them.

Larry Cameron's previous novels, As Darkness Came and The Red River, have both received high literary acclaim, but are very different books in both style and substance to his latest offering.

This is not just an old world tale for academics or those studying literature at university. This book will appeal to a much wider audience than that. It would appear that, at 81 years old, Cameron has found a new depth to his writing. He is able to tap into not only the deeper feelings of Theo and Eleanor but also into the feelings and emotions of his readers. This is what is going to set this book apart from his earlier works.

The Cliff's Edge has already been shortlisted for a number of literacy prizes and is expected to do well both in awards and in sales.

The Cliff's Edge, by Larry Cameron is published by Bumble Publishing.

The Cliff's Edge, by Larry Cameron
Reviewed by Renee Park

The Cliff's Edge is an engaging story of growing up in the newly established United States of America in the late 18th century. It follows the unlikely couple of Theo and Eleanor through those turbulent years, as they seek out their fortunes in this rapidly changing land.

Despite Cameron's great writing, that sets the scene so beautifully and so effortlessly takes us on a journey though those often forgotten times, the relationship between Eleanor and Theo is just a step too far. The narrative is smooth and his attention to historical detail is unmatched in any other contemporary author, but it is hard to see how this novel will appeal to any wider audience than his previous works have.

Critically acclaimed it may be and a relaxing read for a long plane ride, but not a blockbuster that will fly off the shelves in most neighborhood bookstores.

196. What do the two reviews agree on?

(A) That academics will like the book
(B) That the book is similar to his previous books
(C) That sales of the book will be very good
(D) That the relationship between Theo and Eleanor is well written

197. Which dates are the most probable for the books setting?

(A) 1779 – 1799
(B) 1790 – 1810
(C) 1875 – 1895
(D) 1750 – 1770

198. How many awards has The Cliff's Edge won?

(A) One award
(B) Two awards
(C) Many awards
(D) No awards

199. Who finds parts of the book hard to accept?

(A) Simon Adam
(B) Theo
(C) Renee Park
(D) Larry Cameron

200. What would you NOT expect to find in The Cliff's Edge?

(A) Romance
(B) City life
(C) Death
(D) A surprising ending

Part 7. 單篇／雙篇文章理解

第 153-154 題

收件人：Christine Taylor
寄件人：High Pacific Bank
已經收到你的要重新換發密碼的要求。要完成程序，請點選以下連結，並輸入你的臨時密碼。連結與臨時密碼只能使用一次。
你的臨時密碼：Mj459AtvQ
點選這裡重設你的密碼。
這封郵件只是要確認你的電子信箱。請在重設密碼後刪除此郵件。
如果你有任何更進一步的問題，請寄郵件至：customerassist@hpbank.com 或致電 24 小時顧客協助服務櫃台 677 4446749
謝謝
High Pacific 銀行管理中心

153. 答案 (A) 最可能的是已發生了什麼事？

(A) Christine Taylor 忘了她的銀行密碼
(B) Christine Taylor 正要開一個新的電子信箱帳號
(C) Christine Taylor 忘了她的密碼是 Mj459AtvQ.
(D) Christine Taylor 無法聯絡顧客協助服務櫃台

解說 原文第一段第一句，"Your request to reset your password has been received"，表示 Christine Taylor 要求重新換發密碼，所以可能是因為已經忘記密碼才要重換，故選 (A)。

154. 答案 (D) Christine Taylor 下一步應該做什麼？

(A) 輸入密碼 Mj459AtvQ (B) 檢查郵件
(C) 致電顧客協助服務櫃台 (D) 點選連結

解說 原文第三段，"Click Here to Reset Your Password"，是郵件中給 Christine Taylor 的下一步指示，故選 (D)。選項 (A) 是在點選連結後才要做的事，選項 (C) 原文第五段，"If you have any further problems please email: customerassist@hpbank.com or call the 24hr

Customer Assistance Desk on 677 4446749"，表示若有更進一步的問題才需要再寫郵件或打電話。

字彙：

reset [ri`sɛt] *(v.)* 重換／ request [rɪ`kwɛst] *(v.)* 要求；請求／ temporary [`tɛmpəˏrɛrɪ] *(adj.)* 臨時的／ confirm [kən`fɝm] *(v.)* 確認／ delete [dɪ`lit] *(v.)* 刪除／ assistance [ə`sɪstəns] *(n.)* 幫助／ administration [ədˏmɪnə`streʃən] *(n.)* 管理／ password [`pæsˏwɝd] *(n.)* 密碼

第 155-156 題

Watson's 電腦商店

商用和家用電腦的專家

個人電腦	印表機	電纜線
商用電腦	平板電腦	軟體
膝上型輕便電腦	網路	供電器

所有我們賣出的電腦均延長保固

完全的修繕服務

不限時段，提供任何人來免費咨詢

有課程——我們會教你怎麼用你購買的物品。

在本市有兩個營業處

Broadoak Mall 商店	Claire 街 219 號	(271) 483-1294
Oldgate Park 商店	Badminton Hill 57 號	(271) 483-2479

營業時間：週一至週六 早上 9 點至下午 5 點

電子信箱：watson@computers.com

電話：(271) 483-7184（24 小時協助專線）

特價商品請瀏覽我們的網站：www.watcomputers.com

155. 答案 (C) 如果你在 Watson's 電腦商店買了一台電腦，他們會免費給你什麼？

(A) 免費咨詢　　(B) 免費課程

(C) 更久的保固　　(D) 免費修繕

解說　原文第六行，"Extended guarantee on all computers we sell"，表示這是購買電腦之後的免費項目，故選 (C)。選項 (A)，原文第八行，"Free advice for anyone anytime"，表示無論購買商品與否，均提供免費咨詢，不符合本題題意。選項 (B)、(D) 在文章中並未表明是否需收費。

156. 答案 (D) 現在是星期一深夜，你的電腦無法正確地運作，你可以做什麼？

(A) 瀏覽 Watson's 電腦商店的網站

(B) 把電腦帶至 Watson's 電腦商店

(C) 買一台新的電腦

(D) 致電 Watson's 電腦商店

解說　原文倒數第二行，Tel: (271) 483-7184 (24h helpline)，以及倒數第四行，Open: Monday – Saturday 9am – 5pm，表示深夜已不在該商店的營業時間內，所以只可撥打 24 小時協助電話，故選 (D)。選項 (A)，網站雖是隨時沒有時間限制可以瀏覽，但是文章中並未提及網站可提供協助。

字彙：

specialist [ˋspɛʃəlɪst] *(n.)* 專家（＋ in）／ computing [kəmˋpjutɪŋ] *(n.)* 使用電腦／ personal [ˋpɝsn̩l] *(adj.)* 個人的／ cable [ˋkebl̩] *(n.)* 電纜／ tablet [ˋtæblɪt] *(n.)* 平板電腦／ laptop [ˋlæptɑp] *(n.)* 膝上型輕便電腦（筆記型電腦）／ guarantee [ˏgærənˋti] *(n.)* 商品保證／ properly [ˋprɑpəlɪ] *(adv.)* 正確地；恰當地

第 157-158 題

收件人：Jackie Lang
寄件人：Samui Resort
謝謝你訂購在美麗的泰國 Koh Samui 島嶼上的 Samui 渡假村。
二月三日至二月八日，一間標準雙人房，含早餐。
已從 Visa 信用卡 7856******** 收到付款
你的訂購憑證號碼是 SR5078976
請接受免費升級至會員雙人房

飯店設施的完整細節，與在 Koh Samui 島可以做些什麼活動的導覽，均可以我們的網站看見：www.samuiresort.com.th

我們期待並歡迎你在二月三日蒞臨。如果有什麼我們要事先協助的，請聯絡我們，我們很樂意提供協助。

157. 答案 (B) Samui 渡假村送給 Jackie Lang 什麼？

(A) 免費早餐
(B) 更好的房型
(C) Koh Samui 島的導覽旅遊
(D) 允許進入他們的網站

解說 原文第七行，"Please accept a complimentary upgrade to our Club Double room"，升級的意思即為更好的房型，文中說明是免費升級，所以是額外送給 Jackie Lang。選項 (A)，原文第四行，"including breakfast"，含早餐表示原先已包含在訂房的房價中，並非額外贈送。

158. 答案 (D) Jackie Lang 在收到這封郵件後應該立即做什麼？

(A) 去機場
(B) 檢查她的信用卡有收到付款
(C) 聯絡 Samui 渡假村關於她對房型的疑問
(D) 她什麼也不用做

解說 原文第十行，"If we can be of any assistance before then, please contact us and we will be happy to help"，表示已完成所有訂購事宜，若有進一步的問題才須提出，故選 (D)。選項 (A)，並不知道郵件的時間，所以無法推測是入住的當天。選項 (B)，原文第五行，"Payment has been received from Visa card 7856********"，表示是渡假村收到

付款，而不是 Jackie Lang。選項 (C)，原文第七行，"Please accept a complimentary upgrade to our Club Double room"，飯店已解釋清楚是免費升級，不是搞錯房型。

字彙：

standard [ˋstændɚd] *(adj.)* 標準的／ payment [ˋpemənt] *(n.)* 付款／ reference [ˋrɛfərəns] *(n.)* 證明／ complimentary [ˌkɑmpləˋmɛntərɪ] *(adj.)* 免費招待的／ facility [fəˋsɪlətɪ] *(n.)* 設施／ contact [ˋkɑntækt] *(v.)* 聯絡／ assess [əˋsɛs] *(v.)* 允許進入／ receipt [rɪˋsit] *(n.)* 收到；收據

第 159-161 題

Davos- 世界經濟研討會

在酷冷高山上的 Davos 的感覺，一定就像反映出人類之後在氣候上遇到的大問題。座落在瑞士阿爾卑斯山脈的滑雪度假村，是本週全球商人和政治菁英們前往參加年度全球經濟研討會 (WEF) 的地方，為期四天仔細研討地球的未來。今年的研討會將會辯論富裕、貧窮，以及經濟的成長，全是一般平常試著讓世界變好的目的。

很多今年的辯論將集中在全球化是如何改造發展中的經濟，有很多投資界對許多新興市場的預期，持懷疑態度，像是中國在追求經濟成長的同時，也常伴隨著股東利潤的支出。

也會被討論的還有貧富差距的問題，一份 WEF 的問卷調查顯示，這是接下來對全世界最大的危險。問卷調查警告那些商人和政治人物，收入不均，以及與之相關所造成的社會動盪，將會快速增加，這將形成下一個十年裡的全球經濟形態。它警示了「失落的世代」，也就是進入勞動年齡層缺乏技能、工作，以及機會的時代。

159. 答案 (C) Davos 是什麼？

(A) 全球經濟研討會　　(B) 新興市場

(C) 瑞士的滑雪度假村　　(D) 人類遭遇的問題

解說　從原文標題 "Davos- The World Economic Forum"，以及原文第一段第二句，"The ski resort in the Swiss Alps is where the global business and political elite are heading to this week"，可以知道

Davos 是研討會的地點，而研討會的地點是瑞士一處滑雪渡假村，故選 (C)。

160. 答案 (A) 哪一個不是今年全球經濟研討會中會提出的顧慮？

(A) 地球未來的氣候　(B) 新興市場

(C) 年青失業人口　(D) 貧窮人口

解說　原文第二段，"with many in the investment community skeptical about prospects in many emerging markets"，説明會討論對新興市場的態度，談到選項 (B)；原文第三段第一句，"Also to be discussed is the widening gap between rich and poor"，表示會也討論貧富差距，談到選項 (D)；原文第三段最後一句，"It warns of a 'lost generation' who enter working age lacking skills, jobs and opportunities"，表示在討論中提出問卷警示勞動年齡在將來會遇到的問題，談到選項 (C)。只有選項 (A) 不會在研討會中提出。

161. 答案 (C) 什麼是今年全球經濟研討會強調，也可能是最重要的議題？

(A) 全球化　(B) 社會動盪

(C) 收入差距　(D) 缺乏青年人口

解說　原文第三段第一句，"this is the biggest risk to the world in the coming year"，以及第二句，"the income disparity and its related social unrest will increasingly shape the world economy in the next decade"，足以推測出這次全球經濟研討會強調的重要議題。選項 (A)、(D) 在文章裡未提及此為討論議題。選項 (B)，是因貧富不均造成的。

字彙：

climate [ˋklaɪmɪt] *(n.)* 氣候／ mankind [mænˋkaɪnd] *(n.)* 人類／ elite[ɪˋlit] *(n.)* 菁英／ ponder [ˋpɑndɚ] *(v.)* 仔細考慮；衡量／ forum [ˋforəm] *(n.)* 研討會／ aim [em] *(n.)* 目的／ reshape [riˋʃep] *(v.)* 重新改造／ skeptical [ˋskɛptɪkḷ] *(adj.)* 懷疑論的

第 162-165 題

收件人：Orchid 花店
寄件人：Green 太太

謝謝你在星期六送達的 24 朵紅玫瑰。他們很美麗。唯一的問題是我不了解為什麼收到他們。

花在星期六早上送達時，我和先生都不在家，而你的送貨人員把花留給我們的鄰居。當我們在下午回到家時，我們收到花，而且很好奇的看了卡片。卡片是寫給住在愛爾蘭，春田市，New 路的 Green 太太。我是英國，春田市，New 路的 Green 太太。

在看了卡片後，我馬上試著撥打送達收據上的電話號碼，但是由電話答錄機接聽，說你們週末期間只有在星期六早上營業。到星期一之前，我沒有任何別的方式聯繫你們，所以我寄給你這封郵件。花在我家客廳看起來非常棒，但是恐怕愛爾蘭的 Green 太太仍等待著她的花。

162. 答案 (B) 為什麼 Green 太太寫電子郵件給 Orchid 花店？

(A) 要抱怨關於花送達的事
(B) 要告知 Orchid 花店他們的錯誤
(C) 要找到為什麼她送到愛爾蘭的花沒有送達
(D) 試著聯繫愛爾蘭的 Green 太太

解說　原文第一段第二句，"I have no idea why I have received them"，以及第二段第二句，"we received the flowers and were curious to read the card. The card was addressed to a Mrs. Green of New Road, Summerfield, Ireland. I am Mrs. Green of New Road, Summerfield, England"，可以知道這封郵件的目的是告知花店他們送花給錯的人。

163. 答案 (D) 為什麼 Green 太太無法用電話聯繫 Orchid 花店？

(A) 因為她找不到 Orchid 花店的電話號碼
(B) 因為 Orchid 花店的電話號碼只有電話答錄機接聽
(C) 因為 Orchid 花店的送貨人員不在辦公室裡
(D) 因為到了 Green 太太收到花朵時，Orchid 花店已經休息了

解說　原文第二段第二句，"When we arrived home in the afternoon"，以及

第三段第一句 "said that you only open on Saturday morning during the weekend. I have no other way of contacting you until Monday, and so I'm sending you this email"，表示 Green 太太下午才到家，而花店只在當天早上營業，所以無法用電話聯繫，故選 (D)。

164. 答案 (A) 兩位 Green 太太有何共同之處？

(A) 他們有一樣的名字　　(B) 他們是朋友

(C) 他們彼此寄送花朵　　(D) 他們住在同一條街

解說 原文第二段第三、四句 "Mrs. Green of New Road, Summerfield, Ireland. I am Mrs. Green of New Road, Summerfield, England"，可以知道他們的名字相同，皆為 Green 太太，故選 (A)。選項 (B)、(C) 在文章中未提及。選項 (D) 錯誤，因為雖然街名相同，但是一處是愛爾蘭，一處是英國，不是同一條街。

165. 答案 (D) 誰訂購了 24 朵玫瑰花？

(A) 英國的 Green 太太　　(B) 愛爾蘭的 Green 太太

(C) Orchid 花店　　(D) 文章沒有說誰訂購花

解說 選項 (A)，原文第一段第三句，"I have no idea why I have received them"，表示英國的 Green 太太是收件者。選項 (B)，原文第二段第三句，The card was addressed to a Mrs. Green of New Road, Summerfield, Ireland.，表示愛爾蘭的 Green 太太是正確的收件人。選項 (C)，原文第二段第一句，"they were delivered on Saturday morning, and your deliveryman left them with our neighbor"，表示花是 Orchid 花店送達的。選項 (D)，並未在文章中敘述。

字彙：

deliver [dɪˋlɪvɚ] *(v.)* 遞送／ receive [rɪˋsiv] *(v.)* 收到／ address [əˋdrɛs] *(v.)* 向…致詞／ upon [əˋpɑn] (prep.) 在…立即／ answering machine [ˋænsərɪŋ] [məˋʃin] *(n.)* 電話答錄機／ unable [ʌnˋebḷ] *(adj.)* 不能的

第 166-168 題

黃石國家公園

黃石國家公園是位於美國西北部的國家公園。它主要是在美國懷俄明州，但是有些地方跨立鄰州的愛達荷州和蒙大拿州邊境。黃石公園被認定為世界上第一個國家公園。它現在是全世界其中一個最受歡迎的國家公園之一，每年有超過三百萬遊客到訪。

美國原住民已在黃石公園區域世代居住了幾千年，但是一直到十九世紀中期，歐洲的開拓者才首次探索該區域。

公園包含山脈、峽谷、河川和湖泊，然而黃石最著名的是它的火山活動。整個公園以火山為中心點，這讓其中一個最著名的特徵出現了一個稱號——老忠實噴泉。有時候被譽為地球上最好預測的地質現象，它大約每九十一分鐘會噴發一次沸騰熱水至空中。

黃石不只因為它的地質著名，也是因為它有眾多植物和動物物種可生長居住的生態系統，其中有一些是已瀕臨絕種的。

166. 答案 (A) 噴泉的名字稱為「老忠實」，是與什麼有關？

(A) 可以信賴它準時表演　(B) 它噴發沸騰熱水至空中

(C) 它每天表演很多次　(D) 它是火山的一部分

解說　原文第三段第二句，"it is this that gives rise to one of its most famous features - the geyser Old Faithful. Sometimes called the most predicable geological feature on Earth, it sprays boiling water into the air approximately once every ninety-one minutes"，表示「老忠實噴泉」的噴發時間十分規律，這是為什麼有這個稱號，故選 (A)。

167. 答案 (B) 黃石保有什麼世界記錄？

(A) 它是世界上最大的國家公園

(B) 世界上第一個國家公園

(C) 它有比其它國家公園更多的遊客

(D) 它比其他國家公園更早有人居住

解說　原文第一段第三句，"Yellowstone is credited with being the world's first national park"，表示是世界上第一個國家公園，所以是全世界歷史

最悠久的國家公園記錄保持者。選項 (A)、(C)、(D) 並未在文章中詳述。

168. 答案 (D) 根據文章，哪一個陳述是事實？

(A)「老忠實」是火山的名字

(B) 歐洲的開拓者在美國原住民之前就到達

(C) 大部分黃石的生態系統已消失殆盡

(D) 公園不全在一個州裡

解說 選項 (A)，原文第三段第三句，"the geyser Old Faithful"，說明「老忠實」是該噴泉的名字，不是火山的名字，故不正確。選項 (B)，原文第二段，"The Yellowstone area has been inhabited by Native American for thousands of years, but it wasn't until the mid 19th century that European settlers first explored the area"，表示黃石在歐洲開拓者於十九世紀中期首次到達前，美國原住民已世代居住幾千年，故不正確。選項 (C)，原文最後一段，"its ecosystem which is home to countless species of plants and animals"，表示生態系統完好，故不正確。選項 (D)，原文第一段第二句，"It is primarily located in the state of Wyoming but also has areas that straddle the border into the neighboring states of Idaho and Montana."，黃石跨立於三個州，故選 (D)。

字彙：

primarily [praɪˋmɛrəlɪ] *(adv.)* 主要／ straddle [ˋstrædḷ] *(v.)* 跨立／ border [ˋbɔrdɚ] *(n.)* 邊境／ inhabit [ɪnˋhæbɪt] *(v.)* 居住／ settler [ˋsɛtlɚ] *(n.)* 開拓者／ encompass [ɪnˋkʌmpəs] *(v.)* 包含／ canyon [ˋkænjən] *(n.)* 峽谷／ ecosystem [ˋɛkoˏsɪstəm] *(n.)* 生態系統

第 169-172 題

線上護照申請

你可以完成線上護照申請，更新你現有的護照或是在現有的護照上加入細節。第一次申請護照請勿用此表格。

如果你將在接下來的十四天內出國請勿用此表格，請聯絡鄰近的護照辦事處了解我們急件處理的細節，急件臨櫃服務會需要先預約。

完成線上申請表格之後，請將文件印出並簽名。然後附上所有需繳交文件，包含相片兩張，寄至表格最上方的地址。

當你在填寫護照申請時，請詳閱需繳交文件的注意事項。沒有附上所有需繳交文件或沒有附上照片，不符合我們嚴謹的標準，將會延誤你申請護照的時間。申請被駁回的原因，比較多是因為照片不符規定，而不是其他原因。

護照申請有時需要六星期的處理時間，尤其是在忙碌的假期期間，所以請儘早申請。

點選這裡申請

169. 答案 (C) 如果某人沒有護照，但是想要在下個星期出國，他應該怎麼做？

(A) 寄出護照申請並要求急件服務

(B) 直接帶著護照申請至鄰近的護照辦事處

(C) 致電給鄰近的護照辦事處，安排何時親洽該辦事處

(D) 線上申請

解說 原文第一段第二句，“Please do not use this form to apply for your first passport”，表示他不適用線上申請表格，以及第二段“If you are traveling within the next fourteen days, do not use this form, contact your nearest passport office for details of our express over the counter service for which an appointment will be necessary”，表示十四天內需要用到護照的申請人，必須先至鄰近辦事處了解細節，並預約親洽時間，故選 (C)。

170. 答案 (A) 什麼是護照申請被駁回最普遍的原因？

(A) 照片有問題

(B) 只寄一張照片，而不是兩張

(C) 沒有詳閱需繳交文件的注意事項

(D) 寄出不正確的需繳交文件

解說　原文第四段第三句，"More applications are rejected because the photographs do not meet requirements than for any other reason"，說明照片不符合規定是護照申請被駁回最多也最常見的問題，故選 (A)。選項 (B)、(C)、(D) 依文章中敘述，亦為會導致申請駁回，但並非最普遍的原因。

171. 答案 (D) 根據文章，下例哪一個陳述是事實？

(A) 你可以線上完成整個護照申請程序

(B) 大部分被駁回的護照申請是因為需繳交文件和照片有問題

(C) 如果你更新護照，你不需要在申請表上簽名

(D) 假期期間也許會需要較長的時間才收到護照

解說　原文第五段，"Passport applications can take up to six weeks to process especially during busy holiday periods, so apply early"，表示有時護照申請會到六星期那麼長的時間才收到，假期期間更是如此，故選 (D)。選項 (A)，不正確，並非所有需求的申請均能透過線上完成。文中提到第一次申請護照和十四天內要出國的人皆不適用網路表格，而且有這類需求的申請者必須將表格印出，簽名並附上照片及文件，寄至辦事處。選項 (B)，不正確，大部分被駁回原因提到的僅是照片的問題。選項 (C)，不正確，原文第三段第一句，"print and sign the document"，已說明需要簽名。

172. 答案 (A) 在下載線上申請表格之後，下一個步驟是什麼？

(A) 列印出申請表　(B) 在申請表上簽名

(C) 附上需繳交的文件　(D) 寄申請表至鄰近的護照辦事處

解說　原文第三段第一句，"After completing the application form online, print and sign the document" 說明在線上完成表格後，要列印出來，再簽名，所以下一個步驟是印出申請表故選 (A)。選項 (B)，是在列印出來後的下一個步驟。選項 (C)，是簽名之後的步驟。選項 (D)，在文章中並未提及。

字彙：

application [ˌæpləˋkeʃən] *(n.)* 申請／renew [rɪˋnju] *(v.)* 更新／update [ʌpˋdet] *(v.)* 為…提供最新訊息／

form [fɔrm] *(n.)* 表格／ express [ɪkˋsprɛs] *(n.)* 快送／ necessary [ˋnɛsə͵sɛrɪ] *(adj.)* 必要的／ fill [fɪl] *(v.)* 填滿／ requirement [rɪˋkwaɪrmənt] *(n.)* 要求

第 173-176 題

搶劫銀行—已成過去式

依據美國與歐洲的統計，搶劫傳統銀行，已很快地成為過去式。搶劫銀行，過去十年在英國已下降 90%，2011 年只有通報 66 件搶劫銀行案件。類似的趨勢也能在美國看到，2012 年全美通報 3,870 搶劫銀行案件，是十年來最低。

一個讓搶劫戲劇性下降的原因，似乎是銀行自己的保全措施，讓傳統的搶劫手法不容易達成。除了平常監視器的覆蓋範圍，銀行現在有更好的防護隔板和柵欄，可在一秒內升起。

更高科技的設備，也可用一種 DNA 煙霧。一開始煙霧會驅散搶匪，但是也會讓搶匪身上覆蓋一層很難洗掉的獨特可追蹤物質。它可以在稍後用來證明嫌犯在犯罪現場。

<u>搶劫銀行率下降的第二個且也許更重要的因素是，現在透過電腦犯罪鎖定銀行，是比拿槍還來得簡單</u>。每天有好幾百萬筆的網路銀行和信用卡交易，這<u>已迅速的成為犯罪的選項</u>。

每天我們聽見新聞播報大量的信用卡盜刷，還有銀行被駭客入侵 。最近一位美國律師評論道，「取而代替槍枝和面具的是，他們現在用筆記型電腦和惡意程式。它也成了國際犯罪結團更能用來跨國犯罪的工具，而且值好幾百萬美金。」

無論讓犯罪行為改變的原因為何，對銀行員工和顧客都是好消息，他們再也不用常經歷銀行搶匪全副武裝所帶來的創傷。

然而全副武裝的銀行搶匪也許仍是電視戲劇和電影裡的好橋段，現實中，他們也許很快成為歷史。

173. 答案 (B) 在第五段，「跨國犯罪」是什麼意思？

(A) 搶匪越過國界，進入另一個國家

(B) 搶匪不在他們搶錢的那一個國家

(C) 搶匪小心地不越過國界

(D) 找不到搶匪

174. 答案 (C) 作者暗示銀行搶劫下降的最大的原因為何？

(A) 愈來愈多搶匪被抓

(B) 一些銀行有 DNA 煙霧

(C) 網路犯罪上升

(D) 更多的國際犯罪集團在搶劫銀行

解說 原文第四段第一句，"A second and probably more important factor in the drop in robberies is that it is now often easier to target a bank through cyber-crime than with a gun"，和第二句，"this is rapidly becoming the crime of choice"，可以知道透過網路犯罪，現在有上升的趨勢。

175. 答案 (B) 全副武裝的銀行搶匪仍在哪裡受歡迎？

(A) 在美國　　(B) 在電影裡

(C) 邊境城鎮　　(D) 在英國

解說 原文最後一段第一句，"While the armed bank robbery may still make great TV dramas and movies"。知道現在也們仍在電視節目和電影裡受歡迎。

176. 答案 (A) 為什麼銀行搶匪最懼怕 DNA 煙霧？

(A) 它能讓他們與罪行連結起來

(B) 他們煙霧裡看不清楚

(C) 只警察能在煙務裡看清楚

(D) 它讓他們變髒

解說 原文第三段第三句，"It can later be used to prove that a suspect was at the crime scene"，表示能在事後追蹤與搶案相關的人。選項 (B)、(C)、(D) 在文章中皆未提及。

字彙：

robbery [ˋrɑbərɪ] *(n.)* 搶劫／ trend [trɛnd] *(n.)* 趨勢／ dramatic [drəˋmætɪk] *(adj.)* 戲劇性的／ tactic [ˋtæktɪk] *(n.)* 手法／ protective [prəˋtɛktɪv] *(adj.)* 防護的／ disperse [dɪˋspɝs] *(v.)* 驅散／ coat [kot] *(v.)* 覆蓋／ trauma [ˋtrɔmə] *(n.)* 創傷

第 177-180 題

誰是 Banksy ？

Banksy 是神祕的街頭名稱也是英國街道牆面藝術家的假名。 他的作品在全世界，從倫敦到紐約的街道牆面和城市裡的橋面上，都可以被發現。藝術作品常是政治和幽默，每每成功引起討論，但是除了報章雜誌上一般的推測，沒有人真正確定知道他是誰。

只知道他在英國西南部的布里斯托市長大，而該城市也是他的藝術作品在 1990 年初期，開始出現的時候。他早期的作品似乎受到那裡的地下塗鴉和音樂背景，很大的影響。

Banksy 開始他的牆面塗鴉藝術時，是用噴漆罐作畫，但是很快地進展成輪廓事先從紙上剪下的版模，然後噴上漆創作出作品。這個版模技術代表完成作品的時間少很多。Banksy 宣稱這個版模的構想，是來自他在垃圾車下面躲警察時，看見垃圾車底下用版模印刷的編號。

Banksy 總是充滿爭議的。他的牆面塗鴉是藝術還是破壞公物？許多當地議會說它是破壞公物，並試著清除它，但是無論何時問民眾，他們的回 大多一定是對畫作支持。

現在 Banksy' 的作品能在世界各地意想不到的地方被發現，甚至在有爭議的領土上，但是背景總是描畫出擁有當地意涵和造成爭論的原因，同時也帶來國際對該議題的關注。

Banksy 的藝術作品在拍賣會上的價格愈來愈高，尤其是自從國際名人購買幾件他的作品之後，包括歌手和好萊塢女星們。 然而因為 Banksy 大部分的作品就只留在磚牆上，不可能拿來賣，儘管如此，這沒有停止一些建築物持有者費了好大一番工夫，為了移除牆面上的整個區域，就為了賣上頭的畫作。

最近在紐約，Banksy 在街角設立了一個攤位，並喬裝成老人，把自己的作品只賣 60 美金。當天只做成四筆交易，這四位幸運的購買者只用 60 美金買到的是價值超過三萬美金的藝術作品。

Banksy 的真實身分也許沒有人知道，但是他藝術作品價值大家一定知道。

177. 答案 (A) 誰／什麼不欣賞 Banksy 的藝術？

(A) 當地的議會　　(B) 建築物的持有人
(C) 好萊塢女星們　　(D) 民眾

解說　原文第四段第三句，"Many local councils call it vandalism and try to remove it" 表示當地的議會並不喜歡他的藝術作品在牆面上，故選 (A)。

178. 答案 (B) 什麼給了 Banksy 使用版模的靈感？

(A) 警察　　(B) 垃圾車
(C) 音樂　　(D) 當地的議會

解說　原文第三段第三句，"the stenciling idea came to him while hiding from the police under a garbage truck and seeing the truck's serial number stenciled underneath it"，說明是躲警察時，垃圾車的編號帶給他的靈感，故選項 (A) 錯誤，選 (B)。選項 (C)、(D) 並未提及。

179. 答案 (D) 什麼是假名？

(A) 一種牆面畫　　(B) 報紙的名稱
(C) 街道的名稱　　(D) 用來保護某人身份而捏造的名字

180. 答案 (B) 大多數 Banksy 的藝術作品結果如何？

(A) 賣很多錢　　(B) 留在戶外
(C) 在街角販售　　(D) 留在垃圾車上

解說　原文第六段第二句，"However as most of Banksy's work is simply left on a brick wall"，表示大多數的作品都留在外面的牆上，故選 (B)。選項 (A)、(C) 在原文第六段第一句，"Banksy's art has been reaching higher and higher prices at auction"，和原文第七段第一句，"Recently while in New York Banksy set up a stall on a street corner"，均在文中有提到，但是並非他大多數的藝術作品。

字彙：

pseudonym [ˋsudnˏɪm] *(n.)* 假名／ speculation [ˏspɛkjəˋleʃən] *(n.)* 推測／ seemingly [ˋsimɪŋlɪ] *(adv.)* 似乎是／ stencil [ˋstɛnsḷ] *(v.)* 用模板印刷／ serial number [ˋsɪrɪəl] [ˋnʌmbɚ] *(n.)* 編號／ controversial [ˏkɑntrəˋvɝʃəl] *(adj.)* 爭議的／ vandalism [ˋvændlɪzəm] *(n.)* 破壞公物的行為／ invariably [ɪnˋvɛrɪəbḷɪ] *(adv.)* 一定地

第 181-185 題

Real World 出版社正在尋找有才華的刊物短篇故事作家。我們有興趣的是原創的兒童短篇故事，字數大約一千字左右，種類如下：音樂的世界、說話的動物、怪物或童話故事。

在八月十五日之前傳一個範例故事至 sherry@rwp.com

請附上你的姓名、地址、電話，以及讓我們知道任何你先前的寫作經驗。

所有錄取者將在九月以電話通知。

收件人：Sherry

寄件人：Tony James

八月十六日

我回覆你尋找有才華作家的廣告。

我已經寫過許多短篇故事，而且有一些已經在雜誌上刊登。我讀高中時獲得過「青少年作家」年度競賽獎，並一直保有寫作熱情的嗜好。

我附上一篇尚未刊出的故事在這封電子郵件的附件中。它叫做「跟老鼠談話」。希望你會喜歡。我還有很多類似的已經寫好。

我的電話號碼是 756 35433438

---

181. 答案 (C) Tony 忘記在電子郵件中附上什麼？

(A) 他的故事範例

(B) 他的寫作經驗

(C) 他的地址

(D) 他贏得「青少年作家」年度競賽獎時的年紀

解說 第一篇原文二段，"Email a sample story" 第三段，"Please include your name, address and phone number, and let us know about any previous writing experience you have"，要求要附上範例、姓名、地址、電話號碼和寫作經驗。第二篇原文第二句，"From: Tony James"，附上姓名；第二段第一句，"I have written many short stories"，附上寫作經驗；第三段第一句，"I am including one unpublished story as an attachment with this email" 附上範例；最後一段，"My telephone number is 756 35433438"，附上電話號碼。只有地址沒附上，故選 (C)。

182. 答案 (C) 為什麼 Tony 很幸運如果他被列入這個寫作工作的考慮名單？

(A) 他沒有足夠的寫作經驗

(B) 小孩不喜歡關於老鼠的故事

(C) 他錯過了提交故事的最後期限

(D) 因為他之前已經有故事刊出過

解說 第一篇原文第二段，"Email a sample story by August 15th"，以及第二一篇原文第三句，"August 16th "，可以知道已經錯過了最後期限。

183. 答案 (A) Tony 的故事會適合哪一個種類？

(A) 說話的動物 (B) 音樂的世界

(C) 童話故事 (D) 怪物

解說 第二篇原文第三段第二句，"It is called "A word with a Mouse". I hope you like it. I have many more like it already written"，足以得知 Tony 寫作許多這類性質的故事。

184. 答案 (A) Tony 在九月接到 Sherry 的來電，可能是關於什麼事？

(A) 她喜歡他的故事

(B) 問他為何他認為老鼠會說話

(C) 問他他的電話號碼

(D) 問他關於他的寫作經驗

解說 第一篇原文最後一句，"All successful applicants will be notified by telephone in September"，可以知到錄取是因為喜歡他寫作的故事。

185. 答案 (C) 文章告訴我們關於 Sherry 的什麼事？

(A) 她喜歡關於兒童的音樂的世界、說話的動物、怪物和童話故事

(B) 她寫作兒童的故事

(C) 她在 Real World 出版社工作

(D) 她想在雜誌上刊出故事

解說 第一篇原文第一句，"Real World Publishers are looking for talented writers of short stories for publication" 可以推測出 Sherry 在該出版社工作。

字彙：

talented [ˋtæləntɪd] *(adj.)* 有才華的／ publication [ˌpʌblɪˋkeʃən] *(n.)* 刊物／ category [ˋkætəˌgorɪ] *(n.)* 種類／ previous [ˋpriviəs] *(adj.)* 先前的／ advertisement [ˌædvɚˋtaɪzmənt] *(n.)* 廣告／ passion [ˋpæʃən] *(n.)* 熱情／ attachment [əˋtætʃmənt] *(n.)* 附件／ submit [səbˋmɪt] *(v.)* 提交

第 186-190 題

New England Park 湖邊高爾夫與 Spa 飯店

五、六月價格。所有每房每晚價格均不含早餐。

豪華套房 - 450 美金

標準套房 - 375 美金

豪華雙人房 - 310 美金

標準雙人房 - 290 美金

豪華雙人房（兩小床）- 295 美金

標準雙人房（兩小床）- 199 美金

單人房（一小床）- 125 美金

早餐每人 25 美金

專案的傍晚 Spa 99 美金 -- 必須在訂房時預訂。

專案的週末高爾夫兩人套裝行程 800 美金方案——包括兩晚豪華雙人房或豪華雙人房（兩小床），以及兩回合高爾夫，含早餐。

所有價格均含稅。

收件人：Mike
寄件人：Carlos

你升遷的大好消息。在最近投入的努力及超時工作，你真的應當得到這樣的結果。新的工作代表你會太忙和我一起去出玩嗎？或是你可以開始在工作上不那麼忙。

看一下這個我在這封郵件附加的傳單。畢竟你欠我一趟旅程。你在六月有時間來場週末高爾夫嗎？你會需要練習揮桿，因為我最近打很多高爾夫。

我們以前幾乎每週末都打高爾夫，但是自從你幾年前開始在Global Technology 工作後，你似乎都沒有空閒時間了。你應該試著受雇於自己，然後你也許會跟我一樣有很多空閒時間！

如果花時間和我一起而不是跟 Susan 一起渡過讓你感到內疚，我可以也帶 Lynette 一起來，然後我們可以在要打高爾夫時，送老婆們去做 spa。

看一下你的日程表，然後打電話給我。

186. 答案 (B) 下列哪一個陳述為事實？

(A) 高爾夫週末兩人套裝行程價格比 800 美金多
(B) 房價均不含早餐
(C) 女人不能參加高爾夫週末
(D) 單人房在七月的房價為 125 美金

解說 第一篇原文第二句，"Rates for May-June. All prices per room per night, excluding breakfast"，說明房價均不含早餐，故選(B)。選項(A)，第一篇原文倒數第二句，"Special Weekend Golf Package for two $800"，以及最後一句，"All prices include tax"，表示就是 800 美金，沒有額外需加上的價格，故不正確。選項(C)、(D) 並未在文章中提及。

187. 答案 (A) 如果Mike 和 Carlos 決定帶他們的老婆和們一起去他們的高爾夫週末，他們需要做什麼？

(A) 在預訂高爾夫套裝行程時安排 spa
(B) 替 Susan 和 Lynette 訂單人房
(C) 替每個人預訂早餐

(D) 練習如何打高爾夫

解說　第二篇原文第四段，"we can send the wives to the spa while we play golf"，和第一篇原文第十一句，"Special Evening Spa $99- Must be reserved at time of booking"，可知道他們計畫在打高爾夫時，讓老婆們去做 Spa，但是會需要先預約。

188. 答案 (D) Carlos 在哪裡上班？

(A) 他在 Global Technology 上班

(B) 他在 New England Park 湖邊高爾夫與 Spa 飯店上班

(C) 他替 Mike 工作

(D) 受雇於自己

解說　第二篇原文第三段第二句，"You should try working for yourself; then you might have as much free time as me"，可以知道他受雇於自己。

189. 答案 (C) 誰會付這個旅程？

(A) Mike 和 Carlos　(B) Global Technology 公司

(C) Mike　(D) Carlos

解說　第二篇原文第二段第二句，"You owe me a trip after all"，可以知道 Mike 欠 Carlos 一趟旅程，所以費用應是 Mike 支付。

190. 答案 (C) 這些文章告訴我們什麼關於 Mike 和 Carlos 之間的關係？

(A) 他們以前一起工作過

(B) Mike 現在是 Carlos 的老闆

(C) 他們已經認識彼此很多年了

(D) Carlos 以前替 Mike 工作

解說　第二篇原文第三段，"We used to play almost every weekend, but since you started working for Global Technology a couple of years ago you never seem to have enough free time"，可以知道他們彼此的交情已經很多年了。

字彙：

deluxe [dɪˋlʌks] *(adj.)* 豪華的／ reserved [rɪˋzɝvd] *(adj.)* 預訂的／ round [raʊnd] *(n.)* 回合／ promotion [prəˋmoʃən] *(n.)* 升遷／ deserve [dɪˋzɝv] *(v.)* 應當／ flyer [ˋflaɪɚ] *(n.)* 傳單／ guilty [ˋgɪltɪ] *(adj.)* 內疚的／ hang out *(ph.)* 跟朋友一起玩

第 191-195 題

BRICS 國家

BRICS 是字母縮略字（每個詞的第一個字母組成的字），與巴西、俄羅斯、印度、中國，以及南非有關。這個專有名詞首先被英國經濟學家 Jim O'Neil 在 2001 年使用。這五個國家都在快速經濟發展中，處於相似的階段。他們卓越的不只是他們大量、急速經濟成長，也是他們對世界上事務的影響力成長。這兩者一起，他們成了從傳統西方國家轉移經濟力量至新興開發中國家的象徵。

南非是最近包含在這個群組裡，而且造成 S 被加在原本的 BRIC 後面。很多人爭論南非不該被包含在內，由於它繁雜的經濟記錄和相較之下的少量人口，加它進去就好像只是因為適合當字母縮略字。

BRICS 國家似乎感激用字母縮略字，並且已形成一個協會以進一步達成彼此的目標。 但是儘管世界上媒體給 BRICS 的所有關注，他們的合併經濟並不被預期，在 2050 年前能勝過那些西方國家。

MINT 國家

MINT 是因把 BRIC 組成一群組而成名的經濟學家，Jim O'Neil，最近期的字母略縮字。MINT 國家是，墨西哥、印尼、奈及利亞，以及土耳其。 O'Neil 指出他們是二十一世紀潛在的經濟發電所。

讓 MINT 國家與別國不同的，是他們的人民。他們有年輕的人口，因為這樣，至少在接下來的二十年，他們將會有最多人進入勞動力，而不是離開。這被視為經濟成功的關鍵，不只已開發國家羨慕，也是許多迅速發展國家所羨慕的。

我們會拭目以待，是否 MINT 國家將會試圖形成某種像 BRICS 的政治性協會。同時，因為爭論持續在哪個國家應該或不應該被包含在群組裡，字母略縮字的數量增加。兩個新的各為 MIKT 和 TIMBI。你能猜到他們代表誰嗎？

191. 答案 (C) 這些文章暗示 BRICS 和 MINT 國家的崛起將造成什麼結果？

(A) 創造出更多字母略縮字

(B) 轉移 BRICS 和 MINT 國家的影響力

(C) 轉移西方國家的影響力

(D) 轉移較年輕族群的影響力

解說　第一篇原文第一段第五句，"they have become a symbol of the shift in economic power away from the traditional western countries to the newly developing ones"，以及第二篇原文第一段第三句，"them as potential economic powerhouses of the twenty-first century"，可以知道這兩個群組的國家將變成最有影響力的國家。

192. 答案 (A) 哪一個理由是南非不應該被例入 BRICS 的原因？

(A) 它的經濟不夠強固　(B) 不適合宜當字母縮略字

(C) 它的人口太多　(D) 它不是協會的成員

解說　第一篇原文第二段第二句，"due to its mixed economic record and comparatively small population"，說明經濟結構不夠強固，也說明與別的國家相較之下人口過少，故選擇 (A)；選項 (C) 不正確。選項 (B)，在第一篇原文第二段第二句，"it would conveniently fit into the acronym"，說明是合字母縮略字，故不正確。選項 (D)，第一篇原文第三段第一句，"BRICS countries seem to appreciate the acronym and have even formed an association"，表示它也是會員之一，故不正確。

193. 答案 (C) 根據這兩個文章，BRICS 國家和 MINT 國家最大不同之處是什麼？

(A) 他們成長中的經濟　(B) 人口的多寡

(C) 人口的年齡　(D) 創造出字母縮略字的人

解說　第二篇原文第二段第一句 "What set the MINT countries apart are their people. They have a younger population"，說明主要的不同為人口年齡。

194. 答案 (B) Jim O'Neil 做了什麼？

(A) 他發明了「acronym」這個專有名詞

(B) 他把 BRICS 國家分組在一起

(C) 他成立 BRICS 國家的協會

(D) 他爭論關於哪個國家要包含在 BRICS 裡

解說　第一篇原文第一段第二句，"The term was first used by the British economist Jim O'Neil"，以及第二篇原文第一段第一句，"Jim O'Neil the economist famous for grouping the BRIC countries together" 說明這個字母縮略字是他創立的。

195. 答案 (D) 哪個國家可能也是包含在 MIKT 和 TIMBI 國家裡？

(A) 奈及利亞　(B) 南非

(C) 俄羅斯　(D) 墨西哥

解說　第二篇原文最後一段第二、三句，“the number of acronyms increases. Two new ones are MIKT and TIMBI”，表示兩者皆為字母縮略字，只有選項 (D) 墨西哥是 M 字母開頭。

字彙：

acronym [ˋækrənɪm] *(n.)* 字母縮略字／ term [tɝm] *(n.)* 專有名詞／ distinguished [dɪˋstɪŋgwɪʃt] *(adj.)* 卓越的／ inclusion [ɪnˋkluʒən] *(n.)* 包括／ conveniently [kənˋvinjəntlɪ] *(adv.)* 合宜地／ association [əˏsosɪˋeʃən] *(n.)* 協會／ surpass [sɚˋpæs] *(v.)* 勝過／ potential [pəˋtɛnʃəl] *(adj.)* 潛在的

第 196-200 題

〈峭壁的邊緣〉，Larry Cameron 著

Simon Adams 書評

「我們經歷其中一個那些海岸的小徑，沿著峭壁的邊緣盤繞，一個藍色的十月曙光。」所以我們在 Larry Cameron 的鉅作〈峭壁的邊緣〉開始了 Theo 和 Eleanor 的史詩的傳說。三百五十頁的愛情、欺騙、失去和背叛，並有個曲折的結局。

Theo 和 Eleanor 在十八世紀晚期，一個美國海岸的城鎮長大。Eleanor 是位來自地位卑微家庭的擠牛奶女工，而 Theo 則是侵佔他人土地的當地地主的兒子。他們接下來二十幾年的故事，記述著他們在與世隔絕社會的生活，相映照他們周遭新的工業化與迅速改變的世界。

Larry Cameron 的前幾本小說，像是〈黑暗來臨〉和〈紅河〉，都收到高度文學的稱讚，但是在風格與本質上，都與他最近期的書十分不同。

這不只是個給學術或那些在大學修文學的人看的老故事。這本書會吸引比那更廣的讀者。看來似乎在 81 歲時，Cameron 發現了他新的寫作深度。 他不只能敲進 Theo 和 Eleanor 的情感深處，也能敲進他讀者們的情緒。這是為什麼能將這本書與他早期的作品做出區隔。

〈峭壁的邊緣〉已入圍幾個文學獎，而且也預期在獲獎與銷售有亮眼成績。

〈峭壁的邊緣〉，Larry Cameron 著，由 Bumble Publishing 出版

〈峭壁的邊緣〉Larry Cameron 著

Renee Park 書評

〈峭壁的邊緣〉是個十八世紀晚期，在新建立的美國長大的迷人的故事。故事訴說在那些動盪不安的年代，Theo 和 Eleanor 這對情侶不太可達成的事，他們在那急速改變的地方追尋他們的命運。

儘管 Cameron 的偉大著作，如此優美與輕鬆地設定背景，帶領我們進入那些常被遺忘年代的旅程，Eleanor 和 Theo 之間的關係，就有點離題得太遠了。故事敘述是流暢的，而他對歷史細節的注意是任何其他當代的作家比不上的，但是很難看出這本小說，會比他先前的作品吸引更廣的讀者。

評論家讚美它會是長途飛行旅程中的輕鬆讀物，但是不是多數鄰近書店裡，會造成大轟動搶購一空的書。

196. 答案 (A) 兩篇書評都一致認為什麼？

(A) 文學界會喜歡這本書

(B) 書和先前的相似

(C) 書的銷售會很好

(D) Theo 和 Eleanor 之間的關係寫得很好

解說 第一篇原文第五段第一句，“The Cliff's Edge has already been shortlisted for a number of literacy prizes”，以及第二篇原文第三段第一句，“Critically acclaimed it may be and a relaxing read for a long plane ride”，可以得知兩篇文章中對此有相同看法。

197. 答案 (A) 哪個時期最可能是書中的設定？

(A) 1779 – 1799　(B) 1790 – 1810

(C) 1875 – 1895　(D) 1750 – 1770

解說 第二篇原文第一段第一句，“The Cliff's Edge is an engaging story of growing up in the newly established United States of America in the late 18th century”，說明故事背景設定為十八世紀晚期。十八世紀指 1700-1799 年。選項 (A)、(D) 皆為十八世紀，但選項 (A) 較 (D) 更為晚期。

198. 答案 (D)〈峭壁的邊緣〉贏了幾個獎？

(A) 一個獎　　(B) 兩個獎

(C) 很多獎　　(D) 沒有

解說　第一篇原文第五段第一句，“already been shortlisted for a number of literacy prizes and is expected to do well both in awards and in sales”，期待會在得獎和銷售上有亮眼成績，就表示尚未知得獎與否。

199. 答案 (C) 誰發現很難接受書中的某些部分？

(A) Simon Adam　　(B) Theo

(C) Renee Park　　(D) Larry Cameron

解說　第二篇原文第二段第一句，“the relationship between Eleanor and Theo is just a step too far”，以及第二句，“it is hard to see how this novel will appeal to any wider audience than his previous works have”，顯示第二篇寫評論的 Renee Park，對這本書有些不認同的地方。

200. 答案 (B) 你不會預期在〈峭壁的邊緣〉中發現什麼？

(A) 浪漫愛情　　(B) 城市的生活

(C) 死亡　　(D) 令人驚訝的結局

解說　第一篇原文第一段第三句，“Three hundred and fifty pages of love, deceit, loss and betrayal, and all with a twist at the end”，表示書有有選項 (A)、(C)、(D)。

字彙：

review [rɪˋvju] *(v.)* 評論／ coastal [ˋkostl̩] *(adj.)* 海岸的／ twist [twɪst] *(v.)* 盤繞／ deceit [dɪˋsit] *(n.)* 欺騙／ poacher [ˋpotʃɚ] *(n.)* 侵入他人地界者／ chronicle [ˋkrɑnɪkl̩] *(v.)* 記述／ literary [ˋlɪtəˏrɛrɪ] *(adj.)* 文學的／ acclaim [əˋklem] *(n.)* 稱讚

Test 4

Part 5. 單句填空

Questions 101-140.

101. It has been shown that alcohol becomes - - - - - - - to health when consumed in large amounts.

(A) harm
(B) harmful
(C) harmfully
(D) harmed

102. Failure to report a serious car accident to the police can lead to a criminal - - - - - - -.

(A) prosecution
(B) persecution
(C) pursuit
(D) practice

103. There has been a steady increase in temperature all summer - - - - - - - has resulted in more forest fires than expected.

(A) what
(B) that
(C) where
(D) whose

104. Following many delays, the new data entry system was tested - - - - - - - overnight.

(A) success
(B) successful
(C) successfully
(D) succeed

105. All customers of Steve's Bar and Grill are kindly asked to refrain ------- smoking on the open air terrace which overlooks the gardens.

(A) in

(B) off

(C) out

(D) from

106. The price of gold is influenced by many ------- which are hard to predict accurately.

(A) ingredients

(B) figures

(C) factors

(D) fractions

107. Tablet computers ------- very popular over the past couple of years, and they are expected to continue to outsell all other types of computers for the foreseeable future.

(A) become

(B) have become

(C) are becoming

(D) had become

108. It has been reported that Horris Foods Inc. will postpone ------- salaries due to its ongoing financial problems.

(A) pay

(B) to pay

(C) paid

(D) paying

109. Antibiotics are an essential component of every hospital's armory; however,- - - - - - - effectiveness is being increasingly compromised by overuse.

(A) it
(B) theirs
(C) itself
(D) their

110. Last year we employed many new workers on temporary - - - - - - -.

(A) contracts
(B) bonds
(C) deals
(D) enrollment

111. Regulators have made the bank - - - - - - - to all customers who were mis-sold investment accounts.

(A) apology
(B) apologize
(C) apologetic
(D) to apologize

112. During the expansion of Hong Kong International Airport, some flights will be - - - - - - - to Macau.

(A) sent
(B) transported
(C) diverted
(D) relocated

113. The guest speaker at the annual conference delivered an - - - - - - - speech which was much appreciated by all those present.

(A) inspiration
(B) inspire
(C) inspirational
(D) inspirationally

114. - - - - - - - all the cell phones reviewed by this magazine in the past year, this is without doubt the best.

(A) Out

(B) In

(C) By

(D) Of

115. Solarink Inc. would like to apologize for the - - - - - - - to its website this morning.

(A) disruption

(B) disintergration

(C) break up

(D) rupture

116. The engineers were - - - - - - - to discover the problem before too much damage had been done to the underground pipes.

(A) possible

(B) impossible

(C) difficult

(D) able

117. In a unanimous decision, Albert Roberts - - - - - - - elected chairman of Tyne Construction.

(A) is

(B) was

(C) has

(D) has

118. All trains to the west coast will now depart from - - - - - - - six until March 17th.

(A) level

(B) area

(C) podium

(D) platform

119. Small businesses often ------- a much more personalized service than their larger competitors.

(A) offered
(B) offer
(C) offering
(D) offers

120. If the accountant had accepted the bribe, he ------- have gone to prison.

(A) will
(B) may
(C) might
(D) can

121. Our community center's sports team was knocked ------- by a better team.

(A) out
(B) over
(C) down
(D) in

122. Extra insurance should be ------- out by all those who plan to participate in the snowboarding activity.

(A) took
(B) take
(C) taken
(D) taking

123. The latest release of data has shown that growth in export markets has helped Germany avoid the expected -------.

(A) regression
(B) receding
(C) retreat
(D) recession

124. Highlands parish council urges everyone within the projected flood area ------- before the river reaches its peak flood level.

(A) to leave
(B) leave
(C) leaving
(D) left

125. All applicants for the position will be considered ------- for this opening.

(A) equal
(B) equally
(C) to equal
(D) equaled

126. There is growing ------- for the need for online marketing within the fashion industry.

(A) accept
(B) accepting
(C) acceptance
(D) accepted

127. London has become the ------- home for people from all over the world.

(A) adopted
(B) borrowed
(C) foster
(D) embraced

128. Your reservation for three nights at the Royal Plaza Hotel ------- all meals is confirmed.

(A) include
(B) included
(C) including
(D) inclusive

129. Despite initial resistance from middle management, the ------- to focus on product placement is now being taken seriously by the board of directors.

(A) suggest
(B) suggested
(C) suggesting
(D) suggestion

130. Parking in this zone is not permitted, you must find ------- else to leave your car.

(A) anywhere
(B) everywhere
(C) nowhere
(D) somewhere

131. Construction of the new leisure center ------- on schedule and will be completed on time and under budget.

(A) had continued
(B) is continuing
(C) will have continued
(D) was continuing

132. Since entering the European market, sales of Lava Motors have been -------.

(A) promise
(B) promising
(C) promised
(D) promisingly

133. Contract negotiations are ongoing, but unlikely to be completed by the May -------.

(A) deadline
(B) border
(C) boundary
(D) margin

134. My boss's daughter has started work at the supermarket - - - - - - - we often shop at.

(A) whose
(B) which
(C) who
(D) where

135. I was glad - - - - - - - my former manager again after so many years at a rival company.

(A) see
(B) to see
(C) seeing
(D) saw

136. The - - - - - - - for running a red light is to be doubled, effective from the start of next year.

(A) retaliation
(B) levy
(C) rebuke
(D) penalty

137. In this county, tuition at university is not paid by the state - - - - - - -.

(A) anyhow
(B) anymore
(C) anyone
(D) anything

138. The most important - - - - - - - sometimes have to be made with very little time to think.

(A) opinions
(B) conclusions
(C) verdicts
(D) decisions

139. Withdrawal from the trade agreement was - - - - - - - but finally rejected.

(A) consider
(B) considering
(C) considered
(D) to consider

140. There has never been a better time to - - - - - - - for a job in the oil industry.

(A) apply
(B) employ
(C) submit
(D) recruit

Part 5. 單句填空

第 101-140 題

101. 答案 (B) 攝取大量酒精，顯示已成為傷害健康的因素。

(A) 傷害 *(v.)*　　(B) 傷害 *(adj.)*
(C) 傷害地 *(adv.)*　　(D) 傷害（過去式動詞）

解說　become「成為」，是連綴動詞，所以後面要加主詞補語，連綴動詞的用法跟 be 動詞相同，本題適用的答案為一個形容詞，故選 (B)。

例句　She has become depressed since she heard the bad news. 自從她聽到惡耗，她變得憂鬱。

102. 答案 (A) 沒有向警方舉報車禍，會導致依犯罪行為起訴。

(A) 起訴 *(n.)*　　(B) 迫害 *(n.)*
(C) 追求 *(n.)*　　(D) 練習 *(n.)*

103. 答案 (B) 整個夏天的氣溫穩定地上升，導致比預期中更多森林大火。

(A) what　　(B) that
(C) where　　(D) whose

解說　that 是關係代名詞，引導形容詞子句，修飾前面的名詞 temperature，故選 (B)。選項 (A)，不是關係代名詞。選項 (C)，where 是關係副詞，修飾前面的名詞，必須是地方，在本題不適用。選項 (D)，whose 是關係代名詞，修飾前面的名詞，必須是某事物的東西，在本題不適用。

例句　The airplane that departed this morning is heading to Canada. 今天早上起程的飛機飛往加拿大。

104. 答案 (C) 伴隨許多延遲，新資料登入系統經整夜測試成功。

(A) 成功 *(n.)*　　(B) 成功的 *(adj.)*
(C) 成功地 *(adv.)*　　(D) 成功 *(v.)*

解說　tested「測試」是過去分詞，詞性為形容詞，副詞修飾形容詞，故選 (B)。

105. 答案 (D) 所有 Steve's 酒吧與燒烤的顧客，被柔性勸導避免在俯瞰花園的開放陽台抽煙。

(A) in　　(B) off
(C) out　　(D) from

解說 refrain from「避免」。

106. 答案 (C) 黃金價格受許多因素影響，很難精準預測。

(A) 材料 (B) 人物

(C) 因素 (D) 小片段

107. 答案 (B) 平板電腦在這幾年已變得十分受歡迎，在可預見的未來，仍預期繼續在銷量上勝過其他種類的電腦。

(A) become (B) have become

(C) are becoming (D) had become

解說 本句的時間為 over the past couple of years「這幾年來」，表示敘述這幾年來已發生的事，用現在完成式。

108. 答案 (D) 報導指出 Horris Foods 有限公司將會延遲支付薪水，由於該公司目前面臨的財務問題。

(A) 支付 *(v.)* (B) 支付 *(inf.)*

(C) 支付（過去式動詞） (D) 支付（動名詞）

解說 postpone「延遲」，是動詞，它後面的動詞必須寫成動名詞，不能寫不定詞。postpone + Ving。

例句 Brandy postponed sending the application form. Brandy 延遲寄出申請表。

109. 答案 (D) 抗生素是每間醫院藥庫裡一項重要的成分；然而它的效用有增加過度使用的危險。

(A) it (B) theirs

(C) itself (D) their

解說 代名詞所有格 their「他們的」，代表 antibiotics「抗生素」。

110. 答案 (A) 去年我們用臨時的合約雇用許多新人。

(A) 合約 *(n.)* (B) 約定 *(n.)*

(C) 交易 *(n.)* (D) 註冊 *(n.)*

111. 答案 (B) 調解會迫使銀行向所有投資帳戶被誤賣掉的顧客道歉。

(A) 道歉 *(n.)* (B) 道歉 *(v.)*

(C) 道歉的 *(adj.)* (D) 道歉 *(inf.)*

解說　make 是不完全及物動詞，需要一個受詞補語在受詞 the bank「銀行」的後面，受詞補語是原形動詞，故選 (B)。

例句　The doctor made the sick boy take medicine. 醫生迫使生病的男孩吃藥。

112. 答案 (C) 在香港國際機場擴建期間，一些航班將會被重新安置到澳門。

(A) 寄送　(B) 運輸

(C) 送達　(D) 重新安置

113. 答案 (C) 年度討論會的客座講者，發表了激勵人心的演說，所有與會者皆十分欣賞。

(A) 靈感 *(n.)*　(B) 激勵 *(v.)*

(C) 激勵 *(adj.)*　(D) 激勵地 *(adv.)*

解說　an inspirational speech「激勵人心的演說」是名詞片語，inspirational「激勵的」是形容詞，修飾名詞 speech「演說」。

114. 答案 (D) 過去一年來這家雜誌檢視的所有手機，這一個無疑是最好的。

(A) Out　(B) In

(C) By　(D) Of

解說　of 介系詞，在這裡表示同位語。本句等於 This is without doubt the best of all the cell phones reviewed by this magazine in the past year.

115. 答案 (A) Solarink 有限公司要對今天早上公司網站的崩壞情況致上歉意。

(A) 崩壞 *(n.)*　(B) 碎裂 *(n.)*

(C) 解散 *(v.)*　(D) 破裂 *(n.)*

116. 答案 (D) 工程師能夠在地下水管有更大損壞之前發現問題。

(A) 可能的　(B) 不可能的

(C) 困難的　(D) 能夠的

解說　主詞是人，只能用選項 (D)，形容詞 able「能；會」。也可以用假的主詞 It 代表句中的 to discover the problem「發現問題」，那麼選項 (A)、(B)、(C) 皆適用，因為這些形容詞不能用來修飾人，人不會是 possible「可能的」、impossible「不可能的」、difficult「困難的」，只有事情才會用這些形容詞。

例句 It was possible to discover the problem before too much damage had been done to the underground pipes. 在地下水管有太大損壞之前發現問題，是可能辦到的。

117. 答案 (B) 決定以不計名方式，Albert Roberts 被選為 Tyne 建設公司主席。

(A) is (B) was

(C) has (D) has

解說 本句是過去式被動語態，主詞＋was/were＋過去分詞，主詞是單數 Albert Roberts，故選 (B)。

例句 Anakin was chosen as class leader. Anakin 被選為班長。

118. 答案 (D) 所有至西部海岸的列車，現在皆在第六月台上車，直到三月十七日為止。

(A) 層 (B) 區域

(C) 指揮臺 (D) 月台

119. 答案 (B) 小商家們常常比他們較大的競爭對手，提供多很多的個人化服務。

(A) 提供（過去式動詞） (B) 提供 *(v.)*

(C) 提供（動名詞） (D) 提供 *(v.)*

解說 頻率副詞 often「常常」，表示事情是常態的，所以是現在式，選擇現在式動詞，故選 (B)。選項 (D) 亦為現在式動詞，但是有加第三人稱單數 s，主詞是複數的 Small businesses「小商家們」，所以不能選 (D)。

120. 答案 (C) 要是會計師接受了賄賂，他可能就已經去坐牢了。

(A) will (B) may

(C) might (D) can

解說 第三條件句用於假設改變過去發生的事。If＋過去完成式子句＋，＋主詞＋would/could/might＋現在完成式。故選 (C)。

例句 If we had caught the bus on time, we might have been at the concert right now. 要是我們及時趕上公車，我們現在就會已經在演唱會會場了。(表示假設改變沒有及時趕上公車的事實。意指沒趕上公車，也沒到達演唱會會場。)

121. 答案 (A) 我們社區中心的運動隊被一隻更好的隊伍擊敗。

(A) out (B) over

(C) down (D) in

解說 選項 (A)，動詞片語 knock out「擊敗」。選項 (B)，動詞片語 knock over「打翻」。選項 (C)，動詞片語 knock down「拆毀」。選項 (D)，動詞片語 knock in「打進」。

122. 答案 (C) 額外的保險應該要從那些計畫參加滑板滑雪活動的人扣除。

(A) took (B) take

(C) taken (D) taking

解說 take out「扣除」，主詞是 extra insurance「額外的保險」，本句是被動語態。被動語態是主詞＋ be 動詞＋過去分詞。

例句 The cub should be taken away from its mother. 幼獸應該被帶離牠的母親。

123. 答案 (D) 最近發佈的資料顯示，輸出市場幫助德國避免預期的衰退。

(A) 退化 *(n.)* (B) 退去（動名詞）

(C) 撤退 *(n.)* (D) 衰退 *(n.)*

124. 答案 (A) Highlands 地方行政議會強烈要求每個預計會在淹水區域的人，在河水上漲至最高到淹水程度之前離開。

(A) 離開 *(inf.)* (B) 離開 *(v.)*

(C) 離開（動名詞） (D) 離開（過去式動詞）

解說 urge「強烈要求」，urge ＋受詞＋不定詞，urge 的受詞補語必須是不定詞，故選 (A)。

例句 The professor urged his students to pay attention in class. 教授強烈要求他的學生在課堂上專心。

125. 答案 (B) 所有此職缺的申請人，將會在這個職位空缺中給予相等程度地考慮。

(A) 相等的 *(adj.)* (B) 相等地 *(adv.)*

(C) 等於 *(inf.)* (D) 等於（過去式動詞）

解說 considered「考慮的」，是形容詞，副詞修飾形容詞，故選 (B)。

126. 答案 (C) 時尚界裡的網路行銷，接受度正在增長中。

(A) 接受 *(v.)* (B) 接受（動名詞）

(C) 接受 *(n.)* (D) 公認的 *(adj.)*

解說 growing「增長中的」，是形容詞，形容詞修飾名詞，故選 (C)。

127. 答案 (A) 倫敦已成為來自世界各地的人的收養家庭。

(A) 收養的 *(adj.)* (B) 借的 *(adj.)*
(C) 養育的 *(adj.)* (D) 包含的 *(adj.)*

128. 答案 (C) 你在 Royal Plaza 飯店的訂位包含所有餐點已確認。

(A) 包含 *(v.)* (B) 被包括的 *(adj.)*
(C) 包括（現在分詞） (D) 包含的 *(adj.)*

解說 副詞子句的主詞與主要子句主詞相同時，可將副詞子句中的連接詞與主詞改成現在分詞，即為分詞構句。including = which includes ，關係代名詞 which，代表 Your reservation「你的訂位」。

129. 答案 (D) 儘管原本來自中階主管的反抗，專注在產品佈置的建議，現在已經被執行長董事會認真看待。

(A) 建議 *(v.)* (B) 建議（過去式動詞）
(C) 建議（現在進行式動詞） (D) 建議 *(n.)*

解說 the 是定冠詞，用在名詞前，故選擇名詞 (D)。

130. 答案 (D) 這個地帶不允許停車，你必須找某個地方停你的車。

(A) 任何地方 (B) 每個地方
(C) 沒有地方 (D) 某個地方

131. 答案 (B) 新休閒中心正持續按照預定時間建造，也將會在預算內準時完工。

(A) had continued (B) is continuing
(C) will have continued (D) was continuing

解說 時間為 on schedule「按照預定時間」，表示正在進行這件事，用現在進行式主詞＋ be 動詞＋ Ving，故選 (B)。

例句 The final exam is continuing on schedule although there has been a blackout. 考試持續按預定時間進行，雖然有發生停電。

132. 答案 (B) 自從進入歐洲市場，Lava 汽車的銷售量大有可為。

(A) 承諾 *(v.)* (B) 大有可為的（現在分詞 adj.）
(C) 承諾（過去式動詞） (D) 大有可為地 *(adv.)*

解說 現在分詞形容詞，表示主動。

例句 The result of the experiment was disappointing. 實驗結果是失望的。

133. 答案 (A) 合約協商正在進行，但是不太可能在五月的期限內完成。

(A) 期限 *(n.)*　(B) 邊境 *(n.)*
(C) 底限 *(n.)*　(D) 邊緣 *(n.)*

134. 答案 (B) 我們老闆的女兒開始在我們常去的超級市場上班。

(A) whose　(B) which
(C) who　(D) where

解說　關係代名詞which，引導形容詞子句，代表前面名詞（事物）the supermarket「超級市場」，故選(B)。選項(D)，是關係副詞where，代表前面的名詞（地方），需要是at the supermarket「在超級市場」地方副詞當先行詞才符合文法。

135. 答案 (B) 我開心在那麼多年後，在競爭對手公司再次見到我的前任經理。

(A) 見到 *(v.)*　(B) 見到 *(inf.)*
(C) 見到（動名詞）　(D) 見到（過去式動詞）

解說　不定詞做形容詞補語，to see「見到」，修飾glad「開心」。主詞是人的時候，形容詞是一種情緒，主詞I「我」，gald「開心」形容詞（一種情緒），故選(B)。例題：We are happy to have you here. 我們高興有你在這裡。

136. 答案 (D) 闖紅燈的罰鍰加倍，從明年初開始生效。

(A) 報復 *(n.)*　(B) 課稅 *(n.)*
(C) 指責 *(n.)*　(D) 罰鍰 *(n.)*

137. 答案 (B) 這個縣市的大學學費，再也不是由政府支付。

(A) 無論如何 *(adv.)*　(B) 再也不 *(adv.)*
(C) 任何人 *(pron.)*　(D) 任何事 *(pron.)*

解說　副詞anymore「再也不」，用在否定句句尾。

例句　Hazel doesn't play piano anymore. Hazel再也不彈鋼琴。

138. 答案 (D) 有時候最重要的決定，必須在很短的考慮時間做出。

(A) opinions　(B) conclusions
(C) verdicts　(D) decisions

解說　以上四個選項皆為名詞，但是有特定的用法。選項(A)，form an opinion「成形一個觀點」。選項(B)，reach a conclusion「得到結論」。選項

(C)，reach a verdict「得到裁定」。選項 (D)，make a decision「做決定」，故選 (D)。

例句 Life is all about making decisions. 人生就是在做決定。

139. 答案 (C) 退出貿易協議被列入考慮，但是最後仍被駁回。

(A) 考慮 *(v.)* (B) 考慮（現在分詞）

(C) 考慮（過去分詞） (D) 考慮 *(inf.)*

解說 過去式被動語態，主詞＋ was/were ＋過去分詞，故選 (C)。

例句 People trafficking was noticed by our government. 人口販運被我們的政府注意到。

140. 答案 (A) 沒有比現在更好的時機來申請油品業的工作。

(A) 申請 *(v.)* (B) 雇用 *(v.)*

(C) 提交 *(v.)* (D) 徵募 *(v.)*

解說 動詞片語 apply for「請求得到」，apply for a job「申請工作」，故選 (A)。

例句 It is time for me to apply for a job. 該是我申請工作的時候了。

Part 6. 短文填空

Questions 141-143 refer to the following warranty.

Krieger Color Plasma TV Warranty

Limited Warranty Coverage

If your TV does not work properly because of a defect in material or -------, Krieger will for a period of one year from the date of purchase

141. (A) produce
(B) produced
(C) production
(D) producing

either repair or replace the product. The decision to repair or replace will be made by the company.

------- the limited warranty period, all labor and replacement parts

142. (A) In
(B) During
(C) When
(D) While

are free of charge. This warranty only applies to the original purchaser, and only covers product purchased as new. A purchase receipt or other proof of the ------- purchase date is required when applying for

143. (A) original
(B) originate
(C) originating
(D) originated

warranty service.

Questions 144-146 refer to the following newspaper article.

Great white sharks live for 70 years

Great white sharks live for longer than previously thought. Researchers have developed new methods of assessing the age of tissue, and they have ------- specimens which have lived into their

144. (A) identifying
(B) identify
(C) identity
(D) identified

70s. Older, more unreliable methods which tried counting growth rings in bone had estimated that they only lived into their 30s.

The researchers report that this has important implications for conservation programs, ------- knowing how fast they grow and when

145. (A) when
(B) as
(C) if
(D) while

they reach adulthood affects projections of the number of young they will produce, and how long it will take for the shark population to recover to previous levels.

Despite what you may think, very little is actually known about these spectacular underwater predators. The public perception of these creatures is not good. Most of the information that the public has comes from movies which portray them as man eaters, but the ------- is that this is a vulnerable species that requires our protection.

146. (A) really
(B) real
(C) reality
(D) realism

Questions 147-149 refer to the following article.

Advertising is big business, and an important part of most multinational businesses.

There are many different ways to advertise, and no one knows for sure what makes a good advertising campaign, but we all know that some advertisements are funny and innovative, whereas others ------- irritate. Advertisers know that it is hard to convince someone to buy something they don't want, but it is possible to persuade them to switch brands for products they regularly buy.

147. (A) simple
(B) simply
(C) simplify
(D) simpleness

It's also hard to figure out exactly how successful advertisements are, as it's ------- to know for sure which sales are as a result of advertisements and which sales would have been made anyway.

148. (A) questionable
(B) hopeless
(C) improbable
(D) impossible

Advertising has changed over the years. A lot of advertising now is done more subtly than simply buying a thirty-second television -------. Many companies pay celebrities to endorse their products in the hope that their fans will buy what they see celebrities using. Also businesses pay huge sums to television and movie production companies to have their products prominently displayed within a movie or TV program.

149. (A) program
(B) slot
(C) time
(D) schedule

Questions 150-152 refer to the following email.

To: Mr. McAlister

From: Wanda Green, Poters Resorts

Thank you for your email on August 17th enquiring about our children's summer camps. Unfortunately Poters Resorts no longer offers overnight summer camps.

We do offer an ------- range of activity days throughout the

150. (A) extent
(B) extensiveness
(C) extensively
(D) extensive

summer, including arts and crafts, archery, swimming, rock climbing and high ropes. But our most popular summer activity day is the 'Mad Scientist' day ------- children get to experience science in a fun

151. (A) who
(B) where
(C) whose
(D) which

hands-on way. All day camps operate from 9am to 6pm and are suitable for children from eight to twelve years old.

All activities can also be enjoyed as part of a family package while staying in our log cabins within the resort. Full details of all packages and activities including dates and prices can be found on our website: www.potersresorts.com

Should you only be interested in overnight camps for children we can ------- camps at our sister resort of Rocks Park in the nearby mountains.

152. (A) recommend
(B) endorse
(C) trust
(D) advise

Part 6. 短文填空

第 141-143 題

Krieger 彩色電漿電視保固

限定保固範圍

如果你的電視沒有正常運作，是因為材質或生產上缺陷，Krieger 將會自你購買日期算起的一年期間，修繕或更換產品。公司會決定採修繕或更換的方式。

141. 答案 (C)

(A) 生產 *(v.)* (B) 生產（過去式動詞）

(C) 生產 *(n.)* (D) 生產（現在進行式動詞）

解說 介系詞 in「在…上」，後面要用名詞，material「材質」與 production「生產」必須是名詞，故選 (C)。

在有限的保固期間裡，所有人力與更換零件皆不需收費。這個保固只適用原購買者，而且只適用於購買新品。購買憑證或其他原購買日期證明的，在你申請保固服務時會需要。

142. 答案 (B)

(A) in (B) during

(C) when (D) while

解說 在…一段期間，用介系詞 during「在…的整個期間」，介系詞後是名詞片語，the limited warranty period「有限的保固期間」，故選 (B)。選項 (A)，是介系詞 in「在…之內」，指期間之前就會結束，而不是整個期間。選項 (C)、(D)，when「當…時」(指短時間)，while「當…(指一段時間)」，是連接詞，連接的子句會有彼此的對應關係。

143. 答案 (A)

(A) 原本的 *(adj.)* (B) 來自 *(v.)*

(C) 來自（現在分詞） (D) 來自（過去分詞）

解說 名詞 purchaser「購買者」，形容詞修飾名詞，需選擇一個形容詞，故選 (A)。

字彙：

warranty [ˋwɔrəntɪ] *(n.)* 保固／ defect [dɪˋfɛkt] *(n.)* 缺陷／ replacement [rɪˋplesmənt] *(n.)* 更換／ original [əˋrɪdʒənl̩] *(adj.)* 原本的／ proof [pruf] *(n.)* 證明／ cover [ˋkʌvɚ] *(v.)* 適用於

第 144-146 題

大白鯊活 70 年

大白鯊活得比先前認為的久。研究人員已研發出新方法來評估動物組織的年齡，並且已經鑑定出活到 70 幾歲的實例。較老舊又不可靠的方法，是試著數骨頭裡的年輪，而且只猜測大白鯊活到三十幾歲。

144. 答案 (D)

(A) 鑑定 *(v.)*（現在分詞） (B) 鑑定 *(v.)*

(C) 身份 *(n.)* (D) 鑑定 *(v.)*（過去分詞）

解說 現在完成式，主詞＋ have/has ＋過去分詞。

研究人員記述，這對自然保存計畫有重要含意，像是知曉他們在達到成年期時成長速度多快，影響他們會產出多少年幼白鯊的預測數值，以及要多久時間才會讓鯊魚數量回復到原先的程度。

145. 答案 (B)

(A) 當 *(conj.)* (B) as 像；如同 *(prep.)*

(C) 如果；假如 *(conj.)* (D) 當…的時候 *(conj.)*

解說 knowing「知曉」是名詞，前面的字必須選擇介系詞。

不管你也許會怎麼想，關於這些驚人的海底掠食者的實際情況，了解很少。大眾對這些生物的觀感並不好。大部份的資訊是來自把牠們描繪成吃人角色的電影，但事實是，這是一個易受傷的物種需要我們的保護。

146. 答案 (C)

(A) 真地 *(adv.)* (B) 真的 *(adj.)*

(C) 事實 *(n.)* (D) 現實主義 *(n.)*

字彙：

specimen [ˋspɛsəmən] *(n.)* 實例；樣本／ implication [ˌɪmplɪˋkeʃən] *(n.)* 含意／ conservation [ˌkɑnsɚˋveʃən] *(n.)*（對自然資源的）保存／ predator [ˋprɛdətɚ] *(n.)* 掠食者／ portray [porˋtre] *(v.)* 描繪

第 147-149 題

廣告是件大事，是多數跨國公司的重要大事。

有很多方式可以廣告，沒有人真的知道什麼會是好的廣告活動，但是我們都知道一些廣告有趣且創新的，反之，其它的簡直令人惱怒。廣告業知道很難說服某人買某些他們不想要的東西，但是很可能說服他們轉換買跟平常不同的品牌。

147. 答案 (B)

(A) 簡單的 *(adj.)*　　(B) 簡直 *(adv.)*

(C) 簡化 *(v.)*　　(D) 單純 *(n.)*

解說　irritate「使惱怒」，是動詞，副詞修飾動詞，故選 (B)。

也很難知道廣告到底有多成功，因為不可能確知哪一個銷量是廣告導致的結果，以及不論如何都會達成哪一個銷量。

148. 答案 (D)

(A) 可疑的 *(adj.)*　　(B) 沒指望的 *(adj.)*

(C) 不太有可能發生的 *(adj.)*　　(D) 不可能的 *(adj.)*

廣告在這幾年來有了改變。很多廣告現在做得比較巧妙，而不是只有單純買下 30 秒的電視空檔時間。很多公司付錢給名人來背書他們的產品，希望他們的粉絲會買他們看見名人使用的東西。商業也付大筆金錢給電視和電影製作公司，好讓他們的產品顯著地在電影或電視節目裡出現。

149. 答案 (B)

(A) 節目 *(n.)*　　(B) 空檔；狹縫 *(n.)*

(C) 時間 *(n.)*　　(D) 日程表 *(n.)*

字彙：

multinational [ˋmʌltɪˋnæʃənl̩] *(adj.)* 跨國公司的／ innovative [ˋɪnoˏvetɪv] *(adj.)* 創新的／ whereas [hwɛrˋæz] (con.) 反之；卻／ irritate [ˋɪrəˏtet] *(v.)* 使惱怒／ switch [swɪtʃ] *(v.)* 轉換／ subtly [ˋsʌtl̩ɪ] *(adv.)* 巧妙地

第 150-152 題

收件人：McAlister 先生

寄件人：Poters 渡假村，Wanda Green

謝謝你在八月十七日來信探詢我們小孩的暑期營隊。很不幸地 Poters 渡假村已不再提供過夜的暑期營隊。

我們有提供的是大範圍的活動日，整個暑期都有，包括美術和工藝、箭術、游泳、攀岩，以及走高空繩索。但是我們最受歡迎的暑期活動日是「瘋狂科學家」日，小孩可以用有趣親手施做的方式體驗科學。所有一日營隊營運時間自早上九點至下午六點，適合八至十二歲的小孩。

150. 答案 (D)

(A) 程度 *(n.)*　(B) 廣闊 *(n.)*

(C) 廣泛地 *(adv.)*　(D) 廣泛的 *(adj.)*

解說　range「範圍」，是名詞，形容詞修飾名詞，故選 (D)。

151. 答案 (B)

(A) who　(B) where

(C) whose　(D) which

解說　關係副詞 where，代表之前的名詞（地方），指參與「瘋狂科學家」日的地方。

所有以上活動可以在入住渡假村木屋期間，視同家庭專案的一部分。所有的專案詳情與活動，包括日期與價格，可上網瀏覽：www.potersresorts.com

若你只對小孩過夜的營隊有興趣，我們可以推薦你我們在鄰近山區的姐妹渡假村，Rocks Park 渡假村。

152. 答案 (A)

(A) 推薦 *(v.)*　(B) 背書 *(v.)*

(C) 信任 *(v.)*　(D) 勸告 *(v.)*

字彙：

enquire [ɪnˋkwaɪr] *(v.)* 探詢／camp [kæmp] *(n.)* 營隊／extensive [ɪkˋstɛnsɪv] *(adj.)* 廣泛的／archery [ˋɑrtʃərɪ] *(n.)* 箭術／operate [ˋɑpəˏret] *(v.)* 營運／endorse [ɪnˋdɔrs] *(v.)* 背書

Part 7. 單篇／雙篇文章理解

Questions 153-154 refer to the following bar chart.

The following bar chart displays the results of a recent study into population migration into urban centers. Both historical and projected future populations for some of the world's biggest cities are shown. From left to right each city has information for 1950, 1970, 2000 and 2015.

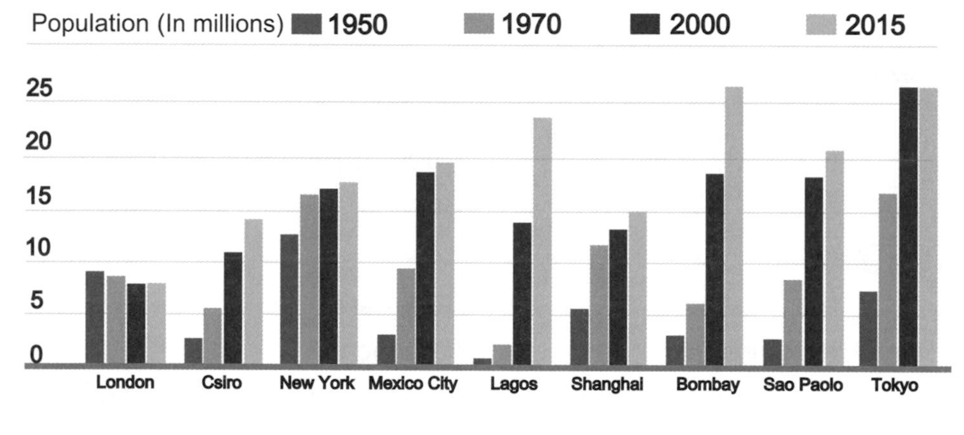

153. Which is the only city that has experienced a decline in population during the period of the study?

(A) New York

(B) London

(C) Shanghai

(D) Bombay

154. Starting from the lowest base level in 1950, which city will have had the most remarkable growth in population by 2015?

(A) Lagos

(B) Shanghai

(C) Cairo

(D) Tokyo

Questions 155-156 refer to the following advertisement.

Champions Tennis Club

Once a year Summer Sale

Annual membership now only $300 until the end of the month

All sports shop equipment reduced by 20%

Many tennis rackets buy one get one free

All members have access to the adjacent open-air swimming pool 365 days a year.

Group tennis lessons available on weekend afternoons from our experienced coaching team. Beginners always welcome. Individual lessons any Monday, Wednesday or Friday evening.

The first five club applications each morning receive free tennis balls.

Free parking always available

Offer ends August 31st

155. Where is the tennis club's swimming pool most likely to be?

(A) In a building next to the tennis courts

(B) Across the road from the tennis courts

(C) By the car park

(D) In the grounds next to the tennis courts

156. Jean and her friend have never played tennis before, when could they have lessons?

(A) Sunday afternoon

(B) Saturday morning

(C) Thursday evening

(D) Wednesday evening

Questions 157-158 refer to the following work tender.

Tender issued for Carter Bridge renovation

The public works bureau is seeking a contractor for major renovations of Carter Bridge on Interstate 67.

The estimated cost of Carter Bridge project is $6 million.

The project involves retrofit to bring the bridge up to new federal earthquake resistance standards and the replacement of deteriorating components, specifically the road surface, sidewalks, lighting system, barriers and the concrete surface of supporting pillars. Work is required to be completed within 94 weeks after the award of the contract.

The successful bidder will be required to retain a state licensed quality verification officer for the duration of the contract.

Bidding will close on March 14

157. What is this tender for?

(A) To test Carter bridge's ability to withstand earthquakes

(B) To build Carter Bridge

(C) To repair Carter Bridge and to bring it up to modern standards

(D) To employ a quality verification officer

158. What happens on March 14?

(A) The contract will be awarded.

(B) No more contractors will be considered.

(C) The work must be completed.

(D) The work must start.

Questions 159-162 refer to the following article.

Every morning, as he has done for thirty years, Daha Abeer walks to a small alley outside New Delhi's high court. He sets up a rickety wooden table and a plastic chair, and carefully places his most prized possession on the table - a twenty-year-old typewriter.

Abeer is one of the last of a long Indian tradition of street typists, but they are dying out fast.

As he sits waiting for his first customer of the day, he reminisces about the past. "A decade ago I wouldn't have had time to chat," he says. "People would be lining up to have things typed. Court papers, legal drafts, wedding invitations and even love letters. I've typed them all, but look at us now." And he points to the few other remaining typists sipping tea at their tables.

Twenty years ago there were over two thousand street typists in New Delhi, now there are only a few dozen left. The local college no longer offers typing classes. Now it is filled with students sitting in front of computers. An old Indian tradition is slowly disappearing.

159. What does Abeer do?

(A) He prepares legal drafts.
(B) He drinks tea.
(C) He writes invitations.
(D) He types other people's documents.

160. What does Abeer say about the past?

(A) That they used to be very busy
(B) That there were over 2,000 typists in New Delhi
(C) That his typewriter is very valuable
(D) That he's waiting for his first customer

161. What does this article tell us about Abeer's typewriter?

(A) That Abeer won it in a competition
(B) That Abeer cares for it a lot
(C) That it's thirty years old
(D) That Abeer wants to replace it with a computer

162. According to this article, which statement is true?

(A) No one ever uses street typists anymore.
(B) Most of the other street typists have died.
(C) Students don't learn typing anymore.
(D) Street typists' services were never very popular.

Questions 163-165 refer to the following email.

To:	Mr. Bailey
From:	Dr. Jackson

I'm writing to remind you that more than a year has passed since your last routine checkup for your diabetes.

It is important that a blood test is performed at least once a year to ensure that your medication is still at the appropriate dosage and that there has been no deterioration in your condition.

Please make an appointment with the clinic receptionist to see the clinic nurse as soon as possible. Unless there is anything you wish to discuss further in person with me, there is no need for a face to face consultation with me at this time.

Diabetes is a serious disease, and although most of its symptoms and long term effects can be treated, they cannot, as I'm sure you are aware, ever be cured. I would therefore like to remind you that it is very important not to become complacent in its treatment.

We look forward to seeing you here at this clinic in the near future.

163. After reading this email, who should Mr. Bailey telephone?

(A) Dr. Jackson

(B) The clinic nurse

(C) The clinic receptionist

(D) He doesn't need to telephone anyone.

164. Why is Dr. Jackson contacting Mr. Bailey?

(A) He wants Mr. Bailey to test to see if he has diabetes.

(B) He wants Mr. Bailey to test to see if he's been cured of diabetes.

(C) He wants Mr. Bailey to test to see if his illness has gotten any worse.

(D) He wants Mr. Bailey to test to see if he has become complacent.

165. According to this email which statement is true?

(A) Diabetes can be cured.

(B) Little can be done to help people with diabetes.

(C) The clinic receptionist can perform the blood test.

(D) Mr. Bailey's diabetes must be monitored.

Questions 166-169 refer to the following article.

A bit of a war has broken out in one well known fast food restaurant in New York between the staff and a group of Korean senior citizens. They come in every morning and apparently stay all day sharing just one carton of fries.

With coffee shops everywhere offering air-conditioning, free wi-fi and comfortable chairs just how many cups of coffee should you buy in order to sit in one all day?

According to the etiquette guide in one online magazine you should buy at least one item every hour so as not to overstay your welcome, but many don't agree. They feel that it is fine to sit on one cup of coffee for hour after hour.

It's a common site, especially in Asia, to see fast food restaurants full of students doing their homework after school, and buying very little. Many restaurants have become a substitute for the library, and many of the restaurant operators seem to have mixed feelings about them.

Some coffee shops have come up with a novel way of dealing with this problem. They offer free tea and coffee, but they charge by the minute.

166. What does this article suggest about many Asian students?

(A) That they spend little time doing their homework
(B) That they prefer fast food restaurants to libraries
(C) That they should drink more coffee
(D) That they have bad manners

167. According to this article what happens in one New York fast food restaurant every day?

(A) The staff argues with a group of elderly customers.
(B) The restaurant becomes like a library.
(C) The staff and customers often fight.
(D) The restaurant's owner gets angry with the staff.

168. What does this article suggest customers do in order to avoid overstaying their welcome?

(A) Read an online etiquette guide
(B) Only buy one cup of coffee at a restaurant
(C) Take advantage of the free wi-fi
(D) Regularly buy things if they stay a long time in a restaurant

169. How is the bill calculated at some coffee shops?

(A) They check how much coffee customers have drunk.
(B) They check how long customers have been there.
(C) They check how many novels customers have read.
(D) They don't charge customers at all.

Questions 170-172 refer to the following diary entries.

Diary entries for a new employee

Day 1: I hate being new! All first days are the same. All I did was fill in countless forms and watch the person who I will be replacing do his job. Hope tomorrow will be better. Got to see the boss a couple of times. He put his head around the door once or twice to see how I was getting on. Seems like a nice guy.

Day2: Still not doing anything. Just trying to learn everyone's names and who does what.

Day 3: Hard to remember who's who, but slowly getting there. All I did today was make a few copies and keep watching other people work.

Day 4: The boss seems to be concerned that I am already getting a little frustrated. Assured him that I am not. Need to do a better job at disguising my feelings.

Day 5: Finally given some work to do. Been checking payments all day. Very boring, but just happy to have finally been given something to do. Could have done this on my first day instead of all the watching. A big relief to be doing something that I know I can do well, and to be contributing something. Looking forward to next week!

170. On day 4, what does the new employee think he/she has to do better?

(A) Pretend that he/she is satisfied

(B) Remember people's names

(C) Work harder

(D) Look more frustrated

171. What is the new employee's main frustration throughout the first four days?

(A) That he/she can't remember everyone's names

(B) That he/she has no real work to do

(C) That the boss is worried about him/her

(D) That the other employees don't like to be watched

172. How does the new employee feel at the end of the week?

(A) Disappointed

(B) Worried

(C) Relieved

(D) Frustrated

Questions 173-176 refer to the following article.

Our son the drummer

A few years ago we decided that Jason, our recently teenage son, needed a new hobby, but something cool that he would accept and that would help him make new friends. So we bought him a drum kit and enrolled him in drum lessons at school.

We knew that it might be loud, but we thought he could practice in the garage, and as long as he didn't play at night the neighbors wouldn't mind.

That was two years ago, and little did we expect that it would become his passion. He practices almost all day in his free time, and to our surprise he has become a very accomplished musician. We even have to admit that it does sound good.

He doesn't have lessons at school anymore, he doesn't need to, and he has joined a band. This is the part that we hadn't anticipated. Since the drums are the biggest equipment in the band, they are hard to move, so the band always comes to our house to practice. The noise is incredible.

The band has played a number of shows. They have never been paid, but they don't expect to be. Hopefully one day they will, but that should be a long time in the future. They all have a lot of growing up to do before they are mature enough for that.

Some of the band members are older than Jason and that was a concern at first, but as we have got to know them, we have realized that they are all good kids just trying to have some fun. Whenever the band plays somewhere else we have to help transport the drums, so at least we always know where they are.

Our main concern was with Jason's grades at school. He was always nearer the bottom of his class than the top, but he's actually improved. He'll never be a straight A's student, but he is getting more of them. Most importantly he is now much happier at school. He has more friends and is even becoming something of star.

173. What were Jason's parents NOT concerned about?

(A) The noise
(B) Jason's grades at school
(C) The other band members
(D) The cost of the drum lessons

174. How old was Jason most likely to have been when his parents bought him the drum kit?

(A) 12 years old
(B) 13 years old
(C) 17 years old
(D) 20 years old

175. What do Jason's parents suggest is true?

(A) The drumming has made Jason more popular.
(B) Jason thinks that drums are cool.
(C) The other band members are too old.
(D) The neighbors often complain about the noise.

176. What happens when the bank play a show?

(A) They get paid.
(B) Jason's parents help with transportation.
(C) The neighbors complain about the noise.
(D) Jason becomes more popular.

Questions 177-180 refer to the following article.

Black Friday

What is Black Friday? You may think it commemorated a disaster, maybe a stock market crash or something to do with Halloween. But you would be wrong. In the United States Black Friday is actually something positive. It is the biggest shopping day of the year and marks the day that shops say that they start making a profit for the year.

Black Friday is the first Friday after Thanksgiving. It is not a public holiday, but many schools and offices do not open on that day. Retailers regard it as marking the start of the Christmas shopping season. Many stores open early, or more recently stay open all night, and major discounts are offered to attract shoppers looking for bargains. Many people try to get all their Christmas shopping on this one day.

The origin of the term is not clear, but records of its use appear in Philadelphia in the late 1950s referring to heavy traffic on the roads the day after Thanksgiving. In the 1970s the term was picked up by major retail stores. According to the explanation, they operated at a financial loss, or “in the red” from January to November. Black Friday was the day of the year that they turned a profit, or “in the black.”

In recent years Black Friday has started to gain a more negative image. Large crowds have been gathering outside major stores waiting for the doors to be opened. There have been many cases where violence has broken out among the queuing crowds with too many people trying to be first in line. Then once inside the stores many fights have been reported over limited stocks of sale merchandise. TV news networks annually show videos of housewives fighting over the last children’s doll.

In the last few years, some international chains have attempted to introduce the Black Friday concept in their stores in other countries, in order to boost their Christmas sales. Black Friday could be coming to a store near you soon!

177. What does Black Friday usually refer to?

(A) The day that stores start to make money
(B) A public holiday
(C) The day that housewives fight for toys
(D) A bad day for major retail stores

178. What does the article say has changed about Black Friday in recent years?

(A) Black Friday is now on the Friday after Thanksgiving.
(B) Black Friday is no longer a public holiday.
(C) Shoppers have become more aggressive.
(D) Black Friday shoppers buy their Christmas presents.

179. What is Black Friday NOT associated with?

(A) Increased traffic on roads
(B) Sales at shops and malls
(C) Christmas shopping
(D) Halloween

180. Where does the term 'Black Friday' come from?

(A) The streets of Philadelphia
(B) Some international chain stores
(C) No one knows for sure.
(D) Christmas shopping

Questions 181-185 refer to the following emails.

📖To:	Alex Wong, First Auto Tech
From:	Jonathan Hague, Sports Auto

I'm writing further to our meeting at the Detroit Auto show last week. I hope that you had a pleasant trip back to Taiwan.

We were very happy to meet you, and we were impressed with your presentation during the show.

As I told you at the show, I would be in contact with you once we were back at our base in Nevada. So this email is just to initiate contact.

We are very interested in your exterior auto accessories. We believe that there is nothing else like it on the market here, and so we would like to open discussions with you about importing them.

📖To:	Jonathan Hague, Sports Auto
From:	Alex Wong, First Auto Tech

Thank you for your email. We had a good flight back to Taiwan.

I recall our meeting at the auto show. If I remember rightly Sports Auto are the biggest customizers of sports cars in the state of Nevada.

I think that we should be able to develop a mutually beneficial partnership to supply our accessories to you for your market.

At this early stage I suggest that you choose some accessories that you think could be suitable for your market, and we can send them to you as samples. After you have a better idea of what you can use, I would be happy to host you for a visit to our factory and offices here in Taiwan.

181. What is the purpose of Jonathan Hague's email?

(A) To introduce himself
(B) To import auto accessories
(C) To initiate email contact
(D) To arrange a meeting

182. What does Sports Auto do?

(A) It manufactures cars.
(B) It alters the appearance of cars.
(C) It makes exterior auto accessories.
(D) It holds auto shows.

183. According to the emails, what will NOT happen?

(A) First Auto Tech will receive a bill for the samples.
(B) Jonathan Hague will visit Taiwan.
(C) First Auto Tech will send some samples.
(D) Sports Auto will customize cars.

184. If things go well in the two company's business relationship, what might happen in the future?

(A) Alex Wong might travel to Nevada.
(B) First Auto Tech might purchase Sports Auto's products.
(C) Jonathan Hague might visit Alex Wong at the Detroit Auto Show.
(D) Jonathan Hague might visit Alex Wong in Taiwan.

185. What would be the most likely next step in the company's relationship?

(A) For Sports Auto to choose which samples they would like
(B) For Jonathan Hague to visit Taiwan
(C) For First Auto Tech to send Sports Auto some samples
(D) For Sports Auto to try to sell First Auto Tech's products in Nevada

Questions 186-190 refer to the following email and travel itinerary.

📖To:	Star Travel
From:	Mary Hamako

My family and I are planning a vacation to Los Angeles next month. Can you please send me flight times, itinerary and prices for your cheapest flight. The family consists of my husband, my teenage son and me.

We are planning to leave Tokyo on Sunday April 27th and to be away for around ten days.

We will be staying with friends in Los Angeles, so we do not require hotel accommodation there.

Thank you for your help in advance.

To:	Mary Hamako
From:	Star Travel

Here is the schedule for the cheapest flight from Tokyo to Los Angeles. This flight is not direct. It requires a change of planes in Hawaii.

OUTBOUND

Flight BN 071	Depart Tokyo 09:15	Arrive Hawaii 16:15
OR		
Flight BN 069	Depart Tokyo 11:25	Arrive Hawaii 18:15
Flight BN 072	Depart Hawaii 18:20	Arrive Los Angeles 05:30 (next day)

INBOUND

Flight BN 053	Depart Los Angeles 08:55	Arrive Hawaii 12:55
Flight BN 051	Depart Hawaii 14:45	Arrive Tokyo 17:30

All flights depart weekdays only
Adult ticket 150,000 Yen
Child (under 12) 110,000 Yen

A two day stopover in Hawaii is available, but you must choose the earlier flight departing Tokyo if you do not wish to stay in Hawaii.

We offer special prices on hotels in Los Angeles, if purchased with your airline tickets. Tours of Los Angeles are also available at great rates. Please let us know if you would like us to book them as well.

Please note all prices are only valid if purchased within a week.

186. Why will the Hamato family have to alter their travel plans?

(A) They do not wish to stopover in Hawaii.

(B) There is no flight from Tokyo on April 27th.

(C) A hotel must be booked with the flight tickets.

(D) The ticket only allows travelers to be away for one week.

187. If the Hamato family don't want to stopover in Hawaii, what will their Tokyo departure time be?

(A) 09:15

(B) 11:25

(C) 18:20

(D) 08:55

188. What hasn't Star Travel paid attention to in Mary Hamato's email?

(A) That the Hamato family want to go to Los Angeles, not Hawaii

(B) That the Hamato family want the cheapest price

(C) That there are three people in the Hamato family

(D) That the Hamato family don't need hotel accommodation in Los Angeles

189. If the Hamato family decide to take this trip, what do they have to do?

(A) Email star travel

(B) Book within the next seven days

(C) Decide on a hotel in Los Angeles

(D) Talk to their friends in Los Angeles

190. How much would be the total cost for the Hamato's tickets?

(A) 410,000 Yen

(B) 450,000 Yen

(C) 370,000 Yen

(D) More than 450,000 Yen

Questions 191-195 refer to the following two articles.

Undergraduate Geology Test: Write 200 words on Earthquakes

Earthquakes: By Linda Miles

An Earthquake is a sudden release of pressure within the Earth's crust that releases waves of movement all the way up to ground level where shaking can be experienced. The intensity (magnitude) of shaking relates to how far away the earthquake was and how deep within the Earth's crust.

Most earthquakes occur around the edges of the Earth's tectonic plates. These giant pieces of the Earth's crust are floating on a sea of molten rock deep within the Earth. These tectonic plates are moving slowly, and although the movement is only a couple of centimeters each year, this movement causes huge pressure and stores of energy to be created where two or more plates collide. This sudden release of energy is an earthquake. The pushing together of tectonic plates has also resulted in the creation of most of the Earth's mountain ranges.

Earthquakes are measured on an open ended magnitude scale. The majority of earthquakes are lower than magnitude 4, and usually go unnoticed. Earthquakes of magnitude 5 to 7 are likely to cause significant problems to the nearby areas. Anything above that can result in extreme damage and loss of life over a large area. The highest recorded earthquake was measured at a magnitude of 9.5 in 1960.

Earthquakes essay- Instructor's comments

This is a clear and concise attempt at the test question. It is well structured and easy to understand.

The explanation on the causes of earthquakes has good detail and is accurate.

The description of the magnitude scale is quite vague and too long for an essay of only 200 words.

Only one example of an earthquake is included in the essay, but despite identifying the correct earthquake the affected country of Chile was not mentioned.

The essay only focuses on earthquakes along tectonic plates. There is no mention of earthquakes in other areas or most importantly of undersea earthquakes and the resulting risk of tsunamis. The relationship between earthquakes and volcanoes was also overlooked.

The inclusion in the essay of an account of how mountain ranges are formed would be more suitable for an essay on plate tectonics, especially as the above topics were not included.

Grade: B+

191. According to these articles, what is the result of the majority of earthquakes?

(A) They cause significant problems.
(B) They cause tsunamis.
(C) They create mountains.
(D) Nobody notices them.

192. According to these articles, what causes an earthquake?

(A) Volcanoes
(B) Tsunamis
(C) The collision of tectonic plates
(D) Molten rock under the Earth's crust

193. According to these articles, where was the biggest earthquake ever recorded?

(A) In Chile
(B) Under the sea
(C) In the earth's crust
(D) On a tectonic plate

194. Which topic did the instructor NOT suggest should have been included?

(A) The cause of earthquakes
(B) Volcanoes
(C) Tsunamis
(D) Undersea earthquakes

195. According to these articles, where can earthquakes be experienced?

(A) Near volcanoes
(B) Along the edges of tectonic plates
(C) In Chile
(D) Anywhere

Questions 196-200 refer to the following articles.

Earning your own money by Debra Gates

All young people know what it is like to ask their parents for money, and I'm no exception. The only difference is that I am 17 years old and I have a job. I didn't want to have to keep seeing the looks on my parents' faces when I asked them for money, so I found a weekend job.

What do I do? I work at the local convenience store. I wasn't sure what would happen when I went for an interview, and I was really surprised when I was accepted. It's hard work though. I often have to stack shelves, and sometimes I work at the cash register. The first time I did that was a little frightening. It was the first time I'd had to deal with money.

I work one shift every Saturday and Sunday. I have to miss some time with my friends, and I still need to get all my schoolwork done, but it's definitely worth it.

I've become much more independent since I started working. I can choose when and where to spend my money. I've found that I even spend less and save more. Even my parents have come around to the idea of me working now, although that was not the case at first.

I'm going to university next year, and I'm very excited about that. I'll definitely keep working then. There is no way that I'll give up my independence now that I have achieved it. By the time I go to university, I should have enough money saved to buy a motorcycle, but that's just between you and me!

Our daughter independent daughter

Our daughter, Debra, is a very headstrong, independent seventeen-year-old. We've always supported her in everything she has done; even when she started working, although she should have at least asked us about it first. She is still a minor after all.

We think that her part-time job at a convenience store is a marvelous idea, and as long as she still has time for all her studies, we're happy for it to continue. We're not so keen on some of the hours she has to work though. Sometimes she has a shift that finishes late at night or even in the early morning on Saturday or Sunday. It's not a good time for her to be coming home on her own, and how does she find the time to sleep?

She'll be leaving home next year for university. We have mixed feelings about this. On the one hand, it'll be great to have the house to ourselves, but we will worry. Debra might be very intelligent, but sometimes she does make some rash decisions without thinking it through.

196. What is one of the main reasons that Debra wanted a job?

(A) To be more financially independent from her parents
(B) To buy more things
(C) To stay out late
(D) To learn how to deal with money

197. What do the two articles disagree about?

(A) Whether Debra should go to university or not
(B) The shifts that Debra has to work
(C) Whether Debra's parents initially supported her or not about her job
(D) Whether Debra has enough time to study or not

198. What concerns Debra's parents about her job?

(A) That Debra spends less time with her friends
(B) What Debra spends the money she earns on
(C) That Debra will buy a motorcycle
(D) The late shifts that Debra has to work

199. What might Debra do at university that her parents consider rash?

(A) Get a job
(B) Buy a motorcycle
(C) Leave home
(D) Become headstrong

200. What annoyed Debra's parents when she started working?

(A) That Debra had become independent
(B) That Debra hadn't discussed it with them first
(C) That Debra can spend her own money
(D) That Debra had a job

Part 7. 單篇／雙篇文章理解

第 153-154 題

以下長條圖展示近期人口遷入城市中心的結果。皆為世界上一些最大城市，歷年與推斷未來人口的現象。從左至右，有每個城市在1950年、1970年、2000年和2015年的資料。

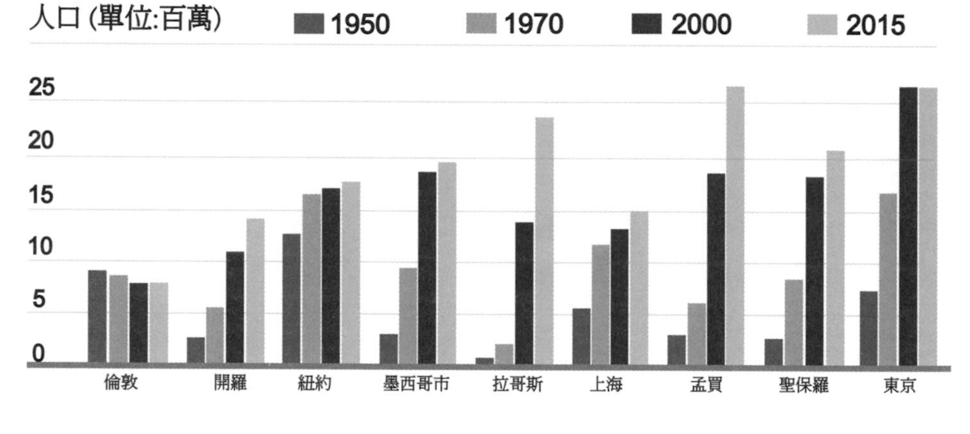

153. 答案 (B) 哪一個是唯一在研究期間，經歷人口下降的城市？

(A) 紐約　　(B) 倫敦

(C) 上海　　(D) 孟買

154. 答案 (A) 以1950年最低基本程度來看，哪一個城市將會在2015年的人口有最驚人成長？

(A) 拉哥斯　　(B) 上海

(C) 開羅　　(D) 東京

字彙：

migration [maɪˋgreʃən] *(n.)* 遷移／ bar chart *(n.)* 長條圖／ historical [hɪsˋtɔrɪkḷ] *(adj.)* 歷年的／ project [prəˋdʒekt] *(v.)* 推斷／ information [ˌɪnfɚˋmeʃən] *(n.)* 資料／ population [ˌpɑpjəˋleʃən] *(n.)* 人口／ remarkable [rɪˋmɑrkəbḷ] *(adj.)* 驚人的／ growth [groθ] *(n.)* 成長

第 155-156 題

冠軍網球俱樂部

一年一次的夏季出清

一年期會員現在只要 300 美金，優惠只到本月底

所有運動配備降價 20%

多款網球拍買一送一

所有會員，全年 365 天可使用毗鄰的露天游泳池。

團體網球課在週末下午有開課，由我們經驗豐富的教練團指導。歡迎初學者。個人課在星期一、三、五傍晚。

每天早上前五位到俱樂部申請，會得到免費的網球。

停車免收費

此優惠到八月三十一日為止

155. 答案 (D) 網球俱樂部的游泳池最可能位於哪裡？

(A) 在網球場隔壁的建築物內 (B) 在網球場對面

(C) 在停車場旁邊 (D) 在網球場隔壁的場地

解說 原文第五行，“the adjacent open-air swimming pool”，說明是毗鄰的露天游泳池，所以不可能是選項 (A) 或 (C)，因為露天不可以在建築物內，而對面並非毗鄰的位置，選項 (C)，比較不合邏輯，因為是網球俱樂部，故最有可能的游泳池地點是在網球場旁邊，故選 (D)。

156. 答案 (A) Jean 和她的朋友以前從來沒打過網球，他們什麼時候有課程可以參加？

(A) 星期日下午 (B) 星期六上午

(C) 星期四傍晚 (D) 星期三傍晚

解說 原文第七和八行，“Group tennis lessons available on weekend afternoons from our experienced coaching team. Beginners always welcome”，說明團體課有週末下午的課程，觀迎初學者，星期六、日是週末，故選 (A)。選項 (D)，是個人課的時間，並未說明初學者可參加。選項 (B)、(C) 的時段皆無課程可供參加。

字彙：

champion [ˋtʃæmpɪən] *(n.)* 冠軍／ equipment [ɪˋkwɪpmənt] *(n.)* 配備／ racket [ˋrækɪt] *(n.)* 球拍／ adjacent [əˋdʒesənt] *(adj.)* 毗鄰的／ experienced [ɪkˋspɪrɪənst] *(adj.)* 經驗豐富的／ coaching [ˋkotʃɪŋ] *(n.)* 當教練；指導／ open-air [ˋopən] [ɛr] *(n.)* 露天／ application [ˏæpləˋkeʃən] *(n.)* 申請

第 157-158 題

發佈更新 Carter 橋的投標

公共營造處正在尋求替 67 號州際公路上的 Carter 橋，進行大更新的承包商。

預計 Carter 橋工程花費約六百萬美金 。

工程包括翻新改進，讓橋達到新的聯邦抗震標準，以及更換退化的組件，尤其是路面、人行道、照明系統、護欄和支柱橋墩的水泥表面。工程需要在授與合約後的 94 週內完工。

成功的得標者，在履行合約期間 ，將需要一位有執照的州品質認證員。

投標將在三月十四日截止

157. 答案 (C) 這個投標是為了什麼？

(A) 測試 Carter 橋對抗地震的能耐

(B) 建造 Carter 橋

(C) 修繕 Carter 橋，並把它弄成符合現代規定

(D) 雇用品質認證員

解說 原文第三段第一句，"retrofit to bring the bridge up to new federal earthquake resistance standards"，表示要翻新並符合新的聯邦抗震規定，故選 (C)。

158. 答案 (B) 三月十四日會發生什麼事？

(A) 將授予合約

(B) 不會再考慮更多的承包商

(C) 工程必須完成

(D) 工程必須開始

解說 原文最後一句，"Bidding will close on March 14"，表示這一天投標結束，不會再收件或是考慮後來才投標的承包商，故選 (B)。

字彙：

tender [ˋtɛndɚ] *(v.)* 投標（＋for）／ issued [ˋɪʃjʊ] *(v.)* 發佈／ renovation [ˏrɛnəˋveʃən] *(n.)* 更新／ bureau [ˋbjʊro] *(n.)*（政府機構的）處；局／ contractor [ˋkɑntræktɚ] *(n.)* 承包商／ interstate [ˏɪntɚˋstet] *(n.)* 州際公路／ deteriorate [dɪˋtɪrɪəˏret] *(v.)* 惡化；退化／ retrofit [ˋrɛtrəfɪt] *(v.)* 做翻新改進

第 159-162 題

每天早晨，一如他三十年來每天做的，Daha Abeer 步行至 新德里的高地外，一處小巷。他設置好一個不牢固的木製桌子和一張塑膠椅，然後小心地擺放他最有價值的財產在桌上，一台用了二十年的打字機。

Abeer 是在印度古老傳統中，碩果僅存的街頭打字員之一，但是這些打字員很快地沒落了。

當他坐著等他今天第一位上門的顧客時，他追憶過去。「十年前，我連閒聊的時間都沒有，」他說。「人會排隊要東西被打字出來。法院文件、法律草案、婚禮邀請函，甚至情書。這些我都打字過，但是看看我們現在的情況。」然後他指向幾個在他們的桌子啜茶，仍從事打字工作的人。

二十年前，在新德里有超過兩千名街頭打字員，現在只有剩下一些。當地大學不再提供打字課程。現在全是坐在電腦前的學生。古老的印度傳統正慢慢地消失。

159. 答案 (D) Abeer 從事什麼樣的工作？

(A) 他準備法律草案　(B) 他喝茶

(C) 他寫邀請函　(D) 他打字別人的文件

解說　原文第三段第三句，“People would be lining up to have things typed. Court papers, legal drafts, wedding invitations and even love letters. I've typed them all,”，可以知道他說的這些項目他的代客打字過，表示他從事替別人打字的工作，故選 (D)。

160. 答案 (A) Abeer 敘述什麼關於過去？

(A) 他們過去十分忙碌　(B) 以前新德里有超過兩千名打字員

(C) 他的打字機十分貴重　(D) 他正在等他第一位上門的顧客

解說　原文第三段第一句，“he reminisces about the past. ‘A decade ago I

wouldn't have had time to chat,' he says. 'People would be lining up to have things typed'"，他回憶道十年之前，他忙碌到連跟客人閒聊的時間都沒有，客人大排長龍要請他將文件打字，故選 (A)。選項 (B)、(C)、(D) 在文章中均有陳述，但不是由 Abeer 敘述。

161. 答案 (B) 這篇文章告訴我們什麼關於 Abeer 的打字機？

(A) Abeer 在比賽中贏得它　　(B) Abeer 很在乎它

(C) 它已經用了三十年　　(D) Abeer 想要以電腦取代它

解說　原文第一段第二句，"carefully places his most prized possession on the table"，顯示 Abeer 對他的打字機的呵護，表示很在乎它，故選 (B)。選項 (A)、(D) 並未在文章中提及。選項 (C)，第一段第二句，"a twenty-year-old typewriter"，表示他的打字機應是用了二十年的打字機，而不是三十年。

162. 答案 (C) 根據這篇文章，以下哪一個敘述為事實？

(A) 再也沒有人用街頭打字員了

(B) 大部分其他街頭打字員都死了

(C) 學生們再也不學習打字

(D) 街頭打字員們的服務從來都不是受歡迎的

解說　原文最後一段第二句，"The local college no longer offers typing classes，表示學校再也沒有打字課，所以學生們不再學習打字，故選 (C)。

字彙：

alley [ˋælɪ] *(n.)* 小巷／ rickety [ˋrɪkɪtɪ] *(adj.)* 不牢固的／ possession [pəˋzɛʃən] *(n.)* 財產／ reminisce [ˏrɛməˋnɪs] *(v.)* 追憶／ sip [sɪp] *(v.)* 啜飲／ draft [dræft] *(n.)* 草稿／ disappear [ˏdɪsəˋpɪr] *(v.)* 消失／ typewriter [ˋtaɪpˏraɪtɚ] *(n.)* 打字機

第 163-165 題

收件人：Bailey 先生
寄件人：Jackson 醫師

我寫信來提醒你，自你最後一次例行性的糖尿病檢查至今，已經過了一年多。

很重要的是，血液檢驗最少要一年進行一次，以確保你的用藥物治療仍在合適的劑量，以及病情沒有惡化。

請與診所接待員預約，儘快回診診所護理人員。除非有任何你想要更進一步與我私下討論的問題，這個時候不需要和我進行面對面的咨詢。

糖尿病是個嚴重的疾病，雖然大部分的症狀和長期影響可以被治療，但是疾病本身無法被治癒，我相信你意識到，是永遠不能被治癒的。因此我想提醒你，很重要的是，不要在它的療法裡變得自滿。

我們期待在不久的未來，在這間診所裡見到你。

163. 答案 (C) 在看完這封郵件之後，Bailey 先生應該會打電話給誰？

(A) Jackson 醫師
(B) 診所的護理人員
(C) 診所的接待員
(D) 他不需要打電話給任何人

解說　原文第三段第一句，"Please make an appointment with the clinic receptionist"，表示醫師建議他先致電診所接待員預約時間，故選 (C)。

164. 答案 (C) 為什麼 Jackson 醫師聯繫 Bailey 先生？

(A) 他想要 Bailey 做檢查看他是否有糖尿病
(B) 他想要 Bailey 先生做檢查看他的糖尿病是否痊癒
(C) 他想要 Bailey 先生做檢查看他的病況是否惡化
(D) 他想要 Bailey 先生 檢查看他是否變得自滿

解說　原文第二段，"It is important that a blood test is performed at least once a year to ensure that your medication is still at the appropriate dosage and that there has been no deterioration in your condition"，顯示他想要確保 Bailey 先生的用藥劑量與病況是否維持良好狀態，故選 (C)。

165. 答案 (D) 根據這封郵件，以下哪一個敘述正確？

(A) 糖尿病可以被治癒

(B) 對患有糖尿病的人能做的幫助不多

(C) 診所接待員能執行血液檢驗

(D) Bailey 先生的糖尿病必須被監控

解說 原文第四段第一句，"although most of its symptoms and long term effects can be treated"，表示病情是可以治療控制的，以及第二句，"not to become complacent in its treatment"，表示不要因為感覺良好就忽視病情的發展，表示 Bailey 先生的糖尿病病情需要追蹤，故選擇 (D)。選項 (A)，原文第四段第二句，"they cannot"，以及 "ever be cured"，明確指出糖尿病永遠無法被治癒。選項 (B)，文章中說明糖尿病的症狀和帶來的影響均可被治療。選項 (C)，文章說明執行血液檢驗的人是診所的護理人員。

字彙：

diabetes [ˌdaɪə`bitiz] *(n.)* 糖尿病／ medication [ˌmɛdɪ`keʃən] *(n.)* 藥物治療／ dosage [`dosɪdʒ] *(n.)* 劑量／ consultation [ˌkɑnsəl`teʃən] *(n.)* 咨詢／ complacent [kəm`plesnt] *(adj.)* 自滿的／ cure [kjʊr] *(v.)* 治癒／ monitor [`mɑnətə] *(v.)* 監控

第 166-169 題

紐約知名速食餐廳，爆發員工和一群年長的韓國紐約市民之間像戰爭的紛爭。他們每個早上都會來，而且顯然地待上一整天，只分著吃一份薯條。

在任何有提供冷氣、免費無線上網，以及舒適坐椅的咖啡 ，為了整天坐在一間咖啡店裡，你應該要買上幾杯咖啡？

依據一個線上雜誌的禮節指南，你應該至少每小時買一項產品，這樣你的光臨才不會讓人覺得逗留過久，但是很多人不同意。他們覺得一個小時接一個小時過去，坐在那只買一杯咖啡沒什麼問題。

它是個普遍的場所，尤其是在亞洲，會看見速食餐廳滿是在放學後寫作業的學生，而且只買很少的東西。許多餐廳已變成圖書館的替代品，許多餐廳經營者似乎對他們有複雜的感覺。

一些咖啡店已想出一個新奇的方法，來處理這個問題。他們提供免費的茶和咖啡，但是他們計時收費。

166. 答案 (B) 這個文章暗示什麼關於許多亞洲學生？

(A) 他們花很少時間寫他們的功課

(B) 他們比較喜歡速食餐廳勝於圖書館

(C) 他們應該喝多一點咖啡

(D) 他們規矩不好

解說 原文第四段第二句，"Many restaurants have become a substitute for the library"，指出餐廳成了圖書館的替代品，暗示很多在速食店做功課的學生，不去圖書館而是去餐廳的原因是比較喜歡在餐廳，故選 (B)。

167. 答案 (A) 依據這篇文章，一間紐約速食餐廳每天發生什麼事？

(A) 員工和一群年老的顧客爭論 (B) 餐廳變得像圖書館

(C) 員工和顧客常常起爭執 (D) 餐廳的老闆對員工生氣

解說 原文第一段第一句，"A bit of a war has broken out in one well known fast food restaurant in New York between the staff and a group of Korean senior citizens. They come in every morning"，說名紐約知名速食餐廳員工與一群年長顧客的紛爭，而且這群顧客每天早上都會來光顧，故選 (A)。

168. 答案 (D) 這篇文章提出顧客可以做什麼，來避免自己的光臨讓人覺得逗留過久？

(A) 閱讀線上禮節指南

(B) 在餐廳只買一杯咖啡

(C) 利用免費無線上網

(D) 如果在餐廳裡長時間停留，規律地買東西

解說 原文第三段第一句，"you should buy at least one item every hour so as not to overstay your welcome"，文章依據一個線上雜誌的禮節指南建議消費者，每個小時購買一項東西，就不會讓店家覺得不歡迎你的光臨，故選 (D)。

169. 答案 (B) 一些咖啡店如何計算帳單？

(A) 他們檢查顧客喝了多少咖啡

(B) 他們檢查顧客在那裡待多久

(C) 他們檢查顧客讀了幾本小說

(D) 他們完全不跟顧客收費

解說　原文最後一段，“Some coffee shops have come up with a novel way of dealing with this problem. They offer free tea and coffee, but they charge by the minute”，説明一些咖啡店採計時收費的新奇做法，故選 (B)。選項 (A)，原文最後一段，提到一些咖啡店提供免費的茶和咖啡，故此選項不正確。選項 (C)，在文章中的 novel「新奇的」，是形容詞而不是名詞的「小説」，文章中未提及咖啡店裡有供應小説。選項 (D)，文章指出，一些咖啡店採計時收費。

字彙：

break out *(ph.)* 爆發／ apparently [əˋpærəntlɪ] *(adv.)* 顯然地／ etiquette [ˋɛtɪkɛt] *(n.)* 行規；禮節／ site [saɪt] *(n.)* 場所／ substitute [ˋsʌbstə͵tjut] *(n.)* 替代物／ operator [ˋɑpə͵retɚ] *(n.)* 經營者／ novel [ˋnɑvḷ] *(adj.)* 新奇的／ overstay [ˋovɚˋste] *(v.)* 逗留過久

第 170-172 題

一名新進員工的日記

第一天：我討厭當新人！所有的第一天都一樣。所有我做的事就是填寫數不清的表格，還有看著我將替補他職位的人做些什麼。希望明天會比較好。必須去見老闆幾次。他探頭在門邊偷看我一兩次，好看我適應的如何。似乎是個很好的人。

第二天：仍然沒有做什麼事。只是試著學每個人的名字與工作內容。

第三天：很難記得誰是誰，但是有慢慢地記起來。今天我做的事只有影印幾張資料，以及繼續看別人工作。

第四天：老闆似乎擔心我已經有點沮喪。我向他保證我沒有。我需要把我的情緒掩飾得更好。

第五天：終於給了我一些工作做。整天都在檢查支付的款項。非常乏味，但是就是很開心終於給了些東西讓我做。大可在第一天就做這件事，而不是只在一旁觀看。知道我能做某件事很好，並貢獻一些心力，讓我鬆了一口氣。期待下星期！

170. 答案 (A) 在第四天，這位新進員工認為他 / 他應該把什麼做得更好？

(A) 假裝他 / 她滿意　　(B) 記得人的名字

(C) 更努力工作　　(C) 看起來更沮喪

解說 原文第四段第一句，"The boss seems to be concerned that I am already getting a little" frustrated，表示老闆擔心他沮喪；第二句，"Assured him that I am not. Need to do a better job at disguising my feelings"，他向老闆保證他沒有沮喪，然後他說自己應該把情緒掩飾的更好，意味他的情緒是沮喪的，要掩飾成相反的滿意樣子，故選 (A)。

171. 答案 (B) 新進員工在整個前四天主要的沮喪是什麼？

(A) 他 / 她不能記得每個人的名字

(B) 他 / 她沒有真正的工作可作

(C) 老闆擔心他 / 她

(D) 其他員工不喜歡被盯著看

解說 原文第一段第二句，"All I did was fill in countless forms and watch the person who I will be replacing do his job"，表示第一天只填表格和在一旁看；第二段第一句，"Still not doing anything"，表示第二天跟第一天一樣什麼也沒做；第三段第一句，"All I did today was make a few copies and keep watching other people work"，表示只印了幾張文件就又在一旁看；第四段第三句，"Need to do a better job at disguising my feelings"，他的沮喪是真的，因為他說必須把自己的情緒掩飾好一點，第五段第一句，"Finally given some work to do"，直到第五天他覺得終於有一些工作可做，代表在那之前他認為自己都沒有做些什麼工作，所以前四天的沮喪是因為這個因素，故選 (B)。

172. 答案 (C) 這名新進員工在一週結束時有什麼感覺？

(A) 失望 (B) 擔心

(C) 放鬆 (D) 沮喪

解說 原文第五段倒數第二句，"A big relief"，以及最後一句，"Looking forward to next week!"，可以知道這名新進員工在過完這一週時感到放鬆了，並期待下星期的到來。

字彙：

entry [ˋɛntrɪ] *(n.)* 作品／ countless [ˋkaʊntlɪs] *(adj.)* 數不清的／ frustrated [ˋfrʌstretɪd] *(adj.)* 沮喪的／ disguise [dɪsˋgaɪz] *(v.)* 掩飾／ payment [ˋpemənt] *(n.)* 支付的款項／ relief [rɪˋlif] *(n.)* 放鬆／ contribute *(v.)* 貢獻／ look forward to *(ph.)* 期待

第 173-176 題

我們的鼓手兒子

幾年之前我們決定，Jason，我們最近進入青少年的兒子，需要一個新嗜好，但是要是某種很酷的事所以他才會接受，才會幫助他交到新朋友。所以我們買了一組鼓給他，並登記他參加學校的打鼓課程。

我們知道那可能會很大聲，但是我們認為他可以在車庫裡練習，而且只要他不在晚上打，鄰居並不介意。

那是兩年前，我們有一點點期待那會成為他的熱忱。他幾乎每天的空閒時間都在練習，並且讓我們驚訝的是，他成為了一個非常有造詣的音樂家。我們甚至必須承認那聽起來很動聽。

他再也沒有上學校的打鼓課了，他不需要，而且他加入了一個樂團。這是我們沒有預料到的部分。由於鼓是樂團裡最大的樂器，很難搬移，所以樂團總是來我們的家練習。那些聲響極好聽。

樂團演奏了幾場表演。他們不曾收到表演費，但是他們也不期待會有。希望有一天會收到表演酬勞，但是那應該會是很久以後的未來。他們都有很大的成長空間，在他們夠成熟收費表演之前。

一些樂團員比 Jason 的年紀還大，而那是一開始擔心的事，但是一旦我們認識他們，我們了解到他們全是只想找點樂趣的好孩子。無論何時樂團在什麼地方表演，我們必須幫忙搬運鼓，所以至少我們都知道他們在哪。

我們主要的擔心是 Jason 的在校成績。他總是接近班上最後的排名而不是前面，但是他真的進步了。他永遠不會是各科滿分的學生，但是他的分數漸漸比較好了。最重要的是，他在學校快樂多了。他有更多的朋友，而且甚至成了一個風雲人物。

173. 答案 (D) Jason 的父母不擔心關於什麼？

(A) 噪音　　(B) Jason 的在校成績

(C) 其他樂團成員　　(D) 打鼓課的價錢

解說　選項 (A)，原文第二段，"We knew that it might be loud, but we thought he could practice in the garage, and as long as he didn't play at night the neighbors wouldn't mind"，表示擔心。選項 (B)，

原文第七段第一句，"Our main concern was with Jason's grades at school"，表示最擔心。選項 (C)，原文第六段第一句，"Some of the band members are older than Jason and that was a concern at first"，表示一開始有擔心。只有選項 (D) 未在文中提及，故選 (D)。

174. 答案 (B) 他的父母買給他一套鼓的時候，Jason 最可能是什麼年紀？

(A) 12 years old　　(B) 13 years old
(C) 17 years old　　(D) 20 years old

解說 原文第一段第一句，"Jason, our recently teenage son,"，青少年是指 13 至 19 歲，剛進入青少年應該選 (B)，選項 (C) 雖也是青少年的年紀，但是較為後期的青少年時期。

175. 答案 (A) Jason 的父母建議何為事實？

(A) 打鼓讓 Jason 更受歡迎　　(B) Jason 認為打鼓很酷
(C) 樂團裡其他成員年紀太大　　(D) 鄰居常常抱怨關於噪音

解說 原文最後一段最後一句，"He has more friends and is even becoming something of star"，表示這讓他更受歡迎，故選 (A)。選項 (B)，原文第一段第一句，"but something cool that he would accept"，是父母認為鼓很酷，不是 Jason 認為。選項 (C)，原文第六段第一句，"Some of the band members are older than Jason"，是指一些年紀比 Jason 大，並沒有說全部都太老。選項 (D)，並未在文中提及。

176. 答案 (B) 當樂團要表演時會發生什麼？

(A) 他們收到表演費　　(B) Jason 的父母會幫忙搬運
(C) 鄰居抱怨關於噪音　　(D) Jason 變得更受歡迎

解說 原文第六段第二句，"Whenever the band plays somewhere else we have to help transport the drums"，表示父母必須幫忙搬運鼓，故選 (B)。選項 (A)，原文第五段第二句，"They have never been paid"，表示不曾收到表演酬勞。選項 (C)、(D) 在原文未提及會在表演時發生。

字彙：

enroll [ɪn`rol] *(v.)* 登記／ accomplished [ə`kɑmplɪʃt] *(adj.)* 有造詣的／ admit [əd`mɪt] *(v.)* 承認／ anticipate [æn`tɪsə͵pet] *(v.)* 預料／ incredible [ɪn`krɛdəbl̩] *(adj.)* 極好的／ mature [mə`tjʊr] *(adj.)* 成熟的／ concern [kən`sɝn] *(v.)* 擔心／ transportation [͵trænspɚ`teʃən] *(n.)* 搬運；運輸

Test 1 Test 2 Test 3 Test 4 Test 5

第 177-180 題

黑色星期五

什麼是黑色星期五？你可能認為它是慶祝災難，也許是股市崩盤或是某種跟萬聖節有關的事。但是你會是錯的。在美國，黑色星期五其實是某種正面的事。它是一年中最大的購物日，並且當天表示店家開始在一年中獲利。

黑色星期五是感恩節後的第一個星期五。不是國定假日，但是很多學校和辦公室在那天不會開。零售商把它視為聖誕季節購物的開始標誌。很多商店很早開門，或是最近地是整晚營業，並提供最大的折扣吸引尋找特價品的購物者。很多人試著在這一天買齊所有聖誕節要採買的東西。

這個專有名詞的原始意涵並不是很確定，但是它的使用記錄是出現在 1950 年代的費城，與感恩節過後隔天的大量繁忙道路交通有關。在 1970 年代，這個專有名被較多的零售商拿來用。依據解釋，自一月至十一月，他們營運呈現財務損失，或是「赤字」。黑色星期五是一年裡，他們轉而獲利，或是「轉為黑字」的一天。

近年來，黑色星期五開始增加更多負面印象。大批群眾聚集在很多商店外面，等待店家開門。有很多案件是插隊，有太多人試著到前排。然後一旦進入了店裡，很多爭吵被報導是因為廉價出售的商品的庫存有限。電視新聞網每年度播放，家庭主婦爭吵搶買最後一個小孩玩偶的錄影帶。

近幾年，一些國際連鎖商店企圖把黑色星期五的概念，引進他們在其他國家的商店，為了促進他們的聖誕銷量。 黑色星期五可能不久會來到你附近的商店！

177. 答案 (A) 黑色星期五通常跟什麼有關？

(A) 商店在新的一年開始賺錢的第一天

(B) 國定假日

(C) 家庭主婦爭玩具的一天

(D) 多數的零售商店的不好的一天

解說 原文第一段第四句，“Black Friday is actually something positive. It is the biggest shopping day of the year and marks the day that shops say that they start making a profit for the year”，實際是開始賺錢的一天，故選 (A)。

178. 答案 (C) 文章裡說關於近年黑色星期五有了什麼改變？

(A) 黑色星期五現在是感恩節後的星期五

(B) 黑色星期五再也不是國定假日

(C) 購物者已變得比較好鬥的

(D) 黑色星期五購物者買他們的聖誕禮物

解說 原文第四段第一句，"In recent years" 和第四第五句，"Then once inside the stores many fights have been reported over limited stocks of sale merchandise. TV news networks annually show videos of housewives fighting over the last children's doll."，表示近年的人變得買不到就用爭吵的。

179. 答案 (D) 黑色星期五和什麼無關？

(A) 路上的交通量變多　(B) 商店和購物中心的廉價銷售

(C) 聖誕節採買　(D) 萬聖節

解說 原文第一段第二句，"maybe a stock market crash or something to do with Halloween. But you would be wrong"，表示萬聖節與它無關，故選 (D)。選項 (A)，原文第三段第一句，"referring to heavy traffic on the roads the day after Thanksgiving"，表示其中一個由來之一。選項 (B)，原文第二段倒數第二句，"and major discounts are offered to attract shoppers looking for bargains"，表示與它有關。選項 (C) 原文第二段最後一句，"Many people try to get all their Christmas shopping on this one day"，表示與它有關。

180. 答案 (C)「黑色星期五」這個專有名詞是從哪裡來？

(A) 費城的街道　(B) 一些國際連鎖的商店

(C) 沒有人真的知道　(D) 聖誕節採買

解說 原文第三段第一句，"The origin of the term is not clear"，表示沒有人知道它真正的由來。

字彙：

commemorate [kəˋmɛməˏret] *(v.)* 慶祝／disaster [dɪˋzæstɚ] *(n.)* 災難／profit [ˋprɑfɪt] *(n.)* 利潤／retailer[ˋritelɚ] *(n.)* 零售商／regard [rɪˋgɑrd] *(v.)* 把…視為／bargain [ˋbɑrgɪn] *(n.)* 特價品／operate [ˋɑpəˏret] *(v.)* ／merchandise [ˋmɝtʃənˏdaɪz] *(n.)* 商品

第 181-185 題

收件人：Alex Wong，First Auto 科技公司
寄件人：Jonathan Hague，Sports Auto 公司

我寫信要更進一步說關於我們上星期，在底特律汽車展的會面。我希望你回到台灣的旅途愉快。

我們十分開心與你會面，我們對你在的展場上的介紹印象深刻。

就如我在展場告訴你的，我一回到我們在內華達州的總部會馬上與你聯擊。所以這封郵件只是開始聯繫。

我們對你們的外部汽車配件十分感興趣。我們相信這裡的市場沒有任何像這樣的東西，所以我們想要與你展開討論，關於進口它們的事宜。

收件人：Jonathan Hague，Sports Auto 公司
寄件人：Alex Wong,，First Auto 科技公司

感謝你的來信。我們回台灣的航程很愉快。

我回憶我們在汽車展的會議。如果我記得沒錯，Sports Auto 公司是位於內華達州，最大的客製跑車商。

我認為我們應該能發展出互利的合作關係，來供應我們的配件給你至你的市場。

在這個早期的階段，我建議你選擇一些你認為會適合你的市場的配件，而我們會寄給你樣品。等你想好可以用我們的什麼商品後，我會很樂意招待你來台灣這裡，造訪我們的工廠及辦公室。

181. 答案 (C) Jonathan Hague 的郵件目的為何？

(A) 介紹他自己　　(B) 進口汽車配件

(C) 開始郵件聯繫　　(D) 安排會面

解說　第一篇原文第三段第二句，“So this email is just to initiate contact”，表明了這封郵件的目的，故選 (C)。

182. 答案 (B) Sports Auto 公司是做什麼的？

(A) 製造車子　　(B) 改裝車子的外觀

(C) 製造外部的汽車配件　　　(D) 舉辦汽車展

解說　從第一篇原文第四段第一句，"We are very interested in your exterior auto accessories"，以及第二篇原文第二段第二句，"Sports Auto are the biggest customizers of sports cars in the state of Nevada"，足以推測出該公司從事客製化跑車外部配件改裝。

183. 答案 (A) 依據這兩封郵件，什麼事將不會發生？

(A) First Auto 科技公司將會收到樣品的帳單

(B) Jonathan Hague 會造訪台灣

(C) First Auto Tech 公司會寄出樣品

(D) Sports Auto 公司會客製化車子

解說　選項 (A)，在郵件中並未提及。選項 (B)，第二篇原文最後一段最後一句，"I would be happy to host you for a visit to our factory and offices here in Taiwan"，代表 Jonathan Hague 可能在未來造訪台灣。選項 (C)，第二篇原文最後一段第一句，"we can send them to you as samples"，表示 First Auto Tech 公司會寄出樣品。選項 (D)，第二篇原文第二段第二句，"Sports Auto are the biggest customizers of sports cars"，得知 Sports Auto 公司會客製化車子。

184. 答案 (D) 如果兩間公司的生意關係進行順利，未來可能發生什麼事？

(A) Alex Wong 可能會到內華達州

(B) First Auto 科技公司可能會買 Sports Auto 公司的產品

(C) Jonathan Hague 可能會到底特律的展場拜訪 Alex Wong

(D) Jonathan Hague 可能會到台灣拜訪 Alex Wong

解說　第二篇原文第三段第一句，"we should be able to develop a mutually beneficial partnership"，以及最後一段最後一句，"I would be happy to host you for a visit to our factory and offices here in Taiwan"，說明如果發展出互利合作關係，Alex Wong 樂意招待 Jonathan Hague 來台灣，故選 (D)。

185. 答案 (A) 以公司的關係來看，下一步最有可能做什麼？

(A) 讓 Sports Auto 公司選擇他們想要的哪些樣品

(B) 讓 Jonathan Hague 造訪台灣

(C) 讓 First Auto 公司寄給 Sports Auto 公司一些樣品

(D) 讓 Sports Auto 在內華達州試著賣 First Auto 科技公司的產品

解說　第二篇原文最後一段第一句，"At this early stage I suggest that you choose some accessories that you think could be suitable for your market"，可得知建議下一步是選擇想要的樣品，故選 (A)。選項 (B)、(C)、(D) 皆為合作順利之後可能會發生的事。

字彙：

pleasant [ˋplɛzənt] *(adj.)* 愉快的／presentation [ˏprizɛnˋteʃən] *(n.)* 介紹／impress [ɪmˋprɛs] *(v.)* 印象深刻／initiate [ɪˋnɪʃɪɪt] *(v.)* 開始／exterior [ɪkˋstɪrɪɚ] *(adj.)* 外部的／import [ˋɪmport] *(v.)* 進口／custermize [ˋkʌstəmˏaɪz] *(v.)* 訂做；客製／mutually [ˋmjutʃʊəlɪ] *(adv.)* 互相；彼此

第 186-190 題

收件人：Star 旅遊
寄件人：Mary Hamako

我和家人正計畫下個月至洛杉磯的渡假。麻煩你寄給我航班時間、你們最便宜航班的價格和路線。家庭成員結構是由我先生、我青少年的兒子，和我。

我們計畫在四月二十七日，星期日離開東京，然後出遊大約十天。

我們在洛杉磯會暫住朋友家，所以在那裡不需要飯店膳宿。

謝謝你在我們出遊前的幫忙。

收件人：Mary Hamako
寄件人：Star 旅遊

這裡是從東京飛到洛杉磯最便宜機票的時間表。這個航班不是直飛。需要在夏威夷轉機。

出境

航班　BN 071　起程　東京　09:15　到達　夏威夷 16:15

或是

航班　BN 069　起程　東京　11:25　到達　夏威夷 18:15

航班　BN 072　起程　夏威夷　18:20　到達　洛杉磯　05:30（隔天）

入境

航班 BN 053 起程 洛杉磯 08:55 到達 夏威夷 12:55

航班 BN 051 起程 夏威夷 14:45 到達 東京 17:30

所有航班僅只在平日起程

成人票價 150,000 日元

兒童票價（12 歲以下）110,000 日元

兩天中途停留夏威夷，但是如果你不希望留在夏威夷過夜，就必需選擇早一點離開東京的那一個航班。

如果跟機票一起訂購洛杉磯飯店，我們提供的特別價格。也提供洛杉磯遊覽的好價格。請讓我們知道你是否要我們也幫你訂這些。

請注意，所有以上價格只在一星期內購買有效。

186. 答案 (B) 為什麼 Hamato 一家必須改變他們的旅行計畫？

(A) 他們不想中途停留在夏威夷

(B) 沒有從四月二十七日起程的航班

(C) 必須跟機票一起訂飯店

(D) 機票只能讓出遊的人在外一個星期

解說 第一篇原文第二段第一句，"We are planning to leave Tokyo on Sunday April 27th"，以及第二篇原文第十二行，"All flights depart weekdays only"，說明原先計畫在四月二十七日，星期日出發，但是航班只在平日起程，勢必須改變旅行計畫，故選 (B)。

187. 答案 (A) 如果 Hamato 一家不想在夏威夷停留一晚，他們在東京的起程時間應該是？

(A) 09:15 (B) 11:25

(C) 18:20 (D) 08:55

解說 第二篇原文第十五行，"but you must choose the earlier flight departing Tokyo if you do not wish to stay in Hawaii"，以及第四行，"Depart Tokyo 09:15"，建議不想停留一晚在夏威夷，就要選早一點離開東京的那一個航班，故選 (A)。

188. 答案 (D) Star 旅遊沒有注意 Mary Hamato 的郵件中的什麼事？

(A) Hamato 一家想要去洛杉磯，不是夏威夷

(B) Hamato 一家想要最便宜的價錢

(C) Hamato 一家成員有三人

(D) Hamato 一家在洛杉磯不需要飯店膳宿

解說 第一篇原文第三段，"We will be staying with friends in Los Angeles, so we do not require hotel accommodation there"，以及第二篇原文第十七行，"We offer special prices on hotels in Los Angeles, if purchased with your airline tickets"，表示在洛杉磯不需飯店，但仍舊回覆建議飯店與訂購方式，故選 (D)。

189. 答案 (B) 如果 Hamato 一家決定做這個旅行，他們必須做什麼？

(A) 寫郵件給 Star 旅遊

(B) 在七天內訂購

(C) 決定一間在洛杉磯的飯店

(D) 跟他們在洛杉磯的朋友談談

解說 第二篇原文最後一句，"Please note all prices are only valid if purchased within a week"，表示若 Hamato 一家決定了這個旅行，必須在一星期也就是七天內訂購，否則價格可能會有所變動，也許就不符合他們的期望，故選 (B)。

190. 答案 (B) Hamato 一家的機票錢總共多少？

(A) 410,000 日元　　**(B) 450,000 日元**

(C) 370,000 日元　　(D) 比 450,000 日元多

解說 第二篇原文第十三、十四行，"Adult ticket 150,000 Yen"，" Child (under 12) 110,000 Yen"，表示成人與兒童票價，第一篇原文第一段第三句，"The family consists of my husband, my teenage son and me"，說明 Hamato 一家的成員是兩名大人，一名青少年，而青少年是指 13 到 19 歲，所以票價與成人相同。一家人的機票花費為三張成人票的價錢，故選 (B)。

字彙：

itinerary [aɪˋtɪnə͵rɛrɪ] *(n.)* 路線／ consist [kənˋsɪst] *(v.)* 構成／ accommodation [ə͵kɑməˋdeʃən] *(n.)* 膳宿／ schedule [ˋskɛdʒʊl] *(n.)* 時間表／ direct [dəˋrɛkt] *(adj.)* 直接的／ depart [dɪˋpɑrt] *(v.)* 起程／ outbound [ˋaʊtˋbaʊnd] *(adj.)* 出境的／ inbound [ˋɪnˋbaʊnd] *(adj.)* 入境的

第 191-195 題

大學生的地質學測驗：寫 200 字關於地震

地震：Linda Miles 寫

地震是地球內部地殼壓力的突然釋放，釋放出移動的振動，一路往上至搖動能被感受到的地表層。搖動的強度與地球的地殼地震點遠近及深度有關。

多數的地震發生在地球地殼構造的板塊邊緣附近。這些巨大的地殼片，漂浮在地球內部深處澆鑄岩石的海面上。這些地殼構造的板塊緩慢地移動，雖然每年只移動幾公分，這個移動造成大量的壓力並儲存能量，能產生兩個或更多板塊的碰撞。這個突然的能量釋放，就是地震。地殼構造的地盤推擠在一起，也創造出地球上大部分的山脈。

地震在無限制的強度量表上測量。多數的地震是強度 4 以下，而且通常不被察覺。地震的強度來到 5 至 7 時，很可能對鄰近的地區造成嚴重問題。任何比那還高的強度，會造成大範圍的極大的災害和傷亡。地震的最高記錄在 1960 年被測得有 9.5 的強度。

地震論說文——講師的評語

這在測驗題的回答是很簡明扼要。結構很好也容易了解。

在地震形成的解釋上，詳述得很好也很正確。

強度量表的敘述有點不明確，而且對只有 200 字的論說文來說太過冗長。

論說文裡只包括了一個地震的範例，但是僅說明正確的地震，卻沒提及受影響的國家，智利。

論說文只注重地殼構造的板塊造成的地震。沒有提及其他地區，或最重要的海底地震，以及導致海嘯風險。 地震和火山之間的關係也漏掉了。

以論說文敘述山脈如何形成，會比較適合用在地殼構造板塊的論說文中，特別是以上的的主題沒有包括在你這篇論說文中。

成績：B +

191. 答案 (D) 根據這兩篇文章，什麼是多數地震的結果？

(A) 造成嚴重的問題　　(B) 造成海嘯

(C) 創造出高山　　(D) 沒有人察覺到

解說　第一篇原文第三段第二句，"The majority of earthquakes are lower than magnitude 4, and usually go unnoticed"，以及第二篇原文第二段第一句，"The explanation on the causes of earthquakes has good detail and is accurate"，說明在論說文中的多數實際發生並測得的地震不被察覺說法是正確的，故選 (D)。

192. 答案 (C) 根據這兩篇文章，什麼會產生地震？

(A) 火山　(B) 海嘯

(C) 地殼構造的板塊碰撞　(D) 地殼下的澆鑄岩石

解說　第一篇原文第二段第三、四句，"huge pressure and stores of energy to be created where two or more plates collide. This sudden release of energy is an earthquake"，以及第二篇原文第五段第一句，"focuses on earthquakes along tectonic plates"，表示第一篇文章只說明這個造成地震的說法，第二篇文章也同意這個原因正確，故選 (C)。

193. 答案 (A) 根據這兩篇文章，最大的地震記錄發生在哪裡？

(A) 智利　(B) 海底

(C) 地殼　(D) 地殼構造的板塊

解說　第一篇原文第三段最後一句，"The highest recorded earthquake was measured at a magnitude of 9.5 in 1960"，以及第二篇原文第四段第一句，"despite identifying the correct earthquake the affected country of Chile was not mentioned"，可以知道記錄中震度最大的發生地是在 1960 年的智利，故選 (A)。

194. 答案 (A) 下例哪一個主題不是講師建議應該包含在內的？

(A) 地震的原因　(B) 火山

(C) 海嘯　(D) 海底地震

解說　第二篇原文第五段第二、三句，"or most importantly of undersea earthquakes and the resulting risk of tsunamis. The relationship between earthquakes and volcanoes was also overlooked"，說明應該在論文中包含選項 (B)、(C)、(D)，故選 (A)。

195. 答案 (D) 根據這兩篇文章，哪裡可以感受到地震？

(A) 靠近火山　(B) 沿著地殼構造板塊的邊緣

(C) 智利　　　　　　　　　　(D) 任何地方

解說　第一篇原文第一段第一句，"all the way up to ground level where shaking can be experienced"，說明只要是在地表層，就會形成有感地震，故選 (D)。

字彙：

undergraduate [ˏʌndəˋgrædʒuɪt] *(adj.)* 大學生的／ geology [dʒɪˋɑlədʒɪ] *(n.)* 地質學／ release [rɪˋlis] *(v.)* 釋放／ crust [krʌst] *(n.)* 地殼／ intensity [ɪnˋtɛnsətɪ] *(n.)* 強度 ／ tectonic [tɛkˋtɑnɪk] *(adj.)* 地殼構造的／ collide [kəˋlaɪd] *(v.)* 碰撞／ concise [kənˋsaɪs] *(adj.)* 簡明的

第 196-200 題

賺屬於你自己的錢　Debra Gates 撰

所有的年青人知道向父母伸手要錢的感覺如何，我也不例外。唯一的不同是我現在 17 歲，而且我有份工作。我不想繼續看見當我向他們要錢時，父母的臉上的神色 ，我找到了一個週末的工作。

我做什麼工作？我在當地的便利商店工作。當我去應徵時，還不確定事情會如何，而且我很驚訝我被他們錄用。它還是份辛苦的工作。我常常必須堆滿架上商品，有時後在收銀台工作。我第一次做的時候有點害怕。那是我第一次必須處理錢。

我每週六和日都輪一班。我必須錯失一些和我的朋友在一起的時間，而且我仍舊必須做完學校作業，但是肯定值得這麼做。

自從我開始工作之後，我已經變得比較獨立。我可以選擇何時何地花錢。我發現了我甚至花較少錢，存較多錢。甚至我的父母現在感覺而我工作後的改變，雖然那不是我一開始的用意。

我明年就要上大學了，我很期待。然後我肯定會繼續工作。我絕不可能放棄我現在已經達到的獨立性。到了我要上大學時，我應該會存足夠的錢買摩托車，但是這件事我們倆知道就好喔！

我們的女兒，獨立的女兒

我們的女兒，Debra，是個非常固執、獨立的十七歲少女。我們總是支持她做的每件事；甚至當她開始工作亦是如此，不過她應該至少先問過我們。畢竟她仍未成年。

我們認為她在便利商店的兼職工作，是個很棒的想法，只要她仍有應付所有課業的時間，我們很樂意她繼續在那裡工作。然而，我們不是很喜歡一些她必須工作的時段。有時候她的上班時段是到深夜，或是在週六或週日的凌晨才下班。那對她自己回家來說不是很好的時間，而且這樣她怎麼有睡覺的時間呢？

她明年將會離家去讀大學。對這一點，我們心裡五味雜陳。一方面，房子裡都只剩我們是很棒的事，但是我們將會擔心她。 Debra 也許是十分聰明的，但是有時候她會沒想清楚就做出一些草率的決定。

196. 答案 (A) 想要一份工作的主要原因之一為何？

(A) 從父母眼中在經濟上更獨立 (B) 買更多東西

(C) 在外面留久一點 (D) 學習如何處理金錢

解說 第一篇原文第一段第三句，“I didn't want to have to keep seeing the looks on my parents' faces when I asked them for money, so I found a weekend job”，說明工作的最初主要原因，故選 (A)。

197. 答案 (C) 這兩篇文章有什麼爭議？

(A) Debra 是否應該上大學

(B) Debra 必須工作的班表

(C) Debra 的父母原先是否支持關於她的工作

(D) Debra 是否有足夠的時間讀書

解說 第二篇原文第一段第二句，“We've always supported her in everything she has done; even when she started working, although she should have at least asked us about it first”，可以得知 Debra 在找工作前並未問過父母，雖然開始工作後父母支持她，但是並不清楚父母原先的立場為何，故選 (C)。選項 (A)、(B)、(D) 在文章中皆詳盡敘述。

198. 答案 (D) 關於她的工作，Debra 的父母憂心什麼？

(A) Debra 花太少時間跟她的朋友在一起

(B) Debra 把她賺的錢花在什麼地方

(C) Debra 將會買一台摩托車

(D) Debra 必須工作的晚班

解說 第二篇原文第二段第三、四句，"Sometimes she has a shift that finishes late at night or even in the early morning on Saturday or Sunday. It's not a good time for her to be coming home on her own, and how does she find the time to sleep"，說明她父母憂心關於她晚上回家的安全性，以及沒有時間睡覺，都是來自她必須在深夜工作的時段，故選 (D)。

199. 答案 (B) Debra 可能在大學做什麼讓她的父母認為是草率的決定？

(A) 找一份工作　　(B) 買摩托車

(C) 離開家裡　　(D) 變得固執

解說 選項 (A)，在第二篇原文第二段第一句，"we're happy for it to continue"，表示他們認為這個決定很好。選項 (C)，在第二篇原文第三段第一句，"She'll be leaving home next year for university"，表示父母認可也預期她會離家。選項 (D)，在第二篇原文第一段第一句，"Debra, is a very headstrong, independent seventeen year old"，表示父母原本就知道 Debra 是固執的。只有選項 (B)，在第一篇最後一句，"By the time I go to university, I should have enough money saved to buy a motorcycle, but that's just between you and me"，表示 Debra 可以認為父母不會認同，所以不跟父母說，這也是可能會讓父母認為這是草率決定。

200. 答案 (B) 當她開始工作時，什麼讓 Debra 的父母惱怒？

(A) Debra 變得獨立　　(B) Debra 沒有先和他們討論

(C) Debra 可以花自己的錢　　(D) Debra 有一份工作

解說 在第二篇原文第一段第二句，"although she should have at least asked us about it first. She is still a minor after all"，表現出父母的不滿，因為他們認為 Debra 尚未成年，要去工作至少要先徵得他們的同意，故選 (B)。

字彙：

exception [ɪk`sɛpʃən] *(n.)* 例外／ definitely [`dɛfənɪtlɪ] *(adv.)* 肯定地／ headstrong [`hɛd͵strɔŋ] *(adj.)* 固執的／ minor [`maɪnɚ] *(n.)* 未成年／ keen on [kin] [ɑn] *(ph.)* 喜愛；熱衷／ intelligent [ɪn`tɛlədʒənt] *(adj.)* 有才智的／ rash [ræʃ] *(adj.)* 草率的

Test 5

Part 5. 單句填空

Questions 101-140

101. ------- analysis of last year's sales will not be available until the end of March.

(A) Complete
(B) Completely
(C) To complete
(D) Completing

102. After months of disagreement and having sold all his remaining stock, the chairman resigned from the board of -------.

(A) supervisors
(B) anchors
(C) directors
(D) administrators

103. Please note that the price of your package tour ------- transport to and from the airport at your destination, but not in your home country.

(A) includes
(B) including
(D) included
(D) has included

104. After moving into its new offices, the sales department was the ------- of the rest of the company.

(A) envying
(B) envious
(C) enviously
(D) envy

105. There is always intense media interest ------- a movie star or chart-topping singer gets arrested.

(A) whoever
(B) whenever
(C) whatever
(D) whichever

106. Delta Data Services ------- beat investor expectations in the second quarter.

(A) comfort
(B) comfortable
(C) comfortably
(D) comforted

107. The ------- president will be remembered at a memorial service marking fifty years since his passing.

(A) old
(B) later
(C) late
(D) belated

108. Hogan Bakery requires the services of a vermin extermination company from time ------- time.

(A) by
(B) to
(C) at
(D) on

109. Regulations only permit residents ------- in this area overnight.

(A) parking
(B) park
(C) parked
(D) to park

110. With - - - - - - - it is easy to say that the problems should have been anticipated.

(A) hindsight
(B) foresight
(C) vision
(D) premonition

111. Despite its best efforts, Loco Media have been unable to locate the missing records - - - - - - -.

(A) everywhere
(B) somewhere
(C) anywhere
(D) nowhere

112. Asia Bank's Internet banking service - - - - - - - essential maintenance between 2:00 A.M. and 5:00 A.M. tonight.

(A) undergoes
(B) has undergone
(C) will be undergoing
(D) will have been undergoing

113. Rita Palmer, a new secretary, has succeeded in - - - - - - - almost everyone in the office with her continuous gossiping.

(A) upset
(B) to upset
(C) upsettingly
(D) upsetting

114. Financial markets reacted positively to the news of a possible merger of the two - - - - - - -.

(A) enemies
(B) rivals
(C) adversaries
(D) foes

115. The state saw recreational drug use ------- after decriminalization last year.

(A) increasing
(B) increase
(C) increased
(D) to increase

116. The response to the new advertising was ------- negative that the company was forced to rethink its whole marketing philosophy.

(A) so
(B) very
(C) much
(D) too

117. Everyone at Sheerwood Furniture hopes that you ------- be happy in your new occupation.

(A) will
(B) should
(C) would
(D) might

118. After dinner, we were ------- by a comedian whose jokes were often quite hard to understand.

(A) entertain
(B) entertaining
(C) to entertain
(D) entertained

119. The problems with the just-in-time supply chain were solved following ------- with the lead suppliers.

(A) demands
(B) arguments
(C) negotiations
(D) concessions

120. Unfortunately the expected end-of-year orders never - - - - - - -, leaving the company order book nearly empty.

(A) come in
(B) came in
(C) had come in
(D) has come in

121. Please contact us for any - - - - - - - information on our extensive range of products and services.

(A) farther
(B) further
(C) furthered
(D) furthering

122. Reliability is the cornerstone of Cabot Engineering's success, and so it is the responsibility of all employees to guarantee - - - - - - -.

(A) it
(B) them
(C) its
(D) that

123. After the accident, all electrical - - - - - - - must be checked before any further use.

(A) facilities
(B) hardware
(C) assets
(D) equipment

124. After opening, re-seal the package to keep the remaining product - - - - - - -.

(A) fresh
(B) freshly
(C) freshness
(D) refreshed

125. This is the final - - - - - - - for flight AX217 leaving for Tokyo from gate 37.

(A) shout
(B) call
(C) cry
(D) hail

126. For most city dwellers, it is hard to imagine - - - - - - - without a roof over one's head.

(A) sleep
(B) slept
(C) sleeping
(D) to sleep

127. Anyone who objects - - - - - - - the proposed location for the new supermarket must register their opposition within fourteen days.

(A) of
(B) by
(C) in
(D) to

128. The cost of the storm cannot be measured simply in dollars, but in lives - - - - - - -.

(A) lose
(B) lost
(C) losing
(D) losable

129. Since obtaining his doctor's license, Dr. Adams has often returned to the hospital at - - - - - - - he was born.

(A) where
(B) which
(C) whose
(D) that

130. The after dinner comments made by the company chairman were greatly ------- by all employees.

(A) appreciate
(B) appreciated
(C) appreciating
(D) to appreciate

131. Paparazzi photographers are ------- known for their intrusive methods of following celebrities wherever they go.

(A) very
(B) good
(C) badly
(D) well

132. ------- on the outcome of the enquiry, new procedures will be implemented.

(A) Depend
(B) Depended
(C) Depending
(D) To depend

133. The town re-elected the mayor by a ------- of more than 10% over his nearest rival.

(A) margin
(B) amount
(C) quantity
(D) measure

134. It is right ------- the minister resigned after the scandal.

(A) which
(B) that
(C) what
(D) who

135. When it opens, the new children's hospital ------- a level of care greater than that offered at any other hospital in the region.

(A) will provide
(B) provides
(C) has provided
(D) is providing

136. The man talking on the radio about the lack of ------- after the accident at the oil refinery is getting increasingly angry.

(A) payment
(B) refunds
(C) remittance
(D) compensation

137. The warning to the lower management about the lax style of management was delivered by the company vice president very -------.

(A) force
(B) forceful
(C) forcefully
(D) forcefulness

138. Shoe manufactures are well aware of the speed at which children grow ------- new shoes.

(A) out of
(B) up to
(C) in of
(D) on to

139. For all art students at this institution, ------- is essential.

(A) imagine
(B) imagined
(C) imaging
(D) imagination

140. The points ------- at the shareholders' annual meeting were too important to be disregarded without further discussion.

(A) elevated
(B) raised
(C) lifted
(D) risen

Part 5. 單句填空

第 101-140 題

101. 答案 (A) 完成的去年銷售分析，將不會在三月底前可以取得。

(A) 完成的 *(adj.)* (B) 完成地
(C) 完成 *(inf.)* (D) 完成（動名詞）

解說 形容詞 complete「完成的」加名詞 analysis「分析」，complete analysis「完成的分析」是名詞片語。

102. 答案 (C) 在幾個月持不同意見，以及賣掉所有他剩下的股票，主席請辭執行長董事一職。

(A) 監督人 (B) 錨
(C) 執行長 (D) 行政官員

103. 答案 (A) 請注意你套裝行程的價格，包括從機場至你的目的地的接送，但是不是在你自己的國家內。

(A) includes (B) including
(C) included (D) has included

解說 時態為現在式，選用現在式動詞 include「包括」，主詞為 the price of your package tour「套裝行程的價格」，是第三人稱單數，所以動詞要加 s，故選 (A)。

104. 答案 (D) 搬至新的辦公室之後，銷售部是公司其它部門的羨慕的對象。

(A) 羨慕（現在分詞） (B) 羨慕的 *(adj.)*
(C) 羨慕地 *(adv.)* (D) 羨慕的對象 *(n.)*

解說 定冠詞 the，後面只能加名詞，故選 (D)。The sales department was the envy of the rest of the company. 可以寫作 The rest of the company envied / were envious of the sales department. 意思是相同的。

105. 答案 (B) 媒體總是有強烈的興趣，無論什麼時候電影明星或最流行的歌手被逮捕。

(A) 無論誰 *(pron.)* (B) 無論何時 *(conj.)*
(C) 不論什麼 *(pron.)* (D) 不論哪個 *(pron.)*

106. 答案 (C) Delta 資料服務安逸地勝過投資者在第二季的預期。

(A) 安逸 *(n.)* (B) 安逸的 *(adj.)*

(C) 安逸地 *(adv.)* (D) 安慰（過去式動詞）

解說 副詞 comfortably「安逸地」修飾動詞 beat「勝過」，故選 (C)。

107. 答案 (C) 已故的總統將會在紀念活動被緬懷，自他過世算起已五十個年頭了。

(A) 老的 *(adj.)* (B) 較晚的 *(adj.)*

(C) 已故的 *(adj.)* (D) 遲來的 *(adj.)*

解說 late 用在名詞片語 the late president 裡，有「死亡」之意。

例句 My late wife would have loved it. 我已故的太太會喜愛它。

108. 答案 (B) Hogan Bakery 有時需要殲滅害蟲 公司的服務。

(A) by (B) to

(C) at (D) on

解說 from time to time「有時」＝ sometimes。

例句 The chef checks on the new apprentice from time to time. 廚師每隔幾天（有時）檢查新來的學徒。

109. 答案 (D) 在這一個區域，法規只允許居民的車停過夜。

(A) parking (B) park

(C) parked (D) to park

解說 不完全及物動詞 permit「允許」，後面可以有受詞，若是有受詞，受詞補語必須是不定詞。permit ＋受詞＋不定詞。

例句 The library permits students to come on Sundays. 圖書館允許學生星期日來，故選 (D)。選項 (A) 不正確，如果 permit「允許」是作完全及物動詞用，必須直接加動名詞 parking，即 permit parking「允許停車」。

110. 答案 (A) 有了事後的了解，很容易說問題應該早先就預期到。

(A) 後見之明 *(n.)* (B) 先見之明 *(n.)*

(C) 洞察力 *(n.)* (D) 預告 *(n.)*

解說 選項 (B)、(C)、(D) 通常與未來的事物有關，不是過去已發生的，本句時態為現在完成式，表示事件已發生過。hindsight「後見之明」，表示在事情發生後所得到的認知與了解，故選 (A)。

111. 答案 (C) 儘管盡最大的努力，Loco 媒體仍到處都找不到不見的唱片。

(A) 每個地方　　(B) 某地方

(C) 任何地方　　(D) 沒有地方

112. 答案 (C) 亞洲銀行的網路銀行服務在今晚凌晨2時至5時之間，將會進行基本維護。

(A) undergoes　　(B) has undergone

(C) will be undergoing　　(D) will have been undergoing

解說　本句時間為 between 2:00 A.M. and 5:00 A.M. tonight「今晚凌晨2時至5時之間」，表示這個時間還未發生，是未來進行式，故選(C)。選項(A)，是現在式動詞。選項(B)是現在完成式。選項(D)，是未來完成進行式。

113. 答案 (D) Rita Palmer，新來的祕書，隨著她持續的傳播流言蜚語，成功地讓幾乎每位在辦公室裡的人心煩。

(A) 使心煩 *(v.)*　　(B) 使心煩 *(inf.)*

(C) 心煩意亂地 *(adv.)*　　(D) 使心煩（動名詞）

解說　succeed in ，in 是介係詞，所以後面要用名詞，必須寫成動名詞，故選(D)。

114. 答案 (B) 財經市場對兩間同業競爭對手可能併購的消息，有正面地反應。

(A) 敵人　　(B) 同業競爭對手

(C) 敵手　　(D) 敵軍

解說　這四個選項皆有敵對之意，但是只有選項(B)會用在商務上，表示同業競爭對手，故選(B)。

例句　Both friend and foe respect his intelligence. 友軍和敵軍都敬重他的智慧。Birds are the enemy of worms. 鳥是蟲的天敵。The once good friends became adversaries in the competition. 一度十分好的朋友在競賽中成了敵手。

115. 答案 (B) 政府發現用於娛樂消遣的藥物使用，在去年合法化之後增加。

(A) 增加（動名詞） (B) 增加 *(v.)*

(C) 增加（過去式動詞） (D) 增加 *(inf.)*

解說 see 是及物動詞，受詞為名詞片語 recreational drug use「娛樂消遣的藥物使用」，後面需要一個受詞補語，受詞補語是原形動詞，故選 (B)。要注意，drug use 是名詞。

例句 The interviewer saw an enormous cockroach crawl on the carpet during the interview. 面試官在面試期間看見一隻偌大的蟑螂爬在地毯上。

116. 答案 (A) 對新廣告的回應是如此地負面，以致於公司被迫重新思考整個行銷哲學。

(A) so *(adv.)* (B) very *(adv.)*

(C) much *(adv.)* (D) too *(adv.)*

解說 四個選項皆為「很；太；如此地」的意思。本句有 that 子句作形容詞補語用，副詞 so ＋ (adj. / adv.) ＋ that 子句（形容詞補語），「如此地…以致於」，故選 (A)。

例句 The wind was so strong that it blew down the traffic light. 風勢如此地強勁，以致於吹倒了紅綠燈。

117. 答案 (A) 每位在 Sheerwood 傢俱行的人，希望你將會滿意你的新居住環境 。

(A) will (B) should

(C) would (D) might

解說 hope「希望」，在未來達成的事，用 will「將會」，故選 (A)。選項 (B)、(C)、(D) 皆用在 wish「希望；但願」。

例句 I hope that he will pass the driving test. 我希望他會通過駕駛考試。

118. 答案 (D) 晚餐過後，一位笑話常常很難懂的喜劇人員娛樂我們。

(A) 娛樂 *(v.)* (B) 娛樂（現在分詞）

(C) 娛樂 *(inf.)* (D) 娛樂（過去分詞）

解說 過去式被動語態。主詞＋ was/were ＋過去分詞，故選 (D)。

119. 答案 (C) 及時供應連鎖商的問題被解決，接著與重要的供應商協商。

(A) 請求 *(n.)*　(B) 爭論 *(n.)*

(C) 協商 *(n.)*　(D) 讓步 *(n.)*

解說 選項 (D)，concession「讓步」+ to/from。

120. 答案 (B) 不幸地，預期年底的訂單從未進來，留下幾乎空白的公司訂購帳冊。

(A) come in　(B) came in

(C) had come in　(D) has come in

解說 語意中，表示訂單未進來是已發生的事，故是過去式，故選 (B)。come「來」的動詞三態為 come-came-come。

121. 答案 (B) 請聯絡我們，如果需要我們廣大範圍的產品或服務的任何更進一步資料。

(A) 更遠的 *(adj.)*　(B) 進一步的 *(adj.)*

(C) 助長（過去式動詞）　(D) 助長（動名詞）

解說 選項 (B)，形容詞 further「進一步的；更遠的」，可用在形容距離或程度。選項 (A)，形容詞 farther「更遠的」是 far「遠的」的比較級，只能用在形容距離。

例句 Hazel went farther away than she was allowed to. Hazel 步行至她被允許的更遠處。

122. 答案 (A) 可靠性是 Cabot 工程的成功基石，所以保證它的可靠性，是全體員工的責任。

(A) it　(B) 他們（代名詞受格）

(C) 它的（代名詞所有格）　(D) that

解說 代名詞 it「它」，表示主詞 reliability「可靠性」，故選 (A)。

123. 答案 (D) 意外事件之後，所有用電的設備必須在進一步使用之前檢查。

(A) 設施 *(n.)*　(B) 硬體 *(n.)*

(C) 資產 *(n.)*　(D) 設備 *(n.)*

124. 答案 (A) 打開之後，重新閉封包裝來保持商品新鮮。

(A) 新鮮的 *(adj.)* (B) 新鮮地 *(adv.)*

(C) 新鮮 *(n.)* (D) 使清新（過去式動詞）

解說 keep「保持」是連綴動詞，本句的主詞補語是形容詞 fresh「新鮮的」，修飾 package「包裝」，故選 (A)。

例句 After cooking, make sure you tidy the kitchen to keep it clean. 煮完飯之後，確定你整理好廚房保持它的乾淨。

125. 答案 (B) 這是航班 AX217 的最後召集，飛往東京在 37 號登機門。

(A) 大叫 *(n.)* (B) 召集 *(n.)*

(C) 哭喊 *(n.)* (D) 歡呼 *(n.)*

解說 選項 (A)、(B)、(C)、(D) 在文法用法上皆為正確，但是只有選項 (B)，call「召集」，符合題意。

126. 答案 (C) 對大部分的城市居民來說，很難想像睡覺頭上沒有屋頂。

(A) 睡覺 *(v.)* (B) 睡覺（過去式動詞）

(C) 睡覺（動名詞） (D) 睡覺 *(inf.)*

解說 及物動詞 imagine「想像」，後面的動詞必須是動名詞，不能加不定詞，故選 (C)。

例句 When I was a kid, I always imagined flying in the sky. 當我是小孩時，總是想像在天空上飛。

127. 答案 (D) 任何反對新超級市場提出的地點的人，必須在十四天內正式提出他們的反對。

(A) of (B) by

(C) in (D) to

解說 object + to「反對」。

128. 答案 (B) 暴風造成的損失無法簡單地用錢衡量，還有因此失去的生命。

(A) 失去 *(v.)* (B) 失去（過去式動詞）

(C) 損失 *(n.)* (D) 易失的 *(adj.)*

解說 過去式，故選過去式動詞 (B)。lives lost = lives which were lost，which were lost 是形容詞子句，修飾 lives。

129. 答案 (B) 自從獲得他的醫師執照，Adams 醫師常回到他出生的醫院。

(A) where (B) which
(C) whose (D) that

解說 關係代名詞 which，引導形容詞子句，代表在它之前的名詞（地方）。at which = where。

130. 答案 (B) 晚餐過後公司主席做的評語，十分受所有員工感激。

(A) appreciate (B) appreciated
(C) appreciating (D) to appreciate

解說 過去式被動語態，主詞＋ was/were ＋過去分詞，故選 (B)。

131. 答案 (D) 狗仔隊攝影師眾所周知的是他們跟拍名人走到哪跟到哪打擾人的方法。

(A) 非常 *(adv.)* (B) 好的 *(adj.)*
(C) 壞地 *(adv.)* (D) 好地 *(adv.)*

解說 現在式被動語態，well known「眾所皆知」。known「已知的」是過去分詞做形容詞，副詞修飾形容詞，故選 (D)。這裡用副詞在形容詞之前，well known。

132. 答案 (C) 視調查的結果，新程序將會被實施。

(A) Depend*(v.)* (B) Depended（過去式動詞）
(C) Depending（現在分詞） (D) To depend*(inf.)*

解說 分詞構句。副詞子句的主詞與主要子句主詞相同時，可將副詞子句中的連接詞與主詞改成現在分詞，即為分詞構句。此句等同 Whether or not new procedures are implemented depends on the outcome of the enquiry.「新程序是否被實施，要視調查的結果」。動詞 depend「視…而定」。

133. 答案 (A) 鄉長重選，與得票數最接近的對手差幅超過百分之十。

(A) 差數 *(n.)* (B) 數量 *(n.)*
(C) 品質 *(n.)* (D) 尺寸 *(n.)*

134. 答案 (B) 政府部長在醜聞之後請辭是正確的。

(A) which (B) that
(C) what (D) who

解說 that 子句是形容詞補語，故選 (B)。選項 (A)、(D) 為關係代名詞。

135. 答案 (A) 當它開始營業時，新的兒童醫院將會提供比該區任何其它醫院更好程度的照護。

(A) will provide (B) provides

(C) has provided (D) is providing

解說 When it opens「當開始營業時」，表示事情仍未發生，是未來式，故選擇 (A)。動詞 provide「提供」。

136. 答案 (D) 在廣播上談論在油品精練廠發生意外之後關於賠償金不足的男人，愈講愈生氣。

(A) 報償 *(n.)* (B) 退費 *(n.)*

(C) 匯款 *(n.)* (D) 賠償金 *(n.)*

137. 答案 (C) 由公司的副總裁十分強而有力的執行，警告關於鬆散風格的管理方式。

(A) 強迫 *(v.)* (B) 強有力的 *(adj.)*

(C) 強有力地 *(adv.)* (D) 有力 *(n.)*

解說 副詞修飾過去分詞做形容詞的 delivered「執行」，故選 (C)。

138. 答案 (A) 製鞋業十分瞭解小孩因長大而穿不下新鞋子的速度很快。

(A) 因長大而穿不下 (B) 到…程度

(C) 成長為… (D) 對…有愈來愈大的影響

解說 grow out of「因長大而穿不下」。

139. 答案 (D) 對這個機構的所有美術學生們來說，想像力是必備的要素。

(A) 想像 *(v.)* (B) 想像（過去式動詞）

(C) 想像（動名詞） (D) 想像力 *(n.)*

解說 需要名詞做為兩個子句的主詞，本句也可寫作 Imagination is essential for all art students at this institution. ，副詞是 for all art students at this institution，主詞需為名詞，故選 (D)imagination「想像力」。

140. 答案 (B) 在股東年度會議提出的問題太過重要，無法在沒有進一步談論的狀況下漠視。

(A) 舉起 *(v.)* 過去式 (B) 提出 *(v.)* 過去式

(C) 抬起 *(v.)* 過去式 (D) 上升（過去分詞）

解說 會議中提出的問題，為過去式，需選擇過去式動詞。選項 (D)，rise「上升」的動詞三態為 rise – rose –risen 。

Part 6. 短文填空

Questions 141-143 refer to the following article.

Mobile phones

Check the pocket of any teenager in many countries around the -------, and you will almost certainly find a mobile phone, but not just

141. (A) Earth
(B) world
(C) Asia
(D) planet

any phone, most likely a smart phone. The way teenagers interact with ------- has changed dramatically in the last decade. They rarely speak

142. (A) one other
(B) the others
(C) other
(D) each other

face to face with their friends anymore, preferring instead to keep in touch online and on social media.

If you see a group of young people together, more than likely all their eyes are ------- to the screens of their mobile devices. They might

143. (A)stuck
(B) glued
(C) gluing
(D) sticking

even be communicating with someone who is sitting right in front of them.

Questions 144-146 refer to the following announcement.

Band reunion announcement

It's official

iRock to reunite.

The countdown is over. After months of speculation, it's official. The 1980s sensation iRock are to reunite–a twelve venue, four continent world tour is being planned.

The multi Grammy winning iconic rock band, best known for their hits- My Love and Stargazer, will start their ------- at the O2 arena in London in July with other rumored venues being Moscow, Tokyo, Sydney and San Francisco.

144. (A) rebirth
(B) comeback
(C) recovery
(D) renewal

The band hasn't played together for over twenty-five years since their much publicized and messy split in 1989. The band made the announcement via a video message posted on YouTube. The video, which has already had over 1,000,000 hits, also hints at a new single to be released to coincide with the tour. Since the YouTube message, more details of the tour have leaked out including the ------- venues.

145. (A) likely
(B) really
(C) probably
(D) certainly

The bands founding members Brian Clark and Paul Gates have both had success as ------- artists since the breakup, but nothing like the adulation they received with iRock. Fan frenzy has already begun, with the Internet buzzing with messages of excitement on social media.

146. (A) alone
(B) single
(C) solo
(D) solitary

Questions 147-149 refer to the following article.

Redlead Online University

Welcome to the global online community of Redleaf University. Now that you are a registered student why not meet other Redlead online students in your area, and team up to form local study groups to help each other work ------- problems and to celebrate when you achieve your goals.

147. (A) through
(B) by
(C) out
(D) in

If there are no groups in your area, then simply start your own group and plan your first meeting. Here at Redleaf University we believe that face-to-face peer working is an important key to success, and we hope that this greatly improves the experience and ------- of being one of our online students. You might even make new friends in the process.

148. (A) enjoy
(B) enjoyable
(C) enjoyably
(D) enjoyment

We also encourage our students to share their experiences with the rest of our online community outside of their area on Facebook and Twitter.

Remember new online classes are always starting at Redleaf University, so keep an eye on our ------- for news of our latest courses.

149. (A) Internet
(B) website
(C) browser
(D) server

Questions 150-152 refer to the following email.

To: Everclean Cleaning Services

From: Sevenoak Cloth Ltd.

I'm writing to you regarding your office cleaning services. I've been ------- your company by one of our clients, Shane King, at Reed

150. (A) recommend
(B) recommending
(C) recommended
(D) to recommend

Clothing. Sevenoak Cloth Ltd. Is an importer of cloth for the fashion industry with its headquarters here in Cambridge.

Our offices have been cleaned for many years by White Cleaners, but as you will know they suddenly went ------- last week and we

151. (A) bankrupt
(B) destitute
(C) impoverished
(D) sterile

have found ourselves with no cleaners in our office from the start of the week. We require a new cleaning service that can start immediately for our offices which are approximately 2,000 square feet over two floors.

Please can you let me know as soon as possible if you are able to help us and give us details of your charges.

A quick response will be much appreciated, so that you can either start cleaning our offices or we can continue looking -------.

152. (A) somewhere
(B) everywhere
(C) anywhere
(D) elsewhere

Part 6. 短文填空

第 141-143 題

行動電話

檢查全世界許多國家青少年們的口袋，你幾乎必定會找到行動電話，但並非就只是任何款式的電話，最可能的是智慧型手機。青少年們彼此互動的方式，在過去十年已有戲劇性地改變。他們幾乎再也不跟朋友面對面説話，反而比較喜歡在網路上和社群媒體上聯繫。

141. 答案 (B)

(A) 地球　　(B) 世界

(C) 亞洲　　(D) 星球

解說　選項 (A)、(C)，Asia「亞洲」是專有名詞不能加定冠詞 the。

142. 答案 (D)

(A) 其餘的一個　　(B) 其餘的人

(C) 其他的　　(D) 彼此

如果你看見一群青少年在一起，比較可能的是他們的眼睛都被黏在手機設備的螢幕上。他們可能甚至正跟就坐在正前方的人用手機通訊。

143. 答案 (B)

(A) 卡住（過去式動詞 / 過去分詞）

(B) 黏 (過去分詞)

(C) 黏（動名詞）

(D) 卡住（動名詞）

解說　現在式被動語態，主詞＋ is/am/are ＋過去分詞。動詞三態 glue-glued-glued「黏」，故選 (B)。選項 (A)，動詞三態 stick-stuck-stuck「卡住」。

字彙：

smart phone [smɑrt] [fon] *(ph.)* 智慧型手機／ certainly [ˋsɝtənlɪ] *(adv.)* 無疑地；必定／ interact [ˏɪntəˋrækt] *(v.)* 互動／ dramatically [drəˋmætɪklɪ] *(adv.)* 戲劇性地／ device [dɪˋvaɪs] *(n.)* 設備／ communicate [kəˋmjunəˏket] *(v.)* 通訊

第144-146 題

樂團重聚宣佈

是正式的

iRock 樂團再度合體

倒數結束。在幾個月的思索之後，它是正式的。1980 年代當紅樂團 iRock 就要再度合體。正計畫在四大洲、十二個地點舉行的世界巡迴演唱。

贏得多座葛萊美將的偶像搖滾樂團，最為人知的就是他們的成名曲－ My Love and Stargazer，將會在六月，於倫敦 O2 圓形舞台，開始他們的復出表演，也有其他傳聞場地會是在莫斯科、東京、雪梨，以及舊金山。

144. 答案 (B)

(A) 再生 *(n.)* (B) 復出 *(n.)*

(C) 復元 *(n.)* (D) 更新 *(n.)*

這個樂團自從在 1989 年公佈並混亂的解散之後，已經超過 25 年沒有在一起演出。樂團透過張貼在 YouTube 上的錄影檔留言公佈。該影片已經有超過百萬次點閱率，也暗示會在巡迴演唱的同時發行單曲。自 YouTube 錄影檔公佈以來，更多的巡演細節洩漏，包括很可能舉辦的地點。

145. 答案 (A)

(A) 很可能 *(adj.)* (B) 確實 *(adv.)*

(C) 大概 *(adv.)* (D) 必定 *(adv.)*

解說 必須選擇形容詞，修飾名詞 venue「地點」。

樂團的創團成員 Brian Clark 和 Paul Gates，兩人自從離團成為獨立藝人後，均很成功，但是卻不像他們在 iRock 樂團時得到的奉承。粉絲已經開始瘋狂，在社群媒體網路上不斷發出這令人興奮的消息。

146. 答案 (C)

(A) 獨自 *(adj.)* (B) 單一 *(adj.)*

(C) 單獨表演 *(adj.)* (D) 隱居 *(adj.)*

字彙：

publicize [ˋpʌblɪˏsaɪz] *(v.)* 公佈／ coincide [ˏkoɪnˋsaɪd] *(v.)* 同時發生（＋ with）／ leak [lik] *(v.)* 洩漏（＋ out）／ venue [ˋvɛnju] *(n.)* 地點／ adulation [ˏædʒəˋleʃən] *(n.)* 奉承／ frenzy [ˋfrɛnzɪ] *(n.)* 瘋狂

第 147-149 題

Redlead 線上大學

歡迎來到 Redleaf 大學的全球線上社群。現在你已是註冊學生，何不與位於你所在地區的其他 Redleaf 線上學生見面，然後組成當地的讀書社團，幫助彼此在這段期間處理面對難題，並在你們達到目標時一同喝采。

147. 答案 (A)

(A) through *(prep.)*　　(B) by *(prep.)*

(C) out *(prep.)*　　(D) in *(prep.)*

解說　選項 (A)，work through「在…整個期間處理面對」，故選 (A)。選項 (C)，work out「運動；成功」。選項 (B)、(D)，在本題沒有意思。

如果你所在地區沒有社團，那麼就自己發起一個社團，然後計畫第一次地會面。在 Redleaf 大學，我們相信面對面同輩一同讀書的方式，是成功的重要關鍵，我們希望這大大地增進經驗與享受成為我們的線上學生。你甚至可能在過程中交到新朋友。

148. 答案 (D)

(A) 享受 *(v.)*　　(B) 享受的 *(adj.)*

(C) 享受地 *(adv.)*　　(D) 享受 *(n.)*

解說　連接詞 and「和」，連接兩種性質相同的事物，the experience「體驗」是名詞，故需要選擇名詞，故選 (D)。

我們也鼓勵我們的學生，跟其他不在他們那個地區的其他線上社團，在臉書或推特上在分享他們的經驗。

記得新的線上課程總是會在 Redleaf 大學開課，所以密切注意我們網站發佈最近開課課程的消息。

149. 答案 (B)

(A) 網路　　(B) 網站

(C) 瀏覽器　　(D) 伺服器

字彙：

peer [pɪr] *(n.)* 同輩／ enjoyment [ɪn`dʒɔɪmənt] *(n.)* 樂趣／ improve [ɪm`pruv] *(v.)* 增進／ process [`prɑsɛs] *(n.)* 過程／ encourage [ɪn`kɝɪdʒ] *(v.)* 鼓勵／ keep an eye on *(ph.)* 密切注意

第 150-152 題

收件人：Everclean 清潔服務
寄件人：Sevenoak 服飾有限公司

我寫信給你是關於你們的辦公室清潔服務。你們公司的一位客戶向我推薦你們，他是在 Reed 服飾公司的 Shane King 。Sevenoak 服飾有限公司是流行產業的服飾進口商，總部位於劍橋這裡。

150. 答案 (C)

(A) 推薦 *(v.)* (B) 推薦（動名詞）
(C) 推薦（過去分詞） (D) 推薦 *(inf.)*

解說 現在完成式被動語態，主詞＋ have/has ＋ been ＋過去分詞，故選 (C)。

我們的辦公室多年由 White Cleaners 公司負責清潔，但是如你所知，他們在上週突然破產，而我們發現自己的辦公室自週一就沒有清潔人員。我們需要可以馬上開始至我們辦公室清潔的新的清潔服務，兩個樓層，面積大約二千平方英尺。

151. 答案 (A)

(A) 破產的 *(adj.)* (B) 缺乏的 *(adj.)*
(C) 窮困的 *(adj.)* (D) 貧瘠的 *(adj.)*

請儘快讓我們知道你們是否能幫助我們，並請給我們費用明細。

會十分感激你快速地回覆，所以你們可以開始清潔我們的辦公室，或是我們能再繼續找別的地方。

152. 答案 (D)

(A) 某處 *(adv.)* (B) 到處 *(adv.)*
(C) 任何地方 *(adv.)* (D) 別處 *(adv.)*

字彙：

regarding [rɪˋgɑrdɪŋ] (prep.) 關於；就…而論／ importer [ɪmˋportɚ] *(n.)* 進口商／ headquarters [ˋhɛdˋkwɔrtɚz] *(n.)* 總部／ bankrupt [ˋbæŋkrʌpt] *(adj.)* 破產的／ charge [tʃɑrdʒ] *(n.)* 費用／ appreciate [əˋpriʃɪˏet] *(v.)* 感激

Test 1 Test 2 Test 3 Test 4 Test 5

Part 7. 單篇／雙篇文章理解

Questions 153-154 refer to the following announcement.

The Chief Executive Officer of Excon Oil would like to inform the company's shareholders that the recent drop in the price of oil and compensation claims for the oil spill in Nigeria last year will have an adverse effect on revenue in the fourth quarter.

The fall in revenue in the quarter is expected to impact full year results substantially. It is likely that when the full year results for 2013 are released in March, profits for the year will be lower than for 2012.

The outlook for the 2014 and beyond remains uncertain with worldwide oil production at record highs, but demand still dependent on the slow recovery of the global economy.

153. What is the purpose of this announcement?

(A) To report an oil spill in Nigeria

(B) To warn those who own Excon Oil that 2013 was not a good year

(C) To warn that the global economy is not improving fast enough

(D) To report that oil production has hit a new record

154. What is NOT mentioned as affecting Excon Oil's prospects?

(A) How much oil the world produces

(B) How fast the world economy improves

(C) How much oil Excon Oil can sell in Nigeria

(D) The price of oil

Questions 155-156 refer to the following advertisement.

A home away from home
Buy a share of paradise

Beautiful beach front apartments for time-share sale on the magnificent Spanish island of Majorca.
Buy from one week to one month per year at the newest, most exclusive development in Spain, all with a full cleaning and maintenance service.
Prices from 20,000 euros + a yearly maintenance and service charge.
Residents have unlimited access to the complex's pool and park areas.
Go to our website at www.ECOconstruction.com/majorca for a virtual tour.
Never have to worry about booking your vacation again!
Visit us soon to avoid disappointment

155. What is this advertisement selling?
(A) Homes in Spain
(B) Cleaning services
(C) Hotel vacations in Spain
(D) Partial ownership of an apartment

156. What do you get at no extra charge, if you buy a time share?
(A) Use of the swimming pool
(B) Use of the car park
(C) Free cleaning
(D) A virtual tour

Questions 157-158 refer to the following article.

Do you need a financial advisor?

Do you do your own investing? If so, have you ever wondered whether you might be better off getting financial advice from a professional?

There doesn't seem to be a magic number at which people seek financial advice. Some people are happy to invest their life savings themselves, but it's often the receipt of a large sum of money that sends people scurrying though the door of a financial advisor.

Those in the industry say that almost anyone will benefit from visiting one, but expect to pay for the service. Only trust a truly independent financial advisor who is being paid by you to look out for your best interests, not looking for a fat commission on sales.

157. According to this article, who can financial advisors help?

(A) Only people who have suddenly received a lot of money

(B) Only people who have life savings to invest

(C) Only people who pay them money

(D) Most people

158. According to this article, if you want good financial advice, what do you have to do?

(A) Scurry through the door of a financial advisor

(B) Pay the financial advisor for the service

(C) Give the financial advisor a big commission

(D) Invest all your life savings

Questions 159-162 refer to the following email.

To:	Mr. Evans
From:	Richard Cousins, Green Travel

We regret to inform you that your flight WX 041 from London to Singapore on June 9th has been rescheduled to depart at the earlier time of 15:15. We apologize for any inconvenience caused, but as I'm sure you are aware, the airline schedule is beyond our control.

You will now be arriving in Singapore two hours earlier than expected at 05:35. Your itinerary included a shuttle bus transfer to your hotel, unfortunately the shuttle bus does not start to operate until 08:00, so as a token of our appreciation for your goodwill, we have arranged for a free transfer for you to your hotel with our partner in Singapore. Someone from Sunset Tours will be waiting for you at arrivals to pick you up.

The rest of your itinerary is as planned, including a day tour of the city on June 11th and a trip to Singapore Zoo for the night safari on the same day. All services on June 11th are also provided by Sunset Tours.

Remember to be at the airport by at least 13:15 to check in for your flight leaving London. Please call me if I can be of any further help.

159. What is Sunset Tours?

(A) Mr. Evans' travel agent
(B) An airline in Singapore
(C) Part of Singapore Zoo
(D) Green Travel's partner in Singapore

160. What did Green travel do?

(A) Apologize to Mr. Evans
(B) Change the time of Mr. Evans' flight
(C) Tell Mr. Evans to take a shuttle bus in Singapore
(D) Control the airline

161. What does Mr. Evans have to do?

(A) Change his flight to Singapore
(B) Go to the airport earlier than planned on June 9th
(C) Take a shuttle bus to his hotel in Singapore
(D) Telephone Mr. Cousins at Green travel

162. When Mr. Evans arrives in Singapore what should he do?

(A) Check in for his flight
(B) Visit Sunset Tours office
(C) Take a shuttle bus to his hotel
(D) Look for someone from Sunset Tours

Questions 163-165 refer to the following article.

Here are some tips for preparing for a job interview, and making sure that the hiring manager knows that you are right for the job.

First what you do before even applying for a job will go a long way to deciding whether or not you even get to the interview stage. Research the company that you are applying to, not just so that you know what the company is about, but also so that you know that it is really the job that you want.

When called for an interview, think about what the company wants. Do your assets match their requirements? Prepare a list of questions that you are likely to be asked, and practice answering them. Find out who you know that works for the company or has a similar job. Their inside information may give you an edge over other candidates.

Have your interview clothes ready before the day of the interview. Be sure to know how to get to the interview beforehand, take some extra copies of your resume and a list of references and arrive around ten minutes early. Remember to turn off your cell phone before entering the office.

Greet the receptionist and interviewer enthusiastically. Listen to what you are asked and look the interviewer in the eye when answering, and most importantly remember to breathe. If you have prepared well the interview should go well, too.

163. According to this article, which statement true?

(A) You shouldn't waste time researching a company until you get an interview.

(B) You should apply for ever job even if you don't really think it's suitable.

(C) You should pay close attention to what the interviewer says.

(D) You should take a list of questions that you want to ask during an interview.

164. Which statement best describes this articles advice?

(A) Your attitude in the interview is the key to interview success.

(B) Preparation is the key to interview success.

(C) First impressions are the key to interview success.

(D) Friends who can help you are the key to interview success

165. What does this article NOT mention that interview candidates should do?

(A) Visit the office where the interview will take place beforehand

(B) Practice interview questions before the interview

(C) Prepare what you plan to wear in advance

(D) Learn all you can about the company that you will be interviewed at

Questions 166-168 refer to the following article.

I want the name Highcraft Electronics to bring to mind an image of quality. In fact when you think "quality," "reliability" or "value," I want you to think of Highcraft Electronics' products.

We are a leader. Our long history of innovation keeps us ahead of the competition. We want you to rate our customer service on the same level as our technology.

It is my pleasure to introduce the latest version of our Highcraft laptop computer. We've listened to our customers and created a product that not only meets their expectations, but exceeds them. The new Highcraft laptop is the most powerful we have ever built.

And that is just the beginning. Take a moment to look beyond the facts and figures, and you will find a product that is backed up by the largest selection of software ever for a computer at launch.

Visit our website, and see how things have changed. Our customer support network is committed to your satisfaction and welcomes your feedback. We will do all it takes to make your Highcraft purchase the best decision you have ever made.

Thank you for choosing Highcraft Electronics

166. What does this article say that you can do on Highcraft Electronics' website?

(A) You can order their new laptop computer.
(B) You can tell them what you think of their products.
(C) You can look at facts and figures.
(D) You can choose software for your new laptop.

167. What does this article claim about Highcraft Electronics?

(A) That they are better than their competitors
(B) That every customer is satisfied
(C) That they have a longer history than their competitors
(D) That their new laptop computer is the most powerful that you can buy

168. What does Highcraft Electronics want customers to do?

(A) To send more feedback to their customer services
(B) To associate Highcraft Electronics with quality
(C) To think about quality when purchasing products
(D) To help change their website

Questions 169-172 refer to the following company announcement.

We regret to inform you that the consolidation review that was carried out following the merger of Western Union Bank and Southern Perpetual has recommended the closure of Western Union Bank's mortgage division.

All mortgages with Western Union Bank will be transferred to Southern Perpetual over the coming year, and Western Unions Bank's mortgage offices in San Diego will close after the process has been completed. We realize that this news will come as a shock to employees at our San Diego offices.

Every effort will be made to find alternative employment within the organization for affected employees. A limited number of new positions will also become available in Southern Perpetual's mortgage division for those who are willing to relocate to Phoenix.

A voluntary redundancy scheme is to be implemented whereby any employee who wishes to leave within the next three months will be offered a generous severance package. Unfortunately any employee who has not found alternative employment within the organization when the office finally closes will be laid off.

Western Union Bank would like to thank all staff for their hard work, and wishes everyone the best of success in their new positions, wherever that may be.

169. What is the purpose of this announcement?

(A) To tell employees that Western Union Bank and Southern Perpetual are to merge

(B) To tell employees that they will have to move to Phoenix

(C) To tell employees that they will lose their current job

(D) To shock employees

170. Which statement is true?

(A) All employees of Western Union Bank are to lose their jobs.

(B) Western Union Bank will give some money to all of its employees who leave within the next three months.

(C) All Western Union Bank's mortgage division employees can get a new position at Southern Perpetual if they are prepared to move to Phoenix.

(D) Western Union Bank's mortgage division will close in three months' time.

171. What is the relationship between Western Union Bank and Southern Perpetual?

(A) They have become one company.

(B) Southern Perpetual has bought Western Union Bank's mortgage division.

(C) Southern Perpetual has reviewed Western Union Bank and recommended that it closes its mortgage division.

(D) Southern Perpetual has been trying to attract Western Union Bank's employees to come to work for them

172. What has Western Union Bank promised to do?

(A) To find new employment for all its mortgage division employees

(B) To help all its mortgage department employees look for alternative employment

(C) To give money to all employees who lose their job

(D) To work hard to save Western Union Bank's mortgage division

Questions 173-176 refer to the following article.

The most beautiful woman in the world

Hollywood actress Angelina Jolie has often been named as the most beautiful woman in the world by both respected newspapers and gossip magazines. The Oscar winning actress has stared in many blockbuster movies, and, together with partner Brad Pitt, they make the ultimate celebrity couple.

Jolie was born in Los Angeles in 1975 to parents already in the film industry. She made her acting debut at the age of seven in one of her father's films, but despite attending acting school she achieved little success in her teenage years. During this period she also suffered from depression. She had a hard time fitting in during high school and was even bullied over her looks.

Modest acting success followed in her early twenties, but it was not until the 2001 release of Lara Croft: Tomb Raider that she became an international star. Since then her career has been unstoppable and she is now Hollywood's highest paid actress.

Now an established movie star, she has often been in the news more for her private life than for her movies. Married twice, a strained relationship with her father and her engagement to Brad Pitt have all made the headlines.

Jolie has been involved in much charity work, both at home but especially abroad, with various roles for the United Nations. This work helped lead her to the decision to adopt children from some of the countries which she had worked in. Jolie and Pitt now have six children, three of which were adopted from developing nations.

More recently she has attracted attention in her attempt to avoid cancer, a disease which has cost her a number of relatives, including her mother. The publicity which followed her treatment even resulted in changes to the law on patenting genes in the US.

Whether at the movie theater or in its magazines, the world doesn't seem to be able to get enough of Angelina Jolie.

173. What has Angelina Jolie become?

(A) A leader at the United Nations
(B) The Hollywood actress who earns the most money
(C) The wife of Brad Pitt
(D) A model in gossip magazines

174. What is NOT mentioned in this article?

(A) Media attention of Angelina Jolie
(B) Angelina Jolie's family relationships
(C) Angelina Jolie's work in foreign countries
(D) Which countries she adopted her children from

175. When did Angelina Jolie first appear in a movie?

(A) When she was seven
(B) When she was a teenager
(C) In 2001
(D) In 1975

176. Besides the movie industry, what does this article say that Angelina Jolie has influenced?

(A) Adoption rates in developing countries
(B) US law
(C) Bullying at High schools
(D) Understanding of depression

Questions 177-180 refer to the following contract.

CONTRACT OF EMPLOYMENT

REED INDUSTRIES

SYDNEY AUSTRALIA

November 5th

Mr. Brian Gough

312 Lions Avenue

Sydney

Dear Mr. Gough

This letter is to confirm that all the pre-employment checks have been completed, and that your employment with Reed Industries can commence on November 25th. You are required to sign this contract agreeing to the terms and conditions stated below and to return the contract to us by November 20th.

Terms of Employment: This is a full time, permanent position. Working hours are a standard thirty-eight hour week, with ten days paid leave per year. Should either you or the company wish to terminate this agreement, three months' notice must be given in writing.

Job Description: You will be employed as a Laboratory research scientist at our Sydney research and development labs. The job will primarily involve developing and testing new materials for the construction industry, but will also include any day to day work that is required for the running a modern laboratory.

Salary: Your salary is our standard starting package for a graduate research scientist of $35,000 a year, including health benefits. This salary is subject to an annual review of your performance. Your salary will be paid monthly into a bank account of your choice.

Confidentiality Clause: All research at our labs remains the property of Reed Industries. No past, present of future research can be discussed outside of our offices. This is includes during any future employment with any other company.

Please sign the duplicate copies of this contract and send them back to us by November 15th. Only when these documents have been received will a contract exist between you and Reed Industries.

We look forward to seeing you on November 25th.

Yours sincerely

Mrs. Anne Beggs

Director of Human Resources

ENDORSEMENT

I have read the above terms and conditions and accept employment as specified.

Signature .... Date ....

177. After receiving this contract, what should Mr. Gough do next?

(A) Go to work on November 25th.

(B) Apply for a job at Reed Industries

(C) Research new materials for the construction industry

(D) Sign and return the contract

178. What is Mr. Gough forbidden from doing?

(A) Talking about his research with other people who work at Reed Industries

(B) Going on vacation for ten days each year

(C) Discussing the research he's working on with his friends and neighbors

(D) Working for any other company in the future

179. What should Mr. Gough do on November 25th?

(A) Check his bank account for $35,000

(B) Turn up for work at Reed Industries

(C) Take the contract to Reed Industries

(D) Terminate his contract with Reed Industries

180. What will Mr. Gough be expected to do at Reed Industries?

(A) Research in a laboratory

(B) Take tests

(C) Sign the contract

(D) Work on a construction site

Questions 181-185 refer to the following two articles.

Aztec Towers Amusement Park Press Release

Aztec Towers Amusement Park is pleased to announce the opening of its newest roller coaster The Aztec Rocket.

At a height of 147 meters at its highest point, it is set to become the world's highest roller coaster- smashing the previous record by over 7 meters. The Aztec Rocket also reaches a terrifying 105 km/hr.

Designed by R&C International, the manufactures of the world's most famous amusement park rides including the Dubai Flyer and the Georgia Wheel. The Aztec Rocket will be the benchmark for all such rides in the future.

The public opening will be on June 12th, the day of the start of our summer schedule. A media day will be held on May 29th. All journalists wishing to attend must apply for accreditation in advance.

Media Fact Sheet

Name: Aztec Rocket

Manufacturer: R&C International

Construction started: February 2012

Construction completed: September 2013

Length: 3,245 meters

Height: 147 meters (at highest point)

Speed: 105 km/hr (max)

Inversions: 11

Ride duration: 2:50

Trains: 60 trains each with four cars. Riders sit four across in a single row for a total of sixteen riders per train.

Capacity: 1,300 rides per hour

Steel used in construction: 2,150 tons

Cost of construction: $27,000,000

181. How do these articles suggest that riders will feel on the Aztec Rocket?

(A) They will feel that the ride is expensive.

(B) They will feel that the ride is too high.

(C) They will feel that the ride is very new.

(D) They will feel scared.

182. What happens over ten times during each ride?

(A) The train turns upside down.

(B) The train reaches a height of 147 meters.

(C) The train reaches a speed of 105 km/hr.

(D) The train flies in the air in Dubai.

183. What are journalists invited to do?

(A) They are invited to visit the park on June 12th.

(B) They are invited to visit the park on May 29th.

(C) They are invited to ride on the Aztec Rocket.

(D) They are invited to write about the Aztec Rocket.

184. What does the Aztec Rocket set a record for?

(A) Its height

(B) Its speed

(C) Its cost

(D) Its number of riders per hour

185. How many people can ride in one car on the Aztec Rocket?

(A) 16

(B) 4

(C) 60

(D) 1,300

Questions 186-190 refer to the following two emails.

📖To:	Jeff Reagan
From:	Ryan Jones

I'm writing to you in my position as Head Coach at Halifax College. Firstly, head coach to head coach, I'd like to congratulate you on your football team's success last season. Reaching the state play-offs must have given the team a lot satisfaction.

I'd like to see if you would be interested in arranging some pre-season games between our respective colleges for both our football and basketball teams.

We rarely play each other, unless drawn together in the state championship, and I feel that both colleges would benefit from it once the real action begins. Our football team in particular would like to test itself against some of your star players.

📖To:	Ryan Jones
From:	Jeff Reagan

Thanks for the email, and well done to Halifax College's Basketball team. Here at Hamilton College our football team reached to state play-offs, but Halifax College almost won the state basketball championship. That last minute loss in the final must have been heartbreaking.

You are right that our two colleges don't play each other enough. We are located so close together, but maybe rivalry has stopped us taking more advantage of the situation.

I think we can definitely arrange some pre-season games for both our football and basketball teams, and our swimming coach has also asked if the swimming team can be included in the action against your team.

Our pre-season training starts on September 1st, so may I suggest the final two weekends of September as probable dates for any games.

Let me know which weekend you would prefer, and then we can discuss locations and other things in more detail.

186. Who is Jeff Reagan?

(A) The head sports coach at Halifax College
(B) Hamilton College's star football player
(C) The head sports coach at Hamilton College
(D) Hamilton College's football coach

187. Why is Ryan Jones emailing Jeff Reagan?

(A) To arrange dates for their pre-season games
(B) To congratulate Hamilton College on their sporting success
(C) To learn more about Hamilton College's football team
(D) To invite Hamilton College to have closer sporting ties with Halifax college

188. Other than the dates of games, what else do the two colleges have to decide?

(A) Where to play
(B) Whether to play football or basketball
(C) Why the two colleges play each other so rarely
(D) How to test their star players

189. Which statement is true?

(A) Hamilton College's football team won the state championship.
(B) Halifax College's basketball team finished second in the state basketball championship.
(C) Halifax College doesn't have a swimming team.
(D) The two college's sports teams regularly play each other.

190. What is the most probable date for the colleges to agree to play on?

(A) Sunday, September 23rd
(B) Saturday, September 8th
(C) Tuesday, September 11th
(D) Monday, September 24th

Question 191-195 refer to the following articles.

TV schedule for Wednesday, July 17th	
12:00AM	Night Life A look into the night club business
1:30AM	Life on Mars Movie: Can Earth's first colony on Mars survive its first crisis?
3:10AM	The Remix The music show with a difference as guest artists perform some of their best loved songs live.
5:00AM	Sinbad Cartoon: Series 5, Episode 3
6:00AM	Good Morning TV Breakfast with the stars. All you need to start your day. News, music, gossip and much, much more. Get your day off to the perfect start with Good Morning TV.
8:30AM	Shopping
10:30AM	The Culture Show A round-up of all the week's news from movies and music to the arts.
12:00PM	Lunch Time News
12:30PM	Georgie Sitcom: Series 2, Episode 11
1:00PM	A Bold Day Movie: A remake of the 1930s classic
3:30PM	Children's Time Cartoons, stories and fun for the little ones.
5:30PM	Health and Fitness Week five of our fitness program

6:00PM	Oliver Twist Series 1, Episode 1 A modern adaptation of Charles Dickens' classic
7:00PM	The President What's it like to be the president of the USA? Unprecedented access was granted for this behind the scenes look at a day in the life of the president.
9:00PM	World News
9:30PM	Local News
10:00PM	The Police Line Documentary: Can the police hold the line against gang warfare? Only suitable for mature audiences.

Date:	TV review for Wednesday, July17th

Some great viewing could be had on TV last night, but you had to look for it carefully.

Do we really need a new production of Oliver Twist? Has it not already been "remade" about thirty times? So I'm giving that a definite thumbs-down. As for The President, much more like "The Yawn" if you ask me! After two hours, I was waiting for the commercial breaks to help relieve the boredom.

And for the good bits, Health and Fitness seems to be hitting the mark. This no nonsense practical approach to getting active appears to be actually working. Thousands of people up and down the country have taken it up, and I'm one of them.

The Police Line was a brutally honest look at the difficulties city police are facing in some of our inner cities. Often hard to watch, this thought provoking documentary showed us a world few of us imagined existed just a few blocks away from where many of us live. This program was certainly the highlight of the day's TV.

191. Which TV program did the reviewer like the most?

(A) Health and Fitness
(B) The President
(C) The Police Line
(D) Oliver Twist

192. What does the reviewer say about The President?

(A) That she doesn't like the current president
(B) That the advertisements were the best part
(C) That the president's life is very boring
(D) That the police have to work very hard to protect him in the inner cities

193. Which program would be most suitable for someone who only watches programs from the beginning?

(A) Oliver Twist
(B) Sinbad
(C) Georgie
(D) Health and Fitness

194. What does "only suitable for mature audiences" mean?

(A) That the program was made in front of an audience
(B) That the police want a large audience to watch the program
(C) That children should not watch the program
(D) That old people should not watch the program

195. Which program is most likely to make you laugh?

(A) Georgie
(B) The Culture Show
(C) The Police Line
(D) The Remix

Questions 196-200 refer to the following newspaper article and letter.

Sending Gran Abroad

Arjeta Weidler from Geneva, Switzerland, packs her suitcase, heads for the airport and gets on a plane. She is going to Chang Mai in northern Thailand, but she is not going on vacation. She is visiting her mother.

Arieta is one of a growing number of people who are sending their elderly relatives to care homes abroad.

"When I told people what I was doing, they were shocked. 'How dare you do this? How can you visit her?' was all I heard," says Weidler.

"But when I visit her, she has forgotten within half an hour, and the level of care she receives in Thailand is far higher than that available here in Switzerland."

Weidler's mother, Hilda, is 93 and suffers from dementia. She was in care in Switzerland for four years before Weidler took the decision to move her to Thailand. "I visit her at least twice a year, and she seems contented with her life now," says Weidler.

A quick look at the figures and it's easy to see why many families are making the same decision as Weidler. The costs are far cheaper, but the reputation for quality is still very high.

In Thailand there are care homes that specialize in caring for foreign clients. Each home has residents from one particular country, so language is never a problem. Most of the residents don't even know that they are in a foreign country, and the climate without the cold European winters is claimed to be better for the elderly, too.

With the ever increasing pressure of an ageing population, and the strains that it is putting on local health providers, maybe more of us will be getting on a plane to visit Gran in the future.

Dear Editor

I was outraged by the recent article in your newspaper "Sending Gran Abroad." How could anyone send their own flesh and blood to live abroad, let alone to the other side of the world?

This all goes to show the lack of respect that the younger generations have for the elderly these days. How can visiting your own mother twice a year be called "care"?

The care that the elderly require is to have their own family around them, not to have strangers from a different culture looking after them.

My wife and I took care of my mother in our own home. She was a happy, important member of our family, always active in family life and in full control of her mind until the day she passed away at 89.

I believe that your article failed to properly investigate the issues introduced, and was far too sympathetic towards Arjeta Weidler, failing to pose any hard questions to her. I believe that this is a failure on the part of your newspaper.

An angry reader

196. From these two articles, what do we know was different between the angry reader's mother and Weidler's mother?

(A) The angry reader's mother was satisfied with the care she received, but Weidler's mother isn't.

(B) Weidler's mother can afford to live in a care home, but the angry reader's mother could not.

(C) The angry reader believes that he was taking care of his mother, but Weidler does not believe that she is taking care of hers.

(D) Weidler's mother suffers from dementia, but the angry reader's mother did not.

197. What do these articles suggest?

(A) That more people may need to send their elderly relatives abroad in the future

(B) That people who suffer from Dementia are better off in Thailand

(C) That people can combine a vacation with visiting a relative in Thailand

(D) That care homes for the elderly in Switzerland are of poor quality

198. When Weidler told people about her plan for her mother, what was their reaction?

(A) They were understanding.

(B) They were outraged.

(C) They forgot within half an hour.

(D) They suffered from dementia.

199. What benefit of sending the elderly to Thailand is NOT given in the article?

(A) The weather is better there.

(B) The elderly receive better care in Thailand.

(C) Paying for the care is easier.

(D) You can visit your relative twice a year.

200. Besides Weidler, who/what else is the angry reader angry with?

(A) The care home in Thailand

(B) The newspaper

(C) Weidler's mother

(D) People in care homes

Part 7. 單篇／雙篇文章理解

第 153-154 題

Excon 油品公司的執行長在此通知公司的股東們，最近油價下跌以及去年油品在奈及利亞漏油意外的賠償金，將會對第四季的收益有不利影響。

該季收益下降，預料會對整年造成相當大地衝擊。很可能當 2013 整年度的營運結果在三月發表時，該年的營利將會比 2012 年低。

2014 年的前景，除了仍存在的不確定性之外，全球石油產量創下有始以來的新高，但需求量仍是取決於全球經濟的慢慢復甦而定。

153. 答案 (B) 這個聲明的目的是什麼？

(A) 報告在奈及利亞的漏油意外

(B) 警告那些持有 Excon 油品公司的人，2013 不是好的一年

(C) 警告全球經濟改善的不夠快

(D) 報告石油產量創新紀錄

解說 原文第一段第一句，"inform the company's shareholders"，以及第二段第二句，"It is likely that when the full year results for 2013 are released in March, profits for the year will be lower than for 2012"，表示通知股東，2013 年的營運沒有比去年好，故選 (B)。

154. 答案 (C) 下列哪一件影響 Excon 油品公司前景的事，沒有在本文提及？

(A) 全世界生產多少油

(B) 世界的經濟改善速度多快

(C) 油品公司能在奈及利亞賣多少油

(D) 油品價格

解說 選項 (A)，原文第三段，"worldwide oil production at record highs"，提到全世界產油量。選項 (B)，原文第三段，"slow recovery of the global economy"，表示世界經濟是慢慢地復甦。選項 (D)，原文第一段，"the recent drop in the price of oil"，提到油價。只有選項 (C) 未在文章中提及，故選 (C)。

字彙：

shareholder [ˋʃɛr͵holdɚ] *(n.)* 股東／ compensation [͵kɑmpənˋseʃən] *(n.)* 賠償／ adverse [ædˋvɝs] *(adj.)* 不利的／ revenue [ˋrɛvə͵nju] *(n.)* 收益／ outlook [ˋaʊt͵lʊk] *(n.)* 前景（＋ for）／ uncertain [ʌnˋsɝtn] *(adj.)* 不明確／ release [rɪˋlis] *(v.)* 發表／ dependent [dɪˋpɛndənt] *(adj.)* 取決於（＋ on）

第 155-156 題

離家遠的另一個舒適的家

入主人間天堂的部分權利

在美不勝收的西班牙馬約卡島上，面臨美麗海灘的公寓，做分時享用的所有權銷售。

可購買從每年一週至一個月入住西班牙近期最新建的住宅區，全都有完整的清潔與維護服務。

價格從 20,000 歐元起 ，外加每年收取一次的維護與服務費。

居住者可無限次使用綜合設施的泳池和公園區。

請至我們的網站觀看虛擬實境導覽 www.ECOconstruction.com/majorca

再也不必擔心訂不到渡假地點！

儘快參觀我們的地方，以免向隅。

155. 答案 (D) 這一則廣告在銷售什麼？

(A) 西班牙的住宅

(B) 清潔服務

(C) 西班牙的飯店假期

(D) 公寓的部分所有權

解說 原文第一段第一句，"Beautiful beach front apartments for time-share sale"，說明公寓是做分時享用的所有權銷售 ，故選 (D)。

156. 答案 (A) 如果你購買分時享用所有權，你會得到什麼不需額外收費？

(A) 使用游泳池

(B) 使用停車場

(C) 免費清潔服務

(D) 虛擬實境導覽

解說　原文倒數第四行，“Residents have unlimited access to the complex's pool and park areas”，說明游泳池和公園可無限次使用，故選 (A)。

字彙：

magnificent [mæg`nɪfəsənt] *(adj.)* 壯麗的／maintenance [`mentənəns] *(n.)* 維護／exclusive [ɪk`sklusɪv] *(adj.)* 高級的／unlimited [ʌn`lɪmɪtɪd] *(adj.)* 無限制的／partial [`pɑrʃəl] *(adj.)* 部分的／virtual [`vɝtʃuəl] *(adj.)* 虛擬的／front [frʌnt] *(adj.)* 正面的／resident [`rɛzədənt] *(n.)* 居住者

第 157-158 題

你需要理財顧問嗎？

你自己做投資嗎？如果是，你是否曾想過是否從專業人士那裡得到一些財務忠告會比較好呢？

人尋求的理財忠告裡，似乎沒有一個魔法數字。一些人樂於自己投資畢生的積蓄，但是常常是收據上出現的大筆金額讓人急匆地跑出理財顧問的大門。

那些從事這行工作的人說，幾乎任何人都會從造訪理財顧問獲得助益，並預計付錢來使用這項服務。只相信真正可靠的理財顧問，支付理財顧問看顧你最好的利息的費用，而不是只看他賣掉的獲利可得到的豐厚佣金。

157. 答案 (D) 根據本文，理財顧問能夠幫助誰？

(A) 只有突然獲得很多錢的人

(B) 只有擁有畢生積蓄可做投資的人

(C) 只有付錢給他們的人

(D) 大多數的人

解說　原文第三段第一行，“almost anyone will benefit from visiting one”，表示理財顧問幾乎對每個人都有益處，故選 (D)。

158. 答案 (B) 根據本文，如果你想要好的理財忠告，你必須做什麼？

(A) 急匆地跑出理財顧問的大門

(B) 支付理財顧問服務的費用

(C) 給理財顧問大額佣金

(D) 投資所有畢生積蓄

解說　原文第三段第二句，“who is being paid by you to look out for your

best interests"，故選 (B)。

字彙：

financial advisor [faɪˋnænʃəl] [ədˋvaɪzɚ] *(ph.)* 理財顧問／ better off [ˋbɛtɚ] [ɔf] *(ph.)* 景況較好／ advice [ədˋvaɪs] *(n.)* 忠告／ scurry [ˋskɝɪ] *(v.)* 急匆地跑／ commission [kəˋmɪʃən] *(n.)* 佣金／ interest[ˋɪntərɪst] *(n.)* 利息／ invest [ɪnˋvɛst] *(v.)* 投資／ saving [ˋsevɪŋ] *(n.)* 積蓄

第 159-162 題

收件人：Evans 先生

寄件人：Richard Cousins，Green 旅行社

我們遺憾通知你，你在六月九日從倫敦飛往新加坡的航班 WX 041，已被重新安排成下午三點十五分起飛。造成你的不便，敬請見諒，但是我想你應能了解，航空公司時程表不在我們能控制的範圍。

你現在會比原先預期的早上五點三十五分更提早兩個小時到達新加坡。你的旅程包括接駁車接送你至下塌飯店，很不幸地，接駁車要到早上八點才開始營運，為了表達我們對你樂意接受此項變動的感謝，我們幫你安排我們在新加坡的關係旅行社，免費接送你至住宿飯店。Sunset 旅行社會派人在入境大廳接你。

你其餘的旅程就照原訂計畫，包括六月十一日的城市導覽半日遊，以及同一天至新加坡動物園來場晚間的旅行隊。所有在六月十一日的服務，也皆由 Sunset 旅行社提供。

記得至少在下午一點十五分到達機場辦理離開倫敦班機的登機手續。如果需要我進一步的協助，請來電。

159. 答案 (D) Sunset 旅行社是什麼？

(A) Evans 先生用的旅行社

(B) 新加坡的航空公司

(C) 新加坡動物園的一部分

(D) Green 旅行社在新加坡的關係旅行社

解說　原文第二段倒數第一、二句，"we have arranged for a free transfer for you to your hotel with our partner in Singapore. Someone from Sunset Tours will be waiting for you at arrivals to pick you up."，說

明 Sunset 旅行社為 Green 旅行社的關係合作旅行社，故選 (D)。

160. 答案 (A) Green 旅行社做了什麼？

(A) 向 Evans 先生致歉

(B) 更改 Evans 先生的航班

(C) 告訴 Evans 到了新加坡搭乘接駁車

(D) 控制航空公司

解說 原文第一段第二句，"We apologize for any inconvenience caused"，表示 Green 旅行社向 Evans 先生致歉，故選 (A)。選項 (B) 不正確，原文第一段第二句，"the airline schedule is beyond our control"，以及第一句，"has been rescheduled"，表示更改航班時間不是旅行社能掌控的。選項 (C) 不正確，原文第二段第二句，"unfortunately the shuttle bus does not start to operate until 08:00"，以及第二段最後一句，"Someone from Sunset Tours will be waiting for you at arrivals to pick you up"，表示要 Evans 先生不要等八點搭接駁車，有人會去接他。

161. 答案 (B) Evans 先生必須做什麼？

(A) 更改要飛往新加坡的航班

(B) 比原先計畫六月九日當天至機場的時間再更早到

(C) 在新加坡搭乘接駁車至他住宿的飯店

(D) 致電 Green 旅行社的 Cousins 先生

解說 原文最後一段第一句，"Remember to be at the airport by at least 13:15 to check in for your flight leaving London"，表示提醒 Evans 先生必須提早至最少在下午一點十五分就要到機場辦理登機手續，故選 (B)。選項 (A) 不正確，更改的是航班的起飛時間，航班並未改變。選項 (C) 不正確，會有人去機場接 Evans 先生至住宿飯店。選項 (D) 不正確，致電給 Cousins 先生除非是有需要更進一步的協助才需要。

162. 答案 (D) 當 Evans 先生到達新加坡時，他應該做什麼？

(A) 辦理登機手續

(B) 去 Sunset 旅行社的辦公室

(C) 搭接駁車至他住宿的飯店

(D) 尋找從 Sunset 旅行社派來的人

解說 原文第二段最後一句，"Someone from Sunset Tours will be waiting

for you at arrivals to pick you up"，說明 Sunset 旅行社的人會在入境大廳接他，故選 (D)。

字彙：

regret [rɪˋgrɛt] *(v.)* 為…抱歉／ reschedule [riˋskɛdʒʊl] *(v.)* 重新安排／ itinerary [aɪˋtɪnə͵rɛrɪ] *(n.)* 旅程；路線／ operate [ˋɑpə͵ret] *(v.)* 營運／ token [ˋtokən] *(n.)* 標記；象徵／ goodwill [ˋgʊdˋwɪl] *(n.)* 樂意；善心／ arrival [əˋraɪvḷ] *(n.)* 到達；入境／ safari [səˋfɑrɪ] *(n.)* 旅行隊；非洲的（狩獵）旅行

第 163-165 題

這裡是一些準備工作面試的訣竅，確保決定人資經理知道你是這分工作的不二人選。

你在申請工作之前所做的事，會對你是否能進行到面試的階段，有很大的關係。研究你要申請工作的公司，不只是要了解公司概況而已，也要知道這個職位是真的是你想要的。

當收到面試召集時，想想公司要的是什麼。你的才能符合他們的要求嗎？準備你可能會被問到的問題清單，練習應答問題。找出你認識在那間公司工作的人。他們的內部消息也許給你在其他候選人中佔優勢。

在面試前一天準備好你的面試服裝。確定事先知道怎麼去面試地點，帶一些多餘的履歷複本，以及參考文件清單，並在十分鐘前提早到達。記得在進入辦公室之前關手機。

熱情地跟接待人員與接見者問好。專心聽你被問到的問題並在回答時看著接見者的眼睛，最重要地，記得呼吸。如果你有準備好，面試應該也會很順利。

163. 答案 (C) 根據本文，下列哪一項敘述為事實？

(A) 你不應該浪費時間研究公司概況直到你得到面試機會

(B) 不管自己真的認為不適合這個職位還是應該申請

(C) 你應該要很注意面試官說的話

(D) 你應該帶面試期間你想發問的問題清單

解說　原文第五段第二句，"Listen to what you are asked"，表示在面試時要注意被問到的問題，故選 (C)。選項 (A) 不正確，應該是要事先就研究好公司概況。選項 (B) 不正確，文中建議要先評估自己的才能是否符合職位需求。選項 (D) 不正確，面試期間應該帶的是參考文件清單。

164. 答案 (B) 下列哪一項敘述最能描述本文的忠告？

(A) 你在面試時的態度，是面試成功的關鍵

(B) 預先準備，是面試成功的關鍵

(C) 第一印象是面試成功的關鍵

(D) 能夠幫助你的朋友，是面試的成功關鍵

解說 原文第三段第三句，"Prepare a list of questions that you are likely to be asked"；第四段第一句，"Have your interview clothes ready before the day of the interview"，以及第五段最後一句，"if you have prepared well the interview should go well, too"，皆表示事先的準備，是面試成功的關鍵，故選 (B) 為本文最佳的描述。

165. 答案 (A) 本文沒有提到面試候選人應該做什麼？

(A) 事先拜訪面試舉行的辦公室

(B) 面試之前練習面試的問題

(C) 事先準備好要穿的衣服

(D) 儘量學得一些你要參加面試的公司訊息

解說 原文第四段第二句，"Be sure to know how to get to the interview beforehand"，文章提到要事先知道怎麼到面試地點，並不是應該事先先到那邊，故選 (A)。選項 (B)，原文第三段第三句，"Prepare a list of questions that you are likely to be asked"，提到應該先練習。選項 (C)，原文第四段第一句，"Have your interview clothes ready before the day of the interview"，提到應該先準備好面試衣服。選項 (D)，原文第二段第二句，"Research the company that you are applying to"；第三段第四句，"Find out who you know that works for the company or has a similar job. Their inside information may give you an edge over other candidates"，提到應該要儘可能的收集要面試的公司訊息。

字彙：

tip [tɪp] *(n.)* 提示；內部情報／ asset [ˋæsɛt] *(n.)* 才能／ requirement [rɪˋkwaɪrmənt] *(n.)* 要求／ edge [ɛdʒ] *(n.)* 優勢／ candidate [ˋkændədet] *(n.)* 候選人／ beforehand [bɪˋfor͵hænd] *(adv.)* 事先／ breathe [brið] *(v.)* 呼吸／ enthusiastically [ɪn͵θjuzɪˋæstɪkḷɪ] *(adv.)* 滿腔熱情地

第 166-168 題

我想要 Highcraft 電器公司帶給人品質好的印象。事實上，當你想到「品質」、「可靠」，或「價值」，我要你想到的是 Highcraft 電器公司的產品。

我們是領導者。我們公司創新的歷史悠久，讓我們保持在競爭的領先地位。我們想要你在我們的顧客服務上評分，就跟對我們的科技程度評分標準一樣。

我很榮幸介紹這款我們最新版的 Highcraft 膝上型輕便電腦。我們傾聽顧客的意見，並創造出不只符合期待，更超越期待的產品。新款 Highcraft 膝上型輕便電腦是我們有始以來，建造出的功能最強大的電腦。

然而這還只是開始而已。花幾分鐘看一下所有你看得到的事實以外的事，你還會發現這是一款已發行的電腦中，由最多系列軟體支援的產品。

參觀我們的網站，並看看最新消息。我們的支持顧客網絡忠於您的滿意度，也歡迎你給我們的意見回覆。我們會盡一切所能，讓你在 Highcraft 的購買，成為你做過的最好決定。

感謝您選擇 Highcraft 電器公司

166. 答案 (B) 本文說你能在 Highcraft 電器公司的網站做什麼？

(A) 你可以訂購他們的新款膝上型輕便電腦
(B) 你可以告訴他們你對他們產品的想法
(C) 你可以看精確的資料
(D) 你可以選擇你的新型膝上型輕便電腦的軟體

解說 原文第五行第一句，"Visit our website, and see how things have changed. Our customer support network is committed to your satisfaction and welcomes your feedback"，提到可至網站看看最新消息，並請不吝給予意見回覆，故選 (B)。

167. 答案 (A) 本文宣稱有關 Highcraft 電器公司的什麼事？

(A) 他們比他們的競爭者優秀
(B) 每位顧客都是滿意的
(C) 他們比他們的競爭者在這一行的歷史更久遠
(D) 他們的新款膝上型輕便電腦是你能買到的功能最強大的一款

解說　原文第二段第一句，“We are a leader. Our long history of innovation keeps us ahead of the competition”，表示 Highcraft 電器公司宣稱自己是業界的領導者，故選 (A)。選項 (B)、(C) 並未在本文提及。選項 (D)，原文第三段最後一句，“The new Highcraft laptop is the most powerful we have ever built”，僅表示是該公司有始以來建造出的功能最強大的電腦，並未說消費者在所有市面上的電腦只能買到這一款才是功能最強大的電腦。

168. 答案 (B) Highcraft 電器公司想要顧客做什麼？

(A) 寄多一點意見回覆至他們的顧客服務

(B) 把 Highcraft 電器公司與品質聯想在一起

(C) 購買產品時要想關於品質

(D) 幫助改變他們的網站

解說　原文第一段，“I want the name Highcraft Electronics to bring to mind an image of quality. In fact when you think “quality,” “reliability” or “value,” I want you to think of Highcraft Electronics' products”，明確的表示出 Highcraft 電器公司想要營造出顧客只要想到「品質」、「可靠」、「價值」，這三者其一時，自然就把它與自己的公司聯想在一起，故選 (B)。

字彙：

reliability [rɪˏlaɪə`bɪlətɪ] *(n.)* 可靠性／ innovation [ˏɪnə`veʃən] *(n.)* 創新／ exceed [ɪk`sid] *(v.)* 超過／ facts and figures [fækt] [ænd] [`fɪgjɚ] *(ph.)* 精確的資料／ network [`nɛtˏwɝk] *(n.)* 網絡／ committed [kə`mɪtɪd] *(adj.)* 忠誠的／ satisfaction [ˏsætɪs`fækʃən] *(n.)* 滿意／ feedback [`fidˏbæk] *(n.)* 反饋的訊息

第 169-172 題

我們很遺憾通知你，合併的評估，在完成接下來的 Western Union 銀行和 Southern Perpetual 合併，建議終止 Western Union 銀行的貸款部門。

所有跟 Western Union 銀行申辦的貸款，將會在接下來的一年，轉換至 Southern Perpetual ，而 Western Unions 銀行位於聖地亞哥的貸款處，將會在此轉換程序完成後結束。我們了解這個消息將會對我們在聖地亞哥的工作同仁們帶來震驚。

我們將會盡一切的努力，在組織裡替受到影響的員工們找到替代的工作。Southern Perpetual 的貸款部門也會釋出名額有限的新職缺，給那些願意被重新安排至鳳凰城上班的人。

提供自願裁退方案，藉以任何希望在接下來三個月內離職的員工，將供以慷慨的遣散費。

很不幸地，沒能在組織裡找到替代工作的員工，當該處最終關閉時，將會被解雇。

Western Union 銀行在此感謝所有員工的辛勞，我們致上最大的祝福，希望每個人無論在哪一個新的職位上，都能成功。

169. 答案 (C) 這則公告的目的為何？

(A) 告訴員工 Western Union 銀行和 Southern Perpetual 要合併

(B) 告訴員工他們將必需移至鳳凰城

(C) 告訴員工他們將會失去目前的工作

(D) 嚇員工

解說 原文第三段第一句，"Every effort will be made to find alternative employment within the organization for affected employees."；第四段第二句，"Unfortunately any employee who has not found alternative employment within the organization when the office finally closes will be laid off"，表示員工受到合併的影響是失去目前的工作，故選 (C)。

170. 答案 (B) 下列哪一項述為事實？

(A) 所有 Western Union 銀行的員工都會失去工作

(B) Western Union 銀行將會給一些錢給它在三個月內離職的員工

(C) 所有 Western Union 銀行的貸款部員工都能在 Southern Perpetual 獲得新的職位，如果他們打算搬到鳳凰市

(D) Western Union 銀行貸款部將會在三個月後結束

解說 原文第四段第一句，"A voluntary redundancy scheme is to be implemented whereby any employee who wishes to leave within the next three months will be offered a generous severance package"，說明三個月內自願離職的員工會收到一筆慷慨的遣散費，故選 (B)。選項 (A) 不正確，只有貸款部門的員工會失去工作。選項 (C) 不正確，Southern Perpetual 釋出的職缺有限，並非每個人都能獲得新工作。選項 (D) 不正確，Western Union 銀行貸款部將在完成合併程序後結束，並未提出明確的時間點。

171. 答案 (A) Western Union 銀行和 Southern Perpetual 的之間的關係為何？

(A) 他們成為一家公司

(B) Southern Perpetual 買下 Western Union 銀行的貸款部門

(C) Southern Perpetual 評估 Western Union 銀行，並建議終止它的貸款部門

(D) Southern Perpetual 試著吸引 Western Union 銀行的員工來替他們工作

解說 原文第一段第一句，"carried out following the merger of Western Union Bank and Southern Perpetual"，表示他們將完成整合成同一家公司，故選 (A)。

172. 答案 (B) Western Union 銀行承諾做到什麼？

(A) 替所有貸款部門的員工找到新的工作

(B) 幫助它的貸款部門員工找替代的工作

(C) 給所有失去工作的員工錢

(D) 努力保有 Western Union 銀行的貸款部門

解說 原文原文第三段第一句，"Every effort will be made to find alternative employment within the organization for affected employees."，表示會努力替貸款部門員工安排替代工作，故選 (B)。

字彙：

consolidation [kən͵sɑlə`deʃən] *(n.)* 合併／ closure [`kloʒɚ] *(n.)* 關閉；終止／ merger [mɝdʒɚ] *(n.)* 合併／ mortgage [`mɔrgɪdʒ] *(n.)* 抵押借款／ organization [͵ɔrgənə`zeʃən] *(n.)* 組織／ relocate [ri`loket] *(v.)* 重新安置／ redundancy [rɪ`dʌndənsɪ] *(n.)* 裁員／ scheme [skim] *(n.)* 方案；計畫

第 173-176 題

世界上最美麗的女人

好萊塢女星，安潔莉娜．裘莉常被受人敬重的報紙和八卦雜誌，被譽為世界上最美麗的女人。奧斯卡獎得主女星演出許多讓人目不轉睛的賣作電影，還有和布萊德．彼特在一起，他們倆的組合成了最終極的名人情侶。

裘莉在 1975 年生於洛杉磯，父母當時已在電影界。她在七歲時，在她父親的一部電影中首次演出，但是儘管就讀戲劇學校，她在青少年時期卻達到很少的成就。在這個時期，她也受憂鬱症之苦。她在高中時很難融入，甚至因外表被欺侮。

她二十出頭時的演技多半是審慎成功的，但是一直到 2001 年《古墓奇兵》發行，她才成為國際巨星。自此之後，她的事業運勢不可擋，而且她現在是好萊塢最高薪的女演員。

現在是已確立地位的電影明星，她常常因私生活出現在新聞上的頻率比電影多。結過兩次婚，她與父親的緊張關係，以及和布萊德．彼特訂婚的消息都成頭條新聞。

裘莉參與許多國內外的慈善活動，尤其是在國外，她替聯合國扮演許多不同角色。這個工作引領她決定，從許多自己曾工作過的國家領養小孩。裘莉和彼特現在有六個小孩，其中三個是從開發中國家領養的。

較近期的，她試著避免癌症引起大家注意，一個讓她許多親戚因此喪命的疾病，包括她的母親。隨著她的療法的宣揚，甚至在美國造成基因專利權的法律有所改變。

無論在電影院或是在雜誌裡，這個世界對安潔莉娜．裘莉的訊息，再多都不會滿足。

173. 答案 (B) 安潔莉娜・裘莉現在變成什麼？

(A) 聯合國領導

(B) 好萊塢賺最多錢的女演員

(C) 布萊德・彼特的老婆

(D) 八卦雜誌模特兒

解說 原文第三段最後一句，she is now Hollywood's highest paid actress，說明她成了好萊塢最高薪的女演員，故選 (B)。選項 (A) 不正確，她從事聯合國慈善活動。選項 (C) 不正確，文中只提到他與布萊德・彼特訂婚的消息，不是結婚的消息。選項 (D) 不正確，是八卦雜誌追蹤她的消息。

174. 答案 (D) 下列哪一項沒有在本文提及？

(A) 媒體對安潔莉娜・裘莉的關注

(B) 安潔莉娜・裘莉的家庭關係

(C) 安潔莉娜・裘莉在外國的工作

(D) 她領養的小孩是來自哪個國家

解說 原文第五段最後一句，"Jolie and Pitt now have six children, three of which were adopted from developing nations"，只說明領養的小孩有三位是來自開發中國家，並未詳述哪一些國家，故選 (D)。選項 (A)，原文最後一段，"the world doesn't seem to be able to get enough of Angelina Jolie"，表示全世界的媒體對她十分關注。選項 (B)，原文第四段第二句，"a strained relationship with her father"，提及她與父親的關係。選項 (C)，原文第五段第一句，"Jolie has been involved in much charity work, both at home but especially abroad"，說明她在國內外皆從事慈善工作。

175. 答案 (A) 安潔莉娜・裘莉何時第一次出現在電影中？

(A) 當她七歲時

(B) 當她是青少年時

(C) 2001 年

(D) 1975 年

解說 原文第二段第一句，"Jolie was born in Los Angeles in 1975"，以及第二句，"She made her acting debut at the age of seven in one of her father's films"，說明她出生於 1975 年，七歲首度在電影中演出，故

選 (A)。選項 (D) 是她出生的那一年，她七歲時是 1982 年，故選項 (C) 也不正確。

176. 答案 (B) 除了電影業，本文說 安潔莉娜．裘莉對什麼造成了影響？

(A) 開發中國家的領養比例

(B) 美國法律

(C) 高中的凌霸

(D) 對憂鬱症的了解

解說 原文第六段最後一句，"The publicity which followed her treatment even resulted in changes to the law on patenting genes in the US"，說明她的療法也改變了美國的基因專利權法律改變，故選 (B)。

字彙：

respected [rɪˋspɛktɪd] *(adj.)* 受敬重的／ stare [stɛr] *(v.)* 目不轉睛／ debut [dɪˋbju] *(n.)* 首次登臺／ depression [dɪˋprɛʃən] *(n.)* 憂鬱症／ bully [ˋbʊlɪ] *(v.)* 欺侮／ release [rɪˋlis] *(n.)* 發行／ strained [ˋstrend] *(adj.)* 緊張的／ adopt [əˋdɑpt] *(v.)* 領養

第 177-180 題

雇用合約

REED 企業

澳洲 雪梨

十一月五日

Brian Gough 先生

Lions 大道 312 號

雪梨

親愛的 Gough 先生

這封信是確認所有預先用前的檢查已完成，你將於十一月二十五日始受雇於 REED 企業。你需要簽名這份合約，同意以下聲明的期限與條款，並在十一月二十日前將合約交回給我們。

雇用期限：這是個全職、永久的職位。工作時數是標準的每週三十八小時，每年享十日帶薪休假。你或公司想終止本約定，必需在三個月前以書面告知。

工作職掌：你將會被雇用為我們位於雪梨研究與開發實驗室的實驗室科學家工作。工作主要牽涉開發與測試新的建築業建材，但是也會包括需要維持現代化實驗室運作的任何日常工作。

薪資：你的薪資是我們給大學研究科學家的標準起薪，年薪三萬五千美元整，包括健康津貼。這個薪水受你年度表現評估管制。你的薪水將會每月轉帳至你選擇的銀行帳號。

機密條款：所有在我們研究室的研究屬於 Reed 企業的資產。過去、現在與未來的研究皆不能在我們辦公室外討論。這包括任何未來與其他公司雇用的期間。

請在這份合約複本上簽名，並在十一月十五日前寄回給我們。只有在我們收到這些文件時，你與 Reed 企業的合約才生效。

我們期待在十一月二十五日與你見面

誠摯的

Anne Beggs 太太

人力資源部主任

背書

我已詳閱以上期間與條款，並接受雇用的具體説明。

簽名：........................ 日期：........................

177. 答案 (D) 收到這份合約之後，Gough 先生下一步應該做什麼？

(A) 十一月二十五日去上班

(B) 在 Reed 企業申請工作

(C) 研究建築業的新建材

(D) 簽名並寄回合約

解說 原文第六段，"Please sign the duplicate copies of this contract and send them back to us by November 15th. Only when these documents have been received will a contract exist between you and Reed Industries"，説明下一步是寄回合約，合約在寄回後始生效，故選 (D)。

178. 答案 (C) Gough 先生被禁止做什麼？

(A) 跟他其它在 Reed 企業上班的人講關於他的研究

(B) 每年去渡假十天

(C) 跟他的朋友和鄰居談論關於他正從事的研究

(D) 未來任職於任何其他公司

解說 原文第五段，"No past, present of future research can be discussed outside of our offices"，機密條款說明在 Reed 企業公司的研究不得在辦公司以外的地方談論，故選 (C)。

179. 答案 (B) Gough 先生應該在十一月二十五日做什麼？

(A) 檢查他的銀行帳戶入帳的三萬五千美金

(B) 出現在 Reed 企業上班 Industries

(C) 把合約帶至 Reed 企業

(D) 終止他與 Reed 公司的合約

解說 原文第一段第一句，"your employment with Reed Industries can commence on November 25th"，以及倒數第七行，"We look forward to seeing you on November 25th"，說明 Gough 先生將受雇 Reed 企業，而他們期待在十一月二十五日見到他，因此得知當天 Gough 先生將會開始至 Reed 企業上班，故選 (B)。

180. 答案 (A) Gough 先生預期在 Reed 企業從事何種工作？

(A) 在實驗室從事研究

(B) 做測試

(C) 簽名合約

(D) 在建築工地工作

解說 原文第三段第一句，"You will be employed as a Laboratory research scientist at our Sydney research and development labs"，說明工作內容是在實驗室裡做開發與研究，故選 (A)。

字彙：

imployment [ɪm`plɔɪmənt] *(n.)* 雇用／ commence [kə`mɛns] *(v.)* 開始／ term [tɝm] *(n.)* 期限／ paid leave [ped] [liv] *(ph.)* 帶薪休假／ terminate [`tɝmə,net] *(v.)* 終止／ subject to *(ph.)* 受…管制／ confidentiality [,kɑnfɪ,dɛnʃɪ`ælɪtɪ] *(n.)* 機密／ duplicate [`djupləkɪt] *(adj.)* 複本的

第 181-185 題

Aztec Towers 遊樂園開放新聞稿

Aztec Towers 遊樂園很開心宣佈最新的雲霄飛車—— Aztec Rocket 開始營運。

在高度 147 公尺的最高點，是設定要成為全世界最高的雲霄飛車——以高出七公尺打破先前記錄。Aztec Rocket 的速度也達嚇人的時速 105 公里。

由世界最知名遊樂園設施製造商，R&C 國際設計，其作品包括杜拜的 Dubai Flyer 和喬治亞的 Georgia Wheel。Aztec Rocket 將會是未來這類設施的基準點。

將會在六月十二日對外開放，當天即開始本園的夏季日程表。五月二十九日將先開放媒體入園。所有想參訪的記者必須事先申請鑑定。

媒體內容概要說明書

名稱：Aztec Rocket

製造商：R&C 國際

起造日：二〇一二年二月

完工日：二〇一三年九月

長度：3,245 公尺

高度：147 公尺（最高點）

速度：時速 105 公里（最大）

倒轉次數：11 次

搭乘期間：兩分鐘五十秒

雲霄飛車：共有 60 輛列車，每輛有 4 節車廂。每節車廂共有 4 排，一排座 4 位乘座人，每列車總共乘載 16 人。

容積：每小時 1,300 趟

建造使用鋼鐵量：2,150 噸

造價：二千七百萬美金

181. 答案 (D) 這兩篇文章提到 Aztec Rocket 的乘坐人將會感覺如何？

(A) 他們會覺得搭乘這項設施很貴

(B) 他們會覺得這項設施太高

(C) 他們會覺得這項設施很新奇

(D) 他們會害怕

解說 第一篇原文第二段第二句，"The Aztec Rocket also reaches a terrifying 105 km/hr"，說明速度是嚇人的，暗示搭乘的人會感到害怕，故選 (D)。選項 (A)、(B)、(C) 屬個人觀感，並未在文章中提到搭乘者的感受。

182. 答案 (A) 什麼會在每次搭乘時發生超過十次？

(A) 列車會上下顛倒

(B) 列車達 147 公尺的高度

(C) 列車達每小時 105 公里的速度

(D) 列車飛進杜拜空中

解說 第二篇原文第八行，Inversions: 11，說明每次乘座時會反轉 11 次，故選 (A)。選項 (B)、(C) 皆為該設施的最高點與最快時速可達到的程度，亦並未說明會在搭乘期間會發生幾次。

183. 答案 (B) 記者受邀做什麼？

(A) 他們受邀在六月十二日參訪遊樂園

(B) 他們受邀五月二十九日參訪遊樂園

(C) 他們受邀搭乘 Aztec Rocket

(D) 他們受邀寫有關 Aztec Rocket 的報導

解說 第一篇原文第四段第二句，"A media day will be held on May 29th"，表示五月二十九日先邀請媒體參訪，故選 (B)。選項 (A)，是向大眾開放該設施的一天。選項 (C)、(D) 在文章中未提及。

184. 答案 (A) Aztec Rocket 以什麼創下新記錄？

(A) 它的高度

(B) 它的速度

(C) 它的造價

(D) 它每小時可乘載的人數

解說　第一篇原文第二段，"At a height of 147 meters at its highest point, it is set to become the world's highest roller coaster- smashing the previous record by over 7 meters"，說明高度打破先前的最記錄，創下新記錄，故選 (A)。

185. 答案 (B) Aztec Rocket 的一個車廂能乘坐幾人？

(A) 16 人

(B) 4 人

(C) 60 人

(D) 1,300 人

解說　第二篇原文第十行，"60 trains each with four cars. Riders sit four across in a single row for a total of sixteen riders per train"，整個車廂說明每列列車有 4 個車廂，每個車廂乘坐 4 人，共可容納 16 人，故選 (B)。

字彙：

press release [prɛs] [rɪ`lis] *(n.)* 新聞稿／ smash [smæʃ] *(v.)* 打破／ benchmark [`bɛntʃ,mɑrk] *(n.)* 基準點／ accreditation [ə,krɛdə`teʃən] *(n.)* 鑑定／ fact sheet [fækt] [ʃit] *(ph.)* 內容概要說明書／ inversion [ɪn`vɝʃən] *(n.)* 倒轉／ duration [djʊ`reʃən] *(n.)* 期間／ steel [stil] *(n.)* 鋼鐵

第 186-190 題

收件人：Jeff Reagan
寄件人：Ryan Jones

我以 Halifax 學院總教練的身分寫信給你。首先，以總教練對總教練的程度上，我想恭賀你們學校的橄欖球隊在上一季的成功。打進州際決賽加時賽，一定讓球隊很滿意。

我想看是否你會有興趣替我們各自學院的橄欖球和籃球隊安排一些季前賽。我們鮮少對打，除了在州際錦標賽被安排在一起，我覺得一旦真的有這樣的行動開始，我們兩所學院都會受益。尤其是我們的橄欖球隊，很想與你們隊上一些明星球員切磋。

收件人：Ryan Jones
寄件人：Jeff Reagan

謝謝你的來信，Halifax 學院的籃球隊表現得很好。我們 Hamilton 學院的橄欖球隊有打入州際決賽加時賽，但是 Halifax 學院可是差點就抱回州際籃球賽冠軍獎座。在最後時刻失分一定很心痛。

你説對了，我們兩所學院太不常對打了。我們的地點如此地靠近，但是也許競爭的行為，阻撓了我們在這樣的清況下獲得更多優勢。

我認為我們一定可以替我們的橄欖球和籃球隊安排一些季前賽，還有我們的游泳教練也在問，是不是也可以包括游泳隊在這個活動內，讓他們與你們學校的隊伍比賽。

我們的季前訓練會在九月一日開始，所以我是否可以建議九月最後兩週的週末，因為是最可能可以用來做任何比賽的日期。

讓我知道你比較想要在哪一個週末比，然後我們能再討論地點和其他更詳盡的事項。

186. 答案 (C) 誰是 Jeff Reagan ？

(A) Halifax 學院的體育總教練
(B) Hamilton 學院的橄欖球明星球員
(C) Hamilton 學院的體育總教練
(D) Hamilton 學院的橄欖球教練

解說 第二篇原文，"From: Jeff Reagan"；第一段第一句，"Here at Hamilton College" 表示寄件人為 Jeff Reagan"，提到我們 Hamilton College，就表示 Jeff Reagan 是 Hamilton 學院的人，以及第一篇原文第一段第二行，"Firstly, head coach to head coach"，説明 Jeff Reagan 是 Hamilton 學院的總教練，故選 (C)。

187. 答案 (D) 為什麼 Ryan Jones 寫郵件給 Jeff Reagan ？

(A) 安排他們季前賽的日期
(B) 恭賀 Hamilton 學院在運動賽事上的成功
(C) 學更多關於 Hamilton 學院橄欖球隊的事
(D) 邀請 Hamilton 學院與 Halifax 學院在運動比賽項目上有更緊密合作

解說　第一篇原文第三段第一句，"We rarely play each other, unless drawn together in the state championship, and I feel that both colleges would benefit from it once the real action begins"，表示很少有對打的機會，邀請可以讓兩所學院互相比賽切磋，故選 (D)。選項 (A)，第一篇的文章中未提已要安排時間，尚未徵求到另一所學院的同意。選項 (B)，有恭賀，但並非寫信的原因。選項 (D)，本中提尤其想跟 Hamilton 橄欖球員的明星球員切磋。

188. 答案 (A) 除了比賽的日期，兩所學院還必須決定什麼？

(A) 在哪裡進行比賽

(B) 看是要打橄欖球或籃球

(C) 為什麼兩間學院那麼少對打

(D) 如何測試他們的明星球員

解說　第二篇原文最後一段第一句，"Let me know which weekend you would prefer, and then we can discuss locations"，表示決定完時間後，必須再討論地點，故選 (A)。

189. 答案 (B) 以下哪一個敘述為事實？

(A) Hamilton 學院的橄欖球隊贏了州際錦標賽

(B) Halifax 學院的籃球隊在州際錦標賽榮獲第二名

(C) Halifax 學院沒有游泳隊

(D) 兩所學院的體育隊很常彼此對打

解說　第二篇原文第一段第二句，"but Halifax College almost won the state basketball championship. That last minute loss in the final must have been heartbreaking"，表示 Halifax 在最後一刻失分，差點贏得冠軍，代表是贏得第二名，故選 (B)。選項 (A) 不正確，第一篇原文第一段第三句，"Reaching the state play-offs must have given the team a lot satisfaction"，說明 Hamilton 學院只打進決賽加時賽，並未贏得冠軍。選項 (C) 不正確，第二篇原文第三段，"and our swimming coach has also asked if the swimming team can be included in the action against your team"，表示也想要兩學院之間的游泳隊互相比賽。選項 (D) 不正確，第二篇原文第二段第一句，"our two colleges don't play each other enough"，說明兩所學院之間很少對打。

190. 答案 (A) 兩所學校最有可能同意的對打日期為何？

(A) 九月二十三日，星期日

(B) 九月八日，星期六

(C) 九月十一日，星期二

(D) 九月二十四日，星期一

解說 原文第二篇第四段第一句，"so may I suggest the final two weekends of September as probable dates for any games"，說明最可能的日期為九月最後兩週，即約在九月十四之後，週末為週六或週日，故選項 (A) 是最符合本文敘述的答案。

字彙：

respective [rɪˋspɛktɪv] *(adj.)* 各自的／ championship [ˋtʃæmpɪənˏʃɪp] *(n.)* 錦標賽／ loss [lɔs] *(n.)* 輸；失去／ heartbreaking [ˋhɑrtˏbrekɪŋ] *(adj.)* 令人心碎的／ rivalry [ˋraɪvl̩rɪ] *(n.)* 競爭行為／ probable [ˋprɑbəbl̩] *(adj.)* 很可能發生的／ tie [taɪ] *(v.)* 合／ action [ˋækʃən] *(n.)* 行為；活動

第 191-195 題

七月十七日，星期三　電視時間表

午夜 12 點	《夜生活》 一窺夜店行業
早上 1:30	《火星上的生活》 電影：地球首批至火星的殖民，能在火星第一場災難生存下來嗎？
早上 3:10	《混合》 不同的音樂節目，由客座藝人現場表演一些他們最愛的歌曲。
早上 5:00	《水手》 卡通：第五季，第 3 集
早上 6:00	《早安電視》 與明星共渡早餐時光。所有開啟一天所需 —— 新聞、音樂、八卦，還有更多的內容。與早安電視開啟你美好的一天。
早上 8:30	《購物》
早上 10:30	《文化節目》 從電影和音樂到藝術的整週新聞簡報
中午 12:00	《正午新聞》
下午 12:30	《Georgie》 情境喜劇：第二季，第 11 集

下午 1:00　《A Bold Day》
電影：重新翻拍的 1930 年代經典電影

下午 3:30　《兒童時間》
給小小孩看的卡通、故事與樂趣

下午 5:30　《健康與健身》
我們的第五週健身計畫

下午 6:00　《孤雛淚》
第一季，第 1 集
現代的狄更斯經典改寫版

下午 7:00　《總統》
當美國總統是什麼滋味？始無前例被批准可近身在背後窺探總統的一天生活。

晚上 9:00　《世界新聞》

晚上 9:30　《當地新聞》

晚上 10:00　《警察戰線》
紀錄片：警察能守住與黑幫衝突的防線嗎？只適合成熟的觀眾觀看。

七月十七日，星期三　電視評論

昨晚電視可能有一些可收看的好節目，但是你必須仔細地找。

你真的需要一部新製作的《孤雛淚》嗎？這部片不是已經被「重新翻拍」大概三十次了嗎？所以，我必定給它失敗的評價。至於《總統》，如果你問我的意見，它比較像是「打哈欠」！兩個小時後，我等待商業廣告的休息時間，以減輕無聊。

還有對那些好的部份，《健康與健身》節目，似乎正中紅心。這不是胡謅的以實際步驟變得積極的方式，顯得真的有用。數以千計全國上下的人都開始這麼做，我也是其中一個。

《警察戰線》有點殘忍地坦率，看著城市警察的難處，面對一些我們城市裡的隱晦面。常常很難觀看到，這個讓人認為刺激的紀錄片，帶領我們看見一些我們想像的世界，就真實存在於只距離很多我們住的地方幾個街區。這個節目當然是當天最精彩的電視節目。

191. 答案 (C) 評論家最喜歡哪一個電視節目？

(A)《健康與健身》

(B)《總統》

(C)《警察戰線》

(D)《孤雛淚》

解說 第二篇原文第四段第一句，“The Police Line was a brutally honest look at the difficulties city police are facing in some of our inner cities”；第三句，“This program was certainly the highlight of the day's TV”，評論家表示《警察戰線》是當天最精彩的節目，故選 (C)。

192. 答案 (B) 評論家對《總統》做出什麼評論？

(A) 她不喜歡現任總統

(B) 廣告是最好的部份

(C) 總統的生活是無聊的

(D) 警察必須努力工作以在城市的隱晦面中保護自己

解說 第二篇原文第二段第四句，“As for The President, much more like "The Yawn" if you ask me! After two hours, I was waiting for the commercial breaks to help relieve the boredom”，說明看《總統》時不斷打哈欠，期待廣告時間，因為廣告能減輕無聊感，故最好看的部分，是廣告時間，故選 (B).。

193. 答案 (A) 哪一個節目最適合剛開始看那個節目的人？

(A)《Oliver Twist》

(B)《水手》

(C)《Georgie》

(D)《健康與健身》

解說 第一篇原文倒數第十一行，“Series 1, Episode 1”，說明《孤雛淚》從第一季，第一集開始播出，是最適合剛開始看一個節目的人，故選 (A)。選項 (B)，已播出至第五季，第 3 集。選項 (C)，已播出至第二季，第 11 集。選項 (D)，已播出至第五週。

194. 答案 (C)「只適合成熟的觀眾觀看」是什麼意思？

(A) 節目是在觀眾面前製作的

(B) 警察想要很多觀眾看該節目

(C) 小孩不應該觀看那個節目

(D) 老人不應該看那個節目

195. 答案 (A) 哪一個節目最可能會讓你笑？

(A)《Georgie》

(B)《文化節目》

(C)《警察戰線》

(D)《混合》

解說 第一篇原文第十九、二十行，《Georgie》，Sitcom: Series 2, Episode 11，喜劇最有可能讓你笑，故選 (A)。

字彙：

colony [ˋkɑlənɪ] *(n.)* 殖民／ series [ˋsiriz] *(n.)* 系列／ episode [ˋɛpə͵sod] *(n.)* 集／ round-up [raʊnd] [ʌp] *(n.)* 新聞簡報／ sitcom [ˋsɪt͵kɑm] *(n.)* 情境喜劇 ／ remake [rɪˋmek] *(n.)* 改做物；翻新物／ grant [grænt] *(v.)* 同意；授予／ adaptation [͵ædæpˋteʃən] *(n.)* 改編；改寫本

第 196-200 題

把祖父母輩送出國

Arjeta Weidler 來自瑞士日內瓦，收拾好她的行李箱，前往機場並搭上飛機。她要前往泰國北部的清邁，但是她不是去渡假。她是去探望她的母親。

Arieta 是人數正在成長，把他們年邁親戚送往國外老人照護之家的其中一人「當我跟人說我做了的事，他們都很震驚。『你怎麼膽敢這麼做？你要怎麼去探視她？』這些是我聽到的所有回應，」Weidler 說。

「但是當我探視她，她不到半小時就忘了，而且她在泰國受到的照護程度遠比在瑞士這裡高很多。」

Weidler 的母親，Hilda，是位 93 歲受痴呆之苦的人 。她在 Weidler 準定將她移至泰國之前在瑞士接受照護四年。「我最少一年探視她兩次，而且她現在似乎滿意她的生活。Weidler 說。

很快看這些特點，不難看出為何許多家庭跟 Weidler 做出一樣的決定。花價便宜太多了，但是仍有高度品質好的好名聲。

在泰國有專門從事照護外國客戶的老人之家。每個老人之家都有從同一個國家來的住戶，所以語言向來不是個問題。多數住戶甚至不知道他們身處外國，而且沒有歐洲冬季的寒冷氣候，也主張這點是對老年人較好。

有最大老年人口增加的壓力，以及當地提供醫療服務人員的沉重壓力，也許我們會在未來搭飛機去探視我們的祖父母輩。

親愛的編輯，

我最近對一則在你的報社上刊登的文章感到萬分地憤怒，標題是「把祖父輩送出國」。

怎麼會有人送他們自己的親人去住在國外，讓他孤獨在世界的另外一邊？

這全顯示現在年輕一代對老一輩缺乏尊重。一年探視你母親兩次，算哪門子的「照顧」？

老年人需要的照顧是擁有他們的家人在附近，而不是有來自不同文化的陌生人照顧他們。

我的老婆和我在我們自己的家中一起照顧我的母親。她是個開心、重要的家庭成員，總是積極在家庭生活中，並且完全掌控自己的心智直到她 89 歲過世的那一天。

我相信你的文章沒有完善的調查內文介紹到的事情，而且也太贊同 Arjeta Weidler 的說法，沒有對她提出任何艱深的問題。我相信這是你報社失敗的一部分。

一位憤怒的讀者

196. 答案 (D) 從這兩篇文章，你知道什麼關於憤怒讀者的母親與 Weidler 的母親之間的不同？

(A) 憤怒讀者的母親很滿意她受到的照顧，但是 Weidler 的母親不是這樣

(B) Weidler 的母親能付得起住在老人照護之家，但是憤怒的讀者的母親無法負擔

(C) 憤怒的讀者相信他有照顧好他的母親，但是 Weidler 不認為自己照顧好她的母親

(D) Weidler 的母親受痴呆之苦，但是憤怒的讀者的母親沒有

解說　從第一篇原文第五段第一句，"Weidler's mother, Hilda, is 93 and suffers from dementia"，以及原文第五段第二句，"in full control of her mind until the day she passed away at 89"，可以知道 Weidler 的母親受痴呆之苦，但憤怒的讀者的母親心智清楚直到去世的那一天，故選 (D)。

197. 答案 (A) 這兩篇文章暗示了什麼？

(A) 愈來愈多人未來可能需要把他們的祖父母輩送出國

(B) 受痴呆之苦的人去泰國比較好

(C) 在泰國可以結合渡假和探視親戚

(D) 老人照護之家在瑞士的品質不好

解說　第一篇原文最後一段，"With the ever increasing pressure of an ageing population, and the strains that it is putting on local health providers, maybe more of us will be getting on a plane to visit Gran in the future"，表示在未來的發展，可能有更多人會把祖父母輩送出國養老，第二篇原文第五段第一句，"was far too sympathetic towards Arjeta Weidler"，表示報社刊登的內容太偏袒 Weidler 把母親送出國到老人之家的說法，也可能造成年輕世代在未來採用這樣的做法，故選 (A)。

198. 答案 (B) 當 Weidler 告訴別人關於她對她母親的計畫時，他們的反應如何？

(A) 他們了解

(B) 他們激動憤怒

(C) 他們不到半小時就忘了

(D) 他們受痴呆之苦

解說　第一篇原文第三段，"When I told people what I was doing, they were shocked. 'How dare you do this? How can you visit her?' was all I heard," says Weidler"，說明聽到的人說的都是對她不諒解的生氣責備話語，故選 (B)。

199. 答案 (D) 什麼不是文章裡說明送長輩至泰國的好處？

(A) 那裡的天氣比較好。

(B) 長輩在泰國受到比較好的照護

(C) 照護費用比較容易可負擔

(D) 你可以每年探視親戚兩次

解說 選項 (A)，第一篇原文倒數第二段第三句，"the climate without the cold European winters is claimed to be better for the elderly, too"，表示泰國的氣候是好處。選項 (B)，第一篇原文第四段第一句，"the level of care she receives in Thailand is far higher than that available here in Switzerland"，表示在泰國得到的照護比較好。選項 (C)，第一篇原文第六段第二句，"The costs are far cheaper"，說明費用的部份比較便宜，是好處。只有選項 (D)，在文章中並未提到這算是好處之一，故選 (D)。

200. 答案 (B) 除了 Weidler，誰／什麼也是讓憤怒的讀者感到生氣的事？

(A) 泰國的老人照護之家

(B) 報社

(C) Weidler 的母親

(D) 在老人之家的人

解說 第二篇原文最後一段，"I believe that your article failed to properly investigate the issues introduced, and was far too sympathetic towards Arjeta Weidler, failing to pose any hard questions to her. I believe that this is a failure on the part of your newspaper"，表現出對報社沒有查明事實細節真相就刊登文章，感到憤怒，也因此認定這是間失敗的報社，故選 (B)。

字彙：

dare [dɛr] *(v.)* 敢；膽敢／ dementia [dɪˋmɛnʃɪə] *(n.)* 痴呆／ contented [kənˋtɛntɪd] *(adj.)* 滿意的（＋with）／ reputation [ˏrɛpjəˋteʃən] *(n.)* 名聲／ specialize [ˋspɛʃəˏlaɪz] *(v.)* 專門從事（＋in）／ outrage[ˋaʊtˏrɛdʒ] *(v.)* 激怒／ flesh and blood [flɛʃ] [ænd] [blʌd] *(ph.)* 親人／ sympathetic [ˏsɪmpəˋθɛtɪk] *(adj.)* 贊同的（＋towards）

READING SECTION (TEST 1)

Part 5								Part 6				Part 7							
Nol	ANSWER A B C D	Nol	ANSWER A B C D	Nol	ANSWER A B C D	Nol	ANSWER A B C D	Nol	ANSWER A B C D	Nol	ANSWER A B C D	Nol	ANSWER A B C D	Nol	ANSWER A B C D	Nol	ANSWER A B C D	Nol	ANSWER A B C D
101	ⒶⒷⒸⒹ	111	ⒶⒷⒸⒹ	121	ⒶⒷⒸⒹ	131	ⒶⒷⒸⒹ	141	ⒶⒷⒸⒹ	151	ⒶⒷⒸⒹ	161	ⒶⒷⒸⒹ	171	ⒶⒷⒸⒹ	181	ⒶⒷⒸⒹ	191	ⒶⒷⒸⒹ
102	ⒶⒷⒸⒹ	112	ⒶⒷⒸⒹ	122	ⒶⒷⒸⒹ	132	ⒶⒷⒸⒹ	142	ⒶⒷⒸⒹ	152	ⒶⒷⒸⒹ	162	ⒶⒷⒸⒹ	172	ⒶⒷⒸⒹ	182	ⒶⒷⒸⒹ	192	ⒶⒷⒸⒹ
103	ⒶⒷⒸⒹ	113	ⒶⒷⒸⒹ	123	ⒶⒷⒸⒹ	133	ⒶⒷⒸⒹ	143	ⒶⒷⒸⒹ	153	ⒶⒷⒸⒹ	163	ⒶⒷⒸⒹ	173	ⒶⒷⒸⒹ	183	ⒶⒷⒸⒹ	193	ⒶⒷⒸⒹ
104	ⒶⒷⒸⒹ	114	ⒶⒷⒸⒹ	124	ⒶⒷⒸⒹ	134	ⒶⒷⒸⒹ	144	ⒶⒷⒸⒹ	154	ⒶⒷⒸⒹ	164	ⒶⒷⒸⒹ	174	ⒶⒷⒸⒹ	184	ⒶⒷⒸⒹ	194	ⒶⒷⒸⒹ
105	ⒶⒷⒸⒹ	115	ⒶⒷⒸⒹ	125	ⒶⒷⒸⒹ	135	ⒶⒷⒸⒹ	145	ⒶⒷⒸⒹ	155	ⒶⒷⒸⒹ	165	ⒶⒷⒸⒹ	175	ⒶⒷⒸⒹ	185	ⒶⒷⒸⒹ	195	ⒶⒷⒸⒹ
106	ⒶⒷⒸⒹ	116	ⒶⒷⒸⒹ	126	ⒶⒷⒸⒹ	136	ⒶⒷⒸⒹ	146	ⒶⒷⒸⒹ	156	ⒶⒷⒸⒹ	166	ⒶⒷⒸⒹ	176	ⒶⒷⒸⒹ	186	ⒶⒷⒸⒹ	196	ⒶⒷⒸⒹ
107	ⒶⒷⒸⒹ	117	ⒶⒷⒸⒹ	127	ⒶⒷⒸⒹ	137	ⒶⒷⒸⒹ	147	ⒶⒷⒸⒹ	157	ⒶⒷⒸⒹ	167	ⒶⒷⒸⒹ	177	ⒶⒷⒸⒹ	187	ⒶⒷⒸⒹ	197	ⒶⒷⒸⒹ
108	ⒶⒷⒸⒹ	118	ⒶⒷⒸⒹ	128	ⒶⒷⒸⒹ	138	ⒶⒷⒸⒹ	148	ⒶⒷⒸⒹ	158	ⒶⒷⒸⒹ	168	ⒶⒷⒸⒹ	178	ⒶⒷⒸⒹ	188	ⒶⒷⒸⒹ	198	ⒶⒷⒸⒹ
109	ⒶⒷⒸⒹ	119	ⒶⒷⒸⒹ	129	ⒶⒷⒸⒹ	139	ⒶⒷⒸⒹ	149	ⒶⒷⒸⒹ	159	ⒶⒷⒸⒹ	169	ⒶⒷⒸⒹ	179	ⒶⒷⒸⒹ	189	ⒶⒷⒸⒹ	199	ⒶⒷⒸⒹ
110	ⒶⒷⒸⒹ	120	ⒶⒷⒸⒹ	130	ⒶⒷⒸⒹ	140	ⒶⒷⒸⒹ	151	ⒶⒷⒸⒹ	160	ⒶⒷⒸⒹ	170	ⒶⒷⒸⒹ	180	ⒶⒷⒸⒹ	190	ⒶⒷⒸⒹ	200	ⒶⒷⒸⒹ

READING SECTION (TEST 2)

Part 5								Part 6				Part 7							
Nol	ANSWER A B C D	Nol	ANSWER A B C D	Nol	ANSWER A B C D	Nol	ANSWER A B C D	Nol	ANSWER A B C D	Nol	ANSWER A B C D	Nol	ANSWER A B C D	Nol	ANSWER A B C D	Nol	ANSWER A B C D	Nol	ANSWER A B C D
101	ⒶⒷⒸⒹ	111	ⒶⒷⒸⒹ	121	ⒶⒷⒸⒹ	131	ⒶⒷⒸⒹ	141	ⒶⒷⒸⒹ	151	ⒶⒷⒸⒹ	161	ⒶⒷⒸⒹ	171	ⒶⒷⒸⒹ	181	ⒶⒷⒸⒹ	191	ⒶⒷⒸⒹ
102	ⒶⒷⒸⒹ	112	ⒶⒷⒸⒹ	122	ⒶⒷⒸⒹ	132	ⒶⒷⒸⒹ	142	ⒶⒷⒸⒹ	152	ⒶⒷⒸⒹ	162	ⒶⒷⒸⒹ	172	ⒶⒷⒸⒹ	182	ⒶⒷⒸⒹ	192	ⒶⒷⒸⒹ
103	ⒶⒷⒸⒹ	113	ⒶⒷⒸⒹ	123	ⒶⒷⒸⒹ	133	ⒶⒷⒸⒹ	143	ⒶⒷⒸⒹ	153	ⒶⒷⒸⒹ	163	ⒶⒷⒸⒹ	173	ⒶⒷⒸⒹ	183	ⒶⒷⒸⒹ	193	ⒶⒷⒸⒹ
104	ⒶⒷⒸⒹ	114	ⒶⒷⒸⒹ	124	ⒶⒷⒸⒹ	134	ⒶⒷⒸⒹ	144	ⒶⒷⒸⒹ	154	ⒶⒷⒸⒹ	164	ⒶⒷⒸⒹ	174	ⒶⒷⒸⒹ	184	ⒶⒷⒸⒹ	194	ⒶⒷⒸⒹ
105	ⒶⒷⒸⒹ	115	ⒶⒷⒸⒹ	125	ⒶⒷⒸⒹ	135	ⒶⒷⒸⒹ	145	ⒶⒷⒸⒹ	155	ⒶⒷⒸⒹ	165	ⒶⒷⒸⒹ	175	ⒶⒷⒸⒹ	185	ⒶⒷⒸⒹ	195	ⒶⒷⒸⒹ
106	ⒶⒷⒸⒹ	116	ⒶⒷⒸⒹ	126	ⒶⒷⒸⒹ	136	ⒶⒷⒸⒹ	146	ⒶⒷⒸⒹ	156	ⒶⒷⒸⒹ	166	ⒶⒷⒸⒹ	176	ⒶⒷⒸⒹ	186	ⒶⒷⒸⒹ	196	ⒶⒷⒸⒹ
107	ⒶⒷⒸⒹ	117	ⒶⒷⒸⒹ	127	ⒶⒷⒸⒹ	137	ⒶⒷⒸⒹ	147	ⒶⒷⒸⒹ	157	ⒶⒷⒸⒹ	167	ⒶⒷⒸⒹ	177	ⒶⒷⒸⒹ	187	ⒶⒷⒸⒹ	197	ⒶⒷⒸⒹ
108	ⒶⒷⒸⒹ	118	ⒶⒷⒸⒹ	128	ⒶⒷⒸⒹ	138	ⒶⒷⒸⒹ	148	ⒶⒷⒸⒹ	158	ⒶⒷⒸⒹ	168	ⒶⒷⒸⒹ	178	ⒶⒷⒸⒹ	188	ⒶⒷⒸⒹ	198	ⒶⒷⒸⒹ
109	ⒶⒷⒸⒹ	119	ⒶⒷⒸⒹ	129	ⒶⒷⒸⒹ	139	ⒶⒷⒸⒹ	149	ⒶⒷⒸⒹ	159	ⒶⒷⒸⒹ	169	ⒶⒷⒸⒹ	179	ⒶⒷⒸⒹ	189	ⒶⒷⒸⒹ	199	ⒶⒷⒸⒹ
110	ⒶⒷⒸⒹ	120	ⒶⒷⒸⒹ	130	ⒶⒷⒸⒹ	140	ⒶⒷⒸⒹ	151	ⒶⒷⒸⒹ	160	ⒶⒷⒸⒹ	170	ⒶⒷⒸⒹ	180	ⒶⒷⒸⒹ	190	ⒶⒷⒸⒹ	200	ⒶⒷⒸⒹ

READING SECTION (TEST 3)

Part 5								Part 6				Part 7							
No	ANSWER A B C D	No	ANSWER A B C D	No	ANSWER A B C D	No	ANSWER A B C D	No	ANSWER A B C D	No	ANSWER A B C D	No	ANSWER A B C D	No	ANSWER A B C D	No	ANSWER A B C D	No	ANSWER A B C D
101	Ⓐ Ⓑ Ⓒ Ⓓ	111	Ⓐ Ⓑ Ⓒ Ⓓ	121	Ⓐ Ⓑ Ⓒ Ⓓ	131	Ⓐ Ⓑ Ⓒ Ⓓ	141	Ⓐ Ⓑ Ⓒ Ⓓ	151	Ⓐ Ⓑ Ⓒ Ⓓ	161	Ⓐ Ⓑ Ⓒ Ⓓ	171	Ⓐ Ⓑ Ⓒ Ⓓ	181	Ⓐ Ⓑ Ⓒ Ⓓ	191	Ⓐ Ⓑ Ⓒ Ⓓ
102	Ⓐ Ⓑ Ⓒ Ⓓ	112	Ⓐ Ⓑ Ⓒ Ⓓ	122	Ⓐ Ⓑ Ⓒ Ⓓ	132	Ⓐ Ⓑ Ⓒ Ⓓ	142	Ⓐ Ⓑ Ⓒ Ⓓ	152	Ⓐ Ⓑ Ⓒ Ⓓ	162	Ⓐ Ⓑ Ⓒ Ⓓ	172	Ⓐ Ⓑ Ⓒ Ⓓ	182	Ⓐ Ⓑ Ⓒ Ⓓ	192	Ⓐ Ⓑ Ⓒ Ⓓ
103	Ⓐ Ⓑ Ⓒ Ⓓ	113	Ⓐ Ⓑ Ⓒ Ⓓ	123	Ⓐ Ⓑ Ⓒ Ⓓ	133	Ⓐ Ⓑ Ⓒ Ⓓ	143	Ⓐ Ⓑ Ⓒ Ⓓ	153	Ⓐ Ⓑ Ⓒ Ⓓ	163	Ⓐ Ⓑ Ⓒ Ⓓ	173	Ⓐ Ⓑ Ⓒ Ⓓ	183	Ⓐ Ⓑ Ⓒ Ⓓ	193	Ⓐ Ⓑ Ⓒ Ⓓ
104	Ⓐ Ⓑ Ⓒ Ⓓ	114	Ⓐ Ⓑ Ⓒ Ⓓ	124	Ⓐ Ⓑ Ⓒ Ⓓ	134	Ⓐ Ⓑ Ⓒ Ⓓ	144	Ⓐ Ⓑ Ⓒ Ⓓ	154	Ⓐ Ⓑ Ⓒ Ⓓ	164	Ⓐ Ⓑ Ⓒ Ⓓ	174	Ⓐ Ⓑ Ⓒ Ⓓ	184	Ⓐ Ⓑ Ⓒ Ⓓ	194	Ⓐ Ⓑ Ⓒ Ⓓ
105	Ⓐ Ⓑ Ⓒ Ⓓ	115	Ⓐ Ⓑ Ⓒ Ⓓ	125	Ⓐ Ⓑ Ⓒ Ⓓ	135	Ⓐ Ⓑ Ⓒ Ⓓ	145	Ⓐ Ⓑ Ⓒ Ⓓ	155	Ⓐ Ⓑ Ⓒ Ⓓ	165	Ⓐ Ⓑ Ⓒ Ⓓ	175	Ⓐ Ⓑ Ⓒ Ⓓ	185	Ⓐ Ⓑ Ⓒ Ⓓ	195	Ⓐ Ⓑ Ⓒ Ⓓ
106	Ⓐ Ⓑ Ⓒ Ⓓ	116	Ⓐ Ⓑ Ⓒ Ⓓ	126	Ⓐ Ⓑ Ⓒ Ⓓ	136	Ⓐ Ⓑ Ⓒ Ⓓ	146	Ⓐ Ⓑ Ⓒ Ⓓ	156	Ⓐ Ⓑ Ⓒ Ⓓ	166	Ⓐ Ⓑ Ⓒ Ⓓ	176	Ⓐ Ⓑ Ⓒ Ⓓ	186	Ⓐ Ⓑ Ⓒ Ⓓ	196	Ⓐ Ⓑ Ⓒ Ⓓ
107	Ⓐ Ⓑ Ⓒ Ⓓ	117	Ⓐ Ⓑ Ⓒ Ⓓ	127	Ⓐ Ⓑ Ⓒ Ⓓ	137	Ⓐ Ⓑ Ⓒ Ⓓ	147	Ⓐ Ⓑ Ⓒ Ⓓ	157	Ⓐ Ⓑ Ⓒ Ⓓ	167	Ⓐ Ⓑ Ⓒ Ⓓ	177	Ⓐ Ⓑ Ⓒ Ⓓ	187	Ⓐ Ⓑ Ⓒ Ⓓ	197	Ⓐ Ⓑ Ⓒ Ⓓ
108	Ⓐ Ⓑ Ⓒ Ⓓ	118	Ⓐ Ⓑ Ⓒ Ⓓ	128	Ⓐ Ⓑ Ⓒ Ⓓ	138	Ⓐ Ⓑ Ⓒ Ⓓ	148	Ⓐ Ⓑ Ⓒ Ⓓ	158	Ⓐ Ⓑ Ⓒ Ⓓ	168	Ⓐ Ⓑ Ⓒ Ⓓ	178	Ⓐ Ⓑ Ⓒ Ⓓ	188	Ⓐ Ⓑ Ⓒ Ⓓ	198	Ⓐ Ⓑ Ⓒ Ⓓ
109	Ⓐ Ⓑ Ⓒ Ⓓ	119	Ⓐ Ⓑ Ⓒ Ⓓ	129	Ⓐ Ⓑ Ⓒ Ⓓ	139	Ⓐ Ⓑ Ⓒ Ⓓ	149	Ⓐ Ⓑ Ⓒ Ⓓ	159	Ⓐ Ⓑ Ⓒ Ⓓ	169	Ⓐ Ⓑ Ⓒ Ⓓ	179	Ⓐ Ⓑ Ⓒ Ⓓ	189	Ⓐ Ⓑ Ⓒ Ⓓ	199	Ⓐ Ⓑ Ⓒ Ⓓ
110	Ⓐ Ⓑ Ⓒ Ⓓ	120	Ⓐ Ⓑ Ⓒ Ⓓ	130	Ⓐ Ⓑ Ⓒ Ⓓ	140	Ⓐ Ⓑ Ⓒ Ⓓ	151	Ⓐ Ⓑ Ⓒ Ⓓ	160	Ⓐ Ⓑ Ⓒ Ⓓ	170	Ⓐ Ⓑ Ⓒ Ⓓ	180	Ⓐ Ⓑ Ⓒ Ⓓ	190	Ⓐ Ⓑ Ⓒ Ⓓ	200	Ⓐ Ⓑ Ⓒ Ⓓ

READING SECTION (TEST 4)

Part 5								Part 6				Part 7							
No	ANSWER A B C D	No	ANSWER A B C D	No	ANSWER A B C D	No	ANSWER A B C D	No	ANSWER A B C D	No	ANSWER A B C D	No	ANSWER A B C D	No	ANSWER A B C D	No	ANSWER A B C D	No	ANSWER A B C D
101	Ⓐ Ⓑ Ⓒ Ⓓ	111	Ⓐ Ⓑ Ⓒ Ⓓ	121	Ⓐ Ⓑ Ⓒ Ⓓ	131	Ⓐ Ⓑ Ⓒ Ⓓ	141	Ⓐ Ⓑ Ⓒ Ⓓ	151	Ⓐ Ⓑ Ⓒ Ⓓ	161	Ⓐ Ⓑ Ⓒ Ⓓ	171	Ⓐ Ⓑ Ⓒ Ⓓ	181	Ⓐ Ⓑ Ⓒ Ⓓ	191	Ⓐ Ⓑ Ⓒ Ⓓ
102	Ⓐ Ⓑ Ⓒ Ⓓ	112	Ⓐ Ⓑ Ⓒ Ⓓ	122	Ⓐ Ⓑ Ⓒ Ⓓ	132	Ⓐ Ⓑ Ⓒ Ⓓ	142	Ⓐ Ⓑ Ⓒ Ⓓ	152	Ⓐ Ⓑ Ⓒ Ⓓ	162	Ⓐ Ⓑ Ⓒ Ⓓ	172	Ⓐ Ⓑ Ⓒ Ⓓ	182	Ⓐ Ⓑ Ⓒ Ⓓ	192	Ⓐ Ⓑ Ⓒ Ⓓ
103	Ⓐ Ⓑ Ⓒ Ⓓ	113	Ⓐ Ⓑ Ⓒ Ⓓ	123	Ⓐ Ⓑ Ⓒ Ⓓ	133	Ⓐ Ⓑ Ⓒ Ⓓ	143	Ⓐ Ⓑ Ⓒ Ⓓ	153	Ⓐ Ⓑ Ⓒ Ⓓ	163	Ⓐ Ⓑ Ⓒ Ⓓ	173	Ⓐ Ⓑ Ⓒ Ⓓ	183	Ⓐ Ⓑ Ⓒ Ⓓ	193	Ⓐ Ⓑ Ⓒ Ⓓ
104	Ⓐ Ⓑ Ⓒ Ⓓ	114	Ⓐ Ⓑ Ⓒ Ⓓ	124	Ⓐ Ⓑ Ⓒ Ⓓ	134	Ⓐ Ⓑ Ⓒ Ⓓ	144	Ⓐ Ⓑ Ⓒ Ⓓ	154	Ⓐ Ⓑ Ⓒ Ⓓ	164	Ⓐ Ⓑ Ⓒ Ⓓ	174	Ⓐ Ⓑ Ⓒ Ⓓ	184	Ⓐ Ⓑ Ⓒ Ⓓ	194	Ⓐ Ⓑ Ⓒ Ⓓ
105	Ⓐ Ⓑ Ⓒ Ⓓ	115	Ⓐ Ⓑ Ⓒ Ⓓ	125	Ⓐ Ⓑ Ⓒ Ⓓ	135	Ⓐ Ⓑ Ⓒ Ⓓ	145	Ⓐ Ⓑ Ⓒ Ⓓ	155	Ⓐ Ⓑ Ⓒ Ⓓ	165	Ⓐ Ⓑ Ⓒ Ⓓ	175	Ⓐ Ⓑ Ⓒ Ⓓ	185	Ⓐ Ⓑ Ⓒ Ⓓ	195	Ⓐ Ⓑ Ⓒ Ⓓ
106	Ⓐ Ⓑ Ⓒ Ⓓ	116	Ⓐ Ⓑ Ⓒ Ⓓ	126	Ⓐ Ⓑ Ⓒ Ⓓ	136	Ⓐ Ⓑ Ⓒ Ⓓ	146	Ⓐ Ⓑ Ⓒ Ⓓ	156	Ⓐ Ⓑ Ⓒ Ⓓ	166	Ⓐ Ⓑ Ⓒ Ⓓ	176	Ⓐ Ⓑ Ⓒ Ⓓ	186	Ⓐ Ⓑ Ⓒ Ⓓ	196	Ⓐ Ⓑ Ⓒ Ⓓ
107	Ⓐ Ⓑ Ⓒ Ⓓ	117	Ⓐ Ⓑ Ⓒ Ⓓ	127	Ⓐ Ⓑ Ⓒ Ⓓ	137	Ⓐ Ⓑ Ⓒ Ⓓ	147	Ⓐ Ⓑ Ⓒ Ⓓ	157	Ⓐ Ⓑ Ⓒ Ⓓ	167	Ⓐ Ⓑ Ⓒ Ⓓ	177	Ⓐ Ⓑ Ⓒ Ⓓ	187	Ⓐ Ⓑ Ⓒ Ⓓ	197	Ⓐ Ⓑ Ⓒ Ⓓ
108	Ⓐ Ⓑ Ⓒ Ⓓ	118	Ⓐ Ⓑ Ⓒ Ⓓ	128	Ⓐ Ⓑ Ⓒ Ⓓ	138	Ⓐ Ⓑ Ⓒ Ⓓ	148	Ⓐ Ⓑ Ⓒ Ⓓ	158	Ⓐ Ⓑ Ⓒ Ⓓ	168	Ⓐ Ⓑ Ⓒ Ⓓ	178	Ⓐ Ⓑ Ⓒ Ⓓ	188	Ⓐ Ⓑ Ⓒ Ⓓ	198	Ⓐ Ⓑ Ⓒ Ⓓ
109	Ⓐ Ⓑ Ⓒ Ⓓ	119	Ⓐ Ⓑ Ⓒ Ⓓ	129	Ⓐ Ⓑ Ⓒ Ⓓ	139	Ⓐ Ⓑ Ⓒ Ⓓ	149	Ⓐ Ⓑ Ⓒ Ⓓ	159	Ⓐ Ⓑ Ⓒ Ⓓ	169	Ⓐ Ⓑ Ⓒ Ⓓ	179	Ⓐ Ⓑ Ⓒ Ⓓ	189	Ⓐ Ⓑ Ⓒ Ⓓ	199	Ⓐ Ⓑ Ⓒ Ⓓ
110	Ⓐ Ⓑ Ⓒ Ⓓ	120	Ⓐ Ⓑ Ⓒ Ⓓ	130	Ⓐ Ⓑ Ⓒ Ⓓ	140	Ⓐ Ⓑ Ⓒ Ⓓ	151	Ⓐ Ⓑ Ⓒ Ⓓ	160	Ⓐ Ⓑ Ⓒ Ⓓ	170	Ⓐ Ⓑ Ⓒ Ⓓ	180	Ⓐ Ⓑ Ⓒ Ⓓ	190	Ⓐ Ⓑ Ⓒ Ⓓ	200	Ⓐ Ⓑ Ⓒ Ⓓ

READING SECTION (TEST 5)	Part 5								Part 6				Part 7							
	No	ANSWER A B C D	No	ANSWER A B C D	No	ANSWER A B C D	No	ANSWER A B C D	No	ANSWER A B C D	No	ANSWER A B C D	No	ANSWER A B C D	No	ANSWER A B C D	No	ANSWER A B C D	No	ANSWER A B C D
	101	Ⓐ Ⓑ Ⓒ Ⓓ	111	Ⓐ Ⓑ Ⓒ Ⓓ	121	Ⓐ Ⓑ Ⓒ Ⓓ	131	Ⓐ Ⓑ Ⓒ Ⓓ	141	Ⓐ Ⓑ Ⓒ Ⓓ	151	Ⓐ Ⓑ Ⓒ Ⓓ	161	Ⓐ Ⓑ Ⓒ Ⓓ	171	Ⓐ Ⓑ Ⓒ Ⓓ	181	Ⓐ Ⓑ Ⓒ Ⓓ	191	Ⓐ Ⓑ Ⓒ Ⓓ
	102	Ⓐ Ⓑ Ⓒ Ⓓ	112	Ⓐ Ⓑ Ⓒ Ⓓ	122	Ⓐ Ⓑ Ⓒ Ⓓ	132	Ⓐ Ⓑ Ⓒ Ⓓ	142	Ⓐ Ⓑ Ⓒ Ⓓ	152	Ⓐ Ⓑ Ⓒ Ⓓ	162	Ⓐ Ⓑ Ⓒ Ⓓ	172	Ⓐ Ⓑ Ⓒ Ⓓ	182	Ⓐ Ⓑ Ⓒ Ⓓ	192	Ⓐ Ⓑ Ⓒ Ⓓ
	103	Ⓐ Ⓑ Ⓒ Ⓓ	113	Ⓐ Ⓑ Ⓒ Ⓓ	123	Ⓐ Ⓑ Ⓒ Ⓓ	133	Ⓐ Ⓑ Ⓒ Ⓓ	143	Ⓐ Ⓑ Ⓒ Ⓓ	153	Ⓐ Ⓑ Ⓒ Ⓓ	163	Ⓐ Ⓑ Ⓒ Ⓓ	173	Ⓐ Ⓑ Ⓒ Ⓓ	183	Ⓐ Ⓑ Ⓒ Ⓓ	193	Ⓐ Ⓑ Ⓒ Ⓓ
	104	Ⓐ Ⓑ Ⓒ Ⓓ	114	Ⓐ Ⓑ Ⓒ Ⓓ	124	Ⓐ Ⓑ Ⓒ Ⓓ	134	Ⓐ Ⓑ Ⓒ Ⓓ	144	Ⓐ Ⓑ Ⓒ Ⓓ	154	Ⓐ Ⓑ Ⓒ Ⓓ	164	Ⓐ Ⓑ Ⓒ Ⓓ	174	Ⓐ Ⓑ Ⓒ Ⓓ	184	Ⓐ Ⓑ Ⓒ Ⓓ	194	Ⓐ Ⓑ Ⓒ Ⓓ
	105	Ⓐ Ⓑ Ⓒ Ⓓ	115	Ⓐ Ⓑ Ⓒ Ⓓ	125	Ⓐ Ⓑ Ⓒ Ⓓ	135	Ⓐ Ⓑ Ⓒ Ⓓ	145	Ⓐ Ⓑ Ⓒ Ⓓ	155	Ⓐ Ⓑ Ⓒ Ⓓ	165	Ⓐ Ⓑ Ⓒ Ⓓ	175	Ⓐ Ⓑ Ⓒ Ⓓ	185	Ⓐ Ⓑ Ⓒ Ⓓ	195	Ⓐ Ⓑ Ⓒ Ⓓ
	106	Ⓐ Ⓑ Ⓒ Ⓓ	116	Ⓐ Ⓑ Ⓒ Ⓓ	126	Ⓐ Ⓑ Ⓒ Ⓓ	136	Ⓐ Ⓑ Ⓒ Ⓓ	146	Ⓐ Ⓑ Ⓒ Ⓓ	156	Ⓐ Ⓑ Ⓒ Ⓓ	166	Ⓐ Ⓑ Ⓒ Ⓓ	176	Ⓐ Ⓑ Ⓒ Ⓓ	186	Ⓐ Ⓑ Ⓒ Ⓓ	196	Ⓐ Ⓑ Ⓒ Ⓓ
	107	Ⓐ Ⓑ Ⓒ Ⓓ	117	Ⓐ Ⓑ Ⓒ Ⓓ	127	Ⓐ Ⓑ Ⓒ Ⓓ	137	Ⓐ Ⓑ Ⓒ Ⓓ	147	Ⓐ Ⓑ Ⓒ Ⓓ	157	Ⓐ Ⓑ Ⓒ Ⓓ	167	Ⓐ Ⓑ Ⓒ Ⓓ	177	Ⓐ Ⓑ Ⓒ Ⓓ	187	Ⓐ Ⓑ Ⓒ Ⓓ	197	Ⓐ Ⓑ Ⓒ Ⓓ
	108	Ⓐ Ⓑ Ⓒ Ⓓ	118	Ⓐ Ⓑ Ⓒ Ⓓ	128	Ⓐ Ⓑ Ⓒ Ⓓ	138	Ⓐ Ⓑ Ⓒ Ⓓ	148	Ⓐ Ⓑ Ⓒ Ⓓ	158	Ⓐ Ⓑ Ⓒ Ⓓ	168	Ⓐ Ⓑ Ⓒ Ⓓ	178	Ⓐ Ⓑ Ⓒ Ⓓ	188	Ⓐ Ⓑ Ⓒ Ⓓ	198	Ⓐ Ⓑ Ⓒ Ⓓ
	109	Ⓐ Ⓑ Ⓒ Ⓓ	119	Ⓐ Ⓑ Ⓒ Ⓓ	129	Ⓐ Ⓑ Ⓒ Ⓓ	139	Ⓐ Ⓑ Ⓒ Ⓓ	149	Ⓐ Ⓑ Ⓒ Ⓓ	159	Ⓐ Ⓑ Ⓒ Ⓓ	169	Ⓐ Ⓑ Ⓒ Ⓓ	179	Ⓐ Ⓑ Ⓒ Ⓓ	189	Ⓐ Ⓑ Ⓒ Ⓓ	199	Ⓐ Ⓑ Ⓒ Ⓓ
	110	Ⓐ Ⓑ Ⓒ Ⓓ	120	Ⓐ Ⓑ Ⓒ Ⓓ	130	Ⓐ Ⓑ Ⓒ Ⓓ	140	Ⓐ Ⓑ Ⓒ Ⓓ	151	Ⓐ Ⓑ Ⓒ Ⓓ	160	Ⓐ Ⓑ Ⓒ Ⓓ	170	Ⓐ Ⓑ Ⓒ Ⓓ	180	Ⓐ Ⓑ Ⓒ Ⓓ	190	Ⓐ Ⓑ Ⓒ Ⓓ	200	Ⓐ Ⓑ Ⓒ Ⓓ

NEW TOEIC 新多益 700 分 閱讀特訓班

作者	Matthew Gunton、連緯晏 Wendy Lien
封面設計	KING
內頁構成	華漢電腦排版有限公司
發行人	周瑞德
企劃編輯	徐瑞璞
校對	劉俞青、陳欣慧
印製	大亞印製企業有限公司
初版	2014 年 5 月
定價	新台幣 399 元
出版	倍斯特出版事業有限公司
電話	（02）2351-2007
傳真	（02）2351-0887
地址	100 台北市中正區福州街 1 號 10 樓之 2
Email	best.books.service@gmail.com
港澳地區總經銷	泛華發行代理有限公司
地址	香港筲箕灣東旺道 3 號星島新聞集團大廈 3 樓
電話	（852）2798-2323
傳真	（852）2796-5471

國家圖書館出版品預行編目（CIP）資料

NEW TOEIC 新多益 700 分 閱讀特訓班／ Matthew Gunton,
連緯晏 作 . -- 初版 . -- 臺北市：倍斯特 , 2014.05

面；　公分

ISBN：978-986-90331-6-9（平裝）

1. 多益測驗

805.1895　　103007829